PRAISE FOR *THE SHIMMER*

"It would be easier to explain the phenomena of the Marfa lights than it would be to explain the storytelling genius of David Morrell. It's simply that—genius. Never does it shine through more vividly than in *The Shimmer*."

—SANDRA BROWN, *NEW YORK TIMES*
BESTSELLING AUTHOR OF *SMASH CUT*

"David Morrell's *The Shimmer* showcases a master story-teller at his finest. Mysterious lights, an isolated research facility, and a cast of characters as real as your next-door neighbors elevate this techno-thriller into a masterpiece of suspense, intrigue, and terror. Once cracked open, the book demands to be read in one sitting."

JAMES ROLLINS, *NEW YORK TIMES*
BESTSELLING AUTHOR OF *ALTAR OF EDEN*

" . . . a high caliber, one-of-a-kind action thriller only the creator of "Rambo" could have conceived and executed to perfection. . . . [a] multilayered approach gives the novel depth, texture, scope, dimension and a sense of im-mediacy, lifting it far beyond the level of entertainment fiction."

—*ASSOCIATED PRESS*

"David Morrell has written more good thrillers than just about anyone else alive. . . . *The Shimmer* is an enjoyable story and, even better, a hopeful one."

—*CHICAGO SUN-TIMES*

"*The Shimmer* shines in every way as a thriller, a terrific read that would keep even Scully and Muldur wondering what's going to happen next. And it also solidifies Morrell's status as the best thriller writer of this or any generation."

—*PROVIDENCE JOURNAL*

"[Morrell's] fast-moving plot recalls conspiracy theories à la Roswell and *The X-Files* and will appeal to both fans of that paranormal show and to Morrell's readers."

—*LIBRARY JOURNAL*

" . . . a fine example of how to mix genres effectively."

—*BOOKLIST*

" . . . as impressive as anything he has ever written and as challenging an endeavor as he has attempted to date. . . . Put this one on your must-read list for this year."

—*BOOKREPORTER.COM*

"Morrell is THE master of the thriller, period."

—*CRIMESPREE*

"The latest from thriller writer Morrell is a fast-paced, multi-layered story that will please fans . . . No one else writes like David Morrell."

—*HORROR WORLD*

"A tale that is part adventure, part mystery, even part historical, and yet wholly surprising and gripping. "

—*CEMETERY DANCE*

THE
SHIMMER

Also by David Morrell

Novels

First Blood (1972)

Testament (1975)

Last Reveille (1977)

The Totem (1979)

Blood Oath (1982)

The Brotherhood of the Rose (1984)

The Fraternity of the Stone (1985)

Rambo (First Blood Part II) (1985)

The League of Night and Fog
    (1987)

Rambo III (1988)

The Fifth Profession (1990)

The Covenant of the Flame (1991)

Assumed Identity (1993)

Desperate Measures (1994)

The Totem (Complete and
    Unaltered) (1994)

Extreme Denial (1996)

Double Image (1998)

Burnt Sienna (2000)

Long Lost (2002)

The Protector (2003)

Creepers (2005)

Scavenger (2007)

The Spy Who Came for
    Christmas (2008)

Short Fiction

The Hundred-Year Christmas (1983)

Black Evening (1999)

Nightscape (2004)

Illustrated Fiction

Captain America: The Chosen (2007)

Nonfiction

John Barth: An Introduction (1976)

Fireflies: A Father's Tale of Love
    and Loss (1988)

American Fiction, American Myth
    (Essays by Philip Young),
    edited by David Morrell and
    Sandra Spanier (2000)

The Successful Novelist: A
    Lifetime of Lessons about
    Writing and Publishing
    (2008), expanded
    version of Lessons from a
    Lifetime of Writing: A
    Novelist Looks at His
    Craft (2002)

DAVID MORRELL

THE SHIMMER

A Member of the Perseus Books Group

Copyright © 2009 by David Morrell

Published by Vanguard Press
A Member of the Perseus Books Group

Library of Congress Cataloging-in-Publication Data

Morrell, David.
   The shimmer / David Morrell.
      p. cm.
   ISBN 978-1-59315-537-7 (alk. paper)
   1. Supernatural—Fiction. 2. Spectators—Fiction. 3. Military bases—Fiction. 4. Texas—Fiction. I. Title.
PR9199.3.M65S55 2009
813'.54—dc22
2009000244

Mass Market ISBN: 978-1-59315-580-3

10 9 8 7 6 5 4 3 2 1

AUTHOR'S NOTE

The phenomena described in this novel appear on many nights outside the town of Marfa in west Texas. They were observed as long ago as when only Native Americans occupied the area. No one has adequately explained them.

Are not the days of my life few?
Let me alone that I may recover a little
Before I go whence I shall not return,
To the land of darkness and the shadow of death,
The black, disordered land
Where darkness is the only light.

—THE BOOK OF JOB

ONE

THE BECKONING

1

From fifteen hundred feet off the ground, the blue pickup truck looked like a Matchbox toy. Normally it would have blended with traffic, but on this clear Tuesday afternoon in early June, the pilot watched the truck race past other vehicles and veer back and forth between lanes as the driver searched for any open space he could find.

The aircraft, a Cessna 172, had high wings and a single propeller. Its pilot was a forty-year-old police officer named Dan Page. He knew that the driver of the pickup was male because he monitored a police radio through his headphones and was aware that ten minutes earlier the man had shot and killed another man in a feud between drug dealers at Fort Marcy Park. A police officer driving by saw the shooting. When he sped into the park, the assailant fired through the cruiser's windshield and killed him. Park workers who saw the murders all identified the shooter as a thin, twentyish Anglo with a shaved head and a white T-shirt, the short sleeves of which revealed a large tattoo on his left arm.

This was Page's day off. A private pilot, he enjoyed flying his Cessna from Santa Fe's small airport and, as he phrased it, "getting above it all." But when his police radio transmitted news of the chase, he headed over the four-mile-wide city to where the truck had last been seen, hoping to spot it among Santa Fe's low buildings and provide directions to his fellow officers in the pursuing police cars. Five minutes later, he had it in sight. The truck's frantic, random route would have been difficult to follow on the ground but was obvious from the air.

"He's going east on Peralta," Page said into the microphone on his headset. "Now he's turning right onto Guadalupe, heading downtown."

"I'm five blocks in front of him," another officer's voice answered quickly. "I can cut him off."

"Wait. Now he's veering onto Agua Fria."

Page stared down helplessly as an oncoming car swerved out of the truck's way, lurched onto a sidewalk, and hit an adobe wall, earthen bricks cascading onto the hood. He imagined the sound of the crash, the violence somehow gaining in magnitude because of the distance.

"He's back on Saint Francis Drive," Page warned.

"If he's headed toward the interstate, we've got the ramps blocked," an urgent voice replied.

Again the truck abruptly changed direction.

"He's turning right onto Cerrillos Road," Page yelled.

"I'll intercept him at Cordova!" a different voice blurted.

Peering down toward a crosswalk, Page noticed pedestrians scurrying to avoid the truck. A car was forced off the road.

"Too late! He's past Cordova!"

"We'll set up a roadblock at Saint Michael's Drive."

"Better make it Rodeo Road! He's driving so fast, you won't have time at Saint Michael's!"

Indeed, the speed with which the truck covered distance was astounding. The other vehicles on Cerrillos Road seemed to be standing still.

My God, he's got to be doing over a hundred, Page thought.

Other drivers must have seen the truck speeding toward them in their rearview mirrors, or maybe the fugitive kept blowing his horn. For whatever reason, traffic veered out of the way.

"We've got the intersection at Cerrillos and Rodeo Road closed!" a voice shouted.

Immediately the truck swerved onto another side street.

Page finally understood the pattern. "I think he's got a police radio!"

"What?"

"He changes directions whenever you tell me you've got a street blocked! He must be listening to us! Now he's turning into the Lowe's parking lot!"

Customers leaving the huge hardware store darted to the side as the truck sped toward the movie theater at the end of the lot. It disappeared into a parking garage.

Circling, Page watched for a man in a white T-shirt to leave the garage and try to get away on foot. But in June, a lot of men wore T-shirts, and from this altitude, it was almost impossible to distinguish colors on clothing. Moreover, the color might be irrelevant—the driver could force someone in the garage to give him a different-colored shirt so he could walk away without attracting attention.

Page kept circling.

A car left the garage.

He watched the tiny figures of pedestrians proceeding toward the theater's entrance. He looked for anyone whose pace was hurried.

An SUV left the garage.

He can change vehicles as easily as he can put on another shirt, Page realized.

A sports car left the garage.

From above, Page kept track of all three vehicles and described them to the officers on the ground. The first one reached a lane that took it to the left toward Cerrillos Road. The SUV reached the same lane and turned in the opposite direction, toward a side street. The sports car headed back toward the parking lot in front of the hardware store.

Three different directions.

Meanwhile, the pursuing police cars converged on the area. Page saw their flashing roof lights and imagined the wail of their sirens.

No other vehicles came from the garage. At the hardware store parking lot, a police cruiser stopped the sports car. Page switched his view toward the first vehicle that had left the garage. It was stopped at the entrance to Cerrillos Road, unable to find a break in traffic. In contrast, the SUV faced no obstacles as it drove leisurely in the opposite direction, along the lane toward the side street.

Page had a hunch and followed it. He descended a hundred feet, doing nothing drastic, nothing the FAA would object to, but even so, the downward motion made his engine grow louder.

The SUV seemed to drive a little faster.

He descended another hundred feet, making his engine sound even more insistent.

The SUV increased speed.

"He's below me, in the SUV!" Page yelled into the microphone, testing his theory by flying another hundred feet lower and trying to provoke a response.

He got one. The vehicle surged forward and skidded onto the side street.

"He's heading toward Airport Road!"

The SUV swung onto the multilane road and zigzagged through traffic, its speed so reckless that cars swerved to get out of the way. Two of them crashed against each other. Each time the vehicle abruptly changed lanes, it rocked a little—not as stable as the truck had been.

Page glanced farther along Airport Road, gaping at a gasoline truck that emerged from a service station. *Oh, my God . . .*

When the SUV changed lanes again, the abrupt motion caused it to lean. Instead of tipping, it managed to jolt back onto all four wheels. But as the driver tried to find an open space in another lane, he must have yanked the steering wheel. The vehicle tilted more severely, balanced on two wheels, fell all the way over, and crashed onto its side.

Throwing up a shower of sparks, it slid along the road. *No!*

The SUV hit the tanker, tore a gash underneath, and burst into flames as the sparks ignited the gasoline cascading from the fuel truck's belly.

A fireball swelled upward. Banking from it, Page felt the shock wave. It took several moments before he could make his voice work and radio for an emergency team. Dark smoke drifted past him.

2

The debriefing room consisted of metal chairs arranged in rows before a blackboard. Overhead, fluorescent lights hummed and made everyone look pale as the police chief listened to their reports. Page glanced through a window and saw several television broadcast trucks in the police station's parking lot.

"Okay, you told me what you did right. Now, how about what you did *wrong*?" the chief demanded. "That press conference is in fifteen minutes. I don't want any surprises."

"We weren't chasing him," one of the officers, Angelo, insisted. "We never endangered any civilians. All we did was try to get ahead of him and cut him off."

"Right," another man, Rafael, added. "Even though the bastard shot Bobby, we didn't overreact."

"He was driving a hundred miles an hour," an officer named Vera said. "It's a miracle the only other driver he killed was the poor guy behind the wheel of that gasoline tanker."

The chief looked in Page's direction.

"How about you?"

Page tried not to imagine the agony of the tanker's driver.

"With the state police helicopter in the hangar for maintenance, the only aircraft available for police use was mine. I warned the airport traffic controller to advise other planes not to fly over the city. I stayed above the minimum required altitude. No FAA regulations were broken. Nobody was at risk."

The chief swept his gaze across the group. "Anybody have anything to add? Any screw-up I should know about?"

The group was silent.

"Then I'm ready to talk to the reporters."

The officers looked relieved.

Page hung back as they all rose and began to leave the room.

"Want to join us for a beer?" Angelo asked.

"As soon as I tell my wife I'm okay," Page answered. He didn't need to ask where they'd meet. They always went to the same place—a sports bar on Cerrillos Road.

Once he was alone in the debriefing room, he used his cell phone to call home. It was the fourth time he'd done so since landing—and the fourth time he'd heard his own voice saying, "Please leave a message."

He tried Tori's cell phone, and for the fourth time it was *her* voice saying, "Please leave a message."

Yet again he said into the phone, "Hey, it's me. Call me when you get this."

He glanced at his watch, the digital display of which showed 7:23. *Where* is *she?* he wondered.

3

Turning into the driveway of his single-story home, Page pressed the garage-door opener that was attached to his SUV's sun visor. As the door swung upward, he saw that Tori's Saturn wasn't there. He drove in, turned off the engine, got out of his Grand Cherokee, and closed the garage door.

Entering the shadowy kitchen, he noticed how quiet the house felt.

A note lay on the table.

Gone to see my mother.

This made Page frown because Tori's mother lived in San Antonio, Texas, eight hundred miles away, and Tori hadn't said a word about wanting to visit her mother. What on earth could have caused her to make such a spur-of-the-moment trip? he wondered.

The only explanation he could think of was, *Some kind of emergency. She got a phone call with terrible news from her mother—no, about her mother—so she bought a last-minute plane ticket and hurried down to Albuquerque.*

The state's only big airport was in Albuquerque. The drive down from Santa Fe took an hour and fifteen minutes. Normally Page and Tori used his plane when they visited her mother. But because he'd been flying and couldn't answer his cell phone, Tori hadn't been able to tell him what had happened.

Sure. That makes sense, Page thought.

Nonetheless, he couldn't help rubbing his forehead.

Even if I wasn't able to answer my phone, that wouldn't have prevented her from leaving a message.

The kitchen phone hung on a wall next to the fridge. Page went over to it, looked at a list taped to the side, found the number he wanted, and pressed the buttons. He expected to get the answering machine, but an elderly voice answered.

"Hello?"

"Margaret? Is that you?"

Page didn't talk to Tori's mother often, but she recognized his voice.

"Of course it's me, Dan. Why do you sound so surprised?"

"I didn't think you'd be answering. I just assumed you were sick . . . or something."

"Sick? What would give you *that* idea?"

"I came home and found a note from Tori saying she'd gone to visit you. It's so spur-of-the-moment—I mean, when I left this morning she didn't say a word about going—I assumed something serious had happened. That you'd been in an accident or something like that. Are you sure you're okay?"

"Well, I'm tired from working in the garden all afternoon. Otherwise I feel fine. When Tori called and said she was coming to see me, I was as surprised as *you*."

Page tightened his grip on the phone. "She called you? When?"

"This morning around ten."

As soon as I left to go to the airport, he thought. Tori was a real estate agent. She often spent the morning at home, writing offers or making phone calls.

Page did some quick calculations. There wasn't a direct flight between Albuquerque and San Antonio. Tori would have needed to catch a connecting flight in Dallas. Door to door, the whole trip usually took about seven hours. *Depending on when her flight left, she should be in San Antonio by now*, he thought.

"Is she there? I'd like to talk to her."

"No, I don't expect her for several more hours," the elderly voice replied. "Maybe not until tomorrow."

"Tomorrow?" Confusion made Page's head start to ache. "She must be on a really late flight."

"She's not flying."

That didn't sound right. "Not flying? But then how . . . Are you telling me she's *driving*?"

"That's what she said. It didn't make any sense to me, either. Eight hundred miles—but that's what she told me she wanted to do. You *really* didn't know about this?"

"Nothing. Not a damned thing."

"I asked her why she was driving. She answered that she wanted to see the countryside and think. But she didn't say what was on her mind. Dan, I don't know another way to ask this. Is everything okay between Tori and you?"

His impulse was to blurt, *Absolutely. We get along fine. Things couldn't be better.*

But the words stuck in his throat.

He forced out a different answer. "All she needed to do was tell me she wanted to visit you. I might even have gone with her. She didn't have to keep it a secret. If she drives straight through and gets there tonight, tell her to call me as soon as she arrives. I don't care how late it is."

"Count on me. I'll ask her."

"Not just ask her, Margaret. Please, make sure she does it. Put the phone in her hand and make sure she calls me."

4

After he hung up, Page studied the kitchen. Tori had put the breakfast dishes away. The kitchen counters were bare, and everything was in its place, just as if the house were ready for a real estate showing.

He moved into the living room. Magazines that had been spread across the coffee table were neatly stacked. Cushions that had been in disarray from when he and Tori had watched television the previous night were back in their proper places. He remembered that she hadn't watched TV for long, that she'd gone to bed early, saying she wanted to read.

He walked down the hallway and peered into Tori's office. Her laptop computer was gone. Apart from a lamp, nothing was on her desk.

He entered their bedroom. The bed was made, everything perfectly arranged. Looking in the closet, he discovered that two suitcases were missing. He studied the empty hangers and concluded that Tori had taken most of her casual clothes but none of her business outfits. He checked her bureau drawers and discovered that all her socks and underwear were gone. He glanced toward her side of the bed. A compulsive reader, she normally kept a dozen books stacked there.

All of those were also gone.

Page didn't move for quite a while. When he became aware of the gathering darkness outside, he went into the living room and sat in shadows.

5

Waking with a start on Wednesday morning, Page turned toward the terrible emptiness on Tori's side of the bed. He stared at it for several troubled moments, then quickly got into some jeans, went outside, and grabbed the newspaper from the sidewalk, hurrying back so he wouldn't fail to hear the telephone. But it didn't ring.

The newspaper's headline announced, SHOOTING LEADS TO CHASE AND TANKER EXPLOSION. A photograph showed Bobby in his uniform. Another showed the truck driver. A third showed the twisted metal of the SUV and the gasoline tanker after the intense blaze had fused them together.

Page turned the newspaper over, hiding the photographs.

Unable to wait any longer, he picked up the phone and pressed numbers.

"Margaret, it's Dan."

She responded without any of the ordinary pleasantries: "Tori isn't here yet."

Page's throat felt terribly dry. After swallowing, he managed to speak. "She must have gotten tired and spent the night in a motel." Even as he said it, he didn't believe it.

"Then why didn't she call to tell me not to worry? Which is *exactly* what I'm doing." The elderly voice quavered. "What if she had an accident?"

"I don't think that's likely, or I'd have heard something." Page tried to sound convincing. "But I'll see what I can find out."

→→ ←←

Three hours later, en route to investigate a high school stabbing, he received a call from the duty officer at the police station.

"There's no record that Tori was in a traffic accident either in New Mexico or Texas, and nothing about her being admitted to any hospital along the route she was driving."

Page breathed out in relief, but he knew what the report meant and what he was forced to do next—he didn't see another option.

"Put out a missing-person report."

6

Early Thursday morning, the phone rang. Page set down his coffee cup and grabbed the receiver.

"Hello?"

"Dan Page?" a man's voice asked. It had a Southern accent and a raspy tone, as if it belonged to a smoker.

"Speaking." Page realized how tightly he held the phone.

"This is Police Chief Roger Costigan in Rostov, Texas."

"*Where?*" Page's mind swirled. He reached for a pen.

"Rostov, Texas. We're southeast of El Paso, about fifty miles from the Mexican border."

Page felt a knot in his stomach. "You found my wife?"

"Victoria Page," the voice said, as if reading from a list. "Caucasian. Five foot six. One hundred and twenty pounds. Red hair. Green eyes. Driving a dark-blue 2008 Saturn Outlook." The voice gave the license number.

"That's her." Page's brow felt cold.

"One of my officers spotted her car at the side of a road early this morning. He found her nearby."

Page had the sensation of holding his breath. "Is she . . . ?"

"She's fine. You don't need to worry on that score. She hasn't been hurt. She wasn't in any danger."

"No accident?"

"No, sir."

"She hasn't been injured?"

"That's correct, Mr. Page. She's just fine."

Thank God, Page thought. But troubling questions immediately flooded through him.

"If she wasn't injured, then why was her car at the side of the road?"

"That's difficult to explain."

"I don't understand. Is she there? Can you put her on the phone?"

"No, sir. She isn't with me."

"Then how can I talk to her?"

"I guess that's up to her," the voice replied. "We told her you're looking for her, but she didn't react."

"You're not making sense. Is she alone?"

"As much as I can tell."

"Then what in God's name is she doing in . . ." Page looked at the note he'd made. "Rostov, Texas?"

"It's a little complicated. You'll understand better if I tell you in person. The main thing is, no law's been broken. She's here of her own free will."

"You say it's better if you tell me in person?"

"Maybe 'show you' would be more accurate."

"Why are you being so damned cryptic, Chief?"

"I'm not trying to be. Believe me, this is an unusual situation. I'm afraid I can't explain it over the phone. You'll just have to see for yourself."

"Whatever the hell is going on, you can expect to show me this afternoon."

"Mr. Page, I'm afraid you'll need a lot longer than that to get here. You're in Santa Fe, right?"

"That's correct."

"Well, our nearest major airport is in El Paso, and we're a couple of hundred miles from there. There's no way you can get here by this afternoon."

"Do you have any airport at all?"

"There's a little one that the ranchers use, but . . ."

"Then I'll see you at five o'clock."

7

Page phoned the police station and told the duty officer that he couldn't come to work that day and probably wouldn't be in until Monday. He packed a suitcase, grabbed his flight bag, and drove to Santa Fe's small airport. After carrying his luggage into a reception area, he said hello to a young woman behind a counter. She had the newspaper sitting on the counter in front of her, but before she could mention the front-page article, he turned left into a computer lounge, where he studied reports of the weather in New Mexico and Texas. The forecasts indicated a chance for thunderstorms in a couple of days but no immediate problems.

The last thing he always did was look for announcements about prohibited areas. These warned pilots about airspace they weren't allowed to enter, often because of security issues. A pilot who trespassed into a forbidden area was liable to find his or her plane flanked by fighter jets giving angry orders to land at the nearest airfield.

There weren't any flight restrictions in New Mexico, but Page was surprised to discover that the Rostov area of Texas did have one. Puzzled, he clicked a button to get more information and learned that the prohibition involved an array of radio astronomy dishes twenty miles northwest of the town. The concern wasn't related to national security. Rather, the observatory was off-limits because planes flying over the dishes were liable to cause electrical interference that blocked attempts to collect radio signals from astronomical phenomena such as solar flares and spiral galaxies.

Fine—I'll just stay away from it, Page thought.

He pulled charts from his flight bag and quickly plotted a course to Rostov. As Chief Costigan had told him, the town was a couple of hundred miles southeast of El Paso. Nowhere *near* San Antonio.

His emotions in turmoil, Page stepped through a door onto the airport's tie-down area. There, in warm sunlight, numerous small aircraft were secured to the concrete by ropes attached to their wings and tails. One of them was Page's Cessna. Feeling the pressure of time, he warned himself to slow down as he inspected the plane's exterior. After each flight, he always had the fuel tanks filled. Now he drained a small amount of fuel into a cup to assure himself that there weren't any water bubbles or other contaminants.

Stay focused, he told himself.

After untying the plane, he got inside, attached his maps and flight plan to a clipboard strapped to his thigh, and took a deep breath.

Pay attention, he thought. *No matter how much I want to reach Tori, what matters now is the plane. Pay attention to flying the plane.*

He took another deep breath and went through his preflight checklist.

What in God's name is Tori doing in Rostov, Texas?

He used his radio to ask the ground controller for permission to taxi to the takeoff area. Five minutes later— less than two hours after he'd received the phone call from Chief Costigan—he was in the air, flying to Texas.

8

The man with the M4 carbine stood in the shade of the small concrete-block building and savored the last of his cigarette. The temperature was a pleasant, dry 85 degrees, but habits from his two tours of duty in Iraq stayed with him, and he avoided direct sunlight as much as possible.

Because it was midmorning and the sun was on the opposite side of the tiny building, Earl Halloway wasn't able to enjoy the rugged majesty of the Davis Mountains to the north. Instead his view consisted of seemingly endless clumps of sparse brown grass.

Tumbleweeds stuck to a chain-link fence fifty yards from him. The fence was twelve feet high and topped by barbed wire. Signs along it declared:

SCIENTIFIC RESEARCH AREA
NO ADMITTANCE

To Halloway's left, nine huge radio observatory dishes were pointed in various directions toward the sky, and another was tilted so that it pointed horizontally. It had a truck next to it, along with scaffolding and a small crane, as if it were undergoing repairs. The dishes could be seen from quite a distance, a conspicuous intrusion on the landscape.

At the road ten miles away, a similar warning sign was attached to a locked gate that prevented access to the lane. People who stopped their cars to stare toward the far-off dishes usually lingered for only a short time until boredom prompted them to resume their journey.

The chain-link fence was one of three around the dishes. It wasn't electrified—nobody at the installation wanted the nuisance of dealing with ranchers whose cattle happened to wander up to the fence and get barbecued. Even so, there had never been a case of anyone being foolish enough to climb it. The second fence was constructed entirely of razor wire, and the third fence *was* electrified, its numerous prominent signs warning, DANGER! HIGH VOLTAGE!

Halloway could have sat in an air-conditioned security room and watched monitors that would show any intruder's futile attempt to get over the third fence. If such a thing ever happened, he and the other guards would go out afterward to clean up the mess. No smoking was permitted in the sterile facility, so his cigarette break was the only reason he ever needed to step outside. He justified his addiction by telling himself that cameras and monitors were no substitute for eyeballing the landscape in person to make sure everything was as peaceful as it seemed. After all, one of his fellow Army Rangers in Iraq had been a sniper who could disguise himself so well that an enemy could walk across a field and not know the sniper was there unless the enemy stepped on him.

This line of thought made Halloway uncomfortable. All he'd wanted was a peaceful smoke, and now he'd gotten himself brooding about snipers. *Time to get back inside*, he decided. After taking a final satisfying drag from his cigarette, he dropped it to the ground, crushed it with his boot, and gave the bleak vista a final assessment.

Twenty miles to the southeast was a town called Rostov, but he'd never been to it—*no one* from the facility had ever been there. It was strictly off-limits. *We don't want them thinking about us*, he'd been told emphatically when he'd signed on for what was supposed to be easy duty.

But after three months of being confined here, Halloway couldn't wait for his replacement to arrive—an event that was set to occur in just two weeks. Sure, the food was better than what he'd been given in Iraq. Plus the installation had alcohol, which he *hadn't* been able to get in Iraq. He couldn't complain about the Internet downloads of the latest movies, some of which weren't yet available on DVD.

But what he really wanted was to get laid.

Thinking again about snipers, he tapped the security-code buttons on a pad next to the entrance. When he heard a buzz that indicated the lock had been freed, he opened the metal door and stepped inside. Immediately the observatory's filtered, cooled, sterile air encircled him. He shoved the heavy door back into place, making sure the electronic lock engaged. Then he unlocked a secondary door, stepped through, secured that one as well, and descended metal stairs that ended at a long corridor lit by a row of overhead lights.

9

The underground facility was large. A subtle vibration filled it.

When Halloway had arrived three months earlier, he'd thought nothing of the vibration, but as the days had accumulated, he'd become increasingly sensitive to the faint, omnipresent hum that he suspected had something to do with the installation's electrical generator—or else with the activity of the huge radio dishes. No one else seemed aware of it, but for him it had become distracting enough that, even though he'd taken to wearing earplugs when he went to bed, he wasn't able to sleep soundly.

He passed two doors on the left and turned right into a large room filled with numerous closed-circuit television monitors that showed every approach to the installation. The images were in color and displayed excellent definition. At night they had a green tint as heat sensors registered the difference between the rapidly cooling grassland and the constant temperature of animals or human beings.

His counterpart on this shift, a man with large, strong hands, sat in a metal chair and flipped through a sports magazine, occasionally glancing at the screens. It was poor discipline, but after months of inactivity, Halloway understood how hard it was to keep staring at those damned monitors.

"Smoking's bad for your health," the man said without looking up. His name was Taggard.

"So's getting shot at. I figured a bullet was more to worry about than a cigarette."

"This isn't Iraq."

"Thanks for the geography lesson. Putting on weight isn't good for you, either, but that hasn't stopped you from mainlining those candy bars you keep in your desk. How many do you eat a day? Ten? Fifteen?"

Taggard chuckled. With so little to do, they'd taken to ribbing each other constantly. "Yeah, I really ought to be on the Stairmaster instead of reading these magazines. I'll get on that first thing tomorrow."

"I'm going to take a leak," Halloway said.

"After that, maybe *you* could sit here a while and let *me* wander around."

Now it was Halloway's turn to chuckle.

He stepped back out into the corridor and went farther along. On the left, an open door was marked DATA ANALYSIS. Through the opening, he heard static and peered in at a bored, bald, bespectacled researcher who studied a computer screen. All kinds of electronic equipment occupied the numerous shelves that lined the walls around the room. Red indicator lights glowed, and needles pulsed. One device provided a visual depiction of the static, which looked like chaotically shifting dots. The sound was harsh and brittle and reminded Halloway of a radio searching for a hard-to-find station.

Which is pretty much what's going on, he concluded.

The subtle vibration intensified, giving Halloway the start of a headache.

"It sounds a little different than yesterday," he said, causing the man with the glasses to look up.

"Hello, Earl," the researcher answered. "Yes, there's more activity, and it's getting louder. There's been a general increase all week."

"What do you figure is going on?"

"Probably nothing. Sometimes the static seems to be accumulating toward something. Then it backs off. According to the computer, that's been the rhythm ever since this observatory was built fifteen years ago." The researcher turned toward a sequence of knobs. "I'll realign the dish and see if the pattern gains any definition. Monitoring local ambient electrical discharge is a good way to see if the equipment's functioning properly."

Halloway was aware that the dish the scientist referred to was the one tilted toward the horizon, as if undergoing repairs. He had no doubt, however, that the dish was pointed exactly where it was supposed to be—southeast, toward an area near Rostov.

In theory, the dishes gathered radio pulses from deep space and coordinated them. A lot of heavenly bodies generated them, the researcher had explained, and a lot were still echoing from the Big Bang. A complex computer program translated the signals into images that looked like photographs, depicting nebulae, novas, black holes, and other astronomical wonders.

Halloway hadn't known what any of that meant when he'd arrived at the installation three months earlier, but the sameness of each day had bored the researcher enough that he was happy to explain how a radio observatory worked. Despite the explanations, Halloway had no illusions about what was really going on. A radio observatory didn't need razor wire and high-voltage fences. The M4 with which he and the other guards were equipped was one of the best assault carbines on the planet, complete with a grenade launcher and a laser sighting system. That was a hell of a lot of security to protect a facility that studied black holes.

Even before a helicopter had transported him to this remote area of west Texas, Halloway had been convinced that this felt like a spook operation rather than a project for the National Science Foundation. Within days of his arrival, he'd seen enough to use his laptop to Google information about how radio observatories could be employed by espionage agencies. He'd become convinced that the dishes above this huge bunker weren't pointed at nebulae, novas, and black holes. They were aimed at satellites that scooped radio signals from the atmosphere.

They were also aimed at the moon. Radio signals all over the world "leaked" into outer space, his Internet research had informed him. The moon intercepted many of those signals, however, and a properly focused radio observatory could collect them as they bounced back to Earth. By sorting through the various frequencies and choosing those favored by major terrorist organizations or foreign governments hostile to the United States, a facility like this could relay valuable information to intelligence analysts in places such as Fort Meade, near Washington, D.C.

Halloway hadn't picked that location at random. Fort Meade, he knew, was the headquarters of the National Security Agency. Yes, this was a damned spook operation, he was sure of it, but if the technician—whose name was Gordon—wanted to keep lying, claiming it was a scientific project that mapped deep space, Halloway was fine with that. The little game they played was about the only thing that interested him. That and the mystery of why one dish was aimed horizontally toward Rostov. The technician could jabber all he wanted to about "monitoring local ambient electrical discharge."

Give me a fucking break, Halloway thought. *Something's going on near Rostov, and a lot of this billion-dollar facility is being used to try to figure out what it is.*

10

Page landed midroute at the airport outside Roswell, New Mexico. The sun-baked area was where the American UFO craze had begun in 1947, when a rancher had discovered debris from a large fallen object that the military described first as a flying disc and then as a weather balloon. The different explanations may simply have been an example of flawed communication, but conspiracy theorists had seized on those differences to claim a government cover-up. Ever since then, Roswell had become the unofficial UFO capital of the world, so much so that every Fourth of July the town had a UFO Festival where skeptics and so-called experts debated while actors from science fiction movies signed autographs and enthusiasts dressed up as "little green men."

Page and Tori had flown to the festival a few years earlier and enjoyed the carnival atmosphere of the parades, the costume contest, and the concerts, one of which had featured a band interpreting music from Pink Floyd's album *The Dark Side of the Moon*. They rarely found opportunities to vacation together—his job was too demanding—and he remembered how she had laughed as they watched a group of "Klingons" earnestly performing a wedding ceremony.

The bittersweet memory made Page feel even more anxious to reach Tori. He watched as a fuel truck filled his plane's tanks. He verified that the fuel had the correct color—blue—for the type he needed and that there weren't any contaminants. Then he climbed back into the plane, took off, and continued southeast.

His carefully chosen route allowed him to follow a corridor that passed among large military areas to the north, east, south, and west. These were boldly marked on his aerial map and indicated where fighter jets practiced combat maneuvers. Farther west an even more serious military area was located over the White Sands Missile Range, formerly known as the Alamogordo Bombing and Gunnery Range, where the first atomic bomb had been detonated in 1945.

The rugged vista was breathtaking. Nonpilots often assumed that the appeal of flying involved appreciating the scenery. But Page had become a pilot because he enjoyed the sensation of moving in three dimensions. The truth was that maintaining altitude and speed while staying on course, monitoring radio transmissions, and comparing a sectional map to actual features on the ground required so much concentration that a pilot had little time for sightseeing.

There was another element to flying, though, and it was a lot like the drinking that took place at after-shift decompression sessions with his fellow officers. Page enjoyed flying because it helped him not to think about the terrible pain people inflicted on one another. He'd seen too many lives destroyed by guns, knives, beer bottles, screwdrivers, baseball bats, and even a nail gun. Six months earlier, he'd been the first officer to arrive at the scene of a car accident in which a drunken driver had hit an oncoming vehicle and killed five children along with the woman who was taking them to a birthday party. There'd been so much blood that Page still had nightmares about it.

His friends thought he was joking when he said the reward of flying was "getting above it all," but he was serious. The various activities involved in controlling an aircraft shut out what he was determined not to remember.

That helped Page now. His confusion, his urgency, his need to have answers—on the ground, these emotions had thrown him off balance, but once he was in the air, the discipline of controlling the Cessna *forced* him to feel as level as the aircraft. In the calm sky, amid the monotonous, muffled drone of the engine, the plane created a floating sensation. He welcomed it yet couldn't help dreading what he might discover on the ground.

When he entered Texas, the Davis Mountains extended to his left as far as he could see. They were hardly typical of the rest of the state and in fact reminded him of the aspen- and piñon-covered peaks he was accustomed to seeing in New Mexico.

He monitored the radio frequency for the Rostov airport. He knew from his preflight research that there wasn't a control tower and that he needed to broadcast his intentions directly to any aircraft that might be in the vicinity to make certain no flight paths intersected. During his long approach, he heard from only one other pilot, a woman with a deep Texas accent who reported that she was heading in the opposite direction.

The aerial map made clear where the prohibited airspace of the observatory was located, but even without a map, Page couldn't have missed the installation. The large white dishes reflected the sun and were awesome to behold. They resembled giant versions of the satellite dish on the roof of his Santa Fe home. Incongruous with the flat landscape in which they were situated, they radiated a feeling of sheer power that made them appear huge, even when seen from a distance.

He was puzzled that the observatory was located on comparatively low ground, especially when compared to the distant mountains. Didn't observatories work best when placed at as high an altitude as possible? But his musings came to an end when the practical concerns inherent to flying replaced his curiosity. Careful to stay clear of the dishes, he continued along his course toward Rostov.

Small communities were usually hard to spot from the air, and Rostov was no exception, blending with the seemingly boundless ranchland that stretched everywhere. For a moment, Page felt an eerie sense that he'd been here before, that he'd flown over this exact area on an earlier occasion and had seen these same cattle spread out, grazing. He was particularly struck by a picturesque windmill next to a pond at which cattle drank, a view he was *positive* he'd seen before. But he'd never before been in this area of Texas.

This just happens to look like a place you've flown over in another part of the country, he told himself. *Pay attention to what you're doing.*

His map revealed railway tracks and a road that went through Rostov. Flying parallel to the road—which was easier to spot—he soon noticed a faint cluster of low buildings ahead.

The map indicated that the airport was three miles northeast of the town, but as it came into view and Page prepared to angle in that direction, he felt confused when a second airstrip appeared on the opposite side of town, to the *south*east. It wasn't marked on the map. Flying lower by that time, he was able to take a closer look, and he saw that the runway was cracked and buckled, a lot of it covered with dirt, patches of weeds and cactus growing at random. The crumbled ruins of hangars lay next to it. *Lots* of hangars, he noticed curiously. Many years ago, this had been a sizable facility.

What happened to it? Page wondered.

He noticed something else: an unusual topographical feature that stretched beyond the decayed airstrip. There, contrasting with the rugged brown grassland, was an extensive area of what looked like huge black cinders, seemingly evidence of volcanic activity that eons ago had pushed subterranean debris to the surface. The cinders had formed the rim of a volcanic crater that had eroded over time until only half of it remained visible, barely rising above the surface of the surrounding land.

Whenever the eruption had occurred, the force of it had scattered chunks everywhere. Page had seen other areas like it while flying over Arizona. They were generally called "badlands," a fitting name for something so bleak and forbidding. He couldn't help concluding that the place looked the way he felt.

Increasingly eager to find Tori, he flew from the ruined, uncharted airfield toward the airport that was marked on the map. Again the precision of what he needed to do was the only thing he could allow to occupy his mind. After radioing his intention to land and checking where the windsock was pointed, he reduced the engine's power and glided downward. When he came within a wingspan of the center line on the airstrip, he leveled the plane, felt it float, sensed it begin to settle, eased back on the yoke, and touched down gently on the two main wheels, letting the nose wheel ease down on its own, protecting the strut that supported it.

He taxied to a tie-down area next to a building that looked like an old gas station, except that there weren't any pumps in front of it. Instead the fuel was kept in a small tanker truck. He quickly shut out the memory of the tanker that he'd seen explode in Santa Fe just a few days earlier. Off to the side, a hangar had its doors open, revealing a helicopter and a Lear jet. Their presence in this small community might have been puzzling if not for the fact that this was Texas cattle country. Four propeller-driven aircraft were tied down, all more powerful and expensive than Page's Cessna, another indicator of wealth.

Climbing out of the cockpit, he secured the plane and pulled his bags from the rear seat, but now that his obligation to the aircraft had ended, he found that he couldn't walk. His muscles seemed paralyzed as confusion escaped from the tight mental compartment into which he'd temporarily been able to shut it away. He was no longer above everything. He didn't have a half-dozen things to accomplish in order to control the plane. At once the pressure of the past two days flooded through him again.

Why did Tori leave without telling me?

What's she doing here?

What the hell's going on?

Despite the apprehension that seized him, Page managed to force his legs to work and carried his bags across the hot pavement. The building that reminded him of an old gas station had adobe walls and a corrugated metal roof, the rust on which suggested that the structure dated back many years.

Opening a squeaky screen door, he entered a small reception area that held a battered wooden table and a scuffed leather sofa. A candy machine stood next to a water cooler and a phone that hung on the wall. Another doorway led to an office on the right, from which a heavy, gray-haired man of about sixty appeared. He wore frayed mechanic's coveralls and used a rag to wipe grease from his fingers. Page set down his bags and shook the man's hand, ignoring the grease on it, knowing that he gained a measure of respect by doing so.

"I called you from Santa Fe this morning about renting a car."

"You Dan Page?"

"That's me. I don't know how long I'll be staying, but I'd like to start a credit-card tab so you can charge me for the tie-down fee. Also, I need the tanks filled with 100 LL." Most propeller-driven aircraft used that type of fuel. The LL stood for low lead, one of the few leaded fuels still sold in the United States.

"That'll be fine—the car's behind this building," the mechanic said. "I've got the paperwork ready for you to sign."

Carefully hiding the disarray his emotions were in, Page handed over his driver's license and a credit card.

"We don't have many strangers fly in here," the mechanic added, a polite Texas way of asking why Page had come to town.

Page surprised himself with his reply.

"I've got marriage problems to sort out."

11

The car was a red Toyota Celica. A wall of heat swept out when Page opened the driver's door. He left it open while he set his bags in the trunk, but when he got behind the steering wheel, both it and the seat remained hot to the touch. He started the engine and turned on the air conditioning. As cool air streamed over him, he took a deep breath and tried to steady himself. Then he drove from the airport to where a dirt road led in only one direction, merging with the paved road into Rostov.

A water tower loomed above the low buildings ahead. To the right, cattle pens stretched along the railroad tracks. At Rostov's outskirts, the street expanded to double the width of the road, presumably a vestige from frontier days when cattle had been herded through town.

He passed a feed-and-grain store, a saddle-and-boot shop, and a Ford dealership that seemed to specialize in pickup trucks. He reached blocks of houses that were painted earth colors ranging from sand to tan to brown. In contrast, their front doors were green or blue or red. Colorful flower gardens accentuated the single-story homes.

Where the wide street intersected with another, all of the buildings became businesses—a restaurant, a bank, a hotel, a real estate office (Page was reminded of Tori), and a clothing store. Here, too, the colors were eye-catching. One building was red while another was purple, another yellow, and another green, no hue repeating itself within any block. But despite the fresh look of the buildings, Page had the sense that most of them dated back many years and that at one time they'd been close to collapsing. He sensed something else: that he'd seen these buildings before, not in their present colorful version but the way they'd once been, just as he felt he'd seen the panorama of the cattle grazing outside town even though it was his first visit to this area.

Traffic was light. A woman pushed a baby carriage. A young man sat on a bench and played a harmonica, barely audible through the tightly closed car windows. At the end of the street to the right, Page saw an old-time railroad station. To the left, he saw a playground and a church. Across from them, a building's domed tower made him suspect that it was a courthouse.

12

The floor was dark, worn marble. A door on the left had a frosted-glass window with black letters that told him: POLICE DEPARTMENT.

Inside, behind a counter, an elderly woman wore a leather vest. She looked up at him and smiled.

"Yes, sir?"

"My name's Dan Page. Chief Costigan's expecting me. I said I'd meet him at five o'clock."

"And you're right on time," a raspy voice said.

Page recognized the voice he had heard that morning on the phone. He turned toward an office doorway, where a lanky man stood watching him. The man's face was thin and creased, with the dull gray skin that smokers tend to have. He had a mustache and a small scar on his chin. His salt-and-pepper hair was cut close to his head. His uniform was tan. Although his equipment belt held a modern Glock pistol, Page wasn't surprised to see that he wore cowboy boots.

"What you said about the airport made me curious, so I asked Harry out there to watch for you. He called to tell me when you arrived. You have your own plane?"

"A Cessna 172."

"I get nervous in airplanes." Costigan gestured toward his office. "Come in."

They shook hands as Page stepped through the doorway.

"I don't know any police officers who can afford a plane." Costigan sat behind a vintage wooden desk. His swivel chair creaked loudly.

"I inherited it from my father. He was a mechanic in the Air Force. Listen, I hope you don't mind if we skip the small talk. I need to know about my wife. You said one of your deputies found her car early this morning." Page did his best to keep his emotions steady.

"Yes, sir. At the side of a road. To be precise, out at the observation platform."

"Observation platform?"

"That's one of the things I figured you'd understand better if I showed you rather than told you about it."

Page waited for him to elaborate, but Costigan made no effort to do so.

"Look, I don't understand *any* of this," Page told him sharply. "Are you sure my wife isn't hurt?"

"Absolutely sure."

"And she isn't with anyone?"

"She's alone. She's staying at a motel here—the Trail's End. I'll take you to her when we're finished." Costigan leaned forward, studying him. "How long have you been a police officer?"

"Fifteen years."

Costigan concentrated on the right side of Page's belt, where a chafed area indicated he often wore a holster. "I always feel off balance when I'm not wearing my weapon. Did you bring yours with you?"

"Do you know any police officer who leaves his gun at home? Do you ever go anywhere without *yours*, even when you're off duty?"

Costigan kept studying him.

"It's not my department's gun. It's my own," Page said. "I have a concealed-carry permit for it. Texas and New Mexico have reciprocal arrangements."

"I know the law, Mr. Page. But you haven't answered my question."

"My gun's in my suitcase, which is safely locked in my rental car. Why do you ask?"

"Under the circumstances, I think it would be a good idea if you kept it there."

"'Under the circumstances'?" The words baffled Page until he realized what Costigan was getting at. "Jesus, surely you don't think I'm a threat to my wife?"

"Domestic disputes and guns don't go together."

"But this isn't a domestic dispute." Page tried not to raise his voice.

"Really? Then why did you ask if she was with anyone?

Why did she tell her mother she was going to visit her in San Antonio yet didn't bother to tell *you* before she left?"

Page didn't respond for a moment. Didn't know what to say. Then he spread his hands helplessly, trying to keep his words steady.

"Okay, the truth is, I don't know how to explain this. I have no idea why she left and why she didn't tell me, and I sure as hell have no idea what she's doing here in Rostov."

"Why she's here—you'll understand tonight. As for what's going on between the two of you . . ."

"You promised to take me to her." Page stood. "We're wasting time. Let's go."

"We're not finished talking. Sit down. I'm going to tell you a story."

"A story?" Page stared down at the man behind the desk. "What kind of crazy—"

"Yes, a story. Humor me—it's about my father. He used to be the police chief here in Rostov."

"What's that got to do with—"

"You still haven't sat back down, Mr. Page."

The intensity in the police chief's eyes made him hesitate.

"And then I'll take you to your wife."

Page sat impatiently. "Tell me your story."

"One night my father got a phone call from a terrified boy who said his dad was beating his mom. When the boy gave his last name, my father didn't recognize it right away. The family had moved here from Fort Worth a couple of months earlier. The husband had been out of work, and a relative of his who lived here had found him a job at the stock pens.

"When he wasn't working, the husband liked to go to a local bar, get drunk, and pick fights. It was the hottest September anybody could remember, yet the wife always wore high, buttoned collars and long sleeves. Later it became obvious that she did that to hide bruises. The boy was quiet in school, always fidgeting as if he was afraid he'd make a mistake and get punished.

"That night, when the boy phoned, afraid that his dad was going to kill his mom, my father got in his cruiser and hurried over there. The house was near the stock pens, a run-down adobe with patches of stucco missing on the walls. The lights were on. When my father heard shouting and sobbing, he knocked on the door and identified himself as a police officer. That's how I imagine it anyhow. I've gone over it in my head more times than I care to think.

"The shouting stopped. My father knocked again, and a shotgun blast from inside tore the door in half. It pretty much tore my father in half, also. I doubt he lived long enough to feel himself hit the ground."

Page leaned forward in his chair.

"When my father didn't report back in a half hour, a deputy drove over to the house, where he found my dad spread out on the ground. After the deputy threw up, he managed to control himself long enough to radio for an ambulance. At that time, there weren't any other local police officers. The deputy's only option was to contact the Highway Patrol, but they said they couldn't get there for another half hour, so the deputy sucked up his nerve, drew his gun, and went into the house.

"The wife was on the living room floor with her head shot off. Blood was everywhere. The deputy went into the kitchen. No one was there. He went into the master bedroom. No one. He went into a smaller bedroom— the boy's—and the window was open. The father must have heard the boy leaping out. What the searchers found the next morning made clear that the father chased his son across the road and into a field. Why did he act that way, do you suppose?"

Page inhaled slowly. "A man like that blames his family for making him unhappy. Everything's *their* fault, and they need to be punished."

"You've been taking psychology courses?"

"Increases my pay grade."

Costigan looked beyond Page, as if remembering the night he'd learned that his father had been shotgunned to death. His eyes refocused.

"What you say makes sense. But here's another explanation. Some people are wired wrong. It's their *nature* to cause pain. They're so dark inside that maybe the only word to describe them is 'evil.'"

"Yes, I've met people like that," Page said. "Too many."

"The next morning, the searchers found the boy's corpse in weeds a half mile from the house. The father was lying next to him. After he'd killed his son, he'd put the shotgun in his mouth and pulled the trigger. Coyotes had gotten to them by the time the bodies were found."

Page tasted a familiar sourness in his mouth. He was reminded of the car that had been hit by the drunk driver, of the five children and the woman inside, killed instantly. He thought of the drug dealer who'd shot his friend Bobby, just two days earlier.

"I'm sorry about your father."

"Not a day goes by that I don't remember him. I'll never be the man *he* was. But he wasn't perfect, and what happened that night proved it. He shouldn't have let it happen. What's the most dangerous situation any police officer faces?"

"Family arguments."

"Exactly. Because they're so emotional and unpredictable. After my father knocked, he should have stepped to the side, away from the door and the windows. Or better yet, he should have stayed by his car and used his bullhorn to order the husband to step outside. If the guy had come out with a shotgun, at least my father would have had a chance to defend himself. It didn't need to happen the way it did. But my father had a weak spot. He couldn't stand bullies." Costigan looked directly at Page. "*Especially* when they picked on women."

"Okay," Page said. "I get the point. But I told you, my wife and I aren't arguing. This isn't a domestic dispute."

"So *you* say. But until I'm sure you're not a threat to her, you won't see her without me standing next to you."

13

Although the sun was descending toward the horizon, its rays seemed unusually bright. In the passenger seat of the police car, Page put on his sunglasses. He pulled out his cell phone and called Margaret to let her know that Tori was okay and that he was on his way to see her. He promised to have Tori call but wasn't sure he'd be able to keep that promise.

As they drove through Rostov, he glanced out the window at a muffler shop and a barbecue restaurant called the Rib Palace. Ahead, at the edge of town, a sign announced, TRAIL'S END MOTEL. A row of plain, single-story units formed a U, with the office in the middle.

"Your wife's in number 11," Costigan told him as the car crunched across the gravel parking lot, raising a cloud of dust.

But when they got to number 11, the parking space was empty.

Page felt hollow as he stepped from the cruiser. The drapes were closed, and he couldn't see past them to tell if there was luggage inside.

They walked across the gravel, pushed open a screen door with a loud squeak, and entered the office, which had a soft-drink machine and a small television in a corner. On the screen, a reporter was announcing sports scores.

"Jake," the police chief said to a gangly young clerk behind the counter, "the lady in unit 11. Did she check out?"

"Nope. Paid for the rest of the week. I saw her car go past twenty minutes ago."

Costigan nodded, then gestured toward Page. "Better save a room for this gentleman."

"No need," Page said, annoyed. "I'll stay with my wife."

"As long as it's her idea, but in case it isn't, Jake, save him a room."

The screen door squeaked again when Costigan opened it. Outside, turning from the sunset, he debated for a moment. "She's got a long night ahead of her."

Whatever that means, Page thought. "You said your deputy found her early in the morning. What was she doing until then?"

"That's something you need to see for yourself."

"Chief, I'm getting tired of this."

Costigan didn't seem to hear him. "Maybe she went to get something to eat. Let's try the Rib Palace."

They drove back to the restaurant, but Tori's SUV wasn't in the parking lot. Most of the clientele seemed to drive pickup trucks, Page noted. At the chief's insistence, they went inside. Tori wasn't among the early-evening crowd.

"Fred," Costigan said to an aproned man behind a counter, "did a red-haired woman come in here about twenty minutes ago and buy some take-out food?"

"Sure did. A turkey-and-cheese sandwich, plus iced tea. Don't get much call for turkey. She's lucky we had some."

"You might want to stock some more of it. I have a hunch she'll be back. Give us a couple of burgers and fries to go." Costigan looked at Page. "You're not a vegetarian, I hope."

Page just stared at him. "Burgers are fine," he said. "I'm buying."

The stuffed paper bag had a grease stain on one side. He carried it out to the police car. They got in and drove

east. Patchy brown grass stretched in every direction. Cattle grazed in the dimming sunset.

On the right, they came to a barbed-wire fence beyond
which lay the rusted ruins of collapsed metal buildings.
Signs hung at regular intervals along the fence.

PROPERTY OF U.S. MILITARY

DANGER

HAZARDOUS CHEMICALS

UNEXPLODED ORDNANCE

"That used to be a military training airfield," Costigan
explained. "Back in the '40s."

"I saw it when I flew in. I wondered what happened to
it."

"They shut it down in 1945. Just left it. It's been falling
apart ever since."

A short distance ahead, past what looked like a historical marker of some sort, Page saw a low wooden structure. It had a flat roof and resembled a roadside stand
where vegetables might be sold. But in this case, the section that faced the road was closed, and the open side
was directed toward a fence and the grassland that lay
beyond. Try as he might, Page couldn't figure out what it
was for.

Tori's blue Saturn was parked next to it.

"Yeah, she got here early," Costigan said.

They pulled off the road and stopped behind the Saturn. The wooden structure had a sidewall that prevented
Page from seeing if Tori was inside. At the same time, it
prevented Tori from seeing the police car.

"I guess she figured waiting *here* was better than waiting in her motel room," Costigan said.

"This is the observation platform you mentioned?"

"Yeah, where my deputy found her."

Page reached to open the cruiser's door.

"Wait," Costigan said. "It won't be long now. The sun's almost down. As soon as it gets dark, you'll understand."

Page stared at him. "Why should I . . ."

"You've indulged me this far. Is ten minutes longer going to make a difference?"

"What's so damned important about the sun going down?"

"Eat your burger before it gets cold. I promise you, this'll be a long night."

14

Earl Halloway sat in the air-conditioned control room, scanning the numerous monitors that showed closed-circuit images of the area around the observatory. Taggard sat next to him, chewing on a candy bar. The setting sun cast an orange tint over the array of dishes that towered aboveground. In a while, as darkness settled, the images would become green, indicating that the heat-sensing capability of the cameras had become active. Animals or people would show clearly as a glow, although at the moment not a single cow or even a rabbit was visible out there.

Halloway picked up the sports magazine that Taggard

had been reading. Every minute or so, he glanced up at the monitors. Nothing was happening outside. Nothing *ever* happened outside, which of course was a good thing, especially compared to the ambushes and roadside bombs he'd dodged in Iraq. But God almighty, this assignment was boring.

Down the hall, Halloway heard a door close.

"I'll be right back," he told his partner.

Taggard nodded, taking another bite.

Halloway left the control room and walked along the hall to the door that he'd heard being closed. He knew which door it was because each night it was always the same door, the one marked DATA ANALYSIS.

During the day, Gordon leaves the door open, but at night he always closes it, he thought. *Why? What's he hiding?*

A renewed wave of boredom made Halloway reach for the handle, then open the door. The room was filled with the subtle hum of all the electronic devices that occupied the walls—and the even subtler vibration that he sensed everywhere in the facility and that interfered with his sleep enough to make him always feel on the verge of a headache.

Gordon wore a headset over his hairless scalp. Sitting at a desk that was turned away from the door, he studied rows of numbers accumulating on a computer screen.

When Halloway stepped closer, Gordon sensed the movement and looked in his direction. Surprised, he took off the earphones and pushed his glasses higher on his nose.

"Didn't I lock the door? I *meant* to lock the door."

"Just checking to see that everything's okay."

"Of course it is. Why wouldn't it be?" Gordon asked defensively.

"That's what they pay me to find out."

Halloway heard a noise coming from the headphones that Gordon had set on the table. It was faint compared to when it had come through the speakers during the afternoon. Even so, he could tell that it sounded quite different now, no longer a persistent crackle but a series of wavering tones pitched at various levels, some rising while others descended, many of them occurring in high and low unison.

They had a subtle, sensual quiver. Their languid, arousing rhythm made him step forward.

"Sounds like music," he said.

"I don't mean to be rude, but you need to get out of here," Gordon responded. "I have work to do."

Halloway held up his hands. "Sure. Sorry to disturb you, Gordon. Like I said, I was just checking."

As he stepped back, the noises from the earphones changed again, sounding definitely like music. But it was unlike any music he had ever heard.

As a teenager, he'd dreamed about becoming a rock star. He'd had a garage band and still played an electric guitar damned well. He knew about major and minor keys and four-four and three-four beat patterns. But this music didn't have any key he'd ever heard, and it sure didn't have any beat pattern that he recognized. Faint as it was, the music floated and dipped, glided and sank. The notes merged and separated in a rhythm that was almost like the way he breathed if he were on R & R, lying on a beach in Mexico, enjoying the salt smell of the air, absorbing the warmth of the sun.

"I don't know what that is, but it's the most beautiful thing I ever heard."

Gordon took off his glasses, and to Halloway's surprise, he didn't protest again. Instead, when he spoke, it seemed as if he felt relieved to do so, to share his discovery with someone.

"It *is* beautiful," he said.

"Why didn't we hear it this afternoon?" Halloway asked.

"I have no idea. Whatever this is, it happens only after the sun goes down."

"And you hear that every night?"

"No. Not like that. Until two nights ago, it was always faint and fuzzy, sort of hovering behind the static. I needed to do a lot of electronic filtering to get a sense of what it sounded like."

"What happened two nights ago?"

"Your guess is as good as mine. But all of a sudden, *that's* what I started hearing."

"I can't hear it very well," Halloway said. "Why don't you turn on the speakers?"

Gordon hesitated, evidently concerned that doing so would violate his orders. But then he shrugged as if to say, *What the hell; I can't keep this to myself any longer*, and flicked a switch.

Instantly the floating, gliding, sailing music filled the room, making Halloway feel as if he were standing on a cushion of air. The instruments—whatever they were—had a synthesizer quality that made them impossible to identify. Perhaps it was only his imagination, but the wave-like tones seemed to drift into his ears like the arousing whisper of a woman pressed against him.

"My God, that's beautiful," he repeated. "What's caus-ing it?"

"We've been trying to figure that out since this place was built." Gordon paused, then added, "And apparently a lot longer than that."

Those last words were cryptic, but before Halloway could ask about them, Taggard appeared in the doorway.

"What kind of radio station is that? I've never heard anything like it. Is it on the Internet? How do I download that music?"

"If you tried to record it, somebody would have to shoot you," Gordon said.

Taggard looked surprised.

"That's not a joke," Gordon told him.

Halloway barely paid attention to what they were say-ing. He felt the music drifting around him and then inside him, becoming part of him. The cushion of air on which he seemed to float became even softer. At the same time, the headache he'd been struggling with finally emerged from the hole where he'd managed to suppress it, like something that had festered until it couldn't be denied.

The pain was beautiful.

15

The U.S. Army Intelligence and Security Command, known as INSCOM, is one of the few branches of the U.S. military that is also a branch of a civilian organization, specifically the National Security Agency, the world's largest electronic intelligence-gathering service. Although INSCOM maintains several bases, the one affiliated with the NSA is located at Fort Meade, Maryland, where the NSA is headquartered.

From his office window, Col. Warren Raleigh could see a mile away to the NSA's headquarters, a tall complex of buildings topped by a vast array of antennae and microwave dishes. Two massive black structures dominated the group. During the day, their shiny dark windows reflected the five thousand cars that sat in the sprawling parking lots that surrounded them.

Raleigh thought that the reflection was appropriate. While the NSA's occupants could see out, no one could see in. And the clandestine nature of the agency was represented in another way—although the buildings were huge, there were even more acres of space concealed underground.

His own office was located in a three-story building designed to look bland and unimposing. A metal plaque next to the entrance read, ENVIRONMENTAL WIND AND SOLAR DEVELOPMENT FACILITY, suggesting that the work inside was devoted to finding cheap, renewable sources of energy for the government and the military. In actuality, the plaque was one of Raleigh's jokes. The idea that the government and the military would be interested in cost-cutting or ecological issues was laughable. To him, the E, W, and S of Environmental Wind and Solar actually stood for Experimental Weapons Strategy.

Many of the projects under development in the building were only tangentially related to the NSA's task of gathering intelligence via electronic means, but some—such as the efforts to create lethal rays derived from the microwave beams that transmitted cell-phone messages were logical extensions of the NSA's tools. So were the experiments to develop communications satellites capable of firing laser beams toward enemy positions.

But when it came to his *personal* choice of weapons, as far as Raleigh was concerned, nothing equaled the feel of a firearm. The second of the building's five underground levels featured an extensive gun range, part of which was a so-called shooting house with a maze designed to look like corridors and rooms in an ordinary apartment complex or office building. Along each corridor and within each room, potential threats lurked unseen. As life-sized targets popped up unexpectedly, the objective was to identify them correctly and eliminate armed opponents without injuring innocent bystanders. And the goal was to do so in the shortest possible time, usually no more than two minutes.

On this Thursday in early June, at 9 in the evening, Raleigh was prepared to beat his own record.

"With your permission, Colonel."

"Do your job, Sergeant Lockhart."

"Yes, sir."

Lockhart, a bull of a man, shook Raleigh violently, then spun him.

"You can do better than that, Sergeant!"

"Yes, sir!"

The sergeant shook Raleigh so hard that the colonel's teeth knocked together. Then Lockhart spun him so forcefully that the colonel had the sense of being in a centrifuge. For a moment, he wondered if the sergeant might be enjoying his work too much.

Abruptly Lockhart let go of him, thrust an M4 into his hands, and shoved him into the shooting house.

The sergeant had, indeed, done his job. Raleigh felt so disoriented that the floor seemed to ripple and the walls to tilt. His heart rushed, and his vision wavered.

Each time Raleigh tested himself in the shooting house, Lockhart reconfigured the partitions, arranging the layout in a new and unpredictable design. The one thing Raleigh could be sure of was the familiarity of the weapon in his hands. During his twenty-five-year career, he'd used its forerunner—the M16—in numerous conflicts around the world. He knew how to field-strip and reassemble an M16 in absolute darkness and with amazing speed. He'd learned to appreciate its contours and secret places as he would those of a lover. He could shoot that venerable assault rifle with remarkable accuracy, even when it was switched to full auto.

Still, the M16 had drawbacks, particularly the length of its barrel in the close environments of urban warfare, so the shorter, lighter M4 carbine had been developed. As an officer in the Army, Raleigh had his differences with the Marines, but he definitely agreed with their wisdom in requiring all officers to replace their sidearms with M4s.

At heart, we're all riflemen, Raleigh thought.

Moving warily along a dim hallway, he checked that the M4's selector was set for three-shot bursts. He willed his mind to stop swirling and his legs to become steady. With long-practiced biofeedback techniques, he worked to control his respiratory rate and subdue his pulse.

A target sped out of a doorway ahead.

Raleigh aimed and held his fire. The target was an old man holding up his hands in surrender.

Raleigh peered into the room, saw that it was empty, and continued down the hallway, but at once, a noise behind him made him pivot. Another target sped from the room. Somehow it had been concealed from him. It was a man with a rifle, but before it stopped, Raleigh pulled the trigger, sending three rounds into the opponent's head. He blew another three rounds into the old man's head on the assumption that he was in league with the assailant and that in an actual firefight, the old bastard would probably pick up the dead man's gun the moment Raleigh's back was turned.

Raleigh quickly scanned the rest of the corridor. Ready to shoot, he moved forward through growing shadows. The trick was to keep his weight balanced, never placing one foot too far ahead of the other. Sliding his feet, he progressed in an efficient shuffle, always capable of adjusting to the M4's recoil.

Another target popped from a doorway. Raleigh almost fired before he saw that it was a woman holding a child. But then he realized that the child was actually a doll and that the grip of a pistol projected from behind it. He pulled the trigger and sent three bullets into the woman's brain.

The smell of gun smoke was thick in the corridor now. Although Raleigh wore protective earplugs, his awareness was at such a level that he swore he could hear the clinking sound of his empty shells hitting the concrete floor.

How much time had gone by? How long had he been there?

Don't think about it! Just get the job done!

The corridor went to the right. Raleigh entered an area that had a receptionist's desk and wooden chairs in front of it. Without warning, a target surged up from behind the desk. A man with a handgun!

As Raleigh fired, a figure rushed from an office doorway—a woman in a white medical coat. She held up her hands as yet another target sped into view, this one from another doorway, a man about to throw a grenade.

Raleigh shot him, then shot a target that hurried from a farther doorway, a woman with a rifle, then shot two gunmen who rushed from the corridor on the opposite side of the reception area.

He pivoted, scanning everything that lay before him, on guard against more attacks.

His mouth was dry. His hands sweated on the M4.

The rush of his heart was so powerful that he felt pressure in the veins of his neck. Breathing deeply but not quickly, he assessed the scene before him. Were all the threats eliminated?

No.

The woman in the white medical coat continued to stand before him. Weaponless, her hands were raised.

Is the sergeant setting me up? Raleigh wondered. *Is that a weapon in the pocket of her medical coat?*

He twisted the M4's selector to full auto and emptied the remainder of the magazine into her, the powerful burst blowing the plywood figure apart.

Through his earplugs, he heard a sharp electronic whistle, the signal that the exercise had ended. He pulled out the earplugs and turned toward Sergeant Lockhart, who approached along the corridor.

"I finished before the ninety-second time limit," Raleigh said. "Beat my own record, didn't I?"

"Yes, sir," Lockhart said, but there was doubt in his voice. He glanced behind him, and Raleigh knew he was thinking of the bullet holes in the target that portrayed the old man. Then Lockhart peered ahead toward the disintegrated target of the woman in the white medical coat.

"Collaborators," Raleigh explained. "They'd have moved against me the first chance they had."

"Of course, sir." Lockhart still sounded doubtful.

"Sergeant, don't you like this assignment?"

"Sir, I'm very happy with it."

"I could arrange to have you sent someplace that offers you more of a challenge. Perhaps a war zone."

"I'd prefer you didn't, sir."

"Combat builds character, you know."

"Sir, I've been in combat. With all due respect, I don't think I need any more character."

"Then I'll spare you a repeat of the experience. But since you've been in firefights, there's one relevant thing I'd expect you to have learned."

"Yes, sir. And what is that?"

The colonel gestured toward the disintegrated target of the woman in the white medical coat.

"You don't stay alive long if you take the time to worry about innocent bystanders, especially in a firefight. Sure, maybe some pussy reporter'll accuse you of a war crime, and maybe the Army'll cave in to the grumbling of a bunch of politicians and put you on trial. But you'll still be alive, and ten years of hard labor is better than getting shot to death by a supposed *innocent* bystander who thinks you're a fool for not killing him. Or *her*. There could easily have been a suicide bomb under her medical coat."

"Yes, sir."

"It's going to be hard for anyone to outdo my new record."

"Yes, sir," the sergeant assured him emphatically.

Raleigh's cell phone buzzed. He pulled it from his belt and spoke into it with authority. "Raleigh here."

What he heard made his jaw tighten.

"I'm on my way."

16

The strange sounds seeped past the closed door of the command center one level below the underground shooting house. Raleigh heard them the moment he hurried from the elevator. He passed an armed sentry, jabbed numbers on a security pad, and pushed the door open.

The full volume of the sounds drifted over him. A dozen civilian researchers studied various electronic displays, assessing, measuring, calculating. He'd never seen his research team look so intense. Amid the multitude of glowing instruments and pulsing meters, he hurriedly closed the door and tried to identify what he was hearing. He was reminded of music, but these weren't like any notes he'd ever heard. Granted, they were processed through a computer's synthesizer program, which gave them an artificial tone, but he'd heard synthesizer music before, and that wasn't what created the distinctive feeling these sounds inspired.

First, the rhythm sank into him. It drifted, so hypnotic that it seemed to counteract his quickening heartbeat. Second, the notes vibrated in a way that made the colors in the room appear to intensify. Third, the melody—which didn't have any pattern that he could detect—made his mouth feel as if he'd just sipped . . .

"You're tasting orange juice, aren't you, Colonel?"

Startled, he looked up. A researcher had noticed him draw his tongue along his lips.

"That's right. How did you know?"

"We *all* are. Do the colors seem stronger as well?" The man's eyes flashed with curiosity.

Raleigh nodded, squinting to subdue the sudden intense glow of the monitors.

"You can almost feel the music as much as hear it," the man continued.

"Yes. A ripple of warmth along my skin."

"It's called synesthesia."

Raleigh was blessed with an encyclopedic memory. He quickly identified the word. "A process by which the stimulation of one sense somehow causes other senses to be stimulated as well."

"Exactly," the researcher said. "In this case, we're not only *hearing* these sounds, we're also seeing them, feeling them, and tasting them."

Raleigh glanced from one scientist to another. He

thought of the projects his team had been developing. One of his favorites was a method of transmitting ultralow sound waves that affected the physical and psychological well-being of an enemy. The enemy wouldn't be able to hear the sound and hence wouldn't be aware of the aural bombardment. But the effects would be profound. In the 1990s, an early version had been tested around the isolated community of Taos in northern New Mexico. For months the valley had been saturated by a low-level frequency that in theory should have been beneath the range of what human and animal ears could register but in actuality turned out to be just barely detectable. Locals who were made nervous wrecks by it took to calling it the "Taos hum." Dogs and cats showed visible pain, scratching at their ears until they were bloody. That glitch had been corrected so that no person or animal could hear the low vibration, and Raleigh had enjoyed the power of being able to make people irritable enough to lose their tempers—even attack one another—simply because he had flicked a switch.

But no project had ever offered so much baffling promise as *this* one. It had been in development for decades, since long before Raleigh had maneuvered his career so that he'd been put in charge of it in 1995. It dated back to before INSCOM had been established in 1977, and even before the National Security Agency itself had been created in 1952. This was the culmination of something that had obsessed him since he was a boy, and it presented the chance for him to fulfill a lifelong ambition.

Finally it's my turn.

Leaning over the console and staring at the flickering lights, he addressed his next question to the entire team.

"Usually all we get is static. Why is this happening all of a sudden?"

"It's not just Rostov," a woman scientist murmured as she shook her head as if to free herself from the strange music.

Raleigh turned toward a large computer screen on which a world map showed four widely separated red dots. Each of the dots was pulsing.

"Rostov started first," a man with thick spectacles said. "But then the others began doing the same thing. The static dissolved, and . . ." The man gestured in mystification. "And then we heard *this*."

"The others?" Continuing to taste orange juice, Raleigh moved closer to the map on the screen. One of the flashing dots was situated in west Texas. That was the one he'd automatically looked toward because that was the site on which the research had always been focused. But now he peered at the other locations. Norway, Australia, and Thailand—all sites known to display phenomena similar to those in west Texas.

"What you're hearing is the one in Australia," the woman continued.

"But those areas are even more out of the way than Rostov," Raleigh objected. "Hell, the one in Thailand's on a riverbank in a jungle. The one in Australia's hundreds of miles into the outback. And we don't have monitoring equipment anywhere near them, let alone a radio observatory like the one in west Texas."

"In this case,' there's no need," the man with thick glasses explained. "The signals are so powerful they're leaking out into the atmosphere. We're capturing them off special frequencies on our satellites."

"You said Rostov started to do this first?"

"Yes. Then the others became active."

Raleigh pulled his cell phone from his belt and quickly tapped numbers.

"Sergeant, assemble a team. Civilian identities. Concealed weapons. We're leaving for west Texas at dawn."

17

"It's dark enough now," Costigan said, his figure indistinct in the police car. Neither of them had spoken in so long that his voice seemed extra loud.

"Finally," Page told him. "It's about time I got the answers you promised."

"I didn't promise answers," the police chief replied. "What I promised was that you'd understand."

Page shook his head in annoyance, opened the passenger door, and stepped onto the gravel parking area. He stretched to ease the tight muscles in his legs and shoulders. His companion walked to the back of the cruiser, where he opened the trunk and pulled something out.

"Here." Costigan reached across with a windbreaker. "In a couple of hours, you'll want this. It gets cold out here."

"A couple of *hours*?" Baffled, Page took the wind-breaker but didn't put it on. Everything was shadowy in the dusk. A faint light was mounted on the sidewall of the observation platform, but its effects were minimal. The last glow of sunset disappeared below the horizon.

As he walked past Tori's Saturn, approaching the observation platform, he heard a vehicle behind him and looked back toward the headlights of a Volkswagen van that steered from the road and stopped a short distance from the police car. Puzzled, he stopped to see who had arrived. The van's headlights went off. Then interior lights came on as doors were opened. Page saw the silhouettes of a middle-aged man and woman getting out. They twisted their shoulders, stretching the kinks out after what had evidently been a long drive.

"This better be worth it," the man said irritably. "We're a hundred and fifty miles out of our way."

"You said you wanted to retire early and see the country," the woman replied.

The man surveyed the dark, barren area around him.

"And we're sure as hell in the country. That police car's probably here to keep people from getting robbed. Well, come on, let's get this over with."

The couple shut their doors, extinguishing the van's interior lights. Their footsteps crunched on the gravel as they walked toward the observation platform.

Following their example, Page continued in that direction. Costigan veered off to throw the crumpled paper bag with the remnants of their burgers and fries into a trash can, then followed him across the lot. Before they made it another ten feet, Page heard a second vehicle approaching, then a third. Both turned into the parking area, their headlights sweeping across the structure, but he didn't look back this time.

He came around the sidewall and found an area about thirty feet long and ten feet deep. It had a wooden floor, a roof, and a built-in bench that went all the way along the back wall. Anyone sitting there would face the grassland that stretched beyond the fence.

A solitary figure was in the middle, looking toward the dark horizon.

A woman. She wore sneakers, jeans, and a sweater. She seemed oblivious to the shadows of the middle-aged man and woman, who went over to the fence and stared past it toward the night.

Page concentrated on her, trying to understand.

"I don't see a thing," the man complained.

"Well, we just got here. You need to give it a chance."

A family came around and stepped in front of the platform—parents with a young boy and girl tugging on their hands.

"By the time we get to the motel, it'll be long past their bedtime," the mother said.

"Hey, as long as we're driving by, there's no harm in stopping. It's not as if it's taking us out of our way," the father replied.

"But the temperature's going down. The kids'll probably catch cold."

The woman on the bench seemed oblivious to the family as well. And oblivious to Page. She just kept looking toward the night.

He smelled cigarette smoke and glanced over his shoulder toward where Costigan leaned his tall, thin body against a post that supported the platform's roof. The police chief had put on a cowboy hat and raised a glowing cigarette to his mouth. The woman didn't pay attention to that, either.

Confused, Page looked in the direction that held her gaze. Above the horizon, he saw an amazing number of stars, with more appearing all the time as the last of the sunlight retreated. He studied the dark expanse of the grassland. Forty-five degrees to the right, he noticed the distant specks of headlights as a few vehicles approached Rostov from the Mexican border, which lay fifty miles away.

So what the hell am I supposed to understand? Page wondered. He was beginning to feel like the victim of a scam, yet he couldn't imagine what it might be.

At the fence, the middle-aged man spoke again, echoing his thoughts. "It's just like I told you. *Nothing.* Just some kind of tourist trap. I'm amazed they're not trying to sell us something."

"Honestly," the woman replied, "I don't know where you're in such a hurry to go. Just give it a chance."

Meanwhile, at another section of the fence, the two children tugged harder at their parents' hands.

"Daddy, I don't see anything," the little girl said.

"Here, I'll lift you up," the father said.

"Me, too," the little boy insisted.

"You'll have to wait your turn. I can't lift both of you at the same time."

"I'll do it." The mother picked up the boy.

"I *still* don't see anything," the little girl said. "Daddy, the dark makes me scared."

"Mommy, I'm hungry," the little boy said.

"Okay," the father told them, sounding defeated. "I guess we'd better go after all. Nothing's out there anyhow. Tomorrow morning, maybe we can see where they made that James Deacon movie. The set's supposed to be around here, and I hear the big old ranch house is still standing."

As the parents carried the fidgeting children to the car, two other vehicles pulled in. One was a pickup truck, and when it stopped, three teenagers got out. The other, to Page's annoyance, was a bus labeled TEXAS TOURS, from which about thirty people emerged. A clamor arose as they all felt the need to say whatever flitted through their minds.

Who are all these people? Page wondered. He had come here hoping to talk with his wife and to find out what had possessed her to leave. With every new arrival, a quiet reunion became more and more impossible.

To the woman on the bench, however, none of the other people seemed even to exist. She just kept staring at the horizon, never once moving her head toward the growing distractions.

Page realized that he was hesitating, that despite his effort to get here and his impatience with Costigan for making him wait, he was actually afraid of the answers he might get.

Bracing his resolve, he walked through the darkness toward his wife.

18

She had her head tilted back so that it was leaning against the shadowy wooden wall. Her gaze was straight ahead.

Page stepped up to the side and watched her.

"Tori."

She didn't reply.

In the background, the jabbering conversations of the people who'd gotten off the bus filled the night.

Maybe she didn't hear me, Page thought.

"Tori?" he repeated.

She just kept staring toward the horizon.

He stepped closer. The reflected headlights from another car showed him that her eyes were wide open, and she didn't even seem to be blinking. It was as if she were spellbound by something out there.

Again he turned in the direction she was looking, but all he saw were the dark grassland, the brilliant array of the stars, and another set of headlights off to the right on the road from Mexico.

"Tori, what are you looking at?"

No response.

Stepping closer, Page came within five feet of her and noticed in his peripheral vision that Costigan moved protectively closer, then leaned against another post. The smoke from his cigarette drifted in the air.

Suddenly Page heard her voice.

"Aren't they beautiful?" Tori asked.

"They?" Page turned toward the dark grassland and concentrated. "What do you see?"

"You can't see them?"

"No."

With the noise of the annoying conversations behind him, Page almost didn't hear what Tori said next.

"Then you shouldn't have come."

Baffled, he sat beside her.

Corrigan shifted again.

She still didn't look at him.

"What did you expect me to do?" Page asked, working to keep his voice calm. "You left without telling me. You disappeared for *two days*. I was afraid something had happened to you. When I found out you were here, surely you didn't expect me to stay home."

A half-dozen people stepped onto the observation platform, their feet thunking on the wood, their voices echoing in the enclosure.

"Don't see a thing," one of them said. "What a crock."

"Wait!" someone in the crowd at the fence shouted. "There!

"Where?"

"Over there! Look! Four of them!"

"Yes!" a woman exclaimed.

"I don't see a friggin' thing," a teenager said.

"There!" someone said. With each exclamation, the crowd shifted and turned. The murmur died away as people focused all of their attention, then rose again when some—Page among them—saw nothing.

"You've gotta be shitting me. There's nothing out there," another teenager complained.

The crowd's comments went back and forth. Some people were rapt, while others were frustrated. A few became angry.

Page heard Tori's voice next to him.

"The interruptions go on for a couple of hours," she said.

Bewildered, he studied her. They sat silently for a while, and as some of the onlookers began to leave, the headlights of their cars showed how intense her eyes were as she gazed at the darkness. Her red hair was combed back behind her ears, emphasizing the attractive lines of her face. He wanted to touch her cheek.

"Then it gets peaceful," she said, "and you can really appreciate them."

"Why don't I sit here, and we'll wait for the rest of the crowd to leave? Then you can show me."

"Yes."

Page felt an ache in his chest. His mind raced with questions that had nowhere to go.

Leaning against the nearby post, Costigan dropped his cigarette and crushed it with his boot, all the while continuing to watch carefully.

"When I was ten, my parents took me with them on a car trip," Tori said, staring toward the darkness. Her voice drifted off.

Page didn't understand why she'd told him that. Then she seemed to remember what she'd started to say.

"We lived in Austin back then, and we didn't reach this section of west Texas until dark." She tilted her head toward something in the distance. "My father wanted to visit a cousin of his who'd just gotten a job on a ranch out here. The cousin was only going to be in the area for a couple of months." Again Tori paused, then seemed to remember what she'd started to say. "As you know, all my father's relatives were wanderers."

Including him, Page thought, but he was careful not to interrupt. Her father had deserted the family when Tori had been sixteen.

"Anyway, we drove through here," Tori said.

The exclamations of delight in the crowd contrasted with complaints about the increasing chill and the impatience some felt when they didn't see what others claimed they did. The noise made it difficult for Page to hear what Tori said, but he didn't dare ask her to speak up for fear of having the opposite effect.

She continued, "I needed to go to the bathroom. Even back then, the county had a couple of outdoor toilets here. When I saw them in our headlights, I yelled for him to stop, but my father was in a hurry to see his cousin. He wouldn't have stopped if my mother hadn't insisted. I rushed into one of the toilets, and after I came out, my father was waiting impatiently by the car. Something made me look toward the grassland, and I saw them."

"Saw what?"

Tori seemed not to have heard the question.

"I couldn't help walking toward the fence and staring at them. My mother always took me to church on Sunday, and I thought that when the preacher told us about heaven, this is what he must have been talking about.

"My father ordered me to get in the car, but I couldn't make myself do it. I couldn't bear to stop looking at what was out there. He wanted to know what the hell I thought

I was seeing. I tried to explain, but all he said was something about a damned fool kid's imagination. I remember trying to push him away when he picked me up and carried me to the car. I shouted and pounded him. He literally threw me into the back seat."

"I'm sorry," Page said. "Maybe it was a good thing that he eventually left."

When Tori didn't continue, Page regretted his interruption, but then he realized that she'd stopped only because she'd renewed her attention on the darkness.

"There!" a woman at the fence shouted.

"Yes!" a man joined in.

Another woman pointed. "Five of them!"

"I don't see *anything*!"

Disgusted, the teenagers got into the pickup truck and drove away. A half-dozen people wandered toward the bus, but a surprising number remained, staring toward the darkness.

"There's one on the left!" someone exclaimed.

"What am I supposed to be looking at?" someone else asked.

Page wondered the same thing.

Again Tori spoke, still not looking at him. "I'd forgotten about this place until two days ago."

"The day you started to drive to your mother's house," Page said. The words he almost used were, *The day you left me*.

"I'd gone a little beyond El Paso. It was six in the evening. I was at a truck stop, studying a road map while I drank a cup of coffee. I still had a long way to drive to get to San Antonio, and I wondered if I might need to stop somewhere for the night. Interstate 10 goes south-east along the Mexican border until it gets to a town called Esperanza, where the highway cuts directly east to San Antonio. I figured Esperanza might be a good place to stop." She paused. "Interesting name for a town."

"'Esperanza'?" Page had lived in the Southwest long enough to know that the word was Spanish for "hope."

Tori smiled at something in the darkness. Page waited, beginning to feel afraid. A minute later, she continued. Her voice was so calm that it was as if she were reading a bedtime story to a child.

"I looked toward the bottom of the map to find the inches-to-miles scale and figure out how much farther I needed to go. But as my eyes drifted past the names of towns, one of them caught my attention: Rostov. It must have been tucked away in my memory all these years. Amazing.

"Suddenly that night came back to me as vividly as if it had happened yesterday. I remembered that the roadside toilet had a sign on the door: 'Property of Rostov County.' I remembered coming out of the toilet and seeing what was in the darkness past the fence. I remembered how angry my father got when he didn't understand what I was talking about and threw me into the car. I could feel the tears in my eyes and how I wiped them and stared through the back window toward the darkness until I couldn't see anything out there anymore as we drove away.

"We drove so long that eventually I fell asleep in the back seat. Even then, I dreamed about them."

"There!" someone at the fence exclaimed, pointing.

"So I finished my coffee and folded the map and got in the car," Tori said. "When I reached Esperanza, instead of stopping for the night, I kept driving, but I didn't turn east on Interstate 10 to go to San Antonio. Instead I took a county road and kept following it southeast along the border. The sun went down, but I kept driving until I got here. This observation platform didn't exist back then—there were just the toilets. I was afraid I'd discover that my memory had tricked me, that what I'd seen that night had been only a damned fool kid's imagination, exactly as my father had insisted."

"There's another one!" someone exclaimed.

Tori smiled toward where a man pointed, and she fell silent again. In a while, she continued, "It was late. Hardly anybody was around. I can't describe the relief I felt when I stepped out of the car and looked past that fence and saw that what I'd remembered—and what I realize now I've been dreaming about all these years—was real. I came over and sat on this bench, in the same spot where I'm sitting now and the same spot where I sat last night, and I didn't want to do anything but stay here the rest of the night and look at what I'd seen when I was ten.

"My life might have been so much different if my father had just allowed me to watch a little longer."

"Different?" Page asked. "How?"

Tori didn't answer. That sent a chill through him that had nothing to do with the night air.

"Watch as long as you want," Page said.

"I will."

"I didn't come here to stop you," he tried to assure her.

"I know. Besides, you can't."

Page looked over at Costigan, who continued to lean protectively against the nearby post. He spread his hands as if to say, *Are you starting to get the idea?*

But Page didn't get anything, not anything at all. He was mystified.

And afraid. He worried that Tori was having some kind of breakdown.

If so, he realized, looking around silently, apparently a lot of other people were having the same breakdown.

"Tori . . ."

She continued smiling wistfully toward the darkness.

"I love you," he said. The words came out before he realized. He couldn't remember the last time he'd said them. He didn't get a reaction.

"Tori, tell me what you're seeing. Help *me* see it, too."

"I don't think you can," she said.

"But how do you *know*?"

"For the same reason I left."

The stark acknowledgment of what Page had been dreading made him feel as if a fist had struck his stomach. He remained silent for several long minutes, trying to recover his equilibrium. Trying to think of something he could say that would make things better.

"If you teach me, I can learn," he said. "Whatever it is I've done wrong, I can correct it."

"You didn't do *anything* wrong. There's no blame in being what you are. Or in my being who *I* am."

Page turned toward the darkness, desperate to understand what Tori was talking about. Even though many of the people in the crowd pointed, all he saw were the night-shrouded grassland, the brilliant stars in the sky, and the isolated headlights on the road to the right.

Which of us is crazy? he wondered.

He strained his eyes, trying to adjust to the night and decipher the darkness. He was reminded of something his father had shown him when he was fifteen. Because of his father's skills as a master mechanic in the Air Force, the family had been relocated to numerous bases over the years, including some in Germany, South Korea, and the Philippines. One of those had been MacDill Air Force Base in Tampa, Florida.

On an August Sunday, Page's father had made a rare effort to spend time with his family by taking Page and his mother to the famed Tampa aquarium. They wandered from tank to tank, peering through thick glass walls at various exhibits: sharks, manta rays, moray eels—his father enjoyed looking at anything dangerous—and various schools of brilliantly colored exotic species. But the space behind one glass wall appeared empty except for water, sand, rocks, aquatic plants, and part of a replica of a sunken ship.

"I guess the aquarium's getting ready to stock it with something," Page said, quickly bored, turning away.

"No, it's already stocked," his father replied.

"With what? Nothing's moving in there. It's empty."

"Oh, there's plenty of life in there."

"You mean the plants."

"No. I mean cuttlefish."

"Cuttlefish?"

"They're not really fish. They're in the squid family."

"*Cuttlefish?*" Page repeated.

"With tentacles that project forward. They can be as little as one of your fingers or as long as your arm, sometimes bigger."

"There's no fish in there as long as my arm," he scoffed.

"Squid," his father corrected him.

"Okay, there's no *squid* in there as long as my arm."

"Actually, there are probably a dozen of them."

"You're kidding, right?"

His father gestured toward the glass. "Take a look. A real close look."

Page had long before learned that his father prided himself on an amazing assortment of knowledge about all kinds of unusual subjects. When his father spoke that authoritatively, there was only one way the conversation could end. So Page concentrated on the water in the huge tank.

"Sometimes we see only what we *expect* to see," his father explained. "Sometimes we need to learn to see in a new way."

That made even less sense than the imaginary fish. "I don't know what you . . ."

At once one of the rocks seemed to move a little. Hardly enough to be noticed. Barely a fraction of an inch. But he was certain he'd seen it move. He stepped closer to the glass.

"Ah," Page's father said, apparently detecting his sudden attention. "I think you're starting to catch on."

"That rock. It . . ."

"But it's not a rock," Page's father emphasized.

The object moved another fraction of an inch, and Page realized that his father was right—it *wasn't* a rock.

Page saw a head then, and a tentacle, and another. Not that the object moved any more noticeably than before. But Page's vision had changed—or else it was his *mind* that had shifted focus.

His father said, "Sometimes we see only what we expect to see."

He was beginning to understand. If the only things that were apparent were sand, rocks, underwater plants, and part of a replica of a sunken ship, then the mind took those shapes for granted and didn't bother to recognize what the eyes were seeing.

Amazingly, another rock moved. A patch of sand shifted slightly as well. A section of the sunken ship turned to the side, and one of the plants started walking across the bottom of the tank. The green spikes on it were actually tentacles. Years later, when Page was being trained at the New Mexico police academy, he thought back to that afternoon when he'd realized that there could be a huge difference between what the eyes saw and what was truly before them, that the world was not always what it seemed. Unfortunately, he later discovered, ugliness too often was the truth of what was before him.

But not that afternoon. Excitedly, he began counting the creatures he suddenly noticed. They were everywhere, it seemed.

"One, two, three."

"Four, five, six," his father said.

"Seven, eight, nine," his mother joined in, laughing. That was the summer before she was diagnosed with the breast cancer that would kill her.

His father predicted that there were a dozen cuttlefish

in the tank, but in the end Page counted eighteen, weird, ugly-looking creatures with a strange name for a squid, who'd learned to conceal their ugliness and after a while began to seem beautiful. Within minutes he wasn't able to see the sand, rocks, underwater plants, or replica of the sunken ship because so many cuttlefish were in the way.

"How do they hide like that?" he asked his father, grinning in astonishment.

"Nobody knows. Chameleon lizards are famous for being able to assume the colors of objects around them. Spiders can do it, too. But nothing's as good at it—and as quick at it—as cuttlefish."

"Magic," Page said.

"Nature," Page's father corrected him.

19

Page remembered that long-ago afternoon as he strained to look at the darkness beyond the fence while the crowd of strangers before him marveled at things he didn't see. Some complained that they didn't know what the others were getting so excited about, and Page understood their frustration. Was he witnessing a mass hallucination, some kind of group delusion in which people convinced one another that they were seeing something that wasn't there?

But Tori hadn't been with a group when she'd first seen it, and she hadn't been with a group when she'd come here alone after so many years of remembering and dreaming. If there was a delusion, she'd brought it on herself.

Or maybe I'm the one who's deluded, Page thought. *Hell, all those years and I couldn't even get my wife to share something so important that it brought her back to the middle of nowhere.*

But he had to stay calm.

Remember the cuttlefish, he told himself. *Remember what your father told you. "Sometimes we see only what we expect to see. Sometimes we need to learn to see in a new way."*

Lord knows, I need to learn to see in a new way.

The reality Page thought he knew had been turned inside out. The marriage he'd thought he had, the life he'd prized —*nothing* was what it had seemed to be.

Why? Page shouted inwardly. *How could I not have seen this coming?*

He rose from the bench and stepped to the edge of the observation platform. Vaguely aware of Costigan leaning against the post near him, he stared over the heads of the people in the excited crowd and concentrated on the darkness.

Again he noticed the specks of distant headlights approaching along the road from Mexico. But that couldn't be what the people in the crowd were thrilled about. They were pointing in a different direction altogether.

He studied the brilliant array of stars, surprisingly much brighter and more varied than he was accustomed to in Santa Fe, which was renowned for the clearness of its night sky. Maybe they were why the government had built the radio telescopes nearby. But the people in the crowd weren't pointing toward the stars—their rapt attention was focused entirely on the horizon.

What do they think they're seeing? Page wanted to know.

Remember the cuttlefish, he urged himself.

He focused on the darkness across the grassland.

And saw an almost imperceptible movement, hardly enough to be noticed. . . .

Except that he was sure he *had* noticed it. Either his eyes had shifted focus or his mind had. It wasn't only movement—it was a change in the darkness.

Without warning, there were tiny lights. Some of what he'd thought were stars weren't in the sky—they were hovering over the grassland. At first he suspected they might be distant fireflies, about a dozen of them, but they were brighter than fireflies, and as he began to notice them, they increased in size.

They could have been miles away, yet they seemed close, as if he could reach out and touch them, which he tried to do. That was when he realized the people in the crowd weren't just pointing—they, too, were reaching out.

As he gazed, the distant lights acquired colors—red, green, blue, yellow, and more—all the tints he'd seen on houses and stores in town. Pairs of them merged, becoming larger and brighter. They rose and fell. At the same time, they drifted back and forth across the horizon, as if they floated in a gentle current. They bobbed and pivoted hypnotically.

What am I seeing?

Confused, Page turned toward Costigan, looking for

confirmation that his eyes weren't tricking him, but all the police chief did was spread his hands again.

Page turned back, redirecting his attention to what he saw—or thought he saw—on the horizon. Some of the lights drifted apart, while others continued to merge. They shimmered, gentle and soothing, almost seeming to beckon.

I've never seen anything like them, he thought. *What are they?* Without warning, doubt surged through him. *Why didn't I see them a minute ago? They've got to be an optical illusion.*

Or maybe I'm so eager to see something out there that I strained my eyes until I saw spots before them. Or else I concentrated until I imagined them. How do I know they're what Tori sees—or thinks she does?

What do the others think they're seeing?

Not only seeing, he realized. There was something else associated with the lights, something he couldn't quite identify. It was just on the edge of his perceptions, a sound that hovered at the limit of his ability to hear it.

As Page stepped off the platform, intending to approach and question a teenaged girl who pointed in delight at the grassland beyond the fence, he became aware of a commotion somewhere in the crowd. A single voice rose above the others.

"Don't you see how evil they are?" someone demanded.

Page stopped and tried to determine the direction of the voice. It was deep, strong, and angry. It belonged to a man.

"Don't you realize what they're *doing* to you?"

To his right, Page saw sudden movement, people being jostled aside, a tall, heavy man sweeping through them.

"Stop pushing!" someone complained.

"Get your hand off me!" someone else objected.

The voice just sounded angrier. "Don't you understand that you're all going to hell?"

"A gun!" a woman wailed. "My God, he has a gun!"

As the word sent a wave of alarm through the crowd, Page responded instantly and crouched. Reaching for the pistol that he almost always carried, he realized with dismay that he'd let Costigan talk him into leaving it in his suitcase back in the rental car, which was parked outside the courthouse.

His palms became sweaty.

Crouching lower, feeling his pulse race, he scanned the panicking crowd and flinched at the loud, ear-torturing *crack* of a rifle. He saw the muzzle flash among fleeing men and women, revealing what looked like the barrel of an assault weapon.

Crack. The man fired again, aiming beyond the fence. The muzzle flash projected toward the horizon, toward whatever was out there, toward whatever Page had thought he'd seen.

"Go back to hell where you came from!" the man shouted into the distance, and he kept firing.

Page saw enough of the rifle's silhouette to identify a curved ammunition magazine projecting from the bottom. The profile was that of an AK-47.

Urgently he glanced behind him, toward Costigan, seeing that the police chief had drawn his pistol and was crouching tensely, just as Page was.

The chaos of the crowd now shielded the man with the rifle, and for a moment, he was lost from sight.

Crack. Another muzzle flash projected toward the darkness.

"You're all damned!" But the gunman was no longer yelling toward whatever had entranced them. Instead he turned and began yelling at the crowd. Page had the sickening realization of what was about to happen.

No!

The man fired directly into the crowd. People screamed and smashed against one another, desperate to escape.

A man tripped.

A woman wailed.

Then Page realized that the man *hadn't* tripped. A bullet had dropped him.

The gunman fired yet again.

Page had seldom felt so helpless. Even if he'd had his pistol, the darkness and the commotion would have prevented him from getting a shot at the man with the rifle.

Crack. A woman fell.

Crack. A teenaged boy toppled. The crowd's frightened shouts became so loud that Page almost couldn't hear the rifle. He saw the barrel swing in his direction.

Tori! he thought desperately. Pivoting, he ran toward the observation platform. Costigan was no longer in sight, but Page didn't have time to figure out what the police chief was doing.

Tori!

She was on her feet, so overwhelmed that she didn't have the presence of mind to react. Page had taught her about firearms and had asked her to keep a handgun in her purse. He'd worried about her taking clients out to remote locations where she'd be alone with them, but Tori never carried the gun he'd given her. The truth was, although she was a police officer's wife, her attitudes were those of a civilian.

He put an arm around her and gripped her tightly, rushing her off the platform. Behind him, a bullet hit a board in the back wall. When she cried out in alarm, he pushed her head down, making her stoop as he rushed her around the corner. This was the side opposite from where Costigan had parked the police car, but Page was relieved to see that vehicles were parked here as well, and he tugged her behind a murky pickup truck.

"Are you okay?" he asked, examining her as best he could in the starlight.

She was too disoriented to answer.

A shot echoed from beyond the observation platform.

"Tori, *answer* me. Are you hurt?"

His abrupt tone made her flinch, bringing her to awareness.

"I . . . No. I'm okay. I'm not hit."

"Thank God. Stay here. Keep behind the engine. Bullets can go through the truck's doors, but not through the engine. If you think the shooter's coming in this direction, fall down and pretend you're dead."

In the shadows, she stared at him.

"Tori, tell me you understand."

Beyond the observation deck, two shots were followed by a scream.

She blinked repeatedly. "Keep behind the engine," she

said, swallowing. "If he comes this way, I'm supposed to fall down and pretend I'm dead."

Crack. The gunman fired again.

"I can't stay with you," Page said. "I need to help stop him."

"*Why is he doing this?*"

"I don't know why people do *anything.*"

The next shot Page heard was a loud *pop* rather than a *crack.* A pistol. *Costigan must be returning fire,* he decided.

He squeezed Tori's shoulder and ran from the cover of the pickup truck. At once he heard another pistol shot, then a rifle shot.

And a groan. Its raspy edge left no doubt that it came from Costigan.

20

The turmoil of his heartbeat contrasted with the slowness he forced upon himself when he reached the corner of the wall. His hands trembled. He fought to control them.

The wooden planks of the wall couldn't protect him from an AK-47's high-powered bullet, but at least they concealed him as he crouched beneath the shooter's eye level and peered around the corner.

The faint light from the opposite side of the observation platform showed him a nightmare. Bodies lay all around. Some twitched, but most remained still.

The shooter stalked among them.

"Came from hell!" He fired down at a head, his rifle's muzzle flash casting him in a grotesque silhouette. "Going *back* to hell!"

Where's Costigan? Page wondered frantically.

He inhaled sharply when he saw the police chief's body sprawled on the ground halfway between the observation platform and the crowd. Costigan's pistol lay near his outstretched right hand.

The gunman fired at a twitching body, the muzzle flash revealing a spray of blood. He dropped an empty magazine and inserted a fresh one so quickly that Page didn't have the chance even to think about charging across the parking lot and tackling him.

The man aimed down, about to shoot at another squirming body, but suddenly stopped and lowered the rifle. He turned as if something had caught his attention. Page followed the direction of his gaze.

What the shooter looked at was conspicuous, even in the dark. It was white, so big that it couldn't be ignored. Inside it, people whimpered and wailed.

The tour bus.

My God, Page realized, *before he started shooting, some of the passengers went back to their seats.*

The gunman walked toward it. With his back to Page, he faced the dark windows of the bus. He stood straighter, as if energized, and took long steps over bodies, approaching his new target. As he rounded the front, disappearing toward the door, Page was tempted to hurry from the side of the observation platform, wanting desperately to reach Costigan's pistol. But the sound of his footsteps on the gravel would almost certainly attract attention. There was little chance that he could reach the pistol before the gunman heard him coming and reappeared, shooting.

A fist banged against the opposite side of the bus.

"Open the door!" the gunman demanded.

Page backed along the sidewall of the observation platform and headed toward the dark road.

"*Open the damned door!*"

Page got to the road and hurried along it, his sneakers hushed on the pavement.

Shots clanged through metal. The gunman was firing into the side of the bus. The AK-47's bullets were capable of penetrating the metal, passing straight through, and going out the other side. A human body would barely slow them.

After the next shot into the side of the bus, someone screamed.

Page reduced speed as he came along the road and neared the back of the bus.

The next shot was followed by a cry of pain. Bullets shattered windows. The sound of terrified wailing intensified.

Page was troubled by another sound he began to hear: that of liquid spilling onto the gravel.

"Came from hell!" the man screamed.

The smell of gasoline drifted into Page's nostrils.

"Going *back* there!"

Page's training had taught him that only in the movies did a shot to a vehicle's fuel tank cause a fire, let alone an explosion. This guy could shoot at the bus's fuel tank all night, but unless he had incendiary ammunition, the only effect would be a lot of holes.

And more leaking fuel. The gasoline fumes smelled stronger.

He moved warily, hoping the darkness behind him would conceal his outline. Peering around the back of the bus, he saw the gunman, who was so intent on shooting at the gas tank that he didn't notice anything else. He stepped back from a pool of gasoline that was spreading on the gravel.

Oh, God—surely he isn't . . .

The man set down his rifle and pulled a book of matches from a shirt pocket.

Page charged.

The man tore a match from the book and struck it along the abrasive strip. The match flared.

Then he heard Page coming and turned. The light from the match cast shadows up his face, exaggerating its harsh angles. His eyes reflected the flame, emphasizing their intensity.

He lit the entire book.

Page ran faster, yelling obscenities as fiercely as he could, trying to startle the man, to distract him from what he intended to do.

The shooter dropped the burning matches an instant before Page crashed into him. As they hit the gravel, Page could only pray that they would go out, but instantly he heard a *whoosh* behind him. Flames dispelled the darkness. Heat rushed over his back.

Outraged, he slammed the man's head against the gravel. Hair and bone crunched against the stones. But the man simply roared and swung his arm with such force that he cast Page aside. Even given the man's height and muscular build, his strength was amazing. He had to be on some kind of psychosis-inducing drug.

The flames roared upward, enveloping the rear of the bus. Page squirmed backward to escape them.

Snap, snap, snap.

The heat broke windows. The wails of the people trapped inside became hysterical. Seeing the gunman reach for his rifle, Page came to his feet and charged again. The impact of striking him was so great that it sent both of them farther from the bus.

They hit the gravel and skidded. Landing on top, Page tried to drive a fist into his opponent's larynx, but the man abruptly twisted, and Page connected only with the side of his neck. The man swung his arm again and struck Page's shoulder so hard that he knocked Page off him. The blow jolted Page almost to the point of paralyzing him. Groaning, he stuck out a foot and tripped the man as he ran toward his rifle. The man landed heavily, grunting loudly.

The flames spread along the bus, their heat radiating toward Page's face.

"Open the door! Get off the bus!" he yelled to the people inside.

He grabbed the gunman from behind and clamped his left arm around the man's neck, straining to choke him. Simultaneously he drove his right fist into the man's right kidney, punching him again and again.

The man lurched backward, ramming Page against a car behind him. As he groaned from the impact, the man twisted away from the car and deliberately fell back. Page groaned again when he struck the gravel. He felt crushed by the man's considerable weight landing on him.

He couldn't breathe.

His arm loosened around the man's neck.

In a rush, the man came to his feet, kicked Page in the right side, and lunged again for his rifle. All the while, the flames roared upward from the rear of the bus and spread toward the front. Page felt the heat through his shirt.

Pumped by adrenaline, he forced himself to his feet.

The man picked up the rifle.

Page charged, struck the man from behind, and propelled him into the flames. The fire was so thick that Page couldn't see the rear of the bus, but he heard a *thump* when the man struck it.

The man's clothes caught fire. His hair blazed.

Turning, he seemed to smile—or maybe it was the effect the flames had on his facial muscles. The rifle fell from his burning hands.

He held out his arms and stepped forward.

Page stumbled away from him.

Ablaze, the man kept lurching toward him, his flaming arms outstretched, his mouth spread in a grotesque smile.

Page jolted back against a car. He squirmed along it, trying to get away from the fiery nightmare that kept stalking toward him. The man's smile wasn't defined any longer as flesh shrank away from his teeth. He was terribly close, and the smell of his burning flesh was sickening.

About to give Page a fiery embrace, he abruptly twisted to the side. The sound of a shot was almost absorbed by the roar of the flames. A second shot made him stagger. His face tilted skyward, for the first time showing anguish.

A third and fourth shot dropped him to his knees.

A fifth shot blew a hole through his head.

The man dropped face down, embracing the gravel, his broiling flesh spreading across it.

Page staggered away from him, staring toward his left. The shooter was Tori. She held Costigan's pistol with two hands, her arms extended, her wrists and elbows locked the way Page had taught her. Her face was twisted with fury. She squeezed the trigger again, shooting into the flames that covered the man.

"Bastard!" she screamed. "*Bastard!*"

The door to the bus banged open. A half-dozen people surged out from the smoke. They sobbed and coughed, running toward the cold darkness and away from the bus, which was little more than a flaming coffin now.

Page hurried around the car and approached Tori from the back. As heat swept over them, she shot again toward the flames that consumed the man.

"Now you're the one who's going to hell!" she screamed.

"Tori," Page said. He came up next to her, reaching for the gun. "It's okay now. He can't hurt anybody anymore. Give me the pistol."

She fired again at the burning corpse's back.

"You son of a bitch!"

"He's dead," Page told her. "You don't need the gun anymore."

He put his right hand on the pistol and pressed it down, encouraging her to lower her arms.

"Give it to me."

Gradually the tension in her hands relaxed. Slowly she released the weapon.

Page's cheeks felt raw from the heat. He guided her in a wide arc around the front of the bus, away from the fire. As the air became darker, it cooled his skin.

The people who'd escaped from the bus slumped near the fence, sobbing. Bodies lay everywhere. He counted twenty but knew there were more. A few squirmed in pain. Most had the stillness of death.

"Tori, don't look." He guided her to the Saturn, where he hoped she'd feel sheltered, but the car was locked, and when he felt the front pockets of Tori's jeans, he didn't find the keys. *They must be in her purse*, he thought.

He led her to the bench on the observation platform. He looked around but couldn't find the purse in the darkness. After sitting her down, he promised, "I'll be right back."

He ran to Costigan. The chief's cowboy hat lay beside him. The left side of his head was covered with blood. Page touched his wrist and felt a pulse.

"Hang on," he told him.

He found the car keys in Costigan's pants and ran to the cruiser, pressing the unlock button on the key fob. Inside, he grabbed the radio's microphone.

"Officer down! Officer down!"

"Who's *this*?" a man's angry voice demanded. "How'd you get on this radio?"

"Officer down!" Page had trouble keeping his voice steady enough to identify himself and describe what had happened. "I was with the chief! He's been shot!"

"*What?*"

"At least twenty other people were hit. At the observation platform outside town. A bus is on fire, and . . ." As he supplied more details, the enormity of what had happened struck him. "The assailant's dead, but we need all the help you can bring."

"If this is a joke—"

"Look at the horizon east of town. You ought to be able to see the glow of the fire."

"Just a . . ." The pause was suddenly broken. "Holy . . . I'll get help as quick as I can."

Page sat numbly in the cruiser and stared toward the devastation that lay beyond the windshield. The light from the flames rippled over the bodies. His side aching, he got out of the car and stepped around pools of blood, approaching the people who'd escaped the burning bus.

"Help's on the way," he promised them.

"Thank you," a woman told him through her tears. "Thank you for saving us."

"I was sure I was going to die," a man said, trembling. ". . . Never been so scared."

"Why did he do it?" someone demanded. "*Why?*"

Amid the roar of the flames, Page noticed that more survivors were warily emerging from their hiding places. Some had crawled under vehicles. Others had run across the road and concealed themselves in the darkness of a neighboring field.

An elderly man wavered among the corpses. Smoke drifted over him.

"Where's Beth? Where's . . . ?" The old man stopped and groaned. Grief made him sink to his knees. He cradled the head of one of the bodies.

Heartsick, Page went back to the observation plat-form.

Tori no longer stared toward the grassland. Instead she bent despairingly forward, her face in her hands.

She shivered.

Page noticed the windbreaker on the bench. He got it and draped it over her shoulders. He finally saw her purse on the floor, where she must have dropped it when the shooting had started. He placed it next to her. Numb, he sat beside her, put an arm around her, and listened to the blare of the approaching sirens.

TWO

THE DARKLING PLAIN

21

Brent Loft gave his most amused, sympathetic look to the camera, saying, "Near Arroyo Park, a tearful ten-year-old girl waved for a police car to stop and pointed to where her cat had climbed to the top of a high-voltage utility pole. Workers from El Paso Electric arrived with a crane and very carefully rescued the feline, which, as you can see, was more afraid of being rescued than of staying on top of the pole. The thick, insulated gloves of the man on the crane protected him from more than just the electrical lines."

Next to Loft, his coanchor, Sharon Rivera, chuckled and read the next paragraph on the teleprompter: "The girl and her pet were finally reunited, but apparently this isn't the only time the cat has been rescued. Last month two city workers had to free it from a storm drain."

"Seven more lives to go," Brent said, trying not to gag on the line. He turned toward the man on his left. "Frank, what's the final weather recap?"

"Tomorrow'll be another hot, sunny day with a chance of thunderstorms during the night."

"We can always use the rain," Sharon said.

"Sure can," Brent agreed. "Well, that's it for El Paso's First-on-the-Scene News at 10. Be sure to watch our morning report from 6 to 7. We'll see you tomorrow night at 5, 6, and 10. Thanks for joining us."

With big smiles, they listened to their program's pulsing theme music. The red lights on the cameras stopped glowing. The harsh overhead lights dimmed.

Like the other newscasters, Brent took off his lapel microphone and removed the earbud radio receiver through which the show's producer could give him instructions to cut an item, add a late-breaking story, or make a joke.

Sharon's earbud got caught in her voluminous hair.

"I hate reports about rescued pets," Brent complained.

"Yeah, but people like to go to sleep with a cozy feeling," sports reporter Tom Montoya said as he stood from behind his desk. Tom wore a jacket and tie for the camera, but what viewers at home couldn't see was that—hidden by the desk—the rest of his ensemble consisted of shorts, sweat socks, and sneakers. He'd played basketball between the 6 and 10 newscasts, barely returning to the station in time to refresh his makeup.

Sharon wore an elegant navy blazer and a pale-blue blouse, the tightness of which accentuated her breasts. When she stood from the news desk, her mismatched jeans became visible. Because she had chronic sore feet, she didn't wear shoes. Her socks were thick wool because her feet were sensitive to the cold that came off the studio's concrete floor.

In contrast, Brent wore a full suit, an expensive calfskin belt, and designer shoes that he always buffed before he went on the air. The shoes were the most important feature—he felt that their shine radiated upward and added to the substance of his delivery. From bottom to top, everything counted. He would no more go on the air with scuffed shoes than he would with hair that wasn't carefully blow-dried.

But it had taken all his skill to sound sincere when he'd read that item about the damned cat. The next time the producer wanted a cute story, Brent promised himself he'd make Sharon read all of it.

"Want to go out for a drink?" he asked her.

"Brent, how many times do I need to tell you I'm dating someone?"

"Hey, it never hurts to ask. If you're serious about this guy, why don't you bring him around sometime so we can see what he looks like?"

"He?" She looked at him strangely.

"Very funny," Brent said.

"You've been working here three months, and no one told you I was gay?"

"Yeah, right. Quit kidding around."

"What makes you think I'm kidding?"

"Okay, okay, I can take a joke." At that moment, the producer entered the studio, rescuing him from Sharon's ridiculous act.

"Brent, I need to talk to you."

Brent didn't like his tone. *Something's going to hit the fan*, he predicted.

He had risen through the broadcast markets from a small television station in Oklahoma to a modest-sized one in Kansas to this bigger one in El Paso. Every newscaster's goal was to work for the premium cable news channels—like CNN or Fox—or the network stations in Los Angeles, Chicago, Washington, and New York. Better yet, at the top—to go national on the evening news at ABC, NBC, or CBS.

Brent had rocketed through the lower-level stations, but he was forced to admit that he hadn't gained the momentum he needed to get out of El Paso a year from now, as he'd planned. For one thing, he hadn't managed to bond with the rest of the news team. Perhaps they sensed his determination not to stay in the area any longer than necessary. As a consequence, he hadn't been given any career-advancing stories. Also, he had the sense that the news director regretted hiring him. Presumably he'd decided that Brent looked a little too white-bread for this market.

Shit, he'll probably come down on me for the way I read that piece about the damned cat.

"Sharon, I need to see you, also," the producer said. A somber expression on his face, he looked down at his tennis shoes as if he wanted to avoid eye contact.

"Listen, I can explain about the cat story . . ." Brent said.

The producer peered up, looking distracted. "What are you talking about?"

Sharon padded across the concrete floor on her thick socks. "Has something happened?"

"There's been a mass shooting." The producer's somber expression was replaced with a look of grim resolve.

"What?"

"Outside a town called Rostov. That's about two hundred miles southeast of here. Our contact with the Highway Patrol says as many as twenty people were hit, most of them fatally. It happened at some kind of roadside tourist attraction they have down there."

Brent stepped closer. Even in today's weird world, a mass shooting with five or six victims was news. But *twenty*?

"Who did it?" Sharon asked.

"The gunman hasn't been identified. Apparently a woman on the scene shot and killed him."

"A woman?" *The story's sounding better by the minute,* Brent thought.

"The details are still coming in, but I don't want our viewers to get all their information about it from CNN or Fox. This is a west Texas story. We call ourselves 'First-on-the-Scene,' and by God, we'll prove it. Sharon, go back on the air for 'breaking news.' Our contact with the Highway Patrol agreed to an on-air telephone interview. Brent, the chopper's waiting for you. Fly to Rostov immediately. Find out what's happening. Hopefully you'll be up to speed when Sharon and the broadcast truck reach there in the morning."

As Sharon hurried toward the news desk, the producer called after her, "Sharon, at Rostov you'll give live updates throughout the day. Tomorrow evening, you'll anchor the show with a view of the place where the shootings occurred. This'll be a special broadcast, and we'll make a big deal about it. Squeeze in as much rest as you can. I don't want you looking tired."

"So Sharon and I will be coanchoring there?" Brent asked, already imagining how impressive that would look on his résumé.

"No, *Sharon's* the anchor. You'll contribute background. If you do research all night and all day tomorrow, by the time the broadcast starts tomorrow evening, you'll look like something the cat dragged in." The producer seemed to emphasize the word "cat," but Brent hoped it was just his imagination. "Now, hurry out to the chopper."

"But I need to go home and get some fresh clothes," Brent said. "This suit'll be a mess by tomorrow."

"You don't have time. I want you on the ground before those damned CNN reporters show up." With that, the producer turned toward the three camera operators. "Who wants some serious overtime?"

"I do," a woman said. "The brakes on my car need replacing."

When she stepped from behind the equipment, Brent recognized the cute Hispanic camerawoman who'd recently joined the staff. Her name was Anita something. In her early twenties, she was short and trim, with shiny dark hair pulled back in a ponytail. She wore hiking boots and pants that had twice the usual number of pockets. Her shirt had ample pockets as well.

"Grab a camera and take one of the vans," the producer responded. "Start for Rostov right away. This time of night, you can probably reach there in two and a half hours."

"Less," Anita said confidently.

"Whatever—I don't care how many speeding tickets you get. Just don't crash the van. By the time Brent's done getting overhead shots of the crime scene and providing commentary, you'll need to be close to the area."

"Wait," Brent said, "you want me to operate the chopper's camera, too?"

The producer ignored him and kept talking to Anita.

"There's a good possibility the bodies won't have been removed yet. After the chopper sets Brent down, you and he will start interviewing the police and any witnesses you can find. Brent, I told you to get moving. If we cover this from enough angles, maybe CNN won't bother sending their people. Maybe they'll pay to have Sharon supply live updates. Our competition won't stand a chance in the ratings."

22

The eerie music drifted and dipped, hovered and sailed. Coming from instruments Halloway still couldn't identify, the languid, sensuous melody settled into a lower register. He imagined that he was slow dancing with the most beautiful woman he'd ever met. He smelled cinnamon in her hair and tasted orange juice and vodka.

By now there were seven people in the room: Halloway and his partner, Taggard, another pair of guards who'd kept leaving the surveillance room to listen to the music, and the researcher—Gordon—who'd been joined by two others.

Transported by the sounds, no one spoke. Halloway imagined the woman he danced with pressing against him. She breathed softly into his ear.

Abruptly the music became silent. The woman disappeared.

"Hey, what happened?" Halloway demanded.

Static came from the speakers: harsh, crackly, loud, and aggravating.

"Gordon, what did you do?" he exclaimed. "Where's the music?"

But Gordon looked as surprised—and annoyed—as everyone else.

"I didn't do anything," he protested, holding up his hands as if that would prove it.

"Then what happened? Why did the music stop?"

A researcher pressed buttons and twisted knobs on several of the consoles. "Maybe we have a phasing problem," he offered.

The static's brittle echo rebounded off the walls.

"Phasing, my ass." Halloway clamped his hands to his ears. "Damn it, that *hurts*. Do something."

Another researcher flicked a switch, disengaging the speakers. The static all but disappeared, coming only from headphones on a desk. When Gordon put them on, Halloway couldn't hear the static at all.

What he did hear, though, was the hum of the many electronic devices that were crammed into the room—and the deeper vibration, almost undetectable, that the facility's electrical generator or the huge dishes above-ground sent through the walls.

The music had distracted him from his increasing headache, but now the pain intensified through his skull.

"Where did it come from?"

The researchers gave each other guarded looks, as if hiding something.

"Bring it back!"

"We don't know how we received it in the first place," Gordon explained too quickly, "let alone how to find it again."

"Just bring it back!" Halloway demanded.

"You're not even supposed to be in here," Gordon realized, now that the music no longer occupied his attention. "This area's strictly off-limits. You belong in the surveillance room."

"Like hell. My job's to protect this place. I can go anywhere I want."

"Well, how about protecting it by checking the security monitors? While you've been hanging around in here, a terrorist assault team might have surrounded us."

Buddy, if you hear that music again and you don't let me know, Halloway silently vowed, *terrorists will be the least of your worries.*

23

Dozens of emergency lights flashed in the darkness. Their chaos of orange, blue, and white contrasted starkly with the shimmering colors Page had thought he'd seen earlier. An engine rumbled as firefighters sprayed foam on what was left of the burning bus. Eight Highway Patrol cars were parked next to three police cars from Rostov. Law enforcement officers and medical personnel seemed everywhere. Page heard the wail of a departing ambulance and the roar of a medevac helicopter as it rose from a nearby field, its takeoff lights painfully intense.

From his vantage point a short distance down the road, he watched a patrolman interviewing Tori in her car next to the viewing platform. Page had already spoken to several officers and took for granted that they'd have more questions. Right now he was grateful for the chance to step back from the commotion and try to adjust to the trauma of what had happened.

He found himself next to a metal pole that had a large, brass rectangle attached to the top. Words were embossed on the rectangle. The harsh reflection from the emergency vehicles provided just enough illumination for him to be able to read:

Welcome to the Rostov lights. Many people have claimed to see them, but no one has ever been able to explain them. If you're lucky enough to experience them, decide for yourself what they are.

Footsteps approached. Page turned from the plaque and saw a silhouette of a man in a cowboy hat. As the figure came nearer, he recognized a Highway Patrol captain he'd spoken with earlier. The Hispanic man had a broad face, with prominent cheek- and jawbones. The emergency lights revealed his blue tie and tan uniform. His last name was Medrano.

"We finished interviewing your wife," he announced. "You can take her back to where you're staying."

Page didn't comment on the complexities that lay behind that statement.

"You're done with me, too?"

"For now. All the survivors tell the same story. The guy went crazy. If not for you and your wife, a lot more people would have been killed. You still don't have any idea why he did it?" Medrano looked as if he desperately wanted *something* that would explain what had happened.

"Only that he said the lights were evil."

"The lights? The way you talk about them . . . *You* saw them, too?"

"It took some effort, but yeah. At least, I saw *something*."

The captain looked puzzled. "I live in Harrington, about a hundred miles down the road. It's a big town because of the oil refinery, but there's not a lot to do. Whenever my wife's parents or my brother and his family came to visit, we used to drive here to try to see the lights. I bet I made that trip a dozen times. Never saw a thing. Neither did my wife's parents or my brother and his family, even though strangers standing right next to us claimed they could. We finally gave up and stopped coming. What'd they look like?"

"They seemed miles away, yet I thought they were so close I tried to reach out and touch them. They bobbed and floated, merged and separated, and came together again. They kept changing colors. Once I saw them, I had trouble turning away from them."

Medrano nodded. "That's usually the way they're described."

"The thing is, I'm beginning to wonder if I just *persuaded* myself they were out there. It was like mass hysteria, and I might have just been caught up in it."

"Yeah, that's one explanation—that people talk each other into seeing them."

"*One* explanation? What are the others?"

"Phosphorescent gas that rises from seams in the earth. Another theory suggests that the underground rocks here have a lot of quartz crystals in them. After the heat of the day, the rapid cooling causes the rocks to contract and give off static electricity."

Page looked past Medrano toward the emergency lights, the smoke rising from the shell of the bus—and the corpses.

"All those people died because of static electricity?" He shook his head. "If so, that makes it even more senseless."

"Your wife says the killer shouted to the crowd, 'Don't you realize what they're doing to you?'"

"He meant the lights. Then he started shooting at the horizon. He yelled, 'Go back to hell where you came from.' Then, 'You're all damned.' I thought he meant the lights again, but it turned out he meant that the crowd was damned because the next thing he opened fire on everyone around him."

"Some kind of religious lunatic," Medrano suggested.

"He sure had a fixation on hell. 'Came from hell.' 'Going back to hell.' He said that a couple of times while he was shooting people."

"Well, the fire that burned him gave him a taste of where *he* was going," Medrano said.

"That thought occurred to me, too. Do you know who he was?"

"Not yet—any ID he had on him was destroyed. By process of elimination, we'll figure out which car he used and track its registration number."

"Unless he came on the bus."

"With an AK-47 that nobody noticed?"

"He could have carried it in something like a guitar case," Page offered.

"Yeah, that's possible. You know, you *do* think like a cop. Well, if the shooter arrived on the bus, any evidence was probably destroyed by the fire. That'll make our job a lot more difficult."

Page shivered, perhaps because of the cool breeze or perhaps because he looked toward the corpses again.

"You could use a windbreaker," Medrano said.

"Chief Costigan told me the same thing. Any word about how he's doing?"

"An ambulance driver phoned me from the Rostov hospital. He's in surgery. What about *you*? How are you holding up?"

Page rubbed his right side, where the gunman had kicked him. "I'm not looking forward to seeing the bruise."

"That's not what I meant."

"I know. There's a lot to sort through. For now, I'm just glad to be alive."

"Ever been involved in a shooting before?"

"Once. But nobody died. For certain, my wife was never in a shooting before. If it hadn't been for her, the guy might have reached me."

"She did an amazing thing. We collected six spent pistol cartridges."

"Actually, she fired eight times," Page said.

"And yet she only remembers pulling the trigger *four* times. If you and your wife worked for me, tomorrow morning you'd be talking to a counselor, but there's not much I can do to help outsiders."

"I understand. Thanks for your concern."

Medrano turned toward the western sky, where the roar of a helicopter was rapidly approaching. "Good. Another medevac chopper."

"I'll drive my wife back to the motel."

The emergency lights revealed Tori's silhouette in the front seat of her Saturn. As Page headed in that direction, he heard the helicopter getting louder.

Its lights suddenly blazed, but instead of landing in a nearby field, it hovered over the crime scene—not close enough to the ground to kick up dust or blow objects around and interfere with the investigation, but carefully maintaining a legal altitude.

"What the hell's going on?" Medrano wondered.

But Page had already figured it out, managing to detect four huge letters on the chopper's side.

Medrano shook his fist at the sky. "That's a damned TV news chopper."

24

For a couple of seconds, Brent glimpsed the lights of a town below him. Then the helicopter roared over it, and all he saw was darkness again. At once a cluster of flashing lights appeared ahead.

A *lot* of flashing lights.

Through headphones, he heard the pilot's voice. "There it is."

Smoke rose from a burned-out shell of a bus. Firefighters, police officers, and medical personnel swarmed everywhere he looked.

"Do you see any bodies on the ground?" Brent asked the pilot. "Yes! There!"

Body bags covered human shapes on a gravel parking lot. Brent counted twelve. Others were being placed in ambulances.

His news producer was waiting back at the station, at the other end of a two-way radio. Brent flicked a switch and spoke into his microphone. "I made it here in time. They're just starting to remove the bodies."

"Any other news choppers?"

"None."

"Good. You know what to do."

"Did you find the background material I asked for?" Brent asked. "You didn't give me a chance to do any research. I need to know about this town."

"There's not much," the producer's voice said through the earphones.

"'Not much' is better than 'nothing.'"

"Wikipedia has a small item. Seems the town's main claim to fame is that it was the location for the James Deacon movie *Birthright*."

"It was released on DVD last month. I watched it," Brent said.

"Well, I don't know how that's going to help you."

"Rostov. What kind of name is *that*? Sounds foreign."

"Russian," the producer's voice answered. "The railroad that was built there in 1889 was owned by a husband and wife who stopped in the area when the place was only a water-refilling station. The wife happened to be reading a translation of Tolstoy's *War and Peace*. One of the characters is Count Rostov, so that's the name she gave to the place. If you want to put our viewers to sleep, go ahead and mention that. Also, there's an abandoned military base—just a ruin, really, where they used to train bomber pilots. There are so many unexploded bombs that they had to fence off the area and post warning signs, but there hasn't been an incident in years."

"Anything else?"

"Nothing. Except . . ."

"What?" Brent asked. "I need anything you've got."

"There's something about lights."

"Lights?"

"It calls them, and I quote, 'the mysterious Rostov lights.'"

"What the hell are *those*?"

"All it says is 'colored balls of light in a field.' Along with the old movie set from *Birthright*, they're the big local attraction. Any bets the good citizens of Rostov go out in the field and wave colored flashlights around to attract gullible tourists? But how you're going to use any of that is beyond me."

"You'll be surprised. Get ready."

The pilot had told Brent how to work the camera that was mounted on the chopper's nose. Now he maneuvered controls that allowed him to aim the exterior lens wherever he wanted and zoom in on any detail.

"Transmitting in five, four, three, two, one, *now*," he said. A cockpit monitor showed the images he sent to the station: the flashing lights, the emergency vehicles, the police, the firefighters, the medical team, and the bodies.

If that jerk-off thinks I'm going to play nice and let Sharon have most of the airtime, he's out of his mind. I'll give him stuff that's so much better than she can do, he'll be forced to put me on camera more than her. I've got a feeling this story is big enough to take me to Atlanta.

He let the scene achieve its impact, then gathered his thoughts around the meager information the producer had given him.

"This is Brent Loft reporting from the First-on-the-Scene News chopper. The carnage below me might be mistaken for the aftermath of an attack in a war zone, but this isn't Afghanistan or Iraq. It's peaceful west Texas cattle country, near the sleepy town of Rostov. That name comes from a character in Tolstoy's *War and Peace*—but peace is exactly what Rostov doesn't have tonight. The senseless gunfire that broke out at this scenic vista two and a half hours ago left at least twenty people dead and prompts the question, 'Is any place truly safe anymore?'"

Below, a vehicle backed away from the police cars, ambulances, and a fire truck. Brent aimed the camera toward it, hoping it was an emergency vehicle whose roof lights would suddenly come to life as it raced toward town. But he quickly realized that the vehicle was a civilian SUV, so he redirected the camera toward the firefighters spraying foam on the smoking shell of the bus.

"A half century ago, not far from here, James Deacon starred in the classic film *Birthright*, about a lifelong bitter feud between a wildcat oil driller and a prominent Texas cattle family. It's a gripping saga about how the Old West became the *New* West. But even in the lawlessness of the Old West, the unspeakable massacre that occurred here tonight would have been unimaginable. The New West, as it turns out, is far more violent than the Old. Early reports indicate that the as-yet-unidentified killer was shot by someone on the scene, one of the innocent bystanders he was trying to slaughter. If so, his motive for this shocking outrage might remain as elusive and unexplained as the mysterious Rostov lights that draw tourists to this area."

25

Hearing the roar of the chopper above him, Page drove Tori's Saturn away from the turmoil of the crime scene. As he left the flashing emergency lights behind, he peered over at his wife, troubled by the way she stared straight ahead toward the darkness of the narrow road beyond the car's headlights. Her face was tight. She looked dazed.

"You didn't have a choice," he told her. He kept remembering her frenzied shouts as she repeatedly pulled the trigger, even after the gunman had stopped moving. "You did the right thing. Never forget that."

Tori might have nodded slightly, but perhaps it was only the motion of the car.

"Imagine the alternative," Page said. "If he'd grabbed me, I might have been burned to death. Those people on the bus would have burned to death as well."

"Maybe I shot him once to save you," Tori murmured. Her lips barely moved. As she continued staring ahead, he had to concentrate to decipher what she told him.

"And maybe I shot him a second time to save those other people." She drew a breath, her features more stark. "But I shot him the other times . . . so many . . ."

Page waited.

". . . because he made the lights go away. He ruined the night, the son of a bitch."

The interior of the car became tensely silent.

When they reached the motel, a neon sign said, NO VACANCY. Page stopped in front of unit 11 and recognized one of the cars farther along. The Audi belonged to the mother and father who'd brought their children to the observation area and then had become impatient, wanting to move on. Or at least the mother and the children had wanted to move on. Page remembered how defeated the father had sounded.

Your wife and kids saved your life, he thought.

In the harshly lit parking lot, he helped Tori from the Saturn, took the motel key from her purse, and unlocked the room. The place smelled old and musty.

He switched on the overhead light and saw that the room had two beds. *Just as well*, he thought.

When he secured the deadbolt on the door, the noise

made her turn to him. Page was afraid she was going to say, "I don't want you here." But instead she told him numbly, "I'm going to take a shower."

She opened a suitcase, removed boxer shorts and a T-shirt—her usual pajamas—and went into the bathroom.

She locked it.

Feeling empty, Page studied each bed and noticed that one had books on the table next to it. Choosing the other, he lay on a thin blanket and listened to the sound of the shower. He smelled smoke on his denim shirt and felt a spreading pain where he'd been kicked in the side.

The memory of the gunman's blazing arms reaching out to embrace him made him grimace.

When Tori came out of the bathroom, she wore the boxer shorts and loose T-shirt. Her towel-dried hair was combed back, darker red than usual because it was damp. She went to the door, shut off the light, and crawled beneath the covers on the other bed.

The scent of soap and shampoo drifted from the bathroom.

"Good night," Page said.

He lay in the darkness, waiting for her to reply.

"Good night," she finally told him, her voice so muted he barely heard her.

26

When Page had learned to fly, his dreams had been filled with the sensation of floating, as if he were in the air on a gentle current, drifting over forests and fields. The plane was as silent as a glider.

He hovered.

He turned.

He sailed along the smooth air.

Now he had a version of that dream. But he wasn't above forests and fields. He was in blackness, suspended in a void, settling, then rising, drifting to the left, pausing, then floating to the right, as if on invisible waves.

The way he'd seen the lights moving.

When he wakened, he felt groggy. He gradually opened his eyes and waited for his troubling memories to anchor him. Daylight streamed past the corners of the cheap drapes. He looked toward the other bed and saw that it was empty, its covers piled to the side. Immediately he sat up, realizing that he still wore his smoke-smelling jeans and denim shirt from the night before. He hadn't even taken off his sneakers.

His side ached worse.

"Tori?"

The bathroom door was open. He looked inside, but she wasn't there.

He hurried to the main door and pulled it open, relieved to see Tori's car.

The sun hurt his eyes. A glance at his watch showed him that the time was almost a quarter after three. He recalled checking his watch when he'd driven Tori back to the motel. The time had been a little after one. *My God, I slept more than twelve hours.*

Tori.

Stiff from the pain in his side, he ran through the

afternoon heat to the motel office. Inside, the same gangly young clerk was behind the desk.

"Did you see my wife go past?"

"She walked down the road toward the Rib Palace a half hour ago." He gave Page a vaguely accusing look. "Like Chief Costigan told me, I saved a room for you last night. Could've used it when all that trouble happened. Lots of people coming to town."

"I'll pay for not using it. Give it to someone else now."

"I already did after checkout time. A reporter's got it now."

"Reporter?"

"There's a ton of them."

The clerk pointed toward the television next to the soft-drink machine in a corner of the lobby. On the screen, a handsome man in a rumpled suit held a microphone and looked intently at the camera. His tie was loose and his top shirt button open. His blond hair was in disarray. He had whisker shadow, and his face was drawn with fatigue.

A crowd was gathered behind him. Police officers motioned for people to stay behind barricades. Beyond a cluster of police cars, the observation platform was visible.

"Keep back. This is still a crime scene," a policeman warned, speaking loudly enough for his voice to carry to the microphone.

Meanwhile, the television reporter addressed his viewers. "As you see from the commotion in the background, events are unfolding swiftly. Since First-on-the-Scene News started broadcasting images of the massacre's aftermath early this morning, the eyes of the entire nation have been directed to this quiet Texas town. The gunman's motive appears to have been a religious fixation on the mysterious Rostov lights that attracted the victims here last night. 'You came from hell. Now go back to hell,' witnesses report him shouting before he turned his rifle on them.

"The bizarre circumstances of his rampage prompted many people to start their weekend early and come here to satisfy their curiosity about the unexplained lights that ignited the killer's frenzy. Those lights have been seen in this area for as long as anyone can remember. Tonight, during our special live broadcast at 9, I'll do my best to show them to you and explain what they are. Before then, Sharon Rivera and I will coanchor expanded editions of our 5 and 6 o'clock broadcasts. The bystander who shot the killer was a woman. The police haven't released her identity, but I'll do everything I can to find out who she is and be the first to talk to her. This is Brent Loft. I'll see you at . . ."

"Shit," Page said.

He looked out the window. The previous evening, the road in front of the motel had been almost deserted. Now a stream of vehicles went past, heading to the right, in the direction of the observation platform.

Page realized that Tori's car keys were still in his jeans. He rushed from the office, got into the Saturn, and waited for a break in traffic that allowed him to go in the opposite direction, into town. That side of the road was deserted.

The previous evening, the Rib Palace's parking lot had been only half full, but now it was crammed with vehicles, few of which were pickup trucks. A lot of the cars had rental-company envelopes on the dashboards. Police cruisers were bunched together at one end.

Page hurried inside, where a wave of noisy conversation swept over him. After scanning the animated people at tables and in booths, he caught a glimpse of red hair on his left and noticed Tori sitting at the counter, drinking coffee. An empty plate was in front of her. All the seats were taken, but she was at the counter's end, so he was able to go over and stand next to her.

She glanced in his direction but didn't say anything. He couldn't tell if she looked troubled because of last night or because he stood next to her.

"Are you okay?" He kept his voice low.

"You have my car keys."

"Last night I put them in my jeans by mistake. Sorry." He gave them to her.

"You were sleeping so hard, I didn't want to wake you by searching through your pockets," Tori said.

"It would've been okay. I wouldn't have minded being wakened. We need to . . ."

"Talk. Yes." Tori reached in her purse and put money on a check that the waiter had left.

The smell of hamburgers and French fries filled the air, reminding Page that the last meal he'd eaten had been the night before, but food was the last thing he cared about as he followed her outside.

"Where's my car?" she asked in the parking lot.

"Over there. The second row."

More vehicles drove past, heading in the direction of the observation platform.

When Tori got behind the steering wheel, Page took

the passenger seat, assuming they would sit in the parking lot while he did his best to get her to explain why she'd left him. Instead she started the car and steered toward the road. She found a gap in traffic and joined the vehicles going toward the observation platform. She didn't say a word.

"Please," Page said, "help me understand."

"I have breast cancer," Tori replied.

Page suddenly felt cold. In shock, he managed to ask, "How bad?"

"I'm having surgery this coming Tuesday. In San Antonio."

"San Antonio?"

"My Santa Fe oncologist set it up. The plan is to rest at my mother's house, but I couldn't bring myself to tell her over the phone. I wanted to do it in person."

Page's balance tilted dizzily. "Why didn't you tell *me*? How long have you known?"

"The biopsy results came back a week ago."

"You had a *biopsy*?" Page asked. "I had no idea."

"In my oncologist's office. I didn't need to go to the hospital—she did it with a hypodermic. After you left for the airport on Tuesday, she called to tell me when the surgery was scheduled."

"So you just packed your bags and left?" Page couldn't adjust to his bewilderment. "Why didn't you talk to me about it? You know I'll give you all the support you need."

Tori drove slowly, held back by the line of cars. After a few minutes, she spoke again. "My doctor thinks we found the cancer in time. She thinks surgery, combined with radiation, will get rid of it."

"Under the circumstances, that's the best news you could have."

"I didn't tell you about it because . . ." Tori drew a breath. "Because I'm tired of feeling alone."

"Alone?" Page felt something in him plummet. "I don't understand."

"We live in the same house, but I'm not sure we live *together*. When you come home from work, I ask how your shift went, and you recite a list of crimes that you investigated."

"That's how my shifts usually go."

"It's the way you tell me, cold and flat, as if your shift happened to somebody else and you're disgusted with the world."

"Dealing with terrible things day after day has that effect."

"As often as not, after work you go to a bar and drink with other cops. Do you talk with *them* about the crimes you investigated?"

"It's not like group therapy or anything. We just drink a few beers and tell jokes or whatever."

"Lately you do it after every shift. When you finally get home, we eat something I made in the crockpot. Otherwise the food would burn or get cold because I never know when you'll actually come through the door. Instead of talking, we eat in front of the television. While you keep watching television, I go to bed and read."

"But that's what you like to do," he protested. "You *enjoy* reading."

"I'm not trying to place blame," Tori said. "Each of us is who we are. On the days you're not working, you go to the airport. As you told me once, nonpilots think flying a plane is all about feeling free and enjoying the scenery. But you like to fly because there's so much involved in handling a plane, you can't think about anything else. You can't let the emotions of your job distract you while you're controlling the aircraft. That's your defense against the world.

"When I learned about my cancer, I imagined the clamped-down look you'd get when I told you—the look you always get when you have emotions you don't want to deal with. I decided I couldn't go on that way. If I had a disease that might kill me, I didn't want to feel alone any longer. Going to the airport is your escape. Tuesday morning, after my doctor called, I decided to escape in a different way."

The car became silent.

Needing to distract himself, Page looked toward the sky, where clouds drifted in from the east. He glanced to the right. Beyond a barbed-wire fence, he saw the collapsed, rusted hangars from the military airstrip that had been shut down at the end of World War II. Vehicles were parked along the fence. Ahead, the procession continued, but some of the cars turned into the opposite lane and parked along the other side of the road. A glance toward the side mirror revealed cars stretched out behind the Saturn, some of which were pulling off and parking wherever they found gaps.

Tori broke the silence. "That's why I grabbed at the memory of the lights. When I sat in that coffee shop outside El Paso and noticed Rostov on the map, the excitement of seeing those lights came back to me. Before I knew it, I couldn't wait to get here and see them again. It's been a long time since I felt that kind of emotion."

"I feel as if I'm being compared to the way your father behaved that night."

"Not at all. You're a kind, decent man. My father was impatient and harsh. You're nothing like that. But I need someone who feels positive."

Page thought of the five children and the female driver who'd died in the head-on collision. He thought of the driver of the gasoline tanker who'd burned to death. He thought of his friend who'd been shot to death by the man who'd crashed into the gasoline tanker.

He couldn't free his memory of all the people who'd been shot the previous night.

And now Tori had cancer.

"Feel positive?" He shook his head. "I'm not sure I know how to do that. But I saw the lights, too. That's got to count for something."

Tori didn't respond.

"We'll watch them together," Page said, hoping. "I'll learn from you."

He heard the distant rumble of helicopters. Ahead, three of them hovered a safe distance apart. The choppers all had large letters on the undersides identifying the television stations to which they belonged. Their nose cameras were aimed at the line of vehicles.

Near the observation platform, a crowd faced barricades and the police officers who guarded them. Someone sold food from a van marked BEST TACOS IN TEXAS. Reporters stood in front of cameras next to news trucks with broadcast dishes on top. Page recognized the reporter he'd seen on the television at the motel office, the one with the rumpled suit.

"Tori, don't stop," he warned. "The TV people know a woman shot the killer. Sooner or later, they'll find out it was you. They'll never let you alone."

But she didn't seem to hear. All she did was stare toward the field where she'd seen the lights.

"They're ruining it," she said.

27

As the sun began its descent, the Black Hawk helicopter sped through the sky at 160 miles per hour. Ignoring the muffled vibration of the engines, Col. Warren Raleigh glanced to the left toward where the Davis Mountains stretched along the horizon. A moment later, he peered ahead toward clouds drifting in from the direction of the Gulf of Mexico.

Below, cattle grazed on sparse grassland that seemed to go on forever.

"Big country." The pilot's voice came through Raleigh's headset.

"Some ranchers down there own a half-million acres," Raleigh said into his microphone. "Lots of privacy."

At 6 that morning, Raleigh and his team had flown from Glen Burnie Airport near the NSA's headquarters in Fort Meade, Maryland. Their aircraft had been a Falcon 2000 owned by INSCOM but registered to a fictitious civilian corporation. It flew them two-thirds of the way across the continent to the Army airbase at Fort Bliss in El Paso, Texas. There they'd picked up equipment that Raleigh had ordered to be ready for them. They'd also added two members to their team. One was human—an Army dog handler. The other was a German shepherd.

The helicopter they'd transferred to was unarmed. In its cargo-transport configuration, without the dramatic-looking missile launchers and Gatling guns, it wouldn't attract any more attention than most other helicopters, Raleigh thought, especially in an area where the majority of eyes that would see it belonged to cattle and coyotes.

He glanced at his watch. "We should be there just about now."

"Exactly on schedule, sir." The pilot gestured ahead toward a gleam of white.

The ten radio dishes grew rapidly larger. It had been three years since Raleigh had visited this facility. He'd personally supervised the installation of the new equipment and arranged for one of the dishes to be aimed toward an area near Rostov. Now he was impatient to return.

Through his headset, he heard Sergeant Lockhart telling the men, "One minute to touchdown."

Raleigh watched the dishes get closer. Each was so huge that it dwarfed the combat helicopter. As an array, though, they were beyond huge. The only word that occurred to Raleigh was "monumental." Not easily impressed, he found their intense whiteness to be awesome.

When the helicopter descended past the three concentric rows of fences, its whirling blades created a dust storm. He felt the wheels touch down and the helicopter's weight settle. Then the speed of the blades diminished, their sound becoming a whistle, and Lockhart opened the rear hatch, motioning the men to grab their packs and hurry out.

Raleigh returned the pilot's salute and jumped to the ground, joining his team a safe distance from the swirling dust. As the chopper lifted off and headed back toward Fort Bliss, a second Black Hawk appeared on the horizon.

The eight men were in their midtwenties. Their hair was short but not to the extent that they seemed obviously military. Each wore sturdy shoes, slightly oversized jeans, a T-shirt, and a loose outdoor shirt that hung over his belt, concealing a Beretta 9-millimeter pistol. That handgun wasn't a match for Raleigh's beloved M4, but until somebody figured out a practical way to conceal a carbine, the pistol would have to do. Besides, there were several M4s in the crates of equipment he'd ordered.

Apart from the magnificent observatory dishes, the only aboveground structure was a concrete-block shed from which two guards wearing khaki uniforms emerged into the sunlight. They held their carbines in a deceptively casual way, but Raleigh noted that they could make the weapons operational in an instant.

One of the guards had strained features, as if he were in pain.

"'I hear a voice you cannot hear,'" the man said.

Under other circumstances, his seemingly deranged statement would have made Raleigh frown, but instead he immediately replied, "'Which says I must not stay.'"

The guard continued, "'I see a hand you cannot see.'"

"'Which beckons me away,'" Raleigh said.

With the code recognition completed, the guard saluted. "Welcome to the facility, Colonel."

"Your name is . . . ?"

"Earl Halloway, sir."

Raleigh remembered the name from documents he'd read en route. "Saw combat in Iraq. Former Army Ranger. Correct?"

"Yes, sir."

"Then there's no need to salute me any longer."

"It's a good habit, sir."

"Indeed it is. In case you're curious, those lines come from an eighteenth-century English poet: Thomas Tickell."

"I'm afraid I never heard of him, sir."

"Nobody has. Posterity wasn't kind to him." *But it'll be kind to me*, Raleigh thought. "You look uncomfortable, Earl. Is anything wrong?"

"Just a headache, sir. It's nothing. I took some aspirin. It's going away."

But the tight expression on his face made Raleigh think the headache was doing anything but fading.

The second chopper interrupted them, roaring over the fences and setting down where the first had been. The moment the dust settled, the trainer got out with the German shepherd. Staying clear of the dog, the team hurried to unload wooden crates.

"Earl," the colonel said.

"Yes, sir?"

"When I radioed ahead, I gave instructions for the two Suburbans in the underground garage to be ready to go."

"It's been taken care of, sir," Halloway responded. "They're out back."

"Then all we need is for you to give us the keys."

Halloway hesitated. "You might want to come inside first, sir."

"Oh?" Raleigh frowned. "Why would I want to do that?"

"There's something you should know about." He looked even more pained. "If I'm right, sir, you're here because of the music."

"The music?" Raleigh was astonished. "You actually know about the music?" *How bad has security gotten out here?* he wondered.

"I heard it last night, sir."

"You *heard* it?"

"And not long afterward, you contacted us to say you were coming, so I figured there was a connection. The radio dish that's angled toward Rostov."

"Make your point, Halloway."

"I'm guessing it's aimed toward whatever caused the music."

Raleigh was stunned. One of the military's most secret projects and this former Army sergeant was talking about it as if it were common knowledge.

He tried not to reveal how disturbed he felt.

"All right, Earl, show me what you think I should see."

Leaving the team outside to prepare the vehicles, Raleigh followed the guard into the small concrete-block building. After passing through the two security doors, they went down an echoing metal stairwell into the glowing lights and the filtered, cool air of the underground facility. As they entered a surveillance room, Raleigh heard a voice that he at first suspected belonged to another guard. But then he scanned the numerous monitors that showed the area around the dishes, and to his surprise, one of the screens turned out to be a television set.

"You watch TV in here?" He made no attempt to hide his displeasure.

The screen showed a crowd in front of police barricades. In the foreground, a reporter in a rumpled suit held a microphone and faced a camera.

"What the hell is going on?" Raleigh demanded.

"They started broadcasting this on the early-morning news. You were probably in the air by then, so you didn't hear about it. Twenty people were shot to death last night."

"Bad things happen all the time. Why should it concern me?"

Earl pointed toward the reporter on the television. "This guy was the first reporter on the scene. He kept talking about the lights, whatever *they* are."

"The lights?" Raleigh stepped closer to the television. "Wait a minute. You're telling me the shootings happened in *Rostov*?"

"Five miles away from it at what they call the observation platform. Apparently the gunman went crazy because of the lights. He started screaming, 'You're all going to hell,' and opened fire on a bunch of tourists."

Raleigh's muscles tightened. *It's happening again*, he thought.

"That reporter made a big deal about the lights being the reason for the killings, and all the other reporters followed his lead," Halloway went on. "Now people are coming from every direction to try to see them. The town's turned into a zoo. If you're headed over there, I thought you'd want to know."

Staring at the chaos on the television, Raleigh felt his pulse race as if he were headed into combat.

Just like in 1945.

My God, it's really happening again.

28

The Rostov County hospital was a modest-sized two-story building, its stucco tinted the harsh orange of the late-afternoon sun. Heat radiated off the front steps. Even so, Tori hesitated on them.

Page watched her with concern. "Are you okay?"

"Just thinking about next Tuesday. San Antonio. The hospital."

Page kept remembering that his mother had died from breast cancer. Numbness spread through him. "I'll be there with you."

"I never doubted that. But what happens if life gets back to normal and I'm alone again, even when you're with me?"

"I can change."

"Hard to do."

"For you, I'll do anything. I'll quit being a cop."

Tori looked surprised.

"The job's what makes me shut down my feelings,"

Page said. "To make things better between us, quitting's an obvious start."

"But what would you do?"

"What my father did. Be an airplane mechanic."

Tori considered him a moment longer, then drew a long breath and approached the hospital's front doors. They opened automatically.

Inside a lobby, Page walked past a row of plastic chairs and stopped before a spectacled woman at a desk.

"We're here to check on someone. He was admitted last night with a gunshot wound. Chief Costigan."

"He's not receiving visitors."

"Well, can you tell us how he's doing?"

"Are you family?"

"No, we're—"

"Edith, it's okay," a voice said. "They're not reporters."

Page turned and saw Captain Medrano standing at an elevator, its door closing behind him. He held his Stetson. Each of the upper sleeves on his tan uniform had a red Highway Patrol patch.

"In fact, they're trying to *avoid* reporters," Medrano said. He pushed the elevator's up button, and the doors immediately reopened. "Come on, I'll take you to him."

In the elevator, Medrano looked apologetic. "I finally had to give the media your names. Believe me, I held off as long as I could, but I was starting to look as if I wasn't in control of the investigation."

"If they find out we're at that motel . . . ," Tori said.

"The clerk promised to deny you're staying there."

"I hope he keeps his word. Do you know who the shooter was?" Page asked.

"Edward Mullen. One of the survivors remembered seeing him on the tour bus. We contacted the company that owns the bus. It's based in Austin. The lights are only a brief part of the tour—it also goes to the big ranch house that was built for that James Deacon movie, *Birthright*."

Page nodded. "Last night at the viewing area, someone mentioned that movie set."

"Mostly, though, it's a nature tour that goes through the Davis Mountains. The company gave us a list of everyone who signed up for that particular tour. All the victims had ID on them. We compared their names and those of the survivors to the names on the list. Edward Mullen was the only person we couldn't account for. You were right— according to one of the survivors from the bus, he had a guitar case. The guy remembered because Mullen had a lot of trouble finding a place to put it. That must be where he hid the rifle."

"A lucky guess."

"No. I told you last night, you have the instincts of a good cop."

Page glanced at Tori and found that she was looking at him.

The elevator doors opened. As they stepped into a hospital corridor, Page's nostrils felt pinched by the smell of antiseptic.

"This was the ninth time Mullen had taken the same tour," Medrano continued.

Page stopped walking and frowned at him. "The *ninth*?"

"The tour company gave us the credit-card number

he used. The credit-card company gave us his address. The Austin police went to his apartment."

"Surprise me and tell me he didn't live alone."

"His wife died a year ago," Medrano said. "He didn't have any children."

"Now tell me the apartment wasn't crammed with religious statues and paintings and all kinds of literature about damnation."

"It'd take a truck to carry it all away," Medrano replied. "I'm tempted to go with the theory I had last night: some kind of religious lunatic. But there's a problem with that theory."

"Oh?"

"Mullen has a brother. According to him, Mullen was never religious—never even went *near* a church—until his wife's funeral. Apparently her death hit him so hard that all he did was stay in bed all day. The brother tried to get him interested in things and happened to see a newspaper ad for one of those tours. Before his wife's death, Mullen was a movie buff. If a movie was filmed in Texas, he knew it shot by shot. So when the brother read that the tour included the set for *Birthright*, one of Mullen's favorites, he managed to convince Mullen—'practically twisted his arm' is how he put it—that the two of them should go on the tour. It also included some locations from movies that were made in the Davis Mountains. Before the group reached the movie locations, though, they arrived at that viewing platform. As usual, some people on the tour claimed to see the lights while others wondered what all the fuss was about."

"Did the brother see the lights?" Page asked.

"No, but Mullen claimed they were spectacular. After he got back to Austin, he started filling his apartment with the religious statues and paintings."

A phone rang, distracting Medrano. It came from a nurses' station across from the elevators. Page glanced around and noticed open doors along the corridor, nurses going into some of them, people in civilian clothes coming out of others.

Medrano pointed toward a clock in the nurses' station.

"Almost 5. I'm due at a press conference at the courthouse. I'd better show you where Chief Costigan is."

As they walked along the corridor, Page looked again at Tori, who rubbed the back of her neck, obviously bothered by the smell and feel of being in a hospital. He stepped closer to her, reached out, and discreetly squeezed her hand, but got no reaction.

Medrano entered the second-to-last doorway on the left and stepped out of Page's sight. "Want more visitors?" he asked someone.

"If they're pretty," a raspy voice said.

"One is. The other could use a shave."

Medrano motioned for Page and Tori to enter the room.

Costigan lay in a bed that was tilted up, allowing him to see a news program on a television that was mounted on the opposite wall. The reporter on the screen was the same man Page had seen on the television at the motel office: rumpled suit, mussed blond hair, beard stubble, haggard but handsome features.

"Anything's better than watching that damned fool get everybody fired up," Costigan growled.

The chief pressed the remote control and shut off the TV. Bandages encircled his head, pads making one side thicker than the other. His face looked grayer and thinner. Even his mustache seemed gray.

"Recognize these folks?" Medrano asked.

"Sure do." An IV tube was taped to Costigan's left arm. Wires attached to heart and blood-pressure monitors led under the chest of his hospital gown.

"Glad to hear it," Medrano said. "That's part of the memory test. I need to get to a press conference, but I want this couple to tell a nurse if you start forgetting things, like the fifty dollars I lent you last week."

"I didn't borrow any fifty dollars."

"You're right. Come to think of it, I lent you a *hundred* dollars."

"Get out of here," Costigan said.

After Medrano grinned and left, the chief motioned for them to come closer.

"We brought your windbreaker back," Page said. "Thanks. It came in handy."

"Keep it a while longer. I'm hardly in a position to use it." Costigan studied them. "He called you 'this couple.' Does that mean things are better between the two of you?"

"It's complicated," Page answered.

"Isn't everything? At least you came here together."

Tori changed the subject. "How bad are you hurt?"

"Apparently I've got a hard head. The bullet creased my skull. Didn't fracture it but gave me a hell of a concussion." Costigan winced. "And an even worse headache. If I start to drool, tell the nurse."

Despite the burden of his emotions, Page almost smiled.

"Your head was covered with so much blood," Tori said, "I thought you were dead."

"Scalp wounds are terrible bleeders. Mrs. Page, I heard that you picked up my gun and made good use of it. You saved the lives of a lot of people. You're remarkable."

Tori looked away.

"Sorry. It wasn't my intention to upset you." Costigan changed the subject. "I don't suppose either of you has any cigarettes."

"Afraid not," she said, looking at him again.

"Just as well. They won't let me smoke in here anyhow."

"It's a good time to quit," Tori said.

"Yeah, this wound gives me motivation to stick around as long as I can." Costigan looked at Page. "Before the shooting started, you seemed to see the lights."

Page could tell that Tori was waiting for his answer.

"I did."

"I'm impressed," Costigan said. "Not everybody does. Your wife sure saw them."

"Yes." Tori sounded as if she spoke about a lover.

"But I'm still not sure what it is I saw," Page added. "What's happening here, Chief? What *are* they?"

Costigan pressed a button. A motor under the bed made a whirring sound and raised his head a little more.

"I've heard every kind of explanation you can imagine. Everything from ball lightning to pranksters. If it's pranksters, they're good at it. When I came to town to be the chief after my father was killed . . ."

The harsh memory made Costigan pause. He gradually refocused his thoughts.

"Well, I spent a lot of nights out there, looking for people with flashlights or lanterns or whatever. That's a long way to go for a practical joke. I never saw cars parked along the side roads, and I never heard any noises I couldn't identify. It would take at least a half-dozen people to pull off a prank like that, and I don't know how they could do it quietly. What's more, it's hard to keep a secret. After all these years, someone in town would have hinted about what they were doing. And how many pranksters have the determination to do it night after night after night?"

"What I saw wasn't flashlights or lanterns or pranksters," Tori said.

"No, but there still has to be *some* explanation. I'm not sure you're going to like this, Mrs. Page."

"Please call me Tori. What am I not going to like?"

"I don't think there's anything magical about the lights. On occasion researchers have come here, some from as far away as Japan. They've set up all kinds of scientific instruments, machines that analyzed light and measured distance and . . . I don't pretend to understand it. The best explanation they could come up with is a temperature inversion."

"A what?"

"I said you wouldn't like it. A temperature inversion. The way it was explained to me is, we're five thousand feet above sea level. At this altitude, when the sun sets after a hot day, there can be as much as a fifty-degree difference between the daytime and nighttime temperatures.

That causes an inversion of hot air on top of cold. Under certain conditions, distant lights—from a moving car or a train—can bounce back and forth through the layers. The lights get magnified. They shift up and down and right and left."

"But why would they change colors?"

"The scientists didn't explain that."

"Do the lights appear in the winter?" Tori persisted. "If so, then there wouldn't be as big a difference between the day and night temperatures. So how could there be a temperature inversion in cold weather?"

"The scientists didn't explain that, either." Costigan gingerly touched his bandaged head. "This headache . . . Harriett Ward."

"Excuse me?" The statement seemed to come out of nowhere. Page worried that Costigan was having trouble keeping his thoughts straight.

"Harriett's the person to talk to about the lights. She's the local expert. She runs an antiques store a block south of the courthouse. Lives in a couple of rooms in the back. Given everything that's happening, I doubt many locals will go out this evening, even if it is Friday night. You'll probably catch her at home."

29

The sign had old-fashioned lettering: WEST TEXAS ANTIQUES.

As Tori parked in front, Page noticed a hutch, a rocking chair, and a wooden sink in the store's window. The frame around the window was painted a pastel blue that contrasted with the yellow on the art gallery to the left and the green on the coffee shop to the right.

"Reminds me of the lights," Tori said.

They looked up the wide street toward the courthouse, where numerous vehicles were parked, including several television broadcast trucks. Page estimated that a couple of hundred people stood in front of the steps, presumably listening to Captain Medrano conducting the press conference.

"My rental car's still parked up there. I can't get it until they leave," Page explained to Tori.

The lowering sun cast the street in a crimson glow.

A pickup truck stopped. A teenaged boy leaned from the passenger window.

"Supposed to be some weird lights around here. We came all the way from Lubbock to see them. You know where they're at?"

"We're strangers," Page said. "Just visiting a friend."

A boy in the middle told the driver, "Ed, let's go ask somebody else. Try that crowd up there."

As the truck drove away, Page knocked on the wooden doorframe and peered through the window toward the shadows in the store.

"Maybe the chief's wrong and she's out for the evening," he said.

But after he knocked again, a door opened in the back of the store. A figure approached, passing old tables and cabinets. The figure had white hair that was cut short, like a man's. Then a light came on, and the person stepped close enough for Page to see a lean woman in her sixties. She wore cowboy boots, jeans, a work shirt, and a leather vest. Her skin was brown and wrinkled from exposure to the sun.

When she unlocked the door and peered out, Page noticed a wedding band.

"Mrs. Ward, my name's—"

"Dan Page. And your wife's name is Tori." The woman shook hands with them. "Chief Costigan phoned to say you were coming. Come in. And please call me Harriett."

Won over by the friendliness, Page motioned for Tori to go first, then followed the two women toward the back of the store. He noticed old rifles on a rack on the wall. The wooden floor creaked. Everything smelled of the past.

"I was about to have a drink, but I hate to drink alone," Harriett said. "So I hope you'll join me."

She closed the door after they entered a small living room that was sparsely furnished. The rug had a sunburst pattern. Page didn't see any indication that a man lived there. Thinking of the wedding band Harriett wore, he concluded that she was a widow.

"I've got vodka, bourbon, and tequila," she said.

"What are *you* having?" Tori asked.

"Tequila on the rocks."

"I'll have the same."

Page was surprised. Tori seldom drank hard alcohol.

"Tequila for you also?" Harriett asked him.

"Just a little. I haven't eaten anything in a while."

Harriett's boot heels thumped on the wooden floor as she went into a small kitchen. He heard the clink of ice cubes being dropped into glasses and the splash of liquid being poured over the ice.

"The chief tells me you're interested in hearing about the lights," Harriett said, returning with two glasses.

"According to him, you're the local expert," Page replied.

"I did a lot of research, if that's what he means." Harriett went back for the third glass and also brought a bag of tortilla chips, which she handed to Page. "I dug into history and found hundreds of reports, a lot of them from the old days. But nobody's really an expert when it comes to the lights. Nobody really understands them."

"Why hasn't word about them gotten around?" Tori wondered.

"There was a segment about them on that old TV show, *Unsolved Mysteries*, and a crew from the History Channel did some interviews here about five years ago. Every once in a while, there's an item in a magazine. When that happens, we get a wave of visitors. That's why the county set up that viewing area and the portable toilets. People made so much mess out there that it seemed better to adjust to the tourists than to ignore them— turned out to be good for business, too. But eventually, interest dies down. For one thing, the lights don't photograph well, so camera crews get restless. Plus, a lot of visitors don't see the lights, which is why the county put up that plaque with its warning that people shouldn't feel disappointed if they don't see anything."

Harriett clicked glasses with them and sat.

Although Page made a show of sipping the tequila, he had no intention of finishing it. He merely used it as a prop to encourage Harriett to feel comfortable and keep talking.

"Chief Costigan thinks they're probably lights from a distance, magnified by temperature inversions. But I don't believe that," Tori said firmly.

"You'll hear all kinds of theories. From UFOs to ball lightning."

"Why do some people see them and others don't?" Page asked.

"As I said, there are all kinds of theories. A psychiatrist on *Unsolved Mysteries* claimed it's a form of mass delusion, that some people want their expectations to be fulfilled while others are determined not to be manipulated."

"I don't believe that, either," Tori insisted, looking at Page. "I had no expectations when I first saw the lights, back when I was ten. All I wanted was for my father to stop the car so I could run to a Porta-Potty. When I came out, the lights were the *last* things I expected to see."

"Fred Nolan sure didn't have any expectations when he first saw them back in 1889," Harriett said.

"Fred Nolan?" Tori asked.

30

April 5, 1889.

Nolan watched as the train's crew lowered the spigot from the water tower and filled the steam engine's water compartment. He scanned the few small buildings that provided shelter for the men who hauled wood from the Davis Mountains and stacked it for trains to use as fuel.

Animals bellowed in the cattle cars.

"Slide the hatches open," Nolan told his men.

Wooden planks rumbled as hooves descended into sunlight and open air.

"Keep 'em together," Nolan ordered.

The five hundred cattle were scrawny, purchased cheaply in Colorado after a hard winter had piled so much snow on grassland that the animals couldn't stomp through the drifts to get at it. Many had starved to death. These that survived looked awful.

But they did survive, Nolan thought. *They're strong. They'll make good breeding stock.*

He'd met with railroad executives in Denver, arguing that this water stop in west Texas was a perfect place for the railroad to build a town and sizable cattle pens.

"Sure, the grass is spread out, but there's more land for the cattle to graze on. They thrive if there's an acre per animal."

"An acre per animal?" a cigar-smoking executive scoffed. "In that case, you'd need an awful lot of land to justify the expense you want us to commit to."

"Well, my ranch is small right now, I admit. All I have is a quarter-million acres, but I'm planning to expand."

"*A quarter-million acres?*" The executive sat forward. "Good God, are you telling us you plan to be able to ship a quarter-million cattle through that water stop?"

"For starters. If you build the pens and the town, I'll supply the cattle."

Now Nolan looked toward where the pens would be

situated, the troughs for water and hay, the permanent ramps that would lead up to the cattle cars. He imagined the town's wide streets through which the cattle would be herded to the pens. The stores that would make it easy to get supplies for his ranch. The homes for the people who would manage the stores. Perhaps a doctor and a church. Perhaps even a saloon, carefully monitored, for although Nolan was a devout Presbyterian who'd never touched a drop of alcohol in his life, he understood the needs of the men he employed and reasoned that allowing occasional, carefully controlled recreation would make it easier for him to attract and keep ranch hands.

He admitted that his ambition was greater than his capabilities. He had the quarter-million acres, which his grandfather and father had fought against Mexicans and Indians to keep. But what he needed now was the money to buy more cheaply priced, scrawny but amazingly strong cattle. So far he had a herd of fifty thousand, but he'd need a lot more to breed them into the quarter million he'd promised.

Well, it's a beginning, Nolan thought. *Next week, I'll head for Oklahoma. Their winter was the reverse of Colorado's, so dry that the spring grass isn't coming up. Ranchers'll be culling their herds, willing to sell their worst-looking stock for pennies on the dollar. They'll think I'm a fool, but I know anything that lived through a winter drought has got to be strong.*

"Move 'em out," he told his men.

The angle of the sun warned him that darkness would fall in five hours, and during that time, his men had to drive the cattle eight miles to the stream they had dammed, creating a pond where the cattle could stay in a group and drink. More than a mile an hour. After the long trip in the cattle cars, there was a risk that some animals might collapse before they got to the water. But after that, they'd be able to rest, to do nothing but eat and drink and grow.

They're strong, Nolan thought. *They've been through worse than this. They'll get to the stream.*

As it turned out, two animals died and the others didn't reach the water until after dark, when it was more difficult to control a moving herd and the yelping of coyotes could easily have spooked them. But finally the cattle circled the dammed-up part of the stream, and Nolan told his foreman, "Keep half the men watching the herd. Tell the other half to set up camp."

In the light of the stars and a rising quarter moon, Nolan dismounted, unsaddled his horse, put a rope around the mare's neck, and led her to the water, where he took care that she didn't drink too much. His legs stiffening, he guided the horse to a stretch of grass, hobbled her, and allowed her to graze. The grass was sparse enough that she wouldn't glut herself and get sick after the water she'd consumed.

On the way to the railroad, Nolan's men had brought firewood from the ranch house and left it near the pond. Now, in the darkness, they arranged it in three piles to build campfires.

"Mr. Nolan, what do you suppose *that* is?" his foreman asked, sounding troubled.

"Where?"

"Over there, to the southeast."

Nolan stepped away from the cattle and looked at the murky horizon.

"I don't see anything. What am I supposed to be looking for?"

"There, Mr. Nolan. Those lights."

"Lights?" Nolan stared toward the darkness. "What lights? I don't see . . . Wait a second."

At first Nolan had thought he was looking at stars that glistened on the horizon. But suddenly he realized that whatever he saw was *below* the horizon. On the grassland. Twinkling. At least a dozen lights.

"Tell the men not to build the fires," he ordered with a muted, urgent voice. "Make sure they don't make any noise, either."

As the foreman ran to obey, Nolan hurried to a man on horseback who was watching the herd.

"Get down. Stay low. Don't show your silhouette. Tell the other men to do the same."

"Trouble, Mr. Nolan?"

"Just do what you're told."

Feeling fire in his stomach, Nolan ran to another horseman and gave him the same orders. Stooping, he rushed to his saddle and pulled his Winchester from its scabbard. He always kept a round in the firing chamber, so there wasn't any need to work the lever. All he had to do was pull back the hammer.

He crouched and studied the lights. They seemed to be five or six miles away. Some floated while others shifted from side to side. They were various colors—blue, green, yellow, red—merging, then drifting apart.

Nolan's men gathered nearby while the foreman stooped next to him and murmured, "You figure they're campfires, Mr. Nolan?"

"I never heard of campfires that keep changing their location." Nolan's voice was tense and low.

"Maybe whoever's out there has torches, and they're moving around, doing something."

"Like what?"

"Like a war dance," the foreman said. "You think those are Indians?"

"Those lights are close enough that we'd hear a war dance," Nolan murmured, conscious of the weight of the Winchester in his hands. "Besides, all the Indians around here are mostly peaceful."

"As you say, Mr. Nolan, 'mostly.'"

"Sure, they could be renegades. But those lights are in the direction of Mexico. What I'm thinking is Mexican raiders. If they start shooting, they could stampede the cattle toward Mexico before there's daylight enough for us to chase them."

Nolan couldn't take his eyes off the lights. As much as he felt threatened by them, he also felt hypnotized, drawn. Spellbound.

Inexplicably, he tasted lemonade.

A shiver prickled his skin.

Behind him, the cattle made lowing sounds as they settled for the night.

We caused plenty of noise getting here, Nolan thought. *Whoever's with those lights is bound to know where we are.*

"Tell the men to get their rifles. Put them in groups of

two so they'll keep each other awake. Anybody I catch sleeping will be out of a job in the morning."

"Somehow, Mr. Nolan, I don't think losing their jobs is what they're worried about right now."

"Then tell the men they'll get a bonus if they keep the herd together."

"You bet, Mr. Nolan," the foreman said. Staying low, he rushed to give orders to the men.

Meanwhile, Nolan stared harder toward the shimmering lights. They sank and drifted. They hovered and rippled. Their colors kept changing.

He remembered a couple of years earlier when he'd been in El Paso during a Fourth of July celebration. Chinese vendors had sold firecrackers and skyrockets, but they'd also sold quiet fireworks called sparklers: thick wires that had been dipped in chemicals capable of being ignited with a match. With a hiss that was virtually silent, the wires had erupted in sparks of various colors. At night Nolan had seen children use the sparklers to write their names in the darkness.

Is that what they've got over there? Sparklers? But if they're raiders, why would they let us know they're nearby?

The answer wasn't hard to imagine.

To scare us.

Well, they'll find out I don't scare easily.

Even so, as the lights drifted and changed colors and beckoned during the longest night of his life, Nolan admitted that his fortitude was being tested.

Troubled, he heard faint music, but its melody and instruments were unfamiliar. Under other circumstances, he might have thought that it came from a town across the border, the Mexicans having some kind of celebration. Possibly a tune from a mariachi band had managed to drift this far but was distorted by the distance.

Nolan didn't believe that. As he concentrated on the hard-to-hear notes, the lights seemed to brighten, their colors strengthening. The two were somehow connected.

The cattle became restive, their hooves scraping the dirt. Their lowing sounds had a nervous edge. Praying that they wouldn't stampede, Nolan thought of the land that his grandfather and father had fought so hard to keep, and of the land he was determined to add to it. He thought of the quarter-million head of cattle he'd promised if the railroad built the town and the cattle pens.

He lay on the hard ground with his rifle propped on his saddle. He stared along it toward the lights and silently recited scripture. From the gospel of St. John: "And the light shineth in darkness, and the darkness comprehendeth it not."

That was the first relevant quotation that popped into his mind, but it didn't provide the affirmation he was looking for, so he recalled another, this one from Isaiah: "The people that walketh in darkness have seen a great light. They that dwelleth in the land of the shadow of death, upon them hath the light shone."

The shadow of death.

That quotation didn't provide the affirmation Nolan was looking for, either. Besides, if raiders came for his cattle, the shadow of death would be on *them*. If the lights and the music were indeed made by raiders.

If the cattle didn't stampede.

Nolan went on like that all through the long, cold night, trying to calm himself with the word of God. His eyes aching, he kept aiming at the lights until, as dawn approached, they faded and shrank. With the sun finally rising, he stood stiffly and lowered the hammer on his Winchester.

His ears ached.

He told his foreman, "Take the herd all the way to the house."

"You bet, Mr. Nolan. Just as soon as the men cook something to eat."

"No. Do it now. The men can eat cold biscuits as they ride. I want to make sure the cattle are safe."

"You're the boss, Mr. Nolan." The foreman looked troubled. "What do you figure those lights were? If they weren't Mexican raiders . . ."

"Give me three riders, and I'll find out."

Nolan saddled his horse and rode southeast with the men. During the night, he'd estimated that the lights were five or six miles away, but when he traveled that distance, he didn't find any sign of cooking fires or horse tracks or crushed vegetation that would indicate where a camp had been made.

He was sure that the lights had been in this direction, but darkness could play tricks, so he told his men, "Spread out." Spacing them fifty yards apart, he rode three miles farther but still didn't see any sign of campfires or horse tracks.

He was forced to ride around a section of black, ugly, twisted boulders that looked like huge dead cinders. A minister with whom he'd once traveled on a train through Arizona had told him that sections like this were left over from the pyrotechnics of when God had created the universe. But if this area was supposed to represent God's power, Nolan didn't understand why the Mexicans called them *malpais*.

Badlands.

He rode another five miles but still didn't see any horse tracks.

I was sure the lights were southeast of the herd, he thought. *How could I have misjudged their direction?*

"Mr. Nolan?" one of his men called behind him.

Belatedly Nolan realized that the rider had been shouting his name for some time.

He looked back.

"Sir, if we keep going like this, we'll end up in Mexico."

Nolan suddenly became aware of how high the sun was and how far they'd ridden. Feeling as if he came out of a trance, he stared ahead toward the sparse grassland that seemed to stretch forever. Something wavered on the horizon. Maybe a dust devil. Maybe air rippling as the sun heated it.

I could follow that movement forever and never reach it, Nolan thought.

"We're heading back!" he yelled to the men. "Pick a different section! Keep looking and shout if you find where somebody camped!"

31

"Did Nolan ever find an answer?" Page asked.

"A few Indians worked on his ranch. He figured it was

safer to keep them close than have them fight him," Harriett said. "He'd never been in that area after dark, but it was a good bet the Indians would know if any strange lights had ever been seen over there. To his surprise, they told him there'd *always* been lights in that direction. Their fathers and grandfathers had talked about them. The lights were the spirits of their ancestors, they believed."

"Superstition's even less convincing than temperature inversions," Tori said. "Anyway, I don't want to have the lights explained. I don't want somebody to take away how special they are by telling me they're just ball lightning or ghosts."

"That's the way most everyone here in town feels about them, too," Harriett replied. "When my late husband and I first came here in 1970, we were hippies in an old station wagon that was basically our home. We happened to hear about the lights, so we drove out to where the viewing area is now. We opened the back hatch, sat on our sleeping bags, smoked dope, and ate dry cornflakes. I still don't know if we actually saw the lights or if the dope made us believe we did.

"But the next night, we watched them without being stoned, and the night after that, too, and, well, we never left. Rostov wasn't much back then, but we managed to find jobs, and we didn't need a lot of money to live. Basically, being able to see the lights whenever we wanted seemed reward enough. After a while, we didn't even need to go out there. Somehow we managed to *feel* that the lights were out there without actually seeing them.

"Every couple of months, though, we'd want to see them again, the way people feel the need to go to church. A lot of people in Rostov are like my husband and me. They intended to pass through, but the lights kept them here."

"Or called them back," Tori said with a hushed tone.

"Most people don't see the lights at all, of course, let alone react the way I described," Harriett said. "But many of the people who live here were fortunate enough to have the same experience, and we long ago stopped trying to explain it. The only thing that matters is, the lights make us feel . . . I guess the word is 'blessed.'"

"Things weren't so blessed last night," Page replied.

32

The press conference was finished by the time they left the antiques store and glanced up toward the courthouse. The sun was lower, casting the deserted street in a deeper orange.

Page looked at Tori.

"I need to get my rental car from up there," he said. "Do you want to follow me back to the motel?"

Tori didn't answer right away. "Sure."

But as Page drove to the motel, he glanced in his rearview mirror and there wasn't any sign of Tori's blue Saturn among the traffic that was heading out of town toward the observation platform. He parked in front of unit 11, got out, and waited. Glancing up, he noticed that there were clouds gathering for the first time since he'd been in Rostov.

Fifteen minutes passed and he still didn't see any sign

of her, so he finally took his suitcase from the trunk and moved toward the door.

The gangly motel clerk came from the office and hurried toward him. Page remembered his name.

"Something wrong, Jake?"

"There've been reporters looking for you."

"I hope you didn't tell them we're staying here."

"Captain Medrano said not to. But somehow the reporters found out the woman at the shooting has red hair, and your wife is the only redhead at the motel. I thought I'd better warn you."

"Thanks."

"It was weird."

"Lately *everything's* been weird," Page said. "Did you have anything specific in mind?"

"The reporter who's most determined to find you is the television guy from El Paso. You saw him on the TV in the lobby the last time we talked."

Page thought a moment. "Movie-star jaw. Rumpled suit. Looks like he hasn't slept in a couple of days."

"That's the guy. He was the first reporter to come to town. He's figured out a lot of angles on the story—so many that the other reporters have just been following his lead. I was in the office, watching him on TV. Then the door opened, and I looked over, and by God, there he was, walking toward me. I guess some of what I figured is 'live' must be on tape. Seeing him in two places at the same time felt unreal. Be careful of him. You want your privacy, but the look in his eyes told me he'd do *anything* to put your wife in front of a camera and make her describe how she shot that guy."

"That isn't going to happen," Page said. Before he could say anything more, a phone rang in the office.

"Gotta get back to work." The gangly clerk ran toward the door.

As it banged shut, Page took another look toward the road, hoping their conversation might have given Tori time to catch up. But there was no sign of the Saturn. More clouds had gathered, filling the sky. His side ached when he carried his suitcase into the room.

If things had been different, it would have felt good to shave and shower, to get the smell of the smoke and the violence off him, but all Page thought was that he could bear anything—even what had happened the previous night—if only Tori had followed him to the motel as she'd said she would. If only she hadn't left him again.

If only she didn't have cancer.

The bruise where he'd been kicked was larger than he'd expected, dark purple ringed with orange. Trying to ignore it, he put on a fresh pair of jeans and another denim shirt. *Kind of predictable, pal.* He took the 9-millimeter pistol out of his suitcase, removed the magazine, made sure it was full, and checked to make sure there was a round in the firing chamber. *You examined it before you left the house yesterday,* he thought, aware that people whose occupation involved carrying a gun tended to display obsessive-compulsive behavior.

Or maybe he just needed to narrow his thoughts.

The gun was a Sig Sauer 225. It held eight rounds in the magazine and one in the chamber. Not a lot of firepower compared to pistols with double-stacked magazines, but the 225's virtue was its compact size. He considered it an ideal concealed-carry pistol. The company didn't make them any longer, and this particular gun had belonged to his father.

He holstered it on his belt, put on a windbreaker to conceal it, grabbed a baseball cap from his suitcase, and opened the door, ready to go looking for Tori, although he knew where he'd find her: the viewing area.

About to get into his car, he heard tires crunching on gravel and looked toward the road, surprised to see the blue Saturn coming through the parking lot toward him. Tori's red hair was vivid through the windshield. When she stopped in front of unit 11, his knees felt weak.

"I figured you'd left me behind," he said through the open window.

She showed him a paper bag. "I got this for you."

Page almost frowned in confusion before he smelled the food.

"You said you hadn't eaten since yesterday. I hope a burger and fries work for you. Anything else would have taken too long."

"They're perfect." Emotion made his knees more unsteady. "Thanks."

"You need to keep up your energy. This'll be another long night."

"Thanks. Really. I mean it."

"Get in," she said impatiently.

He did so, and pulled off the baseball cap.

"Better put this on. Reporters are looking for a woman with red hair."

She nodded and took it.

As she drove, Page bit into the hamburger and recalled

uneasily that this was what he and Chief Costigan had eaten the evening before.

"How are you feeling?" he asked.

"When I see the lights again, everything'll be fine. They'll make me forget what happened last night."

"The trick is to distract your mind by paying attention to the small details. But I wasn't thinking about last night. How are you *feeling*?"

Tori hesitated. "I never realized anything was wrong with me until the doctor phoned to tell me the results of my mammogram. Now I'm so self-conscious that I swear I can feel the thing growing in me."

"On Tuesday, it'll be gone."

"I'd like to just reach in and claw it out with my fingers."

"I love you."

Tori looked at him. "You said that last night, too."

Ahead, three TV news helicopters were silhouetted against the dark, cloudy sky. Vehicles were parked along both sides of the road. Taking his own advice, Page distracted himself by paying attention to small details and looked to the right toward the ruin of the World War II airbase.

He saw someone unlocking a gate. The man wore sturdy shoes, loose-fitting pants, a T-shirt, and an over-shirt that hung below his belt. He was in his forties, bald and sinewy, with rigid shoulders and an air of authority. When he motioned for two dark Chevy Surburbans to drive onto the property, he had the manner of someone who was used to giving orders.

There was now a second sign on the gate.

"Tori, I want to check something. Please stop for a second."

She looked at him reluctantly but applied the brakes as they came close to the gate. Page lowered his window and leaned out to get a better view in the dwindling sunset.

The older sign warned:

PROPERTY OF U.S. MILITARY
DANGER
HAZARDOUS CHEMICALS
UNEXPLODED ORDNANCE

The new one announced:

SOON TO BE
AN ENVIRONMENTAL PROTECTION AGENCY
RECLAMATION SITE

The authoritative man stepped through the gate, locked it, and noticed Page.

"Parking's not allowed on this property." He pointed toward the signs. "Restricted area."

Page waved to indicate he understood.

Another man got out of one of the vans. He had a German shepherd on a leash. The authoritative man just stood there, staring at the car until Tori drove on.

"What was *that* about?" she asked.

"I'm not sure." Page looked back and watched as the two Suburbans drove toward the collapsed, weed-choked, rusted airplane hangars.

Finally he couldn't see them any longer, so he directed his attention ahead, toward the crowd. As Tori neared it, Page noticed that the county had brought a half-dozen more portable toilets. But they weren't going to be enough. The crowd filled the entire parking lot all the way to the fence, onlookers standing where corpses had lain the previous night. People were on the road, forcing Tori to steer into the opposite lane. Medrano and other Highway Patrol officers struggled to keep order.

Tori parked at the end of the line of cars. Costigan's windbreaker was on the front seat, and she snatched it up as she stepped from the Saturn. But as she stared toward the crowd a hundred yards up the road, she faltered.

"You okay?" Page asked.

"Too many people. I don't think I want to go any farther."

"Fine. We don't need to do anything you don't want to."

"Maybe I can see the lights just as well from here," Tori said uneasily. "Maybe the viewing area's only an arbitrary spot."

"Why don't we stay here and find out?" Page suggested.

"Yes." She shivered and put on the windbreaker. "After last night, I don't want to go near a crowd."

33

Raleigh waited at the fence until the blue Saturn drove on.

There were several troubling things about the man who'd leaned out the window to read the new sign that explained his team's presence here. The man's features were guarded, revealing nothing about what he thought. His hair was short—not military short but shorter and neater than was common among civilians. And his eyes were attentive, as if he analyzed everything he saw.

Definitely not just a tourist, Raleigh thought.

He kept waiting until the Saturn was obscured by the long line of cars that were parked along the side of the road. Then he turned to the dog trainer who had the German shepherd on a short leash.

"Put the fear of God into anybody who tries to come over that fence."

As the trainer turned on his flashlight, Raleigh walked ahead of the two dark Suburbans, their only illumination coming from parking lights. He motioned for them to follow, leading them along what had once been a heavily traveled dirt road, its furrows now cluttered with weeds.

After a hundred yards, the last rays of sunset showed a wide row of collapsed airplane hangars to the left. Their corrugated metal had long since rusted. Scrub brush grew among them. Dirt had drifted against them. A lot of this was the work of nature, but some of it had been deliberately arranged to make the ruin look more dilapidated than it actually was.

Raleigh held up his hand, signaling for the vehicles to stop. He surveyed the old runway. Its concrete was visible only here and there, most of it covered with dirt. Weeds grew where numerous cracks had been baked into the pavement by the sun.

His grandfather had once stood here. It made Raleigh feel tremendously proud that a circle was about to close, that a mission his grandfather had started so long ago was finally about to be accomplished.

In World War II, when the hangars and the runway were freshly constructed, this would have been a scene of intense noise and activity, enough to make one's heart pound. Hundreds of airmen had trained here every month, practicing bombing runs and aerial dogfights in a place so remote that only the cattle, coyotes, and jackrabbits were inconvenienced by the commotion. But training airmen had just been the cover story.

A breeze swept dust across the decay. When the darkness was thick enough to conceal them from prying eyes, Raleigh pointed toward a hangar that seemed less collapsed than the others. The Suburbans followed, and he tugged away a section of corrugated metal, revealing a space large enough to allow a vehicle to enter the hangar.

Once they were inside, Raleigh pulled out a flashlight and examined a thirty-foot-high pile of debris that appeared to be the result of a clean-up effort long ago. Pushing aside some of the debris, he uncovered the edge of a camouflaged radio dish that was aimed toward a similar dish at the observatory. After verifying that the dish hadn't been disturbed, he edged behind some of the debris and pushed a button.

A portion of the concrete floor rumbled as it descended to form a ramp. Lights shone up from below, activated by the same button. His footsteps crunching on dirt, Raleigh walked down the ramp into a rush of cool underground air. The Suburbans followed him slowly, and the moment they reached the bottom, he stepped to a wall, where he pushed another button. The ramp ascended, becoming part of the ceiling.

As the men clambered out of the vehicle, Raleigh said, "Sergeant, assemble the team."

Seconds later, they stood in a row before him.

"Gentlemen." His voice reverberated off the concrete walls. "You're beneath Hangar 8 of an airfield that was a training facility for U.S. military flight teams during World War II. The hangar and this area weren't part of that effort, however. Only personnel with top-secret clearance were allowed in the hangar, and even fewer were allowed down here. The explanation was that the prototype for a new bomber was being assembled in the hangar and readied for testing. Trainees cycled through the program so quickly that they never stayed long enough to wonder why the bomber wasn't completed and flown.

"You're familiar with the race to develop the atomic bomb during the Second World War. The location for that project's main research facility, Los Alamos, was on a remote, difficult-to-reach mesa in New Mexico. This underground area enjoyed similar advantages and had a similar purpose. If it seems out of the way now, imagine how truly out of the way it was in 1943, when the project began. The objective was to develop a weapon quite different from the atomic bomb. In a way, Hangar 8 and Los Alamos were racing against one another as well as the enemy. Of course Los Alamos won the race. In fact, the first atomic bomb was detonated at what's now called the White Sands Missile Range, just two hundred and fifty miles north of here, and after two of those bombs ended the war in the Pacific, the urgency to develop a parallel weapon lost its force."

Raleigh chose his next words with care. "In addition, there were what might be called difficulties in conducting the research here."

Difficulties, indeed.

Raleigh looked around the subterranean chamber. Even after all these years, rust-colored smears were visible on the walls, but they had nothing to do with rust.

"With the end of the war, there was no longer any need to train massive numbers of military flight teams, and the cover story lost its effectiveness. So for a number of reasons, the airfield was shut down. Except for this underground facility, the base was allowed to deteriorate. This area wasn't exposed to the elements, however, and apart from minor water damage, it adjusted extremely well to remaining in hibernation. Indeed, from time to time, it received maintenance checks in case its mission should ever be reactivated. Fifteen years ago, I did exactly that.

"I reactivated it."

34

"Anita, are you sure this angle will work?"

Brent raised his voice so that he could be heard above the noisy crowd. He and his camerawoman stood on top of a Winnebago motor home that the owner—a local car dealer—had agreed to let them use in exchange for free publicity.

Like Brent, Anita had gotten only a few hours of sleep since coming to Rostov. There'd been too many people to interview, too many locations to scout. Her eyes looked heavy under her baseball cap. Her outdoor clothes, with their numerous pockets, seemed even more baggy than when they'd started.

My suit looks worse, Brent thought. A day earlier, that would have depressed him, but now—as he peered down at his scuffed, dusty shoes—he almost smiled at the new image he was creating for himself.

"You'll be on the right side of the screen," Anita answered. "The horizon'll be on your left." She looked so tired, he wondered how she had the strength to keep the heavy camera balanced on her shoulder. "It's a clear shot. If we tried this on the ground, the crowd would get in the way, but from high up like this, they won't be in the shot at all unless you ask me to tilt down."

"Perfect. Stay focused on me unless I indicate otherwise. Tell Jack and the guy in the chopper to keep their cameras panning across the crowd the entire time, just in case something happens."

"In case *what* happens?"

"Just make sure they're ready. And I definitely want a shot of *that* guy." Brent pointed down toward a tall, gray-bearded man who wore a biblical robe, held a staff, and looked like Charlton Heston playing Moses in *The Ten Commandments*.

He frowned toward the east, where the dark clouds were getting thicker. *That rain better wait until I finish the broadcast*, he thought.

"Okay, time to prep a guest."

"Button your shirt. Straighten your tie," Anita advised.

"No way." Brent rubbed his bristly whisker shadow. "I want CNN to see how hard I'm working."

"How hard we're *all* working."

"Right."

At dawn, after a night of chasing interviews, Brent had experienced a moment of powerful inspiration when he'd seen his reflection in a car window and cringed at how terrible he looked. He'd been reminded of an old black-and-white movie about a reporter racing against the clock to prove the innocence of a prisoner about to be electro-cuted on Death Row. In the movie, the reporter barely had time to eat, let alone change clothes and shave. At the end of the movie, when he burst into the governor's office with the proof, he looked like he'd suffered through hell to get the story.

At that moment, the idea had hit him: *How can the viewers, or the CNN brass, know how hard I'm working if I make it look easy? I've been doing this wrong. What viewer gives a shit if I'm wearing a perfectly pressed suit? Most of them don't even own a sports coat. For them, wearing jeans is dressing up.*

I've got to make them realize that I'm one of them— that I'm killing myself to get the story for them.

And with that epiphany, he had done a complete about-face.

In addition to exhaustion, Brent suffered from too much coffee and not enough real food. Doughnuts and tacos had been just about all he'd eaten, always on the go. Except for when he drove with Anita, he never had a chance to sit down, and even then, he wasn't resting. He was making hurried notes or using his cell phone—which wasn't easy since the reception here was for shit.

He couldn't let up. He needed to make sure he got to anybody who might have even the slightest information to contribute, and he had to get there before the other reporters. He wanted everyone else feeling behind the curve, certain that anything they did would look like an imitation of what he'd already accomplished.

But there was a cost. His stomach had a sharp, burning sensation. His hands had a slight tremor. He felt light-headed from exhaustion and lack of food.

Legs stiff, he climbed down the ladder to the crowd below. The noise of so many impatient conversations gave him a headache. The daylight was gone now, and the sky was black and starless, but there were plenty of other sources of illumination: headlights, spotlights set up by the authorities and the television crews, flashlights carried by the curious. Brightly lit figures cast stark shadows, lending the scene a surreal quality.

His coanchor, Sharon, waited for him at the bottom of the ladder, her big hair sprayed perfectly into place. Anger made her more beautiful.

"Well, I've got to give you credit," she said crisply. "You finally got what you wanted—you really screwed me today."

"Was it as good for you as it was for me?"

Someone bumped against them, shoving through the crowd.

"Keep going," a woman urged her male companion. "We can't see anything from back here. Get close to the fence."

"*I* was supposed to be the one giving the reports to CNN," Sharon complained. "*I* was supposed to anchor today's broadcasts, all by myself."

"Well, while you were nursing your sore feet, I was out doing the interviews."

Someone else bumped against them, almost knocking them together.

"If you ask me, these lights are all a bunch of bullshit," a man complained to his companion. "I don't know why I let you talk me into coming here. It took *six hours*, for Christ's sake. If I'd known there'd be this many people . . ."

Brent faced Sharon again. "Maybe you should try being a reporter for a change. Dig up more stories about rescued cats and the people who love them."

A man pushed a woman in a wheelchair, nearly knocking Brent off his feet and shouting, "Out of the way! Let us through. My wife needs to see the lights! They'll heal her legs! Out of the way . . ."

Brent took advantage of the interruption and turned toward the broadcast truck, which was parked near the Winnebago.

"Mr. Hamilton," he called to someone inside the truck. "We're ready for your interview."

An uneasy-looking man stepped out. Overweight, in his midforties, he wore cowboy boots and jeans with creases down the middle of the legs. His blue-checked shirt had shiny metal snaps instead of buttons.

"I was on the Highway of Death in the First Gulf War, but nothing ever made me nervous like this."

Hamilton's puffy cheeks were flushed. He grinned at his own candor.

"Going on television? I thought car dealers were used to that because of their television commercials," Brent said as he adjusted the tiny microphone clipped to the man's shirt.

"There's no station in Rostov. Hell, I've never seen the inside of one."

"Don't worry about it. I'll ask you some easy questions about what you told me this afternoon. I've never heard anything more fascinating. All you need to do is forget the camera and talk to me the way you'd talk to a customer."

"Well, I can sure do that." Hamilton looked up uncertainly. "But I've never tried to sell anybody anything from the top of a motor home, and in the dark to boot."

Brent leaned inside the broadcast truck. "Harry, brighten the lights up there, will you? There you go, Mr. Hamilton, lead the way. I think you'll enjoy the view."

With that, they walked over to the Winnebago.

"I hope you're not counting on too much," Hamilton said as he started climbing the ladder.

Only a ticket to Atlanta, Brent thought.

On top of the motor home, he arranged Hamilton so that he stood a few feet away, with the crowd below them and the rangeland in the background.

"I just need to talk to somebody for a moment. Then we'll do the interview."

Brent adjusted his earbud so that it wouldn't be conspicuous. Through it, he listened to the producer, who sat below him in the broadcast van.

"Ready in ten," the producer's voice said.

Next to Anita's camera, a face appeared on a monitor, the craggy features of one of television's most well-known personalities.

Hamilton pointed. "Isn't that . . . ?"

Keeping his right hand at his side, Brent motioned for him to be quiet. He was troubled that his hand had a tremor.

The producer's voice finished counting down.

"Go."

On the monitor, the CNN newscaster's thin lips moved, but there was no sound. Brent could hear him through the earbud, though.

"*And for the next hour, we have a special broadcast about a story that stunned the nation. Last night a crazed gunman shot twenty members of a tour group near the remote town of Rostov in west Texas. The killer's rage was evidently set off by mysterious lights that appear almost nightly in that area. Joining us live at the scene of the shooting is Brent Loft, a reporter for El Paso television station . . .*" The famous personality, whose power Brent hoped to have one day, read the station's call letters.

"*Brent, you look as if this story is taking a toll on you.*"

"Things are very emotional here." Brent's words were picked up by a tiny mike clipped to his dusty lapel. "Believe me, there's a lot more information to track down."

"*I understand you're going to tell us more about the mystery of those lights, and why they drove this gunman into a homicidal frenzy.*"

"That's correct. The lights are a local phenomenon that have been here as long as anybody can remember.

On most nights, they appear on the rangeland behind me—but not to everyone. Some people see the lights, while others don't, and that's as much a mystery as what causes them. In a while, we're going to aim our cameras in that direction and see if the nation gets lucky.

"But first, you need to understand what the eager crowd below me is looking for. To provide some context, I want to introduce you to Luther Hamilton, a car dealer here in Rostov who probably knows as much about the lights as anyone. He's one of the few who've seen them up close and personal. In fact, his experience with them nearly cost him his life.

"Mr. Hamilton," Brent stepped toward his guest so that Anita could put them in a two-shot. The crowd milled impatiently below. "In the summer of 1980, you took part in a highly unusual event."

"It sure wasn't ordinary, I'll tell you that," Luther agreed.

"And it occurred in this area?"

"*Exactly* in this area. Right where everybody's standing down below us. There wasn't any observation platform in those days, just a gravel parking lot at the side of the road. On the Fourth of July, 1980, Rostov had a fireworks celebration. After it was over, we drove out here."

"How many people were involved?"

"Almost as many as are here now. At least four hundred."

"And what did you plan to do? Did you have a name for it?"

"We called it the Rostov Ghost Light Hunt."

35

For the second time that day, Luther described what had happened that long-ago summer, and now he understood that the nervousness he'd spoken about hadn't much to do with worrying that he'd forget what he was supposed to say on television. It was nervousness about what he'd started to remember. That afternoon, when he'd told the reporter about the hunt, he'd recalled it through a haze of decades, but now his memory was focusing, remembering details with clarity, and he dreaded returning to that time.

I wish to God I'd never agreed to this interview, he thought. He'd hoped that the publicity would help him sell cars, but all of a sudden, he didn't care.

Rostov's 1980 Fourth of July fireworks had turned out to be the usual joke. They were ignited on the high school football field: less than ten minutes of skyrockets, some of which had more of a pop than a bang. A few never went off, and the principal made a big show of pouring buckets of water on them. The senior class clown, Jeb Rutherford, burned himself with a sparkler. Bits of burned paper drifted from the sky, and Cal Bailey's girlfriend got a speck in her eye. Cal had to drive her to the hospital. The big finish was a rocket that burst into the shape of a huge American flag blazing above the crowd. Smoke and the smell of gunpowder drifted everywhere. Eleven years later, Luther would associate that odor with the smell of gunsmoke from artillery in the First Gulf War.

And then the show was over. Rick Chambers, the president of the student council, murmured to Luther that the fireworks had lasted about as long as it took to have sex. Everybody headed toward their cars or trucks, but a lot of them knew that the festivities were just beginning, and it wasn't just schoolkids who drove out of town to the gravel parking lot. A lot of parents went there, also, and families came from nearby towns.

Johnny Whitlock—the captain of the football team—was the guy who'd thought of it. Johnny was always coming up with crazy schemes, like suggesting that the Homecoming dance should have a Hawaiian theme because nobody ever left Rostov, so how could there be a homecoming? Maybe the dance should be called the "Wish I Could Leave Home" dance. That idea got only one vote—Johnny's. Another time he sneaked over to the school in the middle of the night and managed to reach the flagpole without being spotted by the janitor or a policeman driving past. The next morning, when the students arrived, they found a Mickey Mouse flag grinning over the school. The principal was furious. At a hastily convened assembly, he ranted that somebody had insulted not only the school but also the American flag, and he demanded to know who'd done it. Only Luther and a few other kids had known it was Johnny, and of course none of them said a word—at least not until after that Fourth of July, when it no longer mattered.

"Let's do something *big* this summer," Johnny told Luther and a half-dozen other kids after their final class of the school year.

They were eating burgers at the Rib Palace, and Luther said, "Yeah, like what? You know there's nothing to do around here."

Johnny chewed thoughtfully and grinned. "All we got around here's the lights, right?"

"And that old ranch house where they made that James Deacon movie," Cal Bailey suggested.

"Who cares about *that* old dump? The damned thing's falling apart. No, the lights are the only action we've got. How many times have any of you tried to figure out what they are?"

Everybody shrugged. It was a rite of passage that on your twelfth birthday you sneaked out of the house after your parents went to sleep. You bicycled out to the parking lot, where other kids were waiting to see if you had the guts to climb the fence and hike into the field to try to find what caused the lights. That was tougher than it sounded because the field stretched all the way to Mexico, and it was easy to get lost out there in the dark. Not many kids actually saw the lights to begin with, so most didn't even know what they were looking for, which was why the older kids tried to make things scarier by calling them "Ghost Lights."

Before the birthday boy arrived, other kids hid in the field. When he climbed the fence and started into the darkness, they raised lanterns, but as soon as he headed in their direction, they covered the lights. That made him look around in confusion. The next thing, he saw other lights—more lanterns—and went toward them. Then *they* disappeared. The joke ended when the kids with the lanterns couldn't keep from laughing.

But sometimes the kids who were hiding saw *other* lights, and it was obvious that *those* lights couldn't be lanterns because some of them floated high off the ground. They moved this way and that, and merged and changed colors, and kept getting larger and coming closer. That was another way the joke ended—when it suddenly wasn't funny and the kids with the lanterns decided it was time to go home. That rite of passage ended after the Fourth of July, 1980. No one wanted to go into the field after that, and when Chief Costigan came to town to replace his father, who'd been shot to death, the field remained off-limits because the chief kept driving out there at night to try to figure out what the lights were.

"Sure, we kidded around about the lights," Johnny said that June, lowering his hamburger. "But the truth is, *nobody* knows what they are."

"They're nothing," Jasper Conklin said. "I bet I've been out there a hundred times. Never seen 'em once. People who claim to see 'em are putting you on."

"Well, *I've* seen 'em," Johnny said.

"So have I," Luther added. "And my mom and dad have, too."

"Let's make a difference and do something the town'll remember for a long time," Johnny said. "Let's find out what causes them. Let's have a Ghost Light Hunt."

That was a typical Johnny idea, but the name had a nice shivery sound to it, and he suggested that they do it after the shitty Fourth of July fireworks and make a real celebration.

"Why not?" Jasper said. "We've got nothing better to do."

They mentioned it around town, and then parents heard about it, and some of *them*—especially the editor of the weekly newspaper—thought it might be interesting. So the newspaper printed an article, and the next thing, there was a meeting in the high school gymnasium. A lot of people didn't want anything to do with the hunt— they were happy with the way things were and felt that *some* things shouldn't be explained. But most of the people were tired of not knowing what was out there, and a few had their own reasons for wanting the hunt to take place.

"Hell, before he died, my grandfather told me he saw the lights way back during the First World War," Josh McKinney said. He owned Rostov's only movie theater. "At the time, the town was afraid they were German spies, sneaking across the Mexican border. The Army came out and couldn't figure what was going on, so to be on the safe side, they built that training field out there. Then they reactivated it during the Second World War, when the lights made the military nervous again. All these years, people around here have been trying to figure out what they are, and no one's ever succeeded. Personally I don't think you're going to find out this time, either, but I'm all for trying, 'cause when you fail, it'll only make the lights more mysterious, and we'll get more tourists."

"And more customers for your theater, eh, Josh?" somebody joked from the crowd.

"Well, I wouldn't turn down the chance to sell more popcorn." The way Josh grinned got a laugh, and everybody started talking at once, but the mayor didn't bother calling for order because it was clear there was going to be a Ghost Light Hunt. Those in favor would work out the details on their own.

So that Fourth of July, hundreds of people gathered at the gravel parking lot outside town. All those headlights blazing were a show of their own, Luther thought, and the overwhelming rumble of that many engines, mostly from pickup trucks, was awesome. Johnny arrived on his motorcycle. Luther had a 1960 military-style Jeep he'd bought from a junkyard outside El Paso. A natural mechanic, he'd rebuilt it and painted it yellow. Several cowboys arrived on horseback.

Everybody was talking so much that Waylan Craig—who owned the hardware store—needed to use a bullhorn to get everybody's attention.

"Shut off those engines!" His amplified voice struggled to compete with the noise of the vehicles.

A few people complied, and then others. Before long, Luther could hear everything Waylan said.

"And shut off those headlights! I didn't think I'd need sunglasses at this hour!"

A couple of people chuckled, and soon there were only enough headlights to keep people from stumbling around in the dark. Luther looked up into the cloudless sky and saw the stars of the Milky Way stretching brightly across the sky.

"I brought eight sets of walkie-talkies from my store," Waylan announced, "As soon as you get organized into groups, I'll hand 'em out. Naturally I'd like 'em back when we're finished—unless, of course, some of you want to buy a pair."

That got more chuckles.

"You're supposed to have your own flashlights," Waylan continued, his words echoing into the dark grassland. "But in case you forgot, I brought some of *those* from my store, also."

"And you want them back, too, unless we decide to buy them," somebody yelled from the crowd.

"This week, they're on special."

Even more chuckles.

It wasn't that Waylan was funny. A lot of people in the crowd had come with a supply of beer, and most of the men were sipping from cans. A few kept going back to their trucks to drink from bottles in paper bags. Luther noticed that some of the teenagers had beer cans, too, holding them close to their sides, trying not to be obvious. A breeze carried the smell of alcohol through the crowd.

As a result, it took more than an hour to get organized. Somebody brought wire cutters from his truck and opened a wide section of the barbed-wire fence.

"We'll want to be sure to repair it after we're done," Waylan said.

"Got any tools to sell us to do that?" somebody yelled.

Four pairs of spotters were placed at strategic areas along the fence, about seventy-five yards apart. Each pair had a telescope, a compass, and a walkie-talkie. People went through the gap in the fence and spread out in a line about thirty yards wide.

Mayor Ackerman took charge of the bullhorn.

"Once we get started, just keep walking straight ahead. Use your walkie-talkies to tell us if you see the lights. As soon as we get everything coordinated on a map, we'll send trucks in that direction. They'll get there so fast, whatever's causing the lights won't have a chance to slip away."

"My motorcycle'll get there faster," Johnny said.

Luther almost added, "And my Jeep."

"My horse can get to places nobody else can," a cowboy said.

"Everybody's help is welcome," the mayor assured them through the bullhorn. "Those of you in the line, don't use your flashlights unless you absolutely need to. They'll ruin your night vision. Besides . . . " His tone indicated he was about to make a joke. "We don't want to scare whatever's making those lights. Heck, we may look as mysterious to them as they do to us."

But it didn't get a laugh, and Luther decided that some people in the crowd believed that the mayor was right.

Finally, a half hour before midnight, everybody started. Well, not everybody. Some people got tired and cold and went home. Others had too much to drink and fell asleep in their trucks. Lucky for them. But the majority spread out carefully and started walking into the darkness of the rangeland.

"Happy Fourth of July!" someone shouted.

Luther stayed behind with Johnny, ready to drive into the field if anybody spotted anything. For a while, the backs of the people in the line were illuminated by the few remaining headlights. But despite the cloudless sky, the darkness of the field was murky, and when they disappeared into the darkness, it was like a magic trick.

A breeze cooled Luther's face as he strained to detect any movement out there.

"I see one!" a spotter exclaimed.

"Where?" his partner wanted to know.

"No! I'm wrong! Sorry, everybody! It was just a flashlight somebody turned on and off!"

Another light flickered and vanished. Luther could tell that it, too, was from a flashlight. Then several lights flickered. The temptation to see what was ahead on the ground was evidently contagious. The off-and-on flashlights looked like giant fireflies bobbing and weaving out there.

A spotter yelled into his walkie-talkie, telling the people in the field, "Turn off those flashlights! You're making it hard for us to see what's beyond you!"

"Cut the flashlights!" another spotter shouted.

Gradually they went off, and finally all Luther saw was darkness. The sky was another matter. When he happened to look up, he saw the flashing lights of an airliner speeding toward its distant destination. Another moving light—this one *not* flashing—probably came from a satellite.

"Shit," Johnny said, hugging himself. "If I'd known it'd be this boring, I never would've suggested coming out here. I'm freezing my ass off. This is worse than the stupid fireworks."

Luther was about to agree when he glanced toward the grassland, and something in him came to attention as a patch of darkness seemed to brighten a little.

Probably just another flashlight, he decided.

But it appeared to be far beyond where the searchers were likely to be, and it was different from the darkness around it.

"Johnny." Luther pointed. "Do you—"

"I see something!" a spotter announced.

"So do I!" somebody else exclaimed.

So did Luther. Definitely. A ball of yellow light out there in the distance. Then a ball of green joined it. They bobbed as if floating in water, then merged into a single large ball that was red. A few seconds later, they drifted apart, and there were *three* of them, blue, orange, and a different shade of green.

Luther realized that he'd raised a hand to his right ear. An almost undetectable, high-pitched sound irritated his eardrum. It reminded him of a vibration he'd heard when he'd watched a man repair an old piano that was always stored in a corner of the school's gymnasium. The man had taken a shiny metal object from his toolbox. It had a stem and a two-pronged fork. He tapped it against the side of the piano, and the fork vibrated with a hum, allowing the man to adjust a wire in the piano until the tuning fork and the piano wire hummed identically.

Luther heard something similar now, like a note from an unusual-sounding piano, except that the barely perceptible vibration was annoying, making him imagine a hot needle piercing each of his eardrums.

"I see another one!" a spotter yelled.

"Two hundred degrees!" his companion shouted, checking his compass.

"One hundred and eighty!" someone farther along the fence yelled.

The other spotters made their reports.

"A hundred and seventy!"

"A hundred and sixty-five!"

In a rush, the mayor and two members of the town council leaned over the hood of a pickup truck, one of them pressing down a map while another aimed a flashlight and the mayor drew lines on the paper.

"They intersect at one seventy-five!" the mayor shouted. He used a ruler to measure the distance on the map and compared it to the scale at the bottom. "Looks to be about eight miles out!" he shouted into his walkie-talkie.

Standing nearby, Luther heard a crackly response from the mayor's walkie-talkie. "Eight miles? In the dark? That'll take all night!"

"Just keep the line going! Head for the lights, and make sure nothing gets around you! We'll send the trucks out now! They'll get there in no time!"

Luther heard the sudden roar of an engine and realized that it was Johnny kick-starting his motorcycle. Two trucks started up, but Johnny was the first through the gap in the fence. He had his headlight dimmed, and when the trucks quickly followed, they used only their parking lights. Even so, Luther could see the dust they raised, and the red of their taillights revealed two horsemen riding close behind them.

From the sound of the receding engines, Luther could tell that nobody was speeding, but in the dark, with minimal lights, speeding was a relative term. Twenty-five miles an hour would be plenty.

At once it occurred to him that he'd been left behind.

His Jeep didn't have a top. He leaped over the door, landed in the driver's seat, and twisted the ignition key. As the engine rumbled and his parking lights revealed the fence, he steered into the gap. His Jeep had a stiff suspension. Bumping across the rough grassland jerked his head back.

Man, I hope the other kids saw me make that jump. Luther was reminded of an old movie that he loved to watch whenever it was on television: *Bullitt*. It had the greatest car chase, and Steve McQueen was the coolest driver ever, but not even McQueen could have done that jump better.

Luther's front wheels jolted over rocks. A jackrabbit raced across his path. A night breeze ruffled his long hair. He pulled a luminous compass from his shirt pocket, took a quick glance down at it, and aimed toward 175 degrees.

The darkness formed a wall on either side. Even at this reduced speed, Luther had the sense of hurtling through space. His faint lights allowed him to see only a hundred feet or so ahead of him. Combined with the shudder of the Jeep over holes and rocks, they made it difficult for him to keep a clear, steady gaze on the area he aimed toward. The Ghost Lights were sometimes hard to see, even if he was standing breathlessly still in the gravel parking lot, but now he realized that, under these conditions, he couldn't hope to notice them unless he got very close.

Abruptly he saw movement ahead. *The people in the line!* he realized. Silhouettes materialized. They were scattered to the side, as if they'd scrambled to get away from Johnny's motorcycle and the trucks and the horsemen. Two people writhed in pain on the ground, while someone yelled into a walkie-talkie. Then Luther saw a horse thrashing on the ground, one of its legs bent at a sickening angle. A cowboy lay beside it. He wasn't moving.

The next second there were only rocks and clumps of grass and the elusive darkness beyond his parking lights as he hurried on.

If I'm not careful, I'm going to run into somebody, he realized.

Wary, he put on his headlights and gasped at the black, cinder-like boulders that suddenly appeared before him. They stretched all the way to the right. If he'd been going any faster, he'd have flipped the Jeep as he steered sharply to the left and tore up dust that swirled around his head, blocking his vision.

Keep turning! Keep turning!

The damned Badlands. As he swung clear of the boulders, coughing from the dust, he noticed a glow ahead of him.

I must be closer to the lights than I realized.

They increased until they hurt his eyes, quickly becoming larger and brighter. At first he thought it was because he was gaining on them, but as they intensified, he realized that they were moving, too.

They're coming toward me!

Luther didn't know why that frightened him. The whole point of the hunt was to get close to the lights and explain what caused them, but as they magnified, he felt his stomach contract.

Two of the lights weren't colored, though. Close to the ground, they sped nearer. With a start, Luther had the sick understanding that they were the headlights of a pickup truck.

It's going to hit me!

He swerved to the right and felt the truck speed past him so closely that wind from it hurled grit into his eyes. He braked hard and skidded over rocks and grass. The jolt knocked his teeth together. Frantic, he pawed at his eyes, trying to regain his sight. Dust filled his lungs, making him cough again.

Then his vision became clear enough for him to see a panicked horse galloping toward him. It didn't have a rider. Terrified, Luther raised his arms across his face, certain the frothing animal would collide with the Jeep. He imagined the agony of its weight flipping onto him, crushing him. But at once the hooves thundered past.

He spun to look behind him. Farther back, distant shouts were accompanied by bobbing flashlights that suddenly seemed everywhere. The people in the line had heard the truck and the horse rushing toward them and were running in every direction to avoid getting hit.

A woman screamed. The horse wailed. Or could that terrible animal outcry possibly have come from a human being?

Luther felt paralyzed by the chaos. Then the roar of another engine made him stare ahead again. He saw the colored orbs chasing the headlights of a truck that veered to avoid Luther's car, angling sharply to his right. A single headlight raced next to the truck—Johnny's motorcycle. Continuing to veer to the right, the truck smashed through a barbed-wire fence and detached a sign that flipped through the air. The sign nearly hit Johnny's motorcycle.

Luther knew exactly what the sign said. He'd seen

identical ones on the fences that enclosed the area over there.

PROPERTY OF U.S. MILITARY

DANGER

TOXIC CHEMICALS

UNEXPLODED ORDNANCE

The speeding taillights dimmed, pursued by the colors, which diminished as well, until all Luther saw was the darkness of the grassland.

A far-off rumble sounded like thunder. Several flashes might have been lightning on the horizon or fireworks from a distant town. But Luther had no doubt what really caused the rumble and the flashes. Despite the distance, he thought he heard Johnny screaming.

36

"So the sign didn't exaggerate?" Brent asked as they stood atop the brightly lit motor home and the crowd milled impatiently in the shadowy parking lot below. Anita continued to direct her camera toward him and Hamilton.

"During the Second World War, there was an active military airfield in that area." Hamilton sounded as if he were in pain. "This area's so remote it was a perfect place for flight crews to practice bombing runs. Usually what they dropped didn't have detonators or explosives. But sometimes it was the real thing—to get the crews used to the shock waves. Not all the bombs exploded when they hit the ground. After so many years, the detonators became very unstable."

"And your friend—did he survive?"

"Johnny?" Hamilton grimaced, as if the memory belonged to yesterday. "He and two men in the pickup truck were blown apart when they drove over a couple of the bombs."

"I'm sorry to hear that." Brent, of course, had already known it. Hamilton had told him about it earlier in the day. But Brent needed to put on a grave look of sympathy.

"Nobody dared go looking for them in the dark," Hamilton continued. "A local pilot went up at dawn. She flew over the area and saw the wreckage and gave details about the location. But even then, a recovery team couldn't just rush in for fear of setting off other bombs. It took them until midafternoon to get there." He shook his head and looked as if he might be sick. "By then the coyotes had gotten to what was left of the bodies and—"

Brent decided it was time to change the subject. The program was close to being a tabloid as it was, without describing animals eating corpses.

"And the lights? What happened to *them*?"

"They just disappeared. The next night, they didn't come back—and the night after that. It was a couple of months before they returned."

"You said the lights chased your friend's motorcycle and the truck?"

"And the other truck and the two cowboys. That's the way it looked to me. Of course, it might have been an optical illusion. During the investigation, a psychiatrist claimed that everybody just got carried away, that we saw the lights because we *wanted* to see them, and when one person panicked, everyone panicked. I don't know *what* to believe. That night the lights sure seemed real, and they sure seemed to have a will of their own. They scared one of the horses so bad it broke its leg, and another threw its rider and bolted away. That was the horse I saw galloping toward me. The cowboy broke an arm and his collarbone."

"And what about *you*? From what you've said, the lights didn't bother you."

"I sat in the darkness for a long time, trying to figure out what I'd seen. I tried to tell myself that my eyes had played tricks on me. But if I was seeing some kind of hallucination, Johnny and the guys in the pickup truck must have seen exactly the same hallucination. Why else would they have been driving so fast to get away? When I finally got the strength to turn the Jeep around and go back to this parking lot, I realized that my shirt collar was wet."

"Wet?"

"With blood."

"What?" Hamilton hadn't told him about this before.

"There was a sound."

"A sound?"

"High pitched. Almost impossible to hear. It felt like a hot needle against my eardrums. They broke."

"Broke?"

"My eardrums. Blood flowed out of my ears. I couldn't hear anything for three months. My doctor was afraid I'd be permanently deaf. It's amazing how much of that night I shut out of my memory. Talking about this again . . ."

Hamilton actually looked as if he were going to cry.

Time to wrap this up, Brent thought. He pointed toward the darkness.

"And now, all these years later, another tragedy has happened because of the lights. We're going to take a short break. As soon as we come back, we'll train our cameras on the area behind me and try to find some answers about—"

"I see one!" somebody in the crowd shouted.

"Where?"

"Over there! To the right!"

"I see it, too!"

Brent felt the motor home shake as the crowd pressed in that direction.

"Look! A half dozen of them!"

Brent sensed Anita moving forward with the camera.

"*Where?*" someone shouted. "I still don't see them!"

"To the right!" someone else yelled.

Brent stared in the direction a lot of people were pointing. All he saw was darkness. He hoped that the camera operators on the ground and in the chopper were following his instructions and focusing on the crowd. The *people* were the story. Their reactions were becoming frenzied.

"Yes! My God, they're beautiful!" a woman exclaimed.

At once Brent saw something in the distance. Six lights appeared to float. They converged in pairs, then separated.

"I see them!" Brent said to the viewers at home. "This is extraordinary. You're the first live audience ever to view the mysterious Rostov lights."

Anita was next to him now, aiming the camera toward

the lights. The intense look on her face told Brent that she was getting fabulous images.

"Perhaps this will help us understand what causes them," he told his audience.

"That isn't them," Hamilton interrupted.

Brent continued. "Perhaps we'll be able to—"

"I'm telling you those *aren't* the Rostov lights," Hamilton insisted.

"But I can see them. They're obviously out there."

"Headlights."

"What?"

"You're looking at the road from Mexico. Those are the headlights of cars driving along the highway. The road goes up and down over there. That's why the headlights seem to float. A lot of people have been fooled by that road."

"But . . ."

"The lights don't look anything like that. Besides, it's the wrong direction. That's southwest. You need to look south*east*."

"Over there!" a man yelled.

As one, the crowd turned southeast, and the Winnebago shook again. Several pointed emphatically.

"There!"

Brent turned to stare in this new direction and felt overwhelmed. The first thing he noticed were the *colors*. He'd grown up in Michigan. One disturbing summer night when he was ten, he'd been outside after dark and had seen countless ribbons of colors rippling across the sky. They'd radiated from the north and filled the heavens, eerily lustrous, swirling as if alive.

He'd run into the house and warned his mother, "We're going to die!"

"What?"

"The sky's on fire! It's the end of the world!" His father had died from a heart attack six months earlier. That was probably why death had been on Brent's mind.

When his mother had finally realized what was happening, she'd held his hand and made him go outside with her.

He'd struggled with her. "No! It'll kill us!"

"There's no reason to be afraid. What you're seeing is the *aurora borealis*."

"The what?"

"The Northern Lights. I heard an explanation for them once. Apparently they're magnetic rays from the sun reflecting off the polar ice cap."

What Brent saw now—off in the distance—made him feel as if the Northern Lights had been squeezed into seven shimmering orbs. Their iridescent colors kept changing, rippling from within, giving the impression that something churned at their cores. Their shimmer was hypnotic as they drifted and floated, sank and rose and hovered. Even though they were far away, Brent tried to reach out and touch them.

Many in the crowd felt the same. They reached toward the darkness.

"Get out of my way!" a man yelled.

"You're blocking the view!" somebody complained.

"Move!" a woman insisted. "I need to get closer! I need to be cured!"

"Stop shoving!"

"No, don't . . ."

Everyone surged toward the fence.

"Can't breathe!"

People slammed against the motor home. As it shook, Brent had trouble keeping his balance. When even more people surged, it trembled violently. He reached out for something to hold him up, but all he grasped was air. The next time the Winnebago shook, his knees gave way. Suddenly he was in the air, plummeting toward the crowd. He fell between bodies, struck the gravel, and groaned from the mass of people charging over him.

37

Earl Halloway sat in the harshly lit surveillance room beneath the observatory's dishes. He'd just swallowed six aspirins, for a total of a half bottle today, but he still couldn't control his headache. His stomach burned. The hum from the facility's generator or the dishes or whatever the hell caused it became louder, making him grind his teeth to try to relieve the pressure behind his ears.

This wasn't Halloway's shift, but there was no way he could contain himself enough to watch a movie on the computer in his room. He'd attempted to turn off the lights and lie in bed with a wet washcloth over his closed eyes. But the headache was too excruciating for him to lie still, so he'd come to the security office in the hope that doing something useful would distract him from it.

The harsh lights only made the pressure in his head more intense.

"Are you okay?" one of the other guards asked.

"Why wouldn't I be?"

"You look like hell."

Halloway had given up trying to make anybody else understand about the hum. No one else seemed to hear it.

"Every day's the same. We keep looking at those monitors. Nothing ever happens."

"That's the way I like it," the second guard said. "You'd rather have somebody attack us, just for the excitement? Maybe you didn't get shot at enough over in Iraq."

"As if terrorists care about an observatory," the first guard said. "I have no idea what we're doing here, but the pay's good."

"You got that right. The pay's good. So Earl, just shut up and quit complaining."

The night-viewing function on the cameras outside had been activated several hours earlier. On the monitors, the dishes, the fences, the scrub grass, the dirt, the miles and miles of godforsaken nothing—all of it was tinted green. One of the screens showed three coyotes loping by. Their body heat made them glow brightly. On a different screen, a jackrabbit jerked its head up. Sensing the coyotes, the rabbit bounded away in a panic. It, too, glowed unnaturally.

Moments later a third screen showed the coyotes chasing the rabbit through the green darkness.

"Who says nothing ever happens?" the first guard asked. "Any bets on who wins?"

"My money's on the rabbit," the second guard answered.

"How much? Oops, too late. Just as well you didn't have time to make your bet."

Halloway scowled at the screen. "Man, even blood looks green on those night-vision images." He stood and walked toward the doorway, stumbling slightly.

"Get some sleep," the second guard said.

"If only." Halloway left the room and walked along the stark corridor. His bootsteps echoed irritably.

The door to the Data Analysis area was closed. Wincing from his headache, he put his left ear against it.

You're not supposed to be in here, the researcher named Gordon had told him after Halloway had made an effort to be friends with him. Gordon's eyes had looked stern behind his spectacles. *This area's off-limits. You belong in the surveillance room.*

Try to be nice to people, and they treat you like shit, Halloway thought.

He pressed his ear harder against the cold metal door. All he heard was the hum. Throughout the afternoon, he'd made yet another effort to find what caused it. He'd searched every room in the facility—the latrines, the sleeping quarters, the kitchen, the mess hall, the generator room, the exercise room, the surveillance room—and yet again, he hadn't found any answers.

I didn't get a chance to check the research area again, he thought darkly. *That son of a bitch Gordon decided I wasn't good enough to be allowed in there any longer.*

The hum filled Halloway's head. The only time he hadn't been in pain was last night when he'd listened to the music—the wonderful music that made him feel he was dancing with the most beautiful woman he'd ever seen, smelling her cinnamon hair, tasting orange juice and vodka.

He gripped the doorknob and turned it.

Nothing happened. That bastard Gordon had locked it.

Halloway banged on the door but didn't get a response. He hammered louder.

Down the hall, one of the guards leaned his head out from the surveillance room. "What are you doing?"

"What's it *look* like?"

"We were told to stay out of there."

"I thought I heard somebody shouting for help."

Halloway pounded so hard that his fist throbbed, but the pain was nothing compared to his headache.

Suddenly the door was yanked open. Standing in the harsh lights of the research area, Gordon glared from behind his tortoiseshell glasses. His face was bright red. "What's the matter with you? Damn it, follow orders."

Halloway stared past him toward the other researchers. Amid banks of glowing electronic instruments, they all wore earphones. A headset—presumably Gordon's—was lying on a table.

"You're listening to the music, aren't you? But you didn't let me know."

"You have no idea what you're interfering with. Unless you want to lose your job, leave us alone."

Gordon started to close the door.

Halloway pressed a hand against it and stopped him. "That's what you're doing, right? You're listening to the music."

Gordon put more effort into closing the door.

Halloway rammed it open, knocking him back.

"Hey!" Gordon shouted.

Halloway stalked past him, approaching the table. The other researchers thought he was coming at them and stumbled away. But all he cared about was the earphones. Faintly the music drifted from them. The wonderful, soothing music.

"Gordon, you brought it back, but you didn't tell me."

"Of course we didn't tell you. You're just a damned guard."

"I tried to be friends," Halloway said.

"What?"

"Friendship doesn't mean anything to you."

"What are you talking about?"

A guard appeared in the doorway. He held an M4.

"Is everything all right?"

"Lock this man up until a helicopter comes to fly him out of here," Gordon said. "He's fired."

Halloway picked up the earphones.

The guard came over. "You heard him, Earl. They want you out of here."

Halloway raised the earphones toward his head.

The guard gripped his left forearm. "The music isn't our business, Earl. Make this easy for everybody. Let's go."

Halloway put down the earphones.

The guard looked relieved. "Good. We'll just let these people do their work."

Halloway punched the guard in the throat.

"Uhhhh . . ."

The guard dropped the M4 and raised both hands to his smashed larynx.

Halloway picked up the rifle and fired a three-shot burst into Gordon's face. The tortoiseshell glasses disintegrated.

Hearing screams behind him, he turned and saw the other scientists scrambling for cover.

Aim away from the equipment, he warned himself.

When the second guard rushed into the room, Halloway shot him in the chest.

The panicked scientists ran for the door. Relieved that their direction took them away from the equipment, he shot all of them in the back.

He picked up the second guard's M4 and checked to make sure that its magazine was full. As he stepped into the corridor, he saw Taggard running toward him. Halloway blew his head off.

He searched the facility and shot two maintenance workers crouching behind boxes in a storage room. He found a female scientist hiding beneath a bunk and shot her, also.

Throughout, he was conscious of the terrible hum. He returned to the research area, satisfied himself that the first guard was finally dead, and put on the earphones.

His headache vanished as the music drifted and floated.

38

Beneath the airbase, Raleigh unlocked a metal door and stepped into a room that he hadn't visited for three years.

The smell of dankness and must hung in the air. He saw
tiny red and white lights that might have been the eyes of
animals, but when he flicked a switch on the wall, overhead lamps revealed that they belonged to a vast array of
electronic instruments stacked on floor-to-ceiling shelves.
Needles pulsed, and dials glowed. As he examined them
closely, he saw that they registered an unusually high level
of activity.

Perfect, he thought.

When he had personally supervised the installation of
this array, the equipment had been state-of-the-art. Since
then, major advances had made it necessary to supplement
all the instruments with serious updates that his team had
brought. Even so, the existing equipment was doing its
job, amplifying energy from the source and transmitting
it through the dish concealed in the wreckage of the hangar
above him. That camouflaged dish was synchronized with
the horizontal dish at the observatory.

Tomorrow night the signal would be amplified even
more and beamed through a vertical dish that pointed
toward a satellite.

In previous experiments, the links had failed, sometimes
with disastrous results. But given the improved electronics
that his team was installing, and the unusually powerful
energy the source was giving off, Raleigh believed that this
time he would finally be able to complete a journey that
he'd begun as a boy inspired by his grandfather.

He pressed a button and activated a row of surveillance
monitors. In night-vision green, they showed the ruined
hangars as well as the area around the airbase. The supe-
rior lenses on the hidden cameras allowed him to magnify

images impressively. He watched the dog handler and the German shepherd patrolling the fence.

He switched his attention to the viewing area down the road, where the crowd was out of control, charging toward the fence. He hadn't counted on having human test subjects. The fact that there were hundreds of them provided an even greater benefit.

But what really mattered, he knew, were the test subjects he'd brought with him. The reaction of the men on his team would determine whether or not the project could be reliably continued. They didn't know that by setting up the experiment, they were crucial parts of it.

39

A shoe struck Brent's forehead. For a moment, his vision turned gray.

"Keep the cameras rolling!" he shouted into his lapel mike as people trampled over him. He worried that the director in the station's control room would stop the broadcast if he thought that Brent was being seriously injured on camera, so he did his best to sound in control.

From Brent's perspective on the gravel, everything was a blur of pant legs and dresses. The truth was, he felt smothered. Another shoe struck him, this time on the side of his neck. He wheezed and rolled, trying to get away from the mob. The gravel tore at him. His shoulder banged against the underside of the motor home. Desperate, he squirmed beneath the vehicle as far as he could manage.

From this vantage point, he saw shoes, boots, and pant legs rushing past. The side of his neck throbbed.

Any closer to my throat and I might have been killed, he thought. Suddenly the crowd was gone, and he crawled from under the truck.

"I'm okay! I'm okay!" he shouted into the microphone.

God, I hope the helicopter's getting a shot of this, he thought. The left sleeve of his suit coat was torn open. Blood trickled from his forehead.

Hearing shouts and screams from the crowd, he was about to climb to the top of the motor home and continue broadcasting, but abruptly he saw Anita and Luther Hamilton lying on the gravel. The camera was on its side, its red light still on.

He ran to Anita and heard her groan. "Are you okay? Can you stand?" he asked urgently. "I need to get you away from this crowd!"

He put one of her arms around his neck and raised her. She wavered.

"Come on, I'll take you where it's safe."

The producer and his crew scrambled from the truck. Brent gave Anita to them and hurried over to Luther Hamilton, who coughed and struggled to crawl. Brent helped him stand and guided him toward the back of the truck.

"We need an ambulance!"

"That's for sure." The producer pointed.

Brent turned and gaped at a half-dozen people lying on the gravel.

At the back of the parking lot, people charged against each other, pushing toward the darkness beyond the fence.

"I see them!"

"They're beautiful!"

"Out of my way!"

"Can't breathe!"

Brent picked up Anita's camera and gave it to the producer. "Do you remember how to use one of these?"

"You bet. I even keep paying my union dues."

"Then follow me to the top of the Winnebago."

Brent grabbed the toppled ladder and propped it against the truck. The tremor in his right hand alarmed him. Feeling faint, he struggled up. At the top, he noted that the station's helicopter had activated its landing lights, illuminating the crowd.

Hoarse from the blow to the side of his throat, he spoke into his lapel mike, describing what he saw. "The people at the back are forcing everyone ahead. Those in the middle are being crushed. The ones in front are being squeezed against the barbed-wire fence."

Brent heard wood cracking.

"I think the fence is about to . . ."

Several posts snapped. The fence collapsed. The people in front dropped with it, screaming as they fell onto the barbed wire. The rest of the crowd surged over their backs, charging into the field.

In the distance, the lights continued to shimmer.

"I hear a sound," Brent said into his microphone. "Luther Hamilton mentioned that sometimes a sound accompanies the lights. I wonder if that's happening now. No, I'm wrong. The sound has nothing to do with the lights. It's—"

40

Standing next to a car at the side of the dark road, Page gaped toward the observation area, where the crowd was out of control. If he'd been alone, he'd have run to help the police, although he couldn't imagine how even ten times as many officers would be able to handle what he was witnessing.

Right now, Tori was all he cared about.

"You were right to stay away from the crowd," he said.

He turned.

She wasn't next to him.

He frowned toward the shadowy road, then stepped toward the space between the parked cars, but he still didn't see her.

"Tori?"

He hurried back to her Saturn. She wasn't inside. He studied the darkness on the far side of the row of parked cars. No sign of her.

"Tori!"

Page doubted that she'd have gone toward the crowd, which had become a single mass that was trampling over the barbed-wire fence, crushing people, and disappearing into the night.

But if she hadn't gone in that direction, there was only one other possibility.

Thunder rumbled.

Page swung toward the murky grassland and ran toward it. Tori had been right when she'd guessed that the observation area was an arbitrary spot from which to try to see the lights. They could be detected from other points along the road, and tonight, to his surprise, he'd had no trouble spotting them. When Tori had pointed excitedly toward the dark horizon, he'd seen them immediately.

I must have learned *to see them,* he thought. *The way I learned to see the cuttlefish.*

Or am I just fooling myself?

In the distance, the colors bobbed and drifted. Not only did Page see them much more quickly than on the previous night, but he also saw them more clearly. It was as if a haze had been removed from his eyes. Radiant, they swirled, far away and yet close. His skin seemed to ripple.

"Tori!"

Thunder rumbled louder, the storm approaching rapidly.

Page made his way toward the fence. Thanks to his pilot training, he knew that the best way to see at night was to try to detect objects from the periphery of his vision. Staring straight ahead at something in the darkness achieved less results than if he worked to detect it from the corners of his eyes because the eye cells designed for night vision, known as rods, were located on the eye's perimeter.

He looked obliquely past the barbed wire. To his right, he heard shouts from the viewing area. Over there, wraith-like shadows moved farther into the grassland, attracted to the lights. He also heard groans.

"Damn it, I told you to stop shoving me!" someone yelled.

Lightning flashed, revealing silhouettes in a struggle. A man punched another man in the stomach. When the second man doubled over, the first man knocked him to the ground and kicked him in the head. Other people grappled in similar frenzied fights, so many that Page knew he couldn't stop them.

Then darkness swooped back, seeming deeper than before because Page's night vision was compromised. Unable to wait for his eyes to adjust, he gripped a post and climbed it, using the barbed wire as a ladder, jumping to the ground on the other side. His holstered handgun dug into him.

"Tori!"

A sudden wind hurled dust into his face. He raised his left arm to shield his eyes and moved forward into the murky field. Scrub grass crunched under his sneakers. A drop of rain struck his nose.

He almost tripped over a rock. When he regained his balance, he shifted ahead and tried to continue in a straight line toward the distant lights. The dust made him shut his eyes for a moment. More drops of rain pelted his forehead.

The next flash of lightning revealed silhouettes closer ahead. Once the crowd had reached the field, everyone had separated, desperate to avoid the crush of people that had propelled them over the toppled fence. They looked confused, as if they suddenly realized where they were.

Thunder shook Page's chest. Then he was sightless again, overwhelmed by darkness.

The next moment, the storm unloaded, the force of the downpour making him stoop. Shockingly cold, it enveloped him, obliterating the distant lights. Without them, he had no bearings. Even the lights back at the observation platform were no longer visible.

"Tori!"

Gusts whipped his face. His wet clothes clung to his skin, the cold rain making him shiver. The next flash of lightning struck nearby. He saw its multiple forks and heard a crack. The two-second blaze of light revealed a figure stumbling ahead of him. Then darkness enveloped him again. Propelled by thunder, he shifted toward where his memory told him he'd seen the figure.

Abruptly they collided. He knew at once that the figure was Tori. Ten years of marriage made it impossible for him not to be able to recognize the feel of her body in the dark.

"Thank God, I found you," he said. "Come on. We need to get back to the car."

"No."

The rumble of thunder made him think he hadn't heard her correctly. "What?"

"Leave me alone."

"You're not safe out here."

Page gripped Tori's hand, but the rain slicked her skin, and she was able to pull away, rushing from him.

"Tori!" he yelled. "We need to get back to the car!"

For a panicked moment, Page couldn't see her. Then lightning revealed her outline, and he charged after her.

"Tori, you could get killed out here!"

Page grabbed her shoulders. Standing behind her, he tried to turn her in the direction from which he'd come. She rammed her elbow into his stomach, knocking him away.

The unexpected blow made him struggle to breathe. Holding himself, he realized that she'd disappeared again.

The next time lightning flashed, he saw that she'd gone much farther than he'd expected. He ran to catch up to her. Again he grabbed her from behind, but this time, his arms pinned her elbows to her sides. He linked his hands around her stomach and lifted her, trying to carry her backward.

She kicked her heels against his knees. When the pain in his legs made him drop her, she spun.

"You bastard, don't take me away from the lights again!"

"Again?"

"If you'd let me stay, if you hadn't grabbed me and shoved me into the car—"

Stunned, Page realized she thought he was someone else. "Tori, I'm not your father."

"All I want to do is see the lights! You son of a bitch, you're always yelling at Mom! You're always trying to *touch* me!"

Page was shocked by this further revelation.

"Tori, your father died a long time ago! It's me! Your husband! I love you!"

Lightning showed her frenzied features as she drew back her fist. Drenched by the rain, he waited for the blow.

Her fist struck his mouth. His head jerked back, but as he tasted blood, he kept his feet in place, preparing himself for what he knew would be another blow.

She drew back her fist again. Then darkness made her disappear. The next time lightning flashed, Page saw her staring at him in shock.

Her shoulders heaved. Some of the drops streaming down her face weren't rain, he suspected, but tears. Her mouth opened, releasing a wail of anguish. When she clutched him, pressing herself against him, she did so with the force of a blow. Her arms clung to him tightly. With her head pressed against his chest, she sobbed uncontrollably.

"Scared," she moaned.

He could barely hear her in the roar of the wind and the rain.

"I'm scared, too. But it's going to be all right," he promised, tasting the blood from his swelling lip. "I'll do anything for you. Please, let me help."

"I don't know what's happening to me."

"I don't know what's happening to me, either," Page said close to her cheek. "But believe me, we're going to find out."

With his arm around her, he waited for the next crack of lightning. It split the sky so close to them that he flinched, but its blaze allowed him to orient himself. Behind him, he briefly saw the shape of the observation area and began to recognize the faint illumination of headlights and flashing emergency lights.

Tori must have seen them as well. As thunder coincided with renewed darkness, she plodded forward through the gusting rain. Page took her hand and moved next to her. If the lightning didn't provide more visual bearings, they risked going in circles in the field.

The ground became muddy, their sneakers sinking into it.

"Cold," Tori murmured.

"Think of a hot bath," Page told her. "Dry clothes. Steaming coffee. Warm covers in bed."

"Lost," Tori said.

"Then we're lost together."

Lightning fractured the sky.

Tori pointed. "The fence."

Their shoes were weighed down by mud. They slipped in it, holding each other up.

When they reached the fence, Page shouted to be heard above the wind. "I'll pull the strands of wire apart! Try to squeeze through the gap!"

As he used both hands to yank a middle strand up while pressing down on a lower one with his muddy sneaker, he feared that lightning would strike the fence, rush along the wires, and fry both of them.

"I'm through!" Tori yelled.

Page climbed the post and jumped to the ground, where he skidded in the mud, falling to his right knee. Lightning cracked close enough for him to smell it.

"Are you okay?" Tori asked.

"I *will* be in a minute." Page came to his feet.

Down the road, headlights glared, revealing the row of cars and people hurrying for shelter. Gusts of rain buffeted them. Some wore ripped clothes and held themselves as if injured.

"You're sure you're okay?" Tori shouted.

"Better than the way *they* look," Page answered. He and Tori ran along the line of cars until they reached the Saturn.

Inside, Tori already had the keys from her pocket. She

turned on the engine and started the heater, but the rush of air was cold, and she quickly shut it off.

As rain lashed the windshield, Page shivered.

Tori's teeth clicked together. Her red hair was stuck to her head. Water dripped from her blouse, her muddy clothes clinging to her.

Behind them, more headlights blazed as cars pulled out of the line, retreating to Rostov. Thunder shook the car.

Tori wiped blood from his mouth.

"I'm so sorry," she told him.

Page touched her hand. "It wasn't really you who hit me."

"The past few days, I feel like I stepped out of my life. I don't understand myself any longer. What the hell is happening?"

"Whatever it is, it's happening to both of us." Page held her, grateful that she let him. He loved her so much that he could barely speak. "We'll find out together."

THREE

EYE OF THE BEHOLDER

41

Chilled by his drenched clothes, Brent stood at the back window of the broadcast truck and stared into the murky rain. Behind him, Anita and Luther Hamilton slumped against a wall, sipping tepid coffee from plastic cups.

The news producer watched as a technician and a cameraman finished stowing the equipment. "Time to head back to the motel."

Lightning flashed, showing Brent the last of the crowd hurrying desperately through the rain toward their cars. Several limped or held themselves in pain.

"I wish we could get a shot of that."

"I'm not sending any camera operator out in that lightning," the producer said. "The storm's predicted to last several hours. Nothing else is going to happen here tonight. It's time to get some sleep."

"Who needs sleep when there's a story this big?"

"And who needs a reporter who passes out from exhaustion?"

"Where's Sharon?" Brent asked with suspicion.

"Back at the motel. She's resting so she can anchor the morning broadcast from here."

"No way. I'll coanchor with her."

"Not unless you get some rest. I know you want to show viewers how hard you're working, but you're starting to look scary."

When the truck started, making the floor unsteady, Brent sat next to Anita and fastened his seat belt. "Are you hurt?"

"Bruised."

"You did good work today."

"And last night," Anita emphasized. Something flashed in her dark eyes.

"And last night," Brent acknowledged. "Tomorrow morning, are you ready to do more?"

"My car still needs repairs." Anita's face was pinched with fatigue. She peered up from under her baseball cap toward the producer. "Am I still getting overtime?"

"You bet. CNN is underwriting our expenses."

The truck bumped as the driver steered onto the road.

"But I don't know what else is left in the story," the producer said. "After what happened tonight, the police say they're shutting down the viewing area. Nobody'll be allowed there tomorrow night. Maybe not for a long time to come."

"The police can try, but after what we transmitted just now, there'll be plenty more curiosity seekers here tomorrow," Brent said. "It'll be Saturday. People will make a weekend of it. They won't like coming a long way and not getting a chance to see the lights. Cops, barricades, an angry crowd—all that makes for great television."

"Tomorrow night," the producer agreed. "But what about in the meantime?"

"Lots of angles. I need to track down the woman who killed the shooter. Also, somebody told me there's a radio observatory around here. I bet I can tie that in somehow—extraterrestrials or whatever. And I want to find out more about that airbase from World War II. Maybe we can get a shot of where that kid got himself blown up back in 1980."

"Johnny," Hamilton murmured.

"What?"

"His name was Johnny."

"Right."

The producer said, "Brent, if you start wandering around that airfield, you're liable to get blown up, too." He looked thoughtful. "You know, *that* would make a great story."

42

Raleigh heard the faint rumble of thunder, but apart from some water trickling down a wall, the area beneath the abandoned airbase remained secure. In the cold glare of the overhead lights, he watched his men finish unpacking the last of the wooden crates.

"Sergeant Lockhart, reassemble the team."

"Yes, sir."

Within seconds, they again stood before him in a line.

"Gentlemen, through the door behind you, you'll find

latrines and your sleeping quarters, although you won't spend much time in the latter. There's a kitchen, but it isn't stocked. For now, you'll need to make do with the field rations you unpacked. When the next Black Hawk arrives at the observatory, it'll bring steaks.

"Part of the reason you were chosen for this assignment is that you're experts in electronics. Behind the door to your right, you'll find a monitoring station. It was state-of-the-art three years ago. The equipment we brought will bring it up to speed. But before you install it, I want you to take the closed-circuit cameras you unpacked and mount them on overhead corners in every room and corridor. I want every inch of this facility—including the latrines—to be visible on surveillance screens and every second of what happens down here to be recorded. If we're going to make history, it needs to be documented.

"Each of you will wear your sidearm at all times. You'll also make sure that one of the M4s you unpacked is close to you wherever you go. In addition, you'll wear shooter's earplugs."

Raleigh noted the puzzled look Lockhart gave him.

"Sergeant, do you have a question?"

"Sir, are you expecting us to come under attack?"

"Just taking precautions, given the instability we've seen outside. As far as the earplugs are concerned, there are certain audio characteristics to this project that can have . . . let's call them damaging effects."

A door opened behind Raleigh. He turned to see one of the team members bringing in the dog trainer and the German shepherd. They'd come down via a stairwell—its electronically controlled hatch was concealed among the hangar's piles of wreckage. All three were soaked.

"Any problems up there?" Raleigh asked.

"No, sir," the dog trainer responded. "Nobody came near this area. The crowd was too distracted by what was happening at the viewing area down the road. Things got crazy there. Then the storm started, and everybody left."

"Through that door, you'll find dry clothes."

"Thank you, sir."

As the trainer and the German shepherd left the area, Raleigh motioned for Lockhart to come over.

Raleigh kept his voice low. "If the dog acts strangely in any way, no matter how slight . . ."

"Yes, sir?"

"Shoot it."

43

The Saturn's windshield wipers flapped heavily in the strengthening downpour that pounded the roof and obscured the headlights. Shivering, Tori almost missed the motel's entrance. She turned, drove through rain-churned puddles, and stopped at unit 11. After she and Page ran to the door, Page unlocked it and held it open for her without entering.

"Go ahead, take a bath," he said. "Put on some warm clothes. I'll drive back to the Rib Palace and get some hot coffee for us."

"But you're as cold as I am. Why should *I* go first? That isn't fair."

"The last thing you need is to get sick before your surgery. How about hot soup? You want some?"

Tori barely hesitated. "Yes. That would be great."

Page hurried back through the drenching rain and got into the car, turning up the heater.

Fifteen minutes later, he returned, setting Styrofoam containers of coffee and soup on the unit's small table. The bathroom door was closed. Hearing the splash of water in the tub, he quickly took off his dripping clothes. The room didn't have a closet, but it did have hangers on a rod. He hung his clothes there and dried himself with a blanket he found on a shelf. Even with the blanket draped around him, he couldn't stop shaking.

He hadn't packed a lot of clothes and was forced to put on the jeans and shirt he'd worn the night before. They still had the odor of smoke, but at least they were dry.

When Tori came out of the bathroom, she found him huddled under the covers of his bed, trying to keep his fingers steady while he used both hands to grip his container of coffee.

She wore her usual T-shirt and boxer shorts. Her towel-dried hair was combed back. "Your turn."

"Somehow the idea of getting wet again doesn't appeal to me. I think I'll wait until I'm a little warmer."

"I still feel shaky. What kind of soup did you get?"

"In a place like the Rib Palace, they had only one choice—they call it Fiery Beef."

"Sounds like exactly what I need."

She pulled a blanket off her bed, wrapped it around

her, and sat at the table, opening the container of soup. Watching her, Page sipped his coffee and felt the hot liquid against his bruised lip. She didn't say anything all the while she ate, spooning the soup quickly. Then she opened the coffee, and while she drank it, she remained silent. Finally she turned to him, her features strained with confusion. "If it hadn't been for the storm, I'd have walked forever to try to reach the lights."

"No," Page said. "If it hadn't been for *me*."

"I couldn't resist. They seemed to be *calling* me."

He considered what she'd said, then gave her an extremely direct look.

"Let's pack and get out of here. Not tomorrow. Right now. We can be at your mother's house by morning. Are you ready to do that?"

Tori lowered her head and didn't reply, in effect giving him an answer. He remembered what had happened in the field. After what she had said and done to him, he wasn't about to try to force her to leave. He wasn't even certain he *could* force her to leave. So he came to a decision.

"In that case, I need to be a cop a while longer. This has gone way past the point where I can just let things keep controlling us. I'm going to find out what's going on."

44

Page jerked awake, struck anew by the stark reality of what Tori had told him about her cancer and by what had happened the night before.

So much to adjust to.

Sunlight crept past the cheap drapes, but he didn't feel at all rested, even though a glance at the bedside clock showed him that the time was 1:14 and that he'd slept another twelve hours.

This time Tori remained in her bed.

Groggy, he went into the bathroom, softly closed the door, and shaved, running the water as little as possible, trying not to make noise.

When he came out, Tori was putting on a pair of slacks.

"Sorry if I woke you," he said.

"It wasn't a good sleep."

"The same with me." He touched the shirt and jeans that he'd put on a hanger. "Still wet." He glanced down at the clothes he'd slept in. Wrinkled, they continued to retain the odor of the fire two nights earlier.

"Looks like we need to do some shopping," Tori concluded.

When they stepped from the room and faced the harsh sunlight, Page was troubled by the number of vehicles streaming past the motel—many more than on the previous day. It took even longer for Tori to find a break in the traffic and steer the Saturn onto the road.

In town, the streets were filled with cars. All the parking spaces were occupied. Tori let Page out in front of a store called the Outfitter, where there were so many tourists that he had to wait fifteen minutes to pay for new clothes. It took another fifteen minutes to get into a dressing room. He put on a pair of pants, a T-shirt, and a shirt to wear over it—something that would conceal his handgun.

When he came out with his old clothes in a shopping bag, he heard a customer talking to a female clerk.

"Do people really see lights around here?"

"Yes," the clerk answered. "But it's been years since I went looking for them."

"Aren't you curious what they are?" the customer asked.

"When I was a kid. But I got used to them."

As Page walked toward the front of the store, he heard another customer telling a different clerk, "My wife has diabetes. We heard this place makes miracles happen, like at Lourdes. If she sees the lights, she'll be cured."

Page went out to the sidewalk, where Tori was waiting with two sandwiches and two bottles of water from a restaurant next door.

Cured? he thought. *Wouldn't that be nice?*

They ate while they walked three blocks to the hospital. There Tori again paused nervously on the hot steps outside the entrance.

"Another day closer to the start of the rest of your life," Page tried to reassure her.

She took a breath and forced herself to go in.

Upstairs, in the brightly lit hallway, the sharp odor of disinfectant seemed stronger as they walked toward Costigan's room.

The chief's familiar raspy voice came from it, telling someone, "God help us if the next riot spreads to town. How many people were injured?"

"Twenty-three," a different voice answered. "Twelve got gashed pretty bad on the barbed-wire fence."

"And the others?"

"Six were almost trampled to death. The rest were hurt in fights."

Page was uncomfortable eavesdropping. He motioned for Tori to follow him as he stepped into the doorway.

Their footsteps made a man turn in their direction. He was in his fifties, stocky, with a sunburned complexion. His sport coat had a Western cut and a zigzag design over the left and right breast. He wore a large belt buckle and held a cowboy hat.

"Sorry to interrupt," Page said. "We just wanted to see how Chief Costigan was doing."

"A lot better, thanks." Propped up in bed, Costigan looked less gray. His mustache now had some contrast with his skin, and the heart and blood-pressure monitors were gone. The IV tube had been removed from his arm, although the thick bandage remained around his skull. "They say they'll let me go home tomorrow as long as I remember not to bang my head against anything. This is Hank Wagner. He runs the drugstore in town. More to the point, he's also our mayor, which, at the moment, he wishes he wasn't."

Page shook hands with Wagner.

"Dan Page. This is my wife, Tori."

"The chief told me about you. You're the couple who saved those people on the bus Thursday night. You're the woman who . . ." Seeing her discomfort, the mayor said, "Well, we're grateful for what you did. Without your help, the situation could have been even worse." He looked at his watch. "You'll have to excuse me. I need to get to an emergency town council meeting."

They watched him leave and then redirected their attention toward Costigan.

"Do you really feel better?" Tori asked.

"The headache's not as bad. And I don't have damned needles sticking into me. The doctor finally took me off a diet of broth and Jell-O." Costigan pointed toward Page's bruised mouth. "Looks like you're one of the people who got hurt last night."

"Things were a little crazy. Can I ask you a question?"

"You can ask." Costigan's voice hung in the air, suggesting, *But I might not answer.*

"The man who killed your father . . ."

For a moment, Costigan's pained eyes focused on the past. "What about him?"

"You said he'd come to Rostov only a couple of months earlier."

"He'd lost his job in Fort Worth when the factory he worked for moved to Mexico. He couldn't find anything else. One of his relatives lived here and managed to get him a job at the stock pens."

"You also said he was a drinker, that he got in arguments in bars. His wife buttoned her collars and wore long sleeves even on hot days—to hide her bruises."

"That's right."

"In your place, given what happened to your father, I'd have looked into every aspect of the case. I'd have gone to Fort Worth and talked to people who knew the husband when the family lived there. Did you find out if his behavior changed after he came to Rostov?"

Costigan considered him for a moment. "Yeah, you're a good police officer."

"Well, you know as well as I do, it's all about asking the right questions."

Costigan nodded. "I did some digging. The husband's behavior definitely got worse after he came here. He'd always had a short temper, especially when he drank, but here it became more extreme. People who knew him in Fort Worth figured he got bitter about being forced to leave the big city and live in the middle of nowhere."

"Did you buy that theory?"

"I had a different one."

"And that's the *real* reason you wanted me to keep my gun in my suitcase when I went to the observation area to find out what Tori was doing there, isn't that correct?"

"Correct."

"What am I missing?" Tori asked.

Costigan looked at her. "People either like it here right away, or else they hate it. You saw that on Thursday night. Some got out of their cars and were open to seeing the lights, while others couldn't wait to get back on the road. A few were actually angry because they couldn't see what others claimed to see. It's like the way magnets can repel each other as much as attract."

"Did the man who shot your father ever go out there to look at the lights?" Page asked.

"He tried several times. He finally decided that the people who told him about the lights were trying to make a fool of him."

"And you were worried that if *I* didn't see the lights, I'd get angry—as angry as the man who shot your father."

"Yes."

"Why didn't you tell me?"

"You wouldn't have understood what I was talking about. How could I possibly have explained it? I told you on the phone—you needed to see for yourself."

"Or *not* see," Page added.

Costigan made a gesture of futility. "There's no way to predict who'll see the lights and who won't, or how they'll react. Even those who *don't* see the lights . . ." The chief rubbed his bandaged forehead. "Do you suppose it's possible to *feel* the lights without actually seeing them?"

"Yesterday you told us they were only a mirage caused by a temperature inversion," Tori reminded him.

"That I did."

"But now you seem to think they're a lot more."

"A temperature inversion. Sure. That's the rational explanation. But one thing I've learned in more than twenty years as a police officer is that human beings aren't rational."

45

Harriett Ward's antiques store was crammed with browsers. After the glare of the afternoon sun, Page found the interior shadows soothing. He noted that a man had taken down one of the antique rifles Page had seen on the wall the evening before. The man worked the vintage firearm's lever and aimed the gun toward the ceiling.

"Just like the rifle James Stewart used in that Western," he told his female companion. "*Winchester '73*. Hard to imagine this was made just after the Civil War. What are they charging for it? Twenty-eight hundred dollars? My God, that's a steal!"

"But I don't think we can afford it," the woman said. "Gas and food cost so much. Next week Bobby's nursery school bill is due, and—"

"Hey, you don't see bargains like this every day. We'll put it on one of our credit cards."

Page looked toward the opposite side of the store and saw an older woman with short white hair and a leather vest: Harriett Ward. As he and Tori went over, she was talking to a couple about a wooden cabinet that had large iron handles on the doors.

"I found it in a village in Mexico. It's made of mesquite, which is about as hard as wood can get and not be like these metal handles."

She noticed Page and Tori and nodded. Five minutes later, she made her way over to them.

"I've never had so many people in the store at one time," she said.

"Well, at least there's an upside to what's been happening," Tori said.

"Everybody wants a twenty percent discount and free shipping. Someone tried to buy the antique light fixtures and got upset when I said I needed them. Someone *else* got upset when I told her I didn't have a public restroom. She made a fuss when I wouldn't let her into my apartment so she could use my private bathroom. I'm glad for the business, but I'd forgotten how difficult people can be."

A woman approached them. She had big blond hair and wore an ornate costume that made her look like a country singer.

"Janice, thanks for coming in to help," Harriett said.

"No problem." The woman laughed and spread her sequined green skirt. "I figured I'd wear something the out-of-state customers will remember. They'll go home and say we all dress like we're in one of those old Westerns where everybody sang when they weren't shooting bad guys."

"Do you think you and Viv can handle the store for a while?"

"Of course. We know what to do."

"Just don't sell the light fixtures."

Laughing at what she thought was a joke, Janice went to greet a customer.

Harriett led Page and Tori through the door in back, entered her sparsely furnished living room, locked the door, closed her eyes, and inhaled deeply. When she finally opened her eyes, she said, "You're here to talk about what happened last night?"

"If you're too busy, we can come back later," Tori said.

"No. Come with me—I want to show you something."

46

Harriett's pickup truck headed along the now familiar route.

"You're taking us back to the viewing area?" Page asked. He sat against the passenger door, with Tori next to him.

"Past it," Harriett answered.

Ahead, more cars were parked along both shoulders of the road. Flatbed trucks had concrete barriers on them. A crane was lifting the barriers and placing them in a line along the entrance to the viewing area, forming a high wall. Two men in suits supervised the work. Their hard hats contrasted with the cowboy hats of Medrano and another Highway Patrol officer.

"Looks like they're shutting the place off," Harriett said. "If they're smart, they'll take down the shelter altogether, along with the historical marker, and load the portable toilets onto those trucks. I never approved of what the county did here. The lights shouldn't be a tourist stop. I don't care about the business outsiders bring to town. Keep the lights a secret. Let people discover them if they're *meant* to."

"If they're meant to?" Tori asked.

"Do you think these people deserve to see the lights? Most can't. The others aren't capable of appreciating what they're lucky enough to see." There was a tone in her voice that Page hadn't heard before.

People filled the road, complaining about the tall barricade. Harriett was forced to stop the truck.

"Quit blocking traffic!" Page heard Medrano yell.

Reluctantly the crowd parted.

Harriett drove on, passing the parked cars. Beyond barbed-wire fences, scrub grass stretched in both directions. Five miles later, she steered toward a gate on the left. Page got out, opened the gate, waited for the truck to drive through, then resecured the gate.

They drove along a dirt road. The heat of the day had dried the puddles from the previous night's storm. Dust rose in small clouds to mark their passing. The rugged grassland extended toward the distant mountains, the vast area so flat and treeless that only the grazing cattle provided variation in the landscape.

Wait, Page thought, peering into the distance. *Something's out there.*

He saw a speck at the end of the road. Leaning forward, he tried to identify what it was. As the truck drove nearer, the speck became larger.

"It's a building," Tori said, curious.

"Why do I feel like I've been here before?" Page frowned, recalling his sense of *déjà vu* when he'd flown over the cattle and the windmill on his approach to Rostov. He'd also felt it when he'd first driven along the town's main street.

The building became more identifiable—and more puzzling. It was an impressive three-story ranch house. A covered porch stretched along its wide front. Several chimneys projected from its roofline. A square tower rose on the right corner, ending in a cupola that made the house look like a castle. But as majestic as the place appeared, it had a brooding, gothic quality.

"I've seen this house before," Tori told Page. Abruptly she made the connection. "*Birthright*."

"Of course!" Page said. "That's why everything looked

familiar when I flew here. This is the house Captain Medrano was talking about, the one Mullen took the tour to see."

Page remembered when a restored version of *Birthright* had been shown in theaters to celebrate its fiftieth anniversary. He and Tori had heard so much about the classic film—which had seldom appeared on television—that they'd made a point of seeing it.

"We love that movie," Tori said.

"Yeah, it really makes an impression," Harriett replied, the house becoming more distinct as she drove toward it. "People here in Texas sure admired it. They couldn't stand the novel, which they thought looked down on them, but they felt that the movie showed their strength and determination, not to mention the vastness of the countryside. No fake-looking computer effects in those days. When you saw a hundred thousand head of cattle, every one of them was real. The miles and miles of ranch-land. The endless sky. I don't think a movie has ever looked so big. As big as the state. And the actors matched the bigness of the movie. James Deacon, Veronica Pageant, Buck Rivers. Legends."

Page stared toward the looming house. Its dark, weathered wood reinforced the feeling of gloom that the structure exuded. Soon the truck was close enough for him to see that some of the boards had fallen, that there were gaps in the wall, that the porch was in danger of collapsing.

"Doesn't anybody maintain it?" Tori asked in surprise.

"The movie people left it here, and the family that owns the ranch took care of it for a while, but then they got distracted," Harriett answered. "And anyway, who would they have maintained it for? It's not as if they wanted tourists tromping over their land and leaving the gates open so their cattle would wander down the road and maybe get hit by a car. By the time the parents died, the children had pretty much forgotten about it. When they finally remembered, it was too late. Now the place is in such bad shape that it can't be repaired without basically being rebuilt."

She stopped the truck at decaying steps that led up to collapsed boards on the porch. The ornate front door looked as if it was about to topple from its rusted hinges.

Page got out of the truck, his sneakers crunching on pebbly dirt. He helped Tori down and watched Harriett come around to join them. She put on her cowboy hat. The sun was intense enough that Page wished he'd thought to bring a baseball cap. Tori continued to wear hers, concealing most of her red hair.

"In the movie, a lawn was here," Page said.

"And a curved driveway bordered by flower beds," Tori added. "A cattle stampede tears it all up. Veronica Pageant and Buck Rivers put it all back together. Then they do it again when there's a tornado. Then there's a terrible drought, but somehow they keep building their empire."

"Texas determination," Harriett said.

"And James Deacon's the white trash they humiliate, until he strikes oil and uses his money and power to get even with them. At one point, he drives his battered old truck across the lawn. He's covered with oil from his first well. He jumps out and punches Rivers." Page looked around. "But I don't see any oil wells."

"Forty miles from here," Harriett said. "That's where you'll find them. One reason the movie was made here is that this *isn't* oil country and there weren't any wells to interfere with the illusion that this is what Texas looked like a hundred years ago, before the oil boom." She paused. "I said there weren't computer effects, but that doesn't mean there wasn't any movie magic. Walk around the house, and you'll see what I mean."

Curious, Page and Tori did what Harriett suggested. Stepping around the corner, Page gaped. All he faced was more grassland.

"There *isn't* any house," Tori said in astonishment.

"The only part they built was the front." Page couldn't get over his surprise. "In the movie, you feel like you can walk right into the place."

"Seeing's believing," Harriett told them. "But what you see isn't always what's real."

Like the cuttlefish, Page thought. "You're making a point about the lights?"

"Eye of the beholder," Harriett answered. "Sometimes we see what we want to see, sometimes what we *ought* to see, and sometimes what we shouldn't see."

"I don't understand."

"A lot of people in town were extras in the crowd scenes in *Birthright*, back when they were kids. Ask around, and you'll hear all kinds of stories about what it was like to have movie stars walking the streets of Rostov."

"What does that have to do with the lights?" Tori asked.

"For about three months, the stars lived right here in town. Rostov was even smaller back then, and everything the actors did was pretty much public knowledge, not that any of it was terribly shocking. There was so little to do that the film crew—including the actors—played baseball every Sunday afternoon against a team the townsfolk put together. People invited the actors to barbecues. Every evening, the director put up an outdoor screen and showed everyone the footage he'd shot a couple of days before. Did you know that all three of the stars were only twenty-three years old?"

"*Twenty-three?*" Tori echoed. "But they look like they're in their forties and fifties for half the film."

"The director had two choices: hire forty-year-old actors and use makeup so they'd look young in the early parts of the movie, or else hire young actors and use makeup to age them. The fame of Deacon, Pageant, and Rivers made him decide to appeal to a younger audience. The acting and the makeup were so brilliant, they convinced you that what you saw on the screen was real."

"More illusion," Page said. "Okay, I get it."

"That's not the point I wanted to make, though," Harriett continued. "Deacon starred in only three movies. First, he played the younger brother in a family that runs a fishing boat in northern California."

"*The Prodigal Son,*" Tori said.

Harriett nodded. "Then he made the street-gang movie, *Revolt on Thirty-second Street.* And finally *Birthright.* He filmed all three back-to-back, but he died in a car crash before any of them were released. He never had a chance to find out how big a star he was."

"I knew he died young, but I had no idea it was before his movies came out," Page said.

"The waste," Tori said. Something in her voice made Page wonder if she was thinking about her own disease. "All the other great movies he might have made."

"At the time, his fans were convinced that he hadn't really died in the car crash," Harriett went on. "They believed he was disfigured, that he hid from the public so he wouldn't shock people and ruin his legacy."

She paused, bracing herself for what she wanted to say.

"Deacon was a troubled farm boy from Oklahoma. His mother ran away with the hired hand. His father was as stern and joyless as the father in *The Prodigal Son*. As a teenager, he rebelled to the point that he was accused of stealing a car and almost went to reform school. A teacher got him interested in acting in high school plays. He loved it so much that he found several part-time jobs, saved a hundred dollars, and hitchhiked to New York City, where he convinced Lee Strasberg to let him audition and was allowed to take classes at the Actors Studio.

"What people tend to forget is that at the beginning of Deacon's career, he played bit parts in a couple of movies, but he never made an impression. He had secondary roles in a lot of live television plays, and no one paid attention to those, either—deservedly. Even though he studied with Strasberg, he was terrible. Awkward, dull, lifeless. If he hadn't been so good-looking, he probably would never have been hired.

"Finally he became so discouraged that he gave up and drove his motorcycle across the country. That was in the summer of '56. By the fall, he was back in New York, where he managed to persuade a casting director to give him a small part in a Broadway play. Suddenly he was acting so brilliantly that a Hollywood talent scout gave him a screen test for a small part in *The Prodigal Son*. The test was so spectacular that the director asked for a second one and then gave Deacon the starring role. According to the DVD of the movie, that's one of the great success stories in Hollywood history. What do you suppose made the difference?"

Page shrugged. "I guess the motorcycle trip gave him a chance to get focused."

"Or maybe he had help," Harriett said.

"Help?"

"That summer, Deacon was on his way from El Paso to Big Bend National Park. That's southeast of here. He happened to drive into Rostov."

Tori stepped forward. "He saw the lights?"

"He spent most of August and all of September here. Every night, he drove out to the observation area, which wasn't even a parking lot back then. And every night, he stayed until dawn. Then he drove back into town and slept in a tent he'd put up in the park. Late afternoons, he went around town and made friends. He was so good-looking, I don't imagine that was difficult. Then one day he was gone, returning to New York and his big break."

Page frowned. "You're saying the lights had something to do with it?"

"They were the only thing that was different in his life," Harriett replied. "I can imagine him staring at the lights for all those weeks. Night after night. Spellbound. In Deacon's earlier roles, his eyes are dull. In his last three films, they glow. When he was hired to be one of the stars in *Birthright*, he told the film's director about Rostov and how the area around here would be perfect for location shooting. He was so persuasive that the director came out to take a look and instantly decided to build the ranch house—right here." She gestured at the ruined structure. "Seems awfully coincidental that we're ten miles from the section of road where Deacon first saw the lights."

"Did the director see the lights, too?" Page asked.

"No. Local people who worked on the movie remember that Deacon went there every night and dragged Pageant, Rivers, and the director with him several times. They had no idea what he was talking about. The crew members didn't get it, either, and finally Deacon was the only one who went out there."

Harriett drew a breath.

"He didn't need makeup to look older," she finally said.

Despite the heat, Page felt a cold ripple on his skin. "What do you mean?"

"The director shot the movie in sequence. As Deacon was supposed to look older, he actually *did* look older. The rumor on the set was that he was drinking and taking drugs every night instead of watching the lights, as he claimed. He began to look so wasted that the director begged him to stop abusing himself. There was talk of shutting down the picture and sending Deacon to a hospital to dry out. But every evening, when the town gathered to watch scenes from a few days earlier, Deacon looked so perfectly in character, so real in the part, that the director kept filming. The makeup people needed to use all their talents to get Pageant and Rivers to look as believably older as Deacon did."

Standing in the shadow of the ranch house's ruin, Tori asked, "What made that happen?"

"All I can tell you is that when Deacon finished his last scene and drove away on his motorcycle, people say he looked sixty years old," Harriett answered. "Five days later, he was killed driving his sports car to a race in northern California near where he'd filmed *The Prodigal Son*. He was going a hundred miles an hour when a pickup truck pulled onto the road. A witness saw sunlight glinting off the truck's windshield. The theory was that the glint blinded Deacon and kept him from being able to steer around the truck."

Page stared at the splintered boards lying on the ground. "Why hasn't any of this been talked about?"

"Deacon's death really traumatized everyone associated with the movie. They didn't claim to understand him, but they respected his brilliance, and they didn't want to tarnish his legacy by claiming that he was wasted on booze and drugs. They *certainly* weren't going to make him sound like a nutcase by mentioning the lights, which nobody believed in anyhow."

Harriett lapsed into silence. In the hot sun, the only sounds were cattle lowing in the distance and a breeze scraping blades of scrub grass.

"So the lights inspired Deacon, and then he became so obsessed by them that he was destroyed?" Tori asked.

"It depends on what you mean by destroyed. That final performance bordered on greatness," Harriett answered.

"But the bottom line is, he died," Tori emphasized.

"It could be that's what Deacon wanted. Maybe he'd lived so intensely during the previous year that he couldn't bear it any longer."

"You're suggesting . . . ?"

"The glint on the windshield of the truck he hit. Maybe he was so burned out that he decided to drive into the light."

The breeze faded, everything becoming still.

"Yesterday you told us how blessed the people in town feel because they've seen the lights," Page said.

"That was my experience."

"But not *everybody's* experience," Page added. "Is it possible to have too much of a good thing? In town, I heard a store clerk say that when she was young, she used to go out to see the lights, but now she never does. Yesterday you said *you* stopped going out to see them, also."

Harriett looked pointedly at Tori. "When Chief Costigan phoned yesterday to say you were coming to see me, he explained how fixated you are on the lights. I brought you here to try to make you understand that, yes, it's possible to have too much of a good thing."

47

The crackle of static woke him.

As did his headache.

And the odor.

Halloway lifted the side of his face from a table. His

cheek was numb from having been pressed so long against the wood. The earphones remained on his head. He felt groggy, as if he'd drunk every one of the numerous glasses of vodka and orange juice that the alluring music had made him imagine.

The scent of cinnamon remained in his nostrils. He sensed the lingering warmth of the voluptuous woman with whom he had slow danced in his fantasy.

And danced, and danced . . .

Until he'd passed out.

Halloway was slumped across a desk. When he straightened, he felt wetness in the front of his pants. He raised his head toward the painfully bright overhead lights and took off the staticky earphones. Exposed to air after so long a time, his ears tingled. He'd hoped that—without the aggravating crackle—his headache would lessen, but in fact the pain burrowed deeper into his skull because the crackle no longer kept him from hearing the hum that radiated from every surface of the underground facility.

If I can only find what's causing it.

But Halloway 's headache wasn't the only thing that had intensified. The odor now almost made him gag.

He peered down at the bodies. So many bodies. The scientists. The other guards. Their blood covered the floor, the stench reminding him of a butcher's shop through which he and his Ranger unit had searched for insurgents in Iraq. The electricity to that part of Fallujah had failed, and the meat had been spoiling in the extreme heat.

Here in the observatory, the blood wasn't the worst of it. Foul-smelling body fluids had leaked from several of the corpses. The faces of some had begun to distend.

That shouldn't be happening so soon, Halloway thought. He glanced at his watch and saw that the hands showed seven minutes to 4. His outburst had occurred around 9:30. His muddled thoughts somehow did the math. Less than seven hours.

At once a suspicion made him stand. Uneasy, he stepped over the bodies, doing his best to avoid the blood. He entered the corridor and found another dead guard, this one with features so mutilated by bullets that his face wasn't recognizable.

Halloway turned right and walked along the corridor, the loud echo of his bootsteps failing to shut out the hum. He entered the surveillance room, his mouth dropping open when he saw the images on the monitors. None had the green tint of a night-vision camera. The radio dishes, the three rows of fences, the miles and miles of scrub grass, the distant mountains—all were bathed in the hot glare of sunshine.

Not seven hours, he thought in shock. *Nineteen.*
Dear God, I've never slept that long in my life.

The phone rang. It was one of only four in the facility, all of which were scrambler-equipped. He stared at it and, on the second ring, picked it up.

"Station Zulu," he said.

"This is Alpha Control," a man's voice said impatiently. "Identify yourself."

"Earl Halloway. I'm one of the guards."

"Halloway," the voice responded. "Former Ranger sergeant. Saw combat in Iraq."

Halloway recognized the steely, authoritative tone. It

belonged to the man who led the team that had arrived via chopper yesterday afternoon. Colonel Raleigh. "Yes, sir."

"Well, *former* Sergeant Halloway—" Raleigh's voice exuded venom. "—I've been trying to contact your station for the past six hours. Why in Christ's name isn't anybody answering the phone?"

The heat of adrenaline cleared Halloway's groggy thoughts. "Sir, there was a thunderstorm last night." He had a vague memory of hearing the periodic rumbles as he drank vodka and orange juice, smelled cinnamon, and danced.

"I know all about the damned storm. I'm only twenty miles away from you. We were caught in it, too."

"Well, sir, we got struck by lightning." He was thinking faster now. "It interfered with our communications capabilities."

"You're telling me that some of the best scientists working for the government don't have the combined skills needed to repair the damage from an electrical storm? That facility is grounded all the way to hell. I find it hard to believe that a lightning strike would have any effect whatsoever."

"Sir, with all due respect, I'm not a communications specialist. I'm just repeating what the technicians told me. They took until now to repair the damage."

"And meanwhile, no data was received or transmitted to Fort Meade?" The colonel's voice sounded even more infuriated.

"I'm told that's correct, sir."

"Damn it, when this is over, I'm going to find out who didn't do his job. Right now, I want you to transfer this call to the control room."

Halloway felt a moment's panic. "Sir, I'm afraid I can't do that."

"Can't? What are you talking about?"

"The phone I'm using, the one in the surveillance room, is the only one that's been put back into service."

The line became silent. Halloway imagined that he could feel the colonel's growing fury. He was glad to have a safe distance between them.

"Former Sergeant Halloway, I want you to go to the control room and bring Gordon to the phone."

"Sir? Are you there, sir? I can't hear you."

"What do you mean you can't hear me?"

"Sir?"

"Damn it, I can hear *you* perfectly fine," Raleigh replied, his voice getting louder.

"Sir? If you're still on the line, you're not coming through. The system must be failing again."

"Bring Gordon to the phone, Sergeant!"

"Sir? Sir?"

Halloway set the phone back on its cradle, breaking the connection.

He looked down at the floor and concentrated. Then he returned to the corridor and made his way back to the control room. Although he was combat-hardened from two tours of duty in the most violent parts of Iraq, the stench made him gag.

Gotta clean this place up, he thought. *Can't appreciate the music if I'm sick to my stomach.*

A further thought added to his resolve.

And I can't defend this place if I'm sick, either.

When he checked his watch, he saw with a chill that the time was now almost 5 o'clock. Somehow fifty minutes had sped by. It was as if he'd blacked out again. Time wasn't acting the way it should.

Move, he told himself.

Halloway stooped toward Gordon's corpse, grabbed its two stiff hands, and dragged the body across the floor. Out in the corridor, he kept moving backward past the surveillance room, toward the stairs. He tried tugging Gordon up them, but the dead man's belt caught on the edge of a metal step. A few steps later, it was Gordon's shoes that got snagged.

This is taking too long.

He pulled Gordon's stiff arms upward until the corpse seemed to be standing a few steps below him. He put an arm around Gordon's back, then reached behind his knees—which didn't bend—and lifted him.

The weight made Halloway wince.

How the hell is it possible, he wondered, *that a hundred and eighty pounds of dead weight is heavier than a hundred and eighty pounds of live weight? It ought to be the other way around, 'cause something's missing.*

Breathing hard, he carried the body up the stairs. His echoing footfalls were loud from the weight he carried.

At the top, he wavered, almost toppling back. After managing to catch his balance, he leaned Gordon against the metal railing and opened the first security door.

I tried to be friends with you, Gordon, but you wouldn't let me. All you needed to do was be a buddy and share the music, but no—you wanted it all to yourself. See what happens when you act like a prick?

He pulled Gordon toward the second security door. The movement resembled dancing. Pressing the corpse against the wall, he opened the second door and blinked at the harsh sunlight.

The breeze was sweet after the stench of so much death.

Behind the radio dishes, there's a stretch of ground nobody ever sees, Halloway thought.

He lowered Gordon and started to drag him in that direction. But then he cursed himself for being stupid.

Use the damned truck.

The flatbed truck was always parked next to the dish that was tilted horizontally. The ignition key was always in the truck. Protected by three fences—one of which was constructed of razor wire, another of which was electrified—the truck was hardly in danger of being stolen.

He ran through the fierce sunlight toward the truck and felt his breathing become more difficult.

The array of observatory dishes loomed over him, the metal beams that supported them resembling legs. Brilliantly white, each dish was fifty feet tall. They stretched in a line a half mile long, and as Halloway hurried past them, they made him feel dwarfed.

Insignificant.

Threatened . . .

Sweat soaked his shirt by the time he reached the truck. He scrambled up into the cab, and sure enough, the ignition key was there. He turned it, but the engine chugged with effort.

The battery's almost dead!

He released the key and twisted it again. The engine labored more slowly.

Come on! Come on!

Abruptly the engine roared to life. With a muttered cry of victory, he put it in gear and steered the truck in a half circle. Leaving a cloud of exhaust smoke, he lumbered toward the concrete-block shed. He jumped out, lifted Gordon, and felt his heart pound from the effort of dumping the corpse onto the back of the truck.

Now I've got a system. The others shouldn't be this hard. Need to rush. Need to finish before the music starts.

A further consideration made him frown.

Or before the colonel decides to make a surprise inspection.

Halloway checked his watch again and gaped. The time was now almost twenty to 6. Forty minutes had sped by when he'd have sworn that only twenty minutes had passed. He pressed the numbers on the security pad, opened the heavy metal door, and reached for the interior door.

Need to collect the M4s and all the ammunition I can find. Need to get grenades for the launchers. This place is designed to withstand a major assault. If the colonel shows up and tries to break in, he'll wish to God he'd let me alone.

All I want is to listen to the music.

As he charged down the metal stairs, again gagging from the stench, he realized that he'd need to bury the bodies instead of just dumping them. Otherwise the vultures might swarm toward the corpses and draw attention. He needed to be extra certain that the colonel wouldn't have any suspicion of what had happened here.

The backhoe, Earl remembered. *They left it when they dug a trench to add new fencing. I'll use it to dig the hole. Perfect. Everything's going to work out.*

48

"Sir? If you're still on the line, you're not coming through. The system must be failing again."

"Bring Gordon to the phone, Sergeant!"

"Sir? Sir?"

The line went dead.

Scowling, Raleigh set down the telephone. During the call, Halloway's voice had been so muffled that Raleigh had taken the risk of removing the shooter's earplug from his right ear, then pressing the phone harder against it.

Now he reinserted the plug.

In the monitoring station beneath the abandoned airbase, he watched his team take their positions in front of the new equipment they'd installed. Banks of electronic instruments blinked and glowed—old components connected to new. On some of the computer screens, he saw the chaotic visual equivalent of the static to which some of the audio receivers were tuned.

Cameras hidden among the collapsed hangars aboveground relayed magnified images of the activity in the surrounding area. Where the observation platform stood, he saw a crane setting the final concrete barrier in place as a frustrated crowd increased in size and Highway Patrol officers watched for trouble.

Reminds me of parts of Iraq, where only the walls kept the Sunnis and the Shiites from killing each other, Raleigh thought.

On another television monitor, he saw the dog trainer and the German shepherd patrolling the fence nearest the viewing area lest any of the crowd try to get around the barricade by climbing onto the airbase property and attempting to see the lights from there. A few civilians did pass nearby, but the dog looked so fierce that no one seemed inclined to take that course of action.

Raleigh was reminded of the orders he'd given to Lockhart the previous night when the German shepherd and the trainer had come in from the thunderstorm. *If the dog acts strangely in any way, no matter how slight . . . shoot it.*

The thunderstorm.

Does Halloway honestly expect me to believe that an electrical storm could have knocked out communications at the observatory? This is the fucking NSA, not the phone company.

"Sir? Are you there, sir? I can't hear you. The system must be failing again."

Bullshit, Raleigh thought in disgust.

Apprehension grew in him. *Maybe it's starting there instead of here.*

"Sergeant," he said crisply.

"Yes, sir." Lockhart's voice was muffled by Raleigh's earplugs.

"Come with me."

They left the team in front of the monitoring equipment and stepped through a door into the subterranean chamber where the two Suburbans were parked. Although the time was late afternoon, the harsh overhead lights made the facility feel as if it were perpetually 3 A.M.

Raleigh glanced at the cameras that had been installed on an upper wall of each side of the chamber. Similar cameras were positioned in the monitoring room and everywhere else in the facility. Everything that happened here was now being recorded.

This time there won't be any unanswered questions, Raleigh thought. *Lord knows there were plenty the last time.*

"Sergeant, put an M4 in a rucksack, along with plenty of ammunition."

"You're expecting trouble, sir?"

"As I recall, you enjoy motorcycles."

"I do, sir. I used to race them when I was a kid."

"When you arrived, perhaps you noticed the Harley-Davidson in the far corner."

"I did, sir."

"It's kept here for emergency transportation. In perfect working order, on a storage rack so its tires don't rest on the concrete and disintegrate. You'll need to make sure they're properly inflated and check the battery. There's a fuel can behind it. The crowd up there will notice if you drive one of the Suburbans out of here. But if you walk the Harley to the gate and don't start it until you're on the road, there's a good chance you can leave without attracting attention."

"Where do you want me to go, sir?"

Raleigh told him.

Lockhart frowned.

"It's probably nothing," Raleigh said. "But drive over to the observatory and find out for sure. Here's the key to the gate. Use this two-way radio. When you get to the observatory, tell me everything you're doing. Step by step."

"Absolutely, sir."

"A Black Hawk's scheduled to arrive soon with more equipment. If there's trouble, the men aboard the chopper can be called upon to help."

"Good to know, sir." Lockhart saluted and headed past the Suburbans toward the motorcycle.

As Raleigh watched him, he made a mental note to select someone else on the team to shoot the German shepherd if the dog acted strangely in even the slightest way.

His attention was drawn to the stain on the wall he'd noticed earlier, the faint red of which looked like long-ago faded rust but wasn't.

49

The crowd again parted reluctantly to let Harriett's truck through. Page noticed that Medrano was still there, watching the crane set the final concrete barrier in place. The wall was high enough that nothing could be seen beyond it.

"Harriett, could you stop here for a second?" Page asked.

He got out and walked over to Medrano, whose red Highway Patrol patches were vivid on the upper part of his tan shirtsleeves.

"Be careful. That television reporter might be around here," Medrano warned. "We'll finish questioning you and Tori as soon as things calm down. The first part of the week, you and your wife can be on your way."

"Good, that'll work. It's important for my wife to be in San Antonio by Tuesday morning. Meanwhile, I was wondering if you could give me some information."

Medrano peered at him curiously. "About what?"

"The man who shot all those people Thursday night. You mentioned that the Austin police had spoken with his brother. That's how you found out that the shooter's wife had died." Page couldn't help thinking of Tori's disease and the unendurable grief he would feel if he lost her.

"That's correct," Medrano said.

"I wonder if you have a phone number for the brother, or maybe you could put me in touch with an Austin police officer who could help me do that."

"You're investigating on your own?" Page couldn't tell whether or not Medrano was displeased.

"There's something I'd like to ask him."

"I hope you're not telling anybody that you're a police officer with authority here in Rostov." Yes, Medrano was *definitely* displeased.

"I know the rules," Page said. "But as long as I make it clear I'm just an interested citizen, I don't see the harm."

"Why on earth would he want to talk to *you*, the husband of the woman who shot his brother to death?"

"He doesn't need to know that much. But even if he did, there's nothing wrong with expressing my condolences."

Medrano still looked skeptical. "What's your question? Maybe the Austin police can ask it for you."

"Or maybe you or Chief Costigan could do the asking."

Mcdrano studied him and sighed. "Why do I get the feeling that's what you had in mind all along?"

50

"Mr. Mullen, I'm Captain Medrano of the Texas Highway Patrol."

The speakerphone sat on the table next to Costigan's hospital bed.

"And I'm Roger Costigan, the police chief here in Rostov." Despite his injury, his gravelly voice was strong enough to project to the phone. "That's the town near the area where—"

"I know where Rostov is," the male voice said wearily from the phone.

Page and Tori watched from the foot of the bed.

"Thanks for taking the time to talk to us," Medrano continued. "I'm very sorry to disturb you."

"Your medical examiner still hasn't released Ed's body," the voice said irritably. "I don't even know when I can schedule the funeral."

"That's not acceptable," Medrano said. "I'll take care of that."

"What Ed did was so awful, I still can't believe he did it. But no matter what, he was my brother. Mom and Dad aren't alive anymore. It's up to me to make sure he gets a proper burial. I bet the relatives of the people he shot would say he doesn't deserve it, but he's my brother."

"I learned a long time ago not to judge people," Costigan said.

Page knew the chief was lying. Most police officers expected the worst in people.

"What did you want to talk about?" the tired voice asked. "I told the Austin police everything I know."

"There are just a few loose ends we need to tie up, and we'll try to keep it brief. After your brother's wife died . . ."

"Cancer. It was so damned unfair. Ann was always a saint, always helping people. She was one of the kindest, most generous people I've ever met. People always used to kid Ed and tell him he didn't deserve her. How come serial killers don't get cancer? Why does it always need to be someone who's good and decent?"

At the mention of the word "cancer," Page inwardly winced. He hadn't been told before how Mullen's wife had died. He glanced at Tori. The reference had made her pale.

"You said that before his wife died, your brother wasn't religious," Medrano continued.

"Never went near a church since my parents made us go with them when we were kids," the voice replied.

"But after your brother saw the lights . . ."

"Which I *still* don't believe in. If you want my opinion, people are either playing a joke or hallucinating. *I* didn't see them, and believe me, I tried. But Ed . . ."

Page hurriedly wrote something on a slip of paper.

Medrano looked at it. "Maybe your brother's grief is

what made him think he saw the lights. Do you suppose that's possible?"

"It makes as much sense as anything. Of course I had no idea Ed was going back so many times to that—what do they call it?—observation area. Once was enough for me. I should've made him go to a psychiatrist instead of taking him on that damned tour."

"And that was when he started collecting the religious paintings and statues?" Costigan asked.

The voice sounded exasperated now. "Ed wouldn't let me in his apartment. We always met at my house, or in a park or a restaurant or whatever. I had no idea he had all that stuff until after the police contacted me."

"Did he ever talk about God?"

"All the time. I assumed it was because he missed Ann so much that he was determined to believe in heaven so he could convince himself Ann was in a better place and that he'd join her there one day. He stank."

Costigan sat higher in the hospital bed. "Stank?"

"He wouldn't bathe. He said the hot water felt so good that it made him feel guilty. The only foods he ate were things he hated—turnips, brussels sprouts, pigs' knuckles. He slept on the floor. He set an alarm clock to wake him every two hours. He told me Ann had suffered so much that he didn't have the right to enjoy anything. He said if he did anything that felt good, it would be like admitting he'd never loved her as much as he'd claimed. As far as he was concerned, the only way he could prove how much he loved her was by punishing himself. Lord, I can't tell you how much I wish I'd made him go to a psychiatrist."

Medrano looked at Page as if asking whether he wanted to know anything else.

Saddened by what he'd just heard, Page shook his head.

"Well, thank you for the help, Mr. Mullen," Medrano said. "We're sorry if we disturbed you. I'll speak to the medical examiner about releasing your brother's remains."

"Anything to try to put this behind me. But I don't understand how what I just told you is going to help. We know my brother shot all those people. It's not as if there's a big mystery about who did it."

"The thing is, we'd also like to know *why* he did it."

"There's no mystery about that, either."

"What do you mean?"

"Grief made him crazy."

"I suppose you're right," Costigan said. "Thanks again for your help." He shut off the speakerphone.

No one spoke for several moments. The only sounds came from outside the room—footsteps, hushed voices, a cart being pushed.

"So what did that tell you?" Medrano finally asked Page.

Tori turned to him, seeming to wonder the same thing.

"'Don't you see how evil they are?'" Page asked.

All three of them frowned in surprise, seeming to fear he'd become unbalanced.

"That's the first thing Mullen shouted Thursday night."

When they understood what he meant, they looked relieved.

"Then he yelled to the crowd, 'Don't you realize what

they're doing to you? Don't you understand you're all going to hell?' When he shot at the lights, he screamed, 'Go back to hell where you came from.' Just before he started shooting at the crowd, he shouted, 'You're all damned.'"

"The ravings of a man who'd recently become a religious fanatic," Costigan said.

"But the lights weren't the reason Mullen became a religious fanatic," Page countered. "You heard what his brother said. Mullen suddenly *needed* to believe in God and heaven so he could convince himself that his wife was in a better place and that one day he'd join her there. But the lights are another matter. What they did to him made him furious."

Tori looked as puzzled as Costigan and Medrano.

"They tempted him," Page explained. "They were so alluring that for the first time since his wife died, he felt good. *Better* than good. They filled him with pleasure. That's why he kept coming back—because the lights were like a drug. He fought what they did to him. He bought more religious statues and paintings. He tried to live like a monk and punish himself to prove that he loved his wife, that he was worthy to join her . . . but he couldn't stop thinking about the lights. They were a pleasure he couldn't stop craving. They made him furious because they showed him how weak he was. We'll never know if he truly thought he could destroy the lights by shooting at them. Maybe he just needed a target for his rage."

"And then he chose closer targets," Medrano said, beginning to understand. "Targets he could hit."

Page nodded. "Exactly. He decided that the lights were

evil and that anybody who enjoyed them had to be evil, also."

"Well, you've sure been getting your money's worth from those psychology courses," Costigan said.

Page felt his cheeks turn red with embarrassment. "I admit it's only a theory."

"One that can't be proved."

"Here's *another* theory," Page told them.

They waited. Tori looked at him as if she were seeing him for the first time.

"Assuming the lights are real . . ."

"A big assumption," Medrano said. "I told you, *I've* never seen them, and it isn't for lack of trying."

"That's not surprising."

"How so?"

"If I'm right," Page said, "the lights intensify the personalities of the people who try to see them. As a police officer, you're a professional skeptic. That skepticism becomes emphasized out there. You're too guarded to be able to see them."

Page turned toward Costigan. "The man who killed your father was a drunk and a bully. You told me that after he came here, he got more extreme. One theory was that he felt humiliated by losing his job in Fort Worth and having to come to a small town where a relative managed to find work for him. His humiliation fueled his rage. But I don't believe that. The more I'm in Rostov, the more I talk to people and overhear what they say, the more I think the lights mirror what's going on inside us. They make whatever we are more extreme. Harriett Ward says James Deacon was obsessed with the lights when

Birthright was filmed here. They reflected his need to be a great actor to the point that when he was supposed to age in the story, he actually *did* look older."

"But as you say, that assumes the lights are real," Medrano pointed out.

"If they're *not* real, the idea still works. Under the right circumstances, people who need to see the lights will believe they see them. They'll project their personalities onto what they're imagining. The result will be the same."

"The man who killed my father never saw them," Costigan said.

"And that made him furious," Page replied. "When Tori and I were here earlier, you wondered if people could be affected by the lights even though they didn't see them. Maybe it's not the lights. Maybe it's being out there in the dark, surrounded by nothing. People become more extreme versions of who they are."

"*I* saw them," Costigan said from his hospital bed.

They looked at him in surprise.

"The day of my father's funeral. After I left the cemetery, I drove out to the observation area. I needed to be alone, and nobody was ever out there during the day. I sat in my father's cruiser and thought about what had happened to him. I was on the Dallas police force back then. The Rostov town council had asked me to take over for my father and become the new police chief, but I wasn't sure I wanted to be in law enforcement any longer because people are so disappointing and many of them don't seem worth helping. Gradually I became aware that I'd sat there all afternoon, that the sun was going down.

"Cars began to stop. People got out, waiting for it to

be dark enough to try to see the lights. I kept sitting there. Then the dark settled in, and a few of the people pointed toward the horizon. I glanced in that direction, and by God, there the lights were. I couldn't believe it. Some nights, when I'd visited my father, I'd gone out there to try to see them, but I'd never had any luck, and now, suddenly, there they were. Dancing, drifting, glowing, merging. The colors were soothing.

"I sat there smiling, and I must have dozed off because the next thing I knew, the cruiser's radio woke me. It was my father's deputy. There was a fight in a bar, and he needed my help. He'd been leaving me alone because of the funeral. Now he apologized for needing backup. I looked toward the dark horizon where I'd seen the lights, but they'd disappeared. I told the deputy I was on my way. I don't know what seeing the lights did to me, but that night, I decided to become Rostov's police chief. I went out to the viewing area other times after that to see if I could find kids with lanterns trying to fool people— some way to explain the lights—but I never found practical jokers, and I never saw the lights again. I'm still not sure they were real. Maybe, as you say, I needed to see them."

"Need," Page said. "Some people need to help others. Some people need to hate. Some people need to fill their emptiness."

Page managed not to look at Tori when he said that.

"Another theory," Medrano said. "But how do you prove it?"

"Tonight I'll do my best."

"How?"

"I want to get closer to the lights." Both Costigan and Medrano looked as if they didn't like what he was saying. "Don't worry—I won't do anything that adds to your problems."

"*We*," Tori interrupted. "*We'll* do our best. Whatever you plan to do, I'm going with you."

51

As they stepped from the hospital, Medrano told Page, "I need to get back to the viewing area. I hope you meant what you promised about not adding to my problems."

"Don't worry. I won't go anywhere near you or the crowd, and I won't make trouble by trespassing on anybody's land."

"I'd love to know what you've got in mind."

"You'll get a full report tomorrow morning."

Medrano gave him a penetrating look and went down the steps toward his black-and-white Highway Patrol car.

Page and Tori remained on the steps, heat drifting off the concrete.

"Guess what," she said. "I'm beginning to understand you."

Page turned toward her, conscious of how the scarlet of the lowering sun emphasized her red hair.

"It took ten years of marriage," she said.

"I hope this isn't going to be a bad thing you're talking about."

"No, it's good. Yesterday you said that the way you distract yourself from the pain you see is by concentrating on small details."

"It's true."

"The idea is that the big picture can be overwhelming, but small portions of it can be handled—they become manageable," she said.

"Yeah, that's right."

"Well, if that's the case, I'm learning from you. Yesterday and today I focused on the little things. Then after a while, what I focused on wasn't so little. It was you. You're a really smart guy."

Page tried to make a joke. "You didn't already know that?"

"You're using the lights to distract you from my cancer. You're treating this like a criminal investigation."

"Which it is," he admitted. "Though there's more to it than that. But it helps me get through the moment and prepare for Tuesday."

"It's taking your mind off what we both don't want to think about. I'm using your investigation in the same way. As long as we've got this to do, I think I can be steady." She considered him. "The way you ask questions. The way you assess people and make them do what you need. Yeah, you're a really smart guy."

"I have the feeling you're using my own tactic. You're trying to find out something."

"What are we going to do tonight? How are we going

to get closer to the lights?" At once Tori smiled—one of the few times he'd seen her do that recently. "I get it. You said we won't be near the crowd and we won't be trespassing.

"We're going to use your plane."

52

"What I need is another riot or a shooting to get this story back on track," Brent said as Anita drove.

"Why not an outbreak of bubonic plague?" she offered with muted sarcasm.

"Look, I know everybody thinks I'm an asshole." Brent studied the barren landscape as they passed. Cattle were spread out, eating the meager grass. "But you have to admit I got sensational overnight ratings for us. It's all about the tone. The weird stuff about the lights needs to sound like it's important—like it's actually news. If CNN is going to keep paying us to run with this, everything needs to sound believable, even if it's the weirdest shit I ever came across."

"Then why are we driving out to the observatory? Last night you said something about extraterrestrials. I hope to God you were joking."

"Yeah, it was a joke. Look, I'm winging this, okay? I'll know what I need when I see it. Besides, I don't understand why you're complaining. Do you have anything better to do?"

"Aside from earning as much extra money as I can, nope. And I don't know what gave you the idea I was complaining."

Anita stopped the van at the side of the road. Dust swirled as Brent studied the sign.

U.S. GOVERNMENT OBSERVATORY

RESTRICTED AREA

TRESPASSERS WILL BE PROSECUTED

"Friendly," he said. "Let's get some shots of me standing next to it."

Stepping out into the intense sunlight, he walked through the blowing dust and positioned himself beside the sign. Determined to continue his rugged look, he didn't bother trying to swat any of the dust from his suit. With his tie open and his collar unbuttoned, he raised the handheld microphone to his mouth. The mike had a transmitter that sent audio directly to Anita's camera, but for the first time since coming to Rostov, he realized that he couldn't think of anything to say.

She held the heavy camera on her shoulder, focusing on him. It had a so-called shotgun microphone attached to the top. Projecting like a barrel, the microphone could register nearby sounds, but not as clearly as the one Brent held.

After a long moment of silence, she looked out from behind the camera.

"Cat got your tongue?" she asked.

"Sarcasm isn't welcome."

"Your fans are waiting."

"Hell with it, then. Let's drive up to the observatory and see if anything looks interesting. I can come back later and do the intro at the end."

"Drive up? I don't think so." Anita pointed toward a metal gate that stretched across the lane that led to the observatory. The gate was locked.

"I guess we head back to town." She moved to load the camera back into the truck.

"Maybe not." Brent walked to the opposite side of the gate.

"What are you doing?"

"Ever been on a farm?"

"I went to a zoo once."

"My grandfather owned a hundred acres in Ohio. I used to go there for two weeks every summer. I remember the day when he drove his tractor out to a field but a gate got locked by accident, and he didn't have the key to open it. I'd never heard anybody swear for that long a time." He smiled at the memory while he examined the gate's hinges and nodded. "Give me a hand, would you?"

She set down the camera and walked over. "Your grandfather found a way to get through?"

"Grab the gate on this end and help me lift."

Anita shrugged and got a solid grip on one of the metal poles. They pushed upward. The hinges had metal circles that fitted over small metal posts. It took only a little effort to raise the circles from the posts and push the gate inward. Within minutes, they managed to make just enough room for the van to slip through.

"I guess the government hired somebody local to install the gate. But they forgot to tell the guy that the gate protected an observatory, not a pasture."

"Maybe you didn't read that part of the sign where it says trespassers will be prosecuted," Anita said.

"We'll just say we found the gate off its hinges and worried that another terrible thing had happened. We decided it was our *duty* to investigate." He paused and looked at her. "But don't let me force you to do anything you're not comfortable with. Do you want to stop?"

"No way," Anita told him. "Ever heard of a *cholla*?"

"What's that?"

"A type of cactus. That was my nickname in high school."

"Because?"

"If people messed with me, they felt like a thorn got stuck in them and festered."

Brent considered her. Five feet two inches tall. Maybe a hundred and five pounds. But she hardly looked petite. A long time of holding the twenty-five-pound camera on her shoulder had made her sinewy. And there was something about the strength in her dark eyes.

"Hey, believe me, I'm not trying to mess with you," he said. "If you don't want to go in there, you don't need to. You can wait here for me."

Walking toward the van, Anita replied over her shoulder, "Of *course* I want to go in there." Her ponytail swinging at the back of her baseball cap, she lifted the camera as if it weighed nothing and put it into the van. Then she got in and revved the engine.

Brent waited for her to drive through the opening.

Then he moved the fence back so the hinges seemed intact. He got into the passenger seat, and she drove down the lane. Dust rose behind them.

"If there's a guard, the dust'll warn him we're coming a long time before we get there," Anita observed.

"No problem—I just want to get a shot of the place. Maybe I'll see something that'll help me connect it to the lights, but now that we're out here, I can't imagine what it would be. I hate to admit it, but this story might have played itself out." He thought for a moment. "Unless there's another shooting tonight. We can always hope for that."

He glanced at her left hand on the steering wheel. "You're not wearing a wedding ring, so I'm guessing you're not married. Do you have a boyfriend?"

"Hey, I hope you're not hitting on me."

Anita reached toward one of the many pockets on her khaki pants. A metal clip was attached to the outside of one of them. She pulled on it and revealed that the clip was attached to a black folding knife. She thumbed it open, revealing the blade.

"Remember what I said about my nickname." She gestured with the knife.

"Honest to God, I'm just making conversation. I was trying to figure out how . . . what's the word you used? . . . a cholla . . . sounds like you used to be a biker chick . . ."

"You got it."

". . . how a cholla became a cameraman."

"Camera*woman*. I had a boyfriend. He flipped his motorcycle, showing off. Got himself killed. Of course it didn't help that he wasn't wearing a helmet. A couple of days earlier, he'd dumped me for somebody else. That's when I realized biker chicks don't have a future. When I saw an ad for the community college, I went out there, asked what courses they had, and decided that learning how to handle a television camera might be cool."

"And critics complain that television isn't a positive influence. Is it as cool as you hoped?'

"Look at the wonderful people I get to work with."

Brent laughed.

"For a little while longer, at any rate," Anita added. "Until CNN hires you. That's what you're hoping, isn't it? If that happens and they need a camerawoman, be sure to put in a good word for me."

"Count on it."

"Never give your word unless you mean it."

"I'm telling the truth. If they hire me, I will in fact put in a good word for you. Now you can set down the knife."

It was Anita's turn to laugh. "Look at those observatory dishes." She pointed toward the huge white shapes that seemed to grow from the horizon as she drove closer. "They remind me of the giant robots in a *Terminator* movie."

"Not a bad line," Brent said. "I'll use it."

"Be my guest, since we're going to CNN together. Do you think they have good Mexican food in Atlanta? Chorizo? Lots of jalapeños in chicken enchiladas?"

"Somehow I doubt it."

"In that case, maybe it'll be just you going to Atlanta. Yeah, those dishes look like giant robots."

As they drove closer, Brent was struck by how tall they were. *They've got to be four or five stories high*, he thought. *They're stretched along the equivalent of two or three city blocks. Hell, at least we'll get some impressive images.*

A minute later, he was close enough to be able to count them. Nine. Then he realized that he was wrong. There was a tenth dish, hidden behind the others. It was tilted sideways and seemed to be undergoing repairs.

A chain-link fence came into view, topped with barbed wire.

Not one *fence*, Brent thought. *Three. And the two inside rows look like they're made entirely from razor wire.*

"They really don't want visitors," Anita observed.

"Well, I guess they're afraid the cattle will wander close and bump against the dishes."

The road led to a ten-foot-high gate, its links so thick that they looked capable of stopping a truck. Signs on the third fence warned:

DANGER

HIGH VOLTAGE

"I suppose the high voltage is designed to stop any cattle that climb the first and second fences," Anita said.

"Yeah, there does seem to be a little—pardon the expression—overkill in the design of this place," Brent agreed.

"Maybe kids from town used to vandalize the dishes—spray-painted them or something."

"In which case, that high-voltage fence will teach those kids how seriously the government disapproves of graffiti."

An open-backed truck was parked next to a concrete-block shed.

"Let's get some shots of this place while we have the chance," Brent decided.

"Wait'll I turn the van around."

"So we'll be ready to make a getaway?"

"Don't mock a cholla," she warned.

As the dust settled, they got out and squinted in the bright sun toward the towering white dishes.

"This'll look great." Anita pulled the camera from the side door of the van and attached a fresh battery pack. "Stand by the gate. I'll angle up toward the dishes, then pan down toward the 'high voltage' signs on the interior fences and finally over to you."

"Sounds as if you should be a director, not a cameraman."

"Camera*woman*. Have you figured out what you're going to say this time?"

"The dish that's tilted sideways . . ."

"What about it?"

"It seems pointed in the general direction of Rostov."

"So?"

"Maybe I'll suggest that it's aimed at the lights."

"As if it's receiving a signal from them? You think CNN's going to buy that?" But she glanced at the dish as if intrigued by the idea.

"It's the best I can come up with right now."

"In that case, I'm not the only one who won't be going to Atlanta." But Anita hefted the camera to her shoulder.

"Trust me. As we keep going, I'll think of something better. Just get some shots of the dish that's tilted toward Rostov. I can always dub a voiceover later if I need to."

Abruptly Brent heard a noise behind him. He lowered the microphone to his side, turned, and gazed through the three fences toward a door that opened in a concrete-block shed.

A man appeared. Emerging from the darkness inside, he came out backward, bending over, tugging something that Brent couldn't see. His khaki uniform left no doubt that he was a guard.

The man glanced behind him to make sure of his footing and stopped when he noticed the van. Immediately he set down whatever he was dragging. The darkness beyond the door still concealed it.

He turned and straightened. His hair was extremely short. His features were stern. His chest was muscled, his shoulders broad.

He stepped forward and halted at the front of the truck. "I guess you can't read."

"Excuse me?" Brent asked. He kept the microphone down, concealed behind his right leg.

"The sign at the road. How'd you get through the locked gate?"

"It was off its hinges," Brent replied. "With all the weird things happening, we got suspicious and decided to make sure nothing's wrong."

"Everything's fine. I'll arrange for the gate to be fixed. Why do you suppose it was off its hinges?"

"Kids maybe."

"Kids. Of course."

"My name's Brent Loft. I'm a television reporter." Brent used his left hand—the one that wasn't concealing the microphone—to point toward the station's letters on the side of the van.

"Yeah, I saw you on TV, talking about the shootings."

"Thanks."

The guard's sour expression suggested that his comment hadn't been a compliment. Even so, Brent pressed on. "As long as we're here, this place looks so fascinating, is there someone I can talk to about doing a feature about it?"

He hoped Anita had the camera rolling. He didn't know where this conversation was going, but he had a suspicion he'd be able to use footage from it. The guard was too far away for Brent's microphone to pick up his voice, but Brent was speaking loudly enough that his own portion of the conversation would be recorded.

He expected the guard to say that the person to talk to was gone for the weekend—some sort of polite brush-off. The guard's curt "no" caught him by surprise.

"No?"

"Like the sign says, this is government property. If you want to get prosecuted, just hang around while I call the cops. But if you want to end this with no hard feelings, get in that van and drive back to the road. Now."

Brent's gaze focused on the open door behind the man. The object he'd been dragging lay in the shadows inside the shed. Part of it was round, resembling a soccer ball.

"Well, maybe I could interview *you*," Brent offered. "How does it feel to work here? Is it exciting to be part of a project this big, or, like most jobs, does it get boring after a while?"

The guard squinted harshly.

Brent kept trying. "Does the observatory study only

stars and comets and black holes, or is it also part of the SETI project?"

The guard's squint became more pronounced.

"You know, *SETI*," Brent said. "The Search for Extraterrestrial Intelligence."

Now the guard scowled. "I know what SETI means."

"I didn't mean to suggest otherwise."

"The joke I heard is we ought to be searching for intelligent life on Earth."

Brent focused again on the door that stood open behind the guard. The soccer ball in the shadows beyond it seemed to have hair.

Oh, shit.

Brent tried not to show a reaction.

"Do you live on-site?" Brent managed to keep talking and prayed that Anita did indeed have the camera rolling. "What's *that* like, being out here away from everything?"

The guard's hands were at his side. He bunched his fingers into fists. Opened them. Closed them. Opened them.

"Tell you what. I'll give you exactly a minute to get out of here. If you don't want to be prosecuted, just get in your truck and drive back to the road."

Brent tried to be subtle when he switched his gaze toward the truck next to the guard. Several objects were piled in the back. They came up only slightly higher than the sides, making it difficult to tell what they were. But one of them looked a lot like it might be part of a shirt—still on someone's arm.

"Fine," he said, finding it hard to remain calm. "I'm sorry if we bothered you." The sudden rapid pounding of his heart sickened him. "I just figured this place would make an interesting story. But I can see I was wrong."

The guard was noticing things also. He stared past Brent toward Anita, presumably toward her camera. Then he appeared to realize that Brent was hiding a microphone next to his leg.

"We don't want any trouble," Brent said.

"Of course not. You're right. This place is really fascinating. Why don't you stay right where you are. I'll go find the guy you need to talk to about permission to do a story."

He motioned for them not to move, then turned and went into the small building, where he shifted the object he'd been dragging so it couldn't be seen any longer. Then he disappeared into the darkness.

"Anita, let's go," Brent said urgently. He pivoted and saw that she held the camera at her side, a seemingly innocent position.

But the camera's red light was conspicuous. Regardless of how frightened Brent felt, he was elated that she seemed to have recorded everything.

The van was pointed away from the observatory. Anita rushed to the vehicle's side hatch and shoved the camera onto a seat.

"There are bodies in that truck," she said starkly.

"Yes, and he was dragging another body from that shed. What the hell happened here?" Brent hurried toward the van's passenger door. His lungs felt starved for air, as if he was running a hundred-yard dash.

Anita rushed toward the front of the van, desperate to reach the driver's door as quickly as she could.

Blood spurted from her left arm.

She dropped.

Brent gaped, suddenly aware of shots—loud and rapid, as if from a string of huge firecrackers. Something zipped past him. Metal clanged repeatedly. He swung toward the observatory and saw that the guard was standing in the open door of the shed, firing an assault rifle. The three rows of fences acted like screens, the chain links and wire deflecting a lot of the bullets. Chunks rose from disintegrating metal. High-voltage sparks flew.

Feeling the heat of a bullet nicking his ear, Brent rushed to Anita and dragged her to the front of the van, out of the guard's sight. A month earlier, he'd done a story about a gunfight between three bank robbers and a solitary policeman. The policeman had survived because he'd taken cover behind the front of his cruiser, behind the engine, which—Brent was told—could stop just about any bullet.

"Anita. *Anita.*"

He was relieved to find that she was conscious, but immediately he registered just how wide her eyes were and how rapidly she was blinking in pain. Her dark skin was pale. When he'd dragged her, she'd left a trail of blood on the dirt. The jagged wound in her upper arm was wide, and deep enough to show bone.

She'll bleed to death.

Brent almost threw up.

Straining to remember what he'd learned in a long-ago emergency first-aid class, Brent tugged off his necktie and twisted it around the top of Anita's left arm, above the wound. One of the instructors had insisted, *Improvise.* Sweating, he knotted the tie, pulled a pen from his shirt pocket, and shoved it under the tie. He twisted the pen, tightening the cloth enough to restrict the flow of blood.

"This'll make your arm partly numb." He remembered a doctor telling him that. "It might help with the pain, too."

"God, I hope so." Anita bit her lip.

The shooting stopped. Amid a hot breeze, Brent smelled burned gunpowder. Struggling not to panic, he peered around the front of the van. At the open door to the shed, the guard dropped a magazine from the bottom of the rifle and inserted a new one. The man's face was twisted into a grimace that suggested he was in pain. He finished reloading, looked in Brent's direction, and fired toward the van's rear tires. Again there were sparks and a spray of metallic fragments as the fences deflected many of the bullets, but enough got through to shred the tires. Brent heard them exploding.

The rear of the van sank.

We're going to die, he thought.

No matter how quickly his chest heaved, he couldn't seem to get enough air. He imagined the guard throwing their bodies into the back of the truck with the others. Frantic, he yanked his cell phone from his belt and hit the buttons, but when he held the phone to his left ear, he moaned. All he heard was dead air.

The expression made him taste bile. *Dead air.*

"I bet I can guess what you're doing!" the guard yelled. "You're trying to use your cell phone! Save yourself the trouble! It won't work! There isn't any civilian service this far out!"

"My boss knows we came here!" Brent shouted back. "He'll send people to look for us!"

"When they see the sign, they'll have brains enough not to trespass on government property! How long will your boss wait before he wonders where you are? Two hours? Three? If people *do* come here looking for you, by then—believe me—they won't find you!"

Brent flinched as the guard fired another volley. More of the bullets got past the metal in the three fences and shattered the van's rear windows.

"Don't you wish *you'd* obeyed the sign?" the guard yelled. "I warned you, didn't I? I said you'd be prosecuted! Hey, Mr. Big Deal Reporter, I've got a question for you!"

"Ask me anything!" Brent hoped to stall for time.

"Did you go to announcers' school or something like that?"

What the hell . . . ? Brent had no choice except to humor the guy. Anything was better than being shot at.

"Yes, I have a college degree in broadcasting!"

"That's what I figured! You had to have learned it! No one could be born that full of shit!"

The guard shot more holes in the back of the van.

Brent heard liquid splashing onto the ground. His nostrils felt pinched by the odor of gasoline streaming from holes in the fuel tank.

At once he heard something else—the drone of a distant engine. *Somebody's coming. We'll get help.* He stared down the lane that led to the road, but he didn't see an approaching dust cloud.

The drone became closer and louder, growing into a rumble.

In the air. He turned in the direction of the lowering sun and saw the dark silhouette of a helicopter speeding toward the observatory.

Thank God, he thought.

The guard must have seen it, too. "I'll deal with you in a little while, Mr. Television Reporter!"

Mouth dry from fear, Brent eased his head around the side of the van and saw the guard vanish into the darkness of the doorway. The building was so small that Brent concluded there had to be stairs leading underground.

The last time the guard had gone back inside, he'd returned with an assault rifle. Brent hated to imagine what he would bring next.

Movement made him turn. Groaning, Anita managed to come to a sitting position and prop herself against the front of the van.

"I can't drive with this arm." She cradled it in pain. "The key's in my right pants pocket." Sweat trickled down her cheeks. "Let's get out of here while he's distracted."

Brent fumbled inside her pocket and pulled out the key. He also took the knife she'd returned to that pocket. He had no idea what to do with it. Even so, he shoved it into his pants.

Anita struggled to get to her feet.

Brent moved to help, putting an arm around her, guiding her to the side of the van. His rapid breathing was hoarse as he shoved her up into the passenger seat. He shut the door, trying to minimize the noise, and raced around to the driver's side. Fear made his legs unsteady when he climbed behind the steering wheel. His trembling fingers had trouble inserting the ignition key.

Come on! Finally it slipped in.

He twisted the key, feeling a surge of triumph when the engine roared to life. Abruptly his sense of triumph turned to panic. A glance in the rearview mirror showed the guard rushing from the doorway. The rifle the man held had something thick mounted under the barrel.

Brent stomped the accelerator and felt the flat rear tires try to gain traction. The wheel rims dug into the ground, spraying a dust cloud. He couldn't see the guard.

Maybe the dust'll keep him from aiming!

The van lurched forward sluggishly.

"Ease off on the gas. You're spinning the wheels," Anita found the strength to tell him.

Brent obeyed. The van responded, gaining more distance from the observatory. In the rearview mirror, he saw the dust settling and caught a glimpse of the guard raising the rifle to his shoulder. Above the sound of the van's engine, he heard the helicopter roaring closer, coming in to land.

The van moved a little faster down the lane, its flat rear wheels fighting the dirt.

Frantic, Brent glanced at the rearview mirror again. The guard suddenly changed the direction in which he aimed. He turned west, toward the rumble of the approaching helicopter. In silhouette, the object attached to the rifle's barrel seemed thicker.

Brent stared to his right, past Anita, toward the massive shape of the chopper, which was close enough that he could see the faint shape of the pilot's face through the canopy. He switched his gaze toward the rearview mirror and saw the rifle buck as if it had been fired. Something flew from the object mounted under the barrel.

The front of the chopper exploded. As the shock wave rocked the van, the fireball of a second explosion—perhaps from fuel tanks—tore the aircraft apart. Wreckage flew in all directions. Chunks of rotors, sections of fuselage, fragments of engines crashed onto the dirt. Smoke billowed. Grass started burning. A flaming skeleton of the fuselage hit the ground and rolled, crushing a section of fence.

"*Madre de Dios*," Anita said in shock.

The speedometer showed fifteen miles an hour, probably as fast as the van would go with shredded rear tires and wheel rims grinding into the dirt.

"We're going to make it," she managed to say.

Brent glanced toward the rearview mirror again and felt pressure in his chest, seeing the guard turn toward the van to realign his aim.

"Anita, brace yourself."

Brent saw the rifle jerk upward. Something rushed from the launcher mounted under the rifle's barrel.

Another shock wave rocked the van. In the rearview mirror, Brent saw an explosion tear up dirt.

"We're far enough away!" Brent shouted. "Yes, we're going to make it!"

The words caught in his throat when he saw flames erupt behind the van.

The bullet holes in the fuel tank, he realized. *We're leaving a trail of gasoline.*

His bladder let loose when the flames began to chase the van.

"No!"

The rear of the van heaved as the flames reached the fuel that streamed from the holes in the tank. The impact wasn't like the grenade explosions. It didn't produce a loud roar. It didn't tear the back of the van apart. It was violent nonetheless, filling the rearview mirror with an image of erupting smoke and flames.

Brent stomped the brakes. As the flames spread forward, he was relieved to see Anita muster the strength to open the passenger door and drop to the ground. He shoved the driver's door open, jumped out, and hurried around to where she'd landed. She was on one knee, struggling to stand.

He grabbed her and lunged toward a furrow, collapsing, pushing her down.

The flames spread toward the middle of the van.

"Need the camera," Brent said.

"Don't take the chance. You'll be hit."

His heart pounded so violently that he was certain it would burst against his ribs. He surged upright, sprinted to the van's side door, and shoved it open. Flames licked at him as he grabbed the camera.

Something snapped past him. A bullet.

Coughing from the smoke, he crouched and ran, holding the camera with both arms. Another bullet snapped past him. He reached the furrow and protected the camera by falling onto his back.

"You're a fool." Anita stared through wide eyes and looked paler.

"My mother always thought so."

He pushed the record button and pointed the camera toward the burning van, panning from the fiery back of it until he reached the front seats, which burst into flames. Then he got a close shot of the shredded rear tire on his side of the van, the fire beginning to melt it. The smoke spread dramatically.

"You've been shot," Anita said.

"Where?"

"Your right ear."

Brent reached up and touched the wound, feeling the slippery blood and the gash on his earlobe.

"Blood's streaming down your neck and onto your shoulder," she murmured.

"Good. If I help you position the camera, do you think you can get a shot of it?"

"You really are crazy."

"You expect me to just wait here and do nothing while he tries to kill us? The camera's the only weapon I have. I'm going to record as much of what's happening as I can. If we get out of this, this'll be the story of a lifetime." The word "lifetime" made him pause. Desperate to distract himself, he added, "I can win an Emmy for this."

"We."

"What?"

"*We* can win an Emmy."

"Right." Brent aimed the camera at her, emphasizing the blood that soaked her safari-type jacket. He got a close-up of the tourniquet he'd made for her arm.

The helicopter, he realized. *Need to get video of the helicopter while it's still burning.*

He squirmed along the furrow until he guessed he was far enough that the guard wouldn't look in that direction. Easing up, he saw the smoke and flames rising from the chopper's wreckage. He aimed the camera's lens and zoomed it toward the part of the fuselage that had crushed a section of the fences.

Yeah, he thought, *I'll get an Emmy for this.*

He corrected himself. *The two of us will get Emmies. If we live.*

53

Sergeant Lockhart drove the motorcycle past the TRES-PASSERS WILL BE PROSECUTED sign and stopped at the gate to the observatory. To the west, he heard a faraway helicopter. The lowering sun angled toward his eyes and made it difficult for him to distinguish the enlarging speck of the chopper. Presumably it was the Black Hawk that Colonel Raleigh had told him would be delivering more equipment.

So far no problem. Everything was on schedule.

Plus, Lockhart had gotten the chance to enjoy a motorcycle ride. The truth was, *any* opportunity to get away from the colonel was enjoyable. The guy had threatened to send him to a war zone, and Lockhart had begun to wonder if maybe that would be preferable to his current assignment. Just about any place would be better than that creepy facility under the abandoned airbase.

Shoot the dog? What the hell was that *about?*

The sergeant reached into a jeans pocket and pulled out the key the colonel had given him, preparing to free the lock on the gate. Then he noticed that the barrier felt unsteady. He glanced along it and saw that the opposite end wasn't resting on its hinges.

Frowning, he pushed the gate open. As he guided the motorcycle toward the lane that led to the observatory, a noise made him pause, then crouch protectively. He'd heard the noise many times in Iraq.

The rumble of a distant explosion.

It came from the direction of the observatory.

Moments later, a second explosion followed. Lockhart searched the sky but no longer saw or heard the helicopter. What he saw instead was smoke rising.

A third explosion brought more smoke.

He reached back toward a canvas sack mounted on the rear of the motorcycle. The sack concealed his M4, along with two spare hundred-round magazines and a half-dozen boxes of ammunition—a troubling amount that the colonel had insisted on.

The sack also contained a scrambler-equipped two-way radio that Lockhart hastily withdrew.

54

Holding an earplug in one hand, Raleigh listened to the disturbing report that came through the two-way radio. His mouth was uncharacteristically dry.

"I can't send reinforcements until dark," he said into the radio. "The Suburbans are the only transportation we have. They're so conspicuous, if I send men in the daytime, the crowd down the road is bound to see. We can't compromise our security. Reconnoiter as close to the observatory as you can. Keep reporting back."

Raleigh ended the transmission. When he reinserted his earplug, shutting out two-thirds of the sound in the room, he noted that some of the men in front of the monitoring equipment were glancing curiously in his direction. Even though it was after 6 in the evening, the cold overhead lights continued to make the time feel like 3 o'clock in the morning.

"Is everything adjusted?" His abrupt tone challenged one of the men, suggesting that there were more pressing things to do than eavesdrop on his radio communications.

"Just about, sir," the man quickly answered. "We're starting to amplify the signals."

Raleigh stood behind the man. A computer screen showed random dots that provided a visual correspondence to the static coming from audio monitors on a table near other glowing electronic equipment. Shelves were filled with receivers, analyzers, and decoders. If all went as planned, soon the static would resolve itself into the alluring music he'd heard at Fort Meade, and then the computer screen before him would show the equivalent of gliding, floating, hypnotic lights.

"You're not wearing your earplugs, soldier."

"Sorry, sir. I've been so busy that I forgot."

Raleigh moved to the center of the room and raised his voice.

"All of you, listen up!"

The eight men raised their heads from the electronics they were adjusting.

"*Everybody* wears earplugs." Raleigh pointed toward

his own. "I warned you that the audio component of this project can damage your hearing. I don't want somebody's mama crying to me because you didn't listen to orders and went deaf. Put in the earplugs *now!*"

They hurriedly did so.

"If necessary, add the noise-reducing headphones we brought."

When he was satisfied that everyone had obeyed, he walked toward a metal door that led to the facility's innermost room. In truth, he wasn't worried about his men going deaf. If this experiment went wrong, going deaf would be the least of their problems.

What he hoped was that the earplugs—and if necessary the noise-reducing earphones—would protect their hearing enough to keep them alive.

Once inside the central chamber, he watched a closed-circuit television monitor that showed a view of the abandoned airbase that sprawled above him. Beyond the collapsed, rusted aircraft hangars, he saw the German shepherd and its trainer patrolling the fence. The crowd had spread far enough from the viewing area that some people were talking to the dog's trainer. The animal snapped at them. The people on the other side of the fence held up their hands in a *we don't want a problem* gesture and backed away.

Raleigh wondered if the German shepherd was normally that aggressive.

We'll soon find out. After dark, I'll bring the dog back inside. We'll see how it behaves. Its ears are more sensitive than ours. If there's trouble, it'll react before humans do— and before we need to shoot it.

He studied the room's thick metal door, assuring himself that it could withstand a grenade blast. He verified that his M4 and several loaded one-hundred-round magazines were in a corner. He opened a filing cabinet and made sure that a trauma kit and emergency rations—including water—were inside in case he was forced to barricade himself in this room for a considerable length of time.

What else do I need to plan for? There's always something.

He'd done his best to take everything into account. Nonetheless, he paused to consider the history of this place and search his memory for anything he might have missed. He knew by heart every event that had happened on this spot. He'd read all of the reports. They stretched back long before the military had established a presence here. One of the reports, however, had been passed down not from a historian or a tactician.

It had come from his great-grandmother.

55

January 22, 1916.

The horse became restless. It was normally so well-behaved that its rider—a twenty-nine-year-old schoolteacher named Dani Marie Brown—glanced warily around, assuming that coyotes were in the area.

She was riding on the dusty road that led from Rostov to Loden, a town fifteen miles away where she taught grade school on Thursdays, Fridays, and Saturdays after teaching on Mondays, Tuesdays, and Wednesdays in Rostov. Three days a week was the most that local cattlemen in each place would allow their children to be away from their ranching chores.

Dani sometimes was at school from dawn until dusk, preparing classes or grading tests when the children weren't at their desks. It was a tiring schedule, but she'd been raised in Rostov, and she hadn't liked being away from home while she'd earned her teacher's certificate in noisy, crowded El Paso. Long, quiet hours in this familiar, reassuring area were preferable to the chaos of the unknown, outside world.

During the winter, the early sunset made it necessary for Dani to bundle herself in a sheepskin coat and ride between the towns after dark. This didn't trouble her. The stars and the moon—even if only a portion of the latter was showing—provided sufficient light for her to see the road. On cloudy nights, she held a lantern to show her the way.

An experienced horsewoman, she never worried about her ability to control the chestnut-colored quarter horse her parents had bought for her. But now, as the animal became more skittish, she tugged back the reins and pressed her heels down in the stirrups while she studied the shadowy landscape with greater intensity. In the heat of summer, coyotes weren't the only threat the horse might have sensed—there would have been the risk that a rattlesnake had crawled onto the road to absorb the last of the day's warmth, but that was out of the question tonight, when the temperature was cold enough to put a layer of ice on a pail of water.

Even so, Dani's stomach fluttered.

Until recently she'd felt happily isolated in this quiet corner of Texas, but then her father had ordered a wireless radio from a catalog, and now, on this particular journey, Dani's thoughts were disturbed by the escalation of the European war, which had reached new heights of atrocity and threatened to draw the United States into the fight between Germany and the Allies.

Just before beginning her ride toward Loden, she'd paid a brief visit to her parents and listened to a shortwave radio report about attacks involving chlorine and phosgene gases: the lung destroyers. There were rumors about something even more horrendous being developed: mustard gas, a blisterer that dissolved skin both inside and outside the body. The gas remained active long after it sank into the ground, with the consequence that soldiers kicking up dust as they walked through a field could cause the equivalent of another attack.

And those weren't the only new horrors. Dani could only imagine the pain and terror produced by such recently invented weapons as tanks and flamethrowers. Thus, on this normally quiet ride, her thoughts were in greater turmoil than she would have expected.

Abruptly something on her right caught her attention. She frowned toward some sort of illumination on the southern horizon. Lights bobbed and weaved. Her immediate suspicion was that they came from torches carried by horseback riders. However, the only direction from which those riders could be coming was Mexico.

That thought filled her with dread because Mexico, too, had become a dangerous place. The recent revolution there

had turned the country into warring factions to which
Germany sent soldiers, weapons, and money, hoping the
United States would be so distracted by the violence south
of its border that it wouldn't enter the war in Europe.

My God, Dani thought, *could those be Germans?*

The horse continued to resist her efforts to control it.
Calm down, she warned herself. *The horse senses my
fear. That's what's causing the problem.*

No, those weren't Germans invading from Mexico,
she decided. Now that she paid closer attention, the lights
didn't look at all like riders with torches.

If they weren't torches, though, what else could they
be?

Only gradually did Dani wonder if these might be the
lights she'd heard so much about when she was growing
up. The stories had seemed fanciful, and she'd paid them
no mind because although she knew many people in town
who claimed to have seen them, she had not.

Now, on the distant horizon, the lights took the shape
of luminous balls. Their colors were like segments of a
rainbow. Sometimes they merged, red and blue becoming
purple, or green and red becoming yellow. They drifted
sideways or rose and fell as if in a current.

They got larger and brighter.

Dani became aware of a hum that gradually increased
in pitch, and before she knew it, her ears were in pain.

Suddenly the horse reared up. She pressed down on
its neck while tightening her legs against its flanks. Making
panicked noises, the animal skittered sideways. Again it
attempted to rear up, and suddenly—regardless of her
expert efforts—it charged along the road.

The horse's speed would normally have made it difficult for Dani to see obstacles on the shadowy road, but as she struggled to subdue it, she realized that the road had become unnaturally bright, with vibrant colors flashing toward it. Without warning, the lights were rushing over her, spinning around her, trapping her in a whirlpool.

At once the horse bucked so violently that she flew off the saddle. When she struck the road, pain shot through her ribs. Her vision blurred. Dizzy, she heard the horse neighing in alarm. The pounding of its hooves began again and receded into the distance.

Dani had no idea how long she lay unconscious. When she wakened, the lights were gone. Clouds had drifted in, partially concealing the stars and the moon. In the meager illumination, she squirmed to her feet. Despite the cold, the pain in her ribs made her sweat.

With a weak voice, she called for the horse, but the animal didn't return. She called again, gave up, and struggled to find her bearings. Which way was Rostov? That was the closer town. If she made a mistake in direction, she'd walk toward Loden, and she doubted she had the strength to go that far.

She scanned the heavens in search of the North Star. The pain was so great that she feared she'd collapse.

The Big Dipper. Need to find the Big Dipper.

There. When she'd been a little girl, her father had made sure that she knew how to navigate by the stars in case she ever got lost in the dark. The two end stars on the Big Dipper pointed toward the *Little* Dipper, and the star at the end of the handle part of the Little Dipper was the North Star.

Now Dani could calculate which way was west, the direction that would take her to Rostov. She wavered along the increasingly dark road and stumbled. When she fell, pain jolted her into consciousness. She crawled and finally managed to stand again.

Time lost all meaning.

She felt another jolt of intense pain and realized she'd run into the side of a building. Only then did she understand that she'd reached town. Delirious, she took two wrong turns before she pounded on her father's door.

When he opened it, she collapsed in his arms.

The next morning, word of her ordeal spread through Rostov. Numerous friends came to satisfy their curiosity.

"Germans?" the veterinarian asked. The closest that Rostov had to a doctor, he recommended that Dani wear a corset to protect her ribs while they healed.

"No," she said through the pain. "I don't think so." The corset put so much pressure on Dani's throbbing chest that she had trouble breathing.

"But you told us you saw riders with torches," Dani's father said. "If not Germans, were they Mexicans?"

"No, I only thought—"

"It could have been a scouting expedition," Rostov's mayor decided. "Some of them got close enough to throw their torches at you. Carranza's people are in league with the Germans. Everybody knows that. Maybe Carranza's seeing how far he can sneak into Texas before anybody makes a fuss."

"Or it might have been that bastard Villa," the town's blacksmith suggested. "He's desperate for money and supplies."

"There's nothing between us and the border." Dani's mother looked horrified. "They could murder us in our sleep."

"No, it wasn't people on horseback," Dani insisted tightly.

"What was it you said?" the mayor asked. "Whatever you saw seemed to be on the horizon, and suddenly it was spinning around you. Wasn't that how you described it?"

"Yes." Squeezed by the corset and her pain-swollen ribs, Dani could hardly speak.

"An airplane can do that. I saw one the last time I visited my sister in El Paso."

"But I didn't hear an engine."

"You said you heard *something*."

"A hum," she replied. "I couldn't place it."

"While blinding lights spun around you."

"Yes, but—"

The mayor stood and put on his coat. "I'll contact Fort Bliss. The Army needs to be warned about this."

"Warned?"

"I think the Germans are testing a new weapon."

A day later, a speck emerged from the afternoon sun. The drone of an engine made people look toward the west, where the shape of an airplane gradually became visible, its yellow vivid against the sky. It had two sets of wings, one above the other, and two open seats, one in front of the other. The sole occupant was seated in the back.

He circled the town and the people who'd gathered on the main street. Angling down, the plane seemed to float as it eased toward the dirt road. When it landed, it bounced slightly, then raised a dust cloud, coming to rest on a section of parched grass.

The people crowded toward the field, marveling as the pilot shut off the engine, pushed himself up from the back seat, and jumped to the ground. He wore boots, leather gloves, a leather jacket, a khaki uniform under it, and a matching scarf around his neck. A pistol was holstered to his wide canvas belt, and someone identified it as one of the new Colt .45 semiautomatics. When he took off his goggles, the area around his eyes was white compared to the dust that coated the rest of his face, including his mustache.

"I'm Capt. John Raleigh," he said with a smooth voice that commanded attention. "You can get a little closer if you want." With his boot, he drew a line on the ground. "To here. But don't touch the plane."

"How does it fly?" a man asked in amazement.

"The propeller pushes air past the wings. They're shaped so a high-pressure area forms under them and a low-pressure area forms over them. The difference between the high and low pressure lifts the plane."

Several people frowned as if he spoke gibberish. Others nodded, perhaps pretending they understood.

"What's covering the wings?" another man asked.

"Strips of linen. They're sealed with a waterproofing agent that's like shellac."

"Doesn't sound very strong."

"Strong enough. The plane brought me all the way from El Paso." With that he looked around, then spoke again to the crowd. "Where's your mayor? I came to talk with him."

"That's *me*, Captain. My name's Ted McKinney." The mayor stepped from the crowd and shook hands with him. "Thanks for coming so soon. My office is just down the street."

"Thank *you* for contacting us," Captain Raleigh responded. "I'd like to get started right away. The Army is very interested in your report."

The crowd parted as he and the mayor walked away.

→→ ←←

Mayor McKinney was the president of Rostov's only bank. He and Raleigh remained inside the adobe building for an hour. Many people gathered on the street, curious about what the two men discussed.

When Raleigh and the mayor came out, they crossed the street to the dry-goods store that Dani's parents owned. The couple lived in an apartment behind it, where she was convalescing.

More people gathered on the street.

A half hour later, the mayor left the store. Preceded by the sound of a rattling motor, he returned shortly with his Ford Model T.

Captain Raleigh stepped from the store and held the door open for Dani, who clutched a coat around her and walked stiffly to the car. The captain helped her onto the passenger seat and climbed into the back. The townspeople watched with growing curiosity as Mayor McKinney drove the car out of town, following the road to Loden.

→→ ←←

The winter sun had descended low enough to touch the horizon, and the scarlet glow deepened the brown of Raleigh's leather jacket. The captain leaned forward from the back seat so that Dani could hear him over the clatter of the Model T's engine.

"Thank you for agreeing to do this, Miss Brown. Not many women would be brave enough to return to the scene of where they were attacked."

"I'm not sure it's a matter of bravery, Captain Raleigh," Dani haltingly explained. "I think perhaps it's anger."

"Anger?" He looked curious, and she couldn't help noticing that he was handsome. Standing or sitting, he held his back straight, and she thought he had the makings of a great horse rider.

Dismissing such thoughts, she continued, "Someone found my horse. The skeleton of it anyway, after the coyotes had finished with it. Whatever attacked me is responsible for that."

"I'm sorry to hear about your horse." He sounded as if he truly meant it. "Do you have a sense of where the incident occurred?"

"I set out after dark." As the sunset weakened, Dani

continued to be short of breath. Her words tightened with pain when the vehicle jolted over bumps. "There was light from the stars. Even so, it was hard to know exactly where I was along the road."

"What time did you leave for Loden?"

"At 7:15."

"That's very precise."

"My father has a wireless radio. I was with him when he listened to a report about the gas attacks in the European war. The report came through at 7." Dani forced herself to continue. "After ten minutes, I was so upset that I said good-bye to my parents and went out to my horse. I was on the road by 7:15."

"The way you sit so rigidly straight, you're obviously hurting," he said with concern. "Are you certain you can continue?"

"I'm prepared to do what's required," she answered firmly. "It's just the corset."

"Corset?" Raleigh sounded embarrassed.

"The veterinarian told me to wear a corset to bind my ribs and protect them."

"You went to a veterinarian?" he asked in surprise.

"This is cattle country, Captain Raleigh. It's easier to find a vet than a doctor."

"As soon as you return home, please take the corset off at once. It can kill you."

Dani winced as the mayor drove over another bump. "*Kill* me? What are you talking about?"

"The Army's been studying how wounds are being treated in the war. It's common for tape to be used on broken ribs. But British doctors are discovering that pneumonia is a frequent result. Apparently the tape causes shallow breathing that allows fluid to collect in the lungs. The next thing, the patient is sick from something far worse than broken ribs. After you remove the corset, breathe as deeply as you can. That'll hurt, but it's the only way to stop the fluid from collecting."

The mayor turned on the Model T's lights. "Speaking of the war, Captain, will the U.S. join the fight?"

"Yes, we will," Raleigh answered. "It's only a question of when. That's why the Army sent me here. If the Germans are testing a new weapon, we need to know about it. Miss Brown, can you estimate how long you were on this road before you saw the lights?"

"Perhaps forty minutes."

"At what gait were you riding?"

"A moderate trot. The light from the moon and the stars was sufficient to allow for that speed."

"Which means that you traveled approximately five miles."

The mayor looked at him with even more respect. "I gather you used to be a cavalryman."

"The Eighth Regiment."

"You were in the Philippines?"

"Apparently Miss Brown isn't the only person keeping up with the news." Raleigh scanned the horizon. "Yes, I was in the Philippines. When I heard that the Army was training pilots, I decided it was better to fly over a jungle than ride through it." He paused and peered into the dusk. "Would you say we've traveled five miles yet?"

"That's what the milometer says."

"Then let's stop and enjoy the view."

McKinney eased back on the accelerator and pulled the handbrake. Even at an idle, the vibrations of the engine made the car rattle.

"Miss Brown, you said the lights came from the south?"

"That's correct."

"If you turn off the engine, Mr. McKinney, will you be able to restart it, or will we be stuck out here?"

"I maintain the car in excellent condition," the mayor said. "It will start."

"Then let's enjoy some peace and quiet."

The mayor shut off the engine. The car wheezed and fell silent.

"If I keep the headlights on, the battery'll go dead," McKinney told Raleigh.

"Of course. Please turn them off."

At once darkness surrounded the vehicle. Silence gave the night power.

"Beautiful," Raleigh said as his eyes adjusted to the gloom. "In El Paso, the streetlights keep me from seeing the sky. I seldom see the heavens so bright."

McKinney pointed with a child's enthusiasm. "Look, a shooting star."

It streaked across the sky like silent fireworks.

"Miss Brown, could that be what you saw?" Raleigh asked. "Perhaps a cluster of shooting stars?"

"I've never heard of shooting stars coming across a field and spinning around someone," she replied. "Nor have I ever experienced any that hummed."

"I haven't, either." Raleigh fixed his gaze on the murky area to the south. Somewhere over there, coyotes yipped and howled.

They're on the hunt, he thought.

Or perhaps they're running from something.

"I need to tell you," Dani said, "that I don't think the lights were torches held by German riders."

"Perhaps not Germans. Perhaps it was Carranza's men."

"No. I mean I don't think there were *any* riders."

"But if there weren't any riders, what caused the lights?"

"I don't know. People around here often see lights," she said. "I myself have never seen them, so I can't tell you what they look like, and before the other night I hadn't thought they even existed. Now I'm not certain *what* I think."

"I'm afraid I don't understand."

"Dani's talking about the Rostov lights," McKinney interrupted. "Indians and early settlers used to talk about them. *I've* never seen them, either, but my wife claims she has. That was after we lost a son to cholera. She believed the lights were the soul of our boy. If you ask me, my Emily was so depressed that she convinced herself she saw the lights."

"Well, whatever's going on, we'll soon find out," Raleigh replied confidently.

"You really believe that?"

"Absolutely," he said. "I'm seeing the lights right now."

"What?" McKinney glanced all around.

Raleigh focused all his attention toward the southern horizon, where glowing colors slowly began to appear. They rose and fell. They drifted and floated in a languorous, captivating rhythm. Red merged into blue. Yellow blended with green.

"Mr. McKinney, do you see them?" Raleigh rested his right hand on his pistol.

The mayor didn't answer for a moment.

"God help me, yes."

"Miss Brown, are *they* what you saw?"

"Yes," she said softly. "Before they attacked me."

"Well, they're not riders carrying torches, that's for certain. Does anyone smell flowers?"

"Flowers?"

"Orchids."

"I wouldn't know what orchids smell like," McKinney said.

"In the Philippines, there were hundreds of types of orchids," Raleigh explained. "Amazing colors. Just like what I'm seeing now. In the night in the jungle, as I tried to sleep in my tent, the scent was thick. Orchids pollinated by bees had a perfume of cinnamon. That's what I'm smelling now."

"I smell rotting meat," Dani said.

McKinney raised a hand to his mouth. "So do I."

Raleigh remembered that the orchids in the Philippines didn't always smell like cinnamon. If they were pollinated by flies, sometimes they had the odor of a dead animal that the flies had sat on.

Abruptly the stench hit him, almost making him gag. *Like corpses after a battle*, he thought.

Dani coughed. The reflexive reaction to the odor filled her chest with pain, causing her to wince.

"Something out there is dead," she said.

A new German weapon? Raleigh wondered.

"How far do you suppose they are?" McKinney's voice was unsteady.

"Without a method to triangulate the distance, it's impossible to know," Raleigh answered. "In the dark, our eyes play tricks on us. The lights could be miles away, or less than a hundred yards. The latter would explain how they reached you so quickly, Miss Brown."

The odor of death became stronger.

We're not prepared, Raleigh thought. Mindful of his responsibility for Dani's safety, he kept his voice level. "Let's go back to town."

Two days later, a detachment of cavalry arrived, their dust cloud visible from a distance. At sunset, Raleigh rode with them to the part of the road from which he'd seen the lights.

Their plan was to use surveyor's instruments to get two separate bearings on the lights, plotting map coordinates that would allow them to determine how far away and where the lights were.

But the moment the lights appeared, the horses went crazy. Whinnying loudly, they kicked and bit one another. A trooper on foot, clinging to the reins of his mount, was dragged along the ground. A hoof fractured his skull. The other panicked horses galloped into the gloom, leaving the soldiers to make their cautious way back to town on foot, all the while ready with their rifles.

A week later, eight Army biplanes flew to Rostov from Fort Bliss. The intervening time had given Raleigh the chance to choose a location for an airstrip and start supervising its construction. The rationale for the airstrip was that it provided an out-of-the-way place at which to secretly train pilots for America's entry into the war.

The actual purpose, however, was to establish a location from which the biplanes could conduct aerial surveillance beyond the Mexican border, looking for a weapon that the Germans might be testing. When he wasn't on duty, Raleigh found himself spending more and more time with Dani Marie Brown.

Part of the training for student pilots involved flying at night. He used the night instruction as an opportunity to send his students to try to determine the origin of the lights, but he was forced to discontinue those missions. As the trainees flew toward the lights, they diverted and attacked one another—with apparent deliberation, two planes actually collided, killing the instructor and student in each.

Thereafter training occurred only during daylight.

Fears about an invasion from Mexico were validated on March 9, 1916, when gunmen led by Pancho Villa staged a night attack on the New Mexican town of Columbus. Within two days, Congress voted to pursue Villa. "Black Jack" Pershing led five thousand soldiers into Mexico, where they remained for most of the year. Although they engaged in numerous battles with Mexican troops, they never located Villa, but that didn't matter. The mission was largely a training exercise, allowing American soldiers to absorb battle experience.

In April 1917, America entered the war.

Raleigh participated in the Mexican campaign, using his biplane to scout for enemy positions. Afterward he returned to Rostov and married Dani Marie, but within weeks of his marriage, he was on a ship bound for France.

The lights and the possibility of a new German weapon being tested along the Mexican border were forgotten by the Army. There were too many tangible weapons to worry about, particularly mustard gas. But on many nights, as Captain Raleigh tried not to think about the next day's combat, he longed for his wife and the son she'd given birth to.

After the war ended in November 1918, he returned home in time for Christmas. Snow fell—unusual but not impossible in that area of Texas. He had survived thirty-nine dogfights with German aviators and thanked God that he was able to be with his wife and son. But even though he was finally safe, he had nightmares. Not about the war, though. Instead his disturbing dreams made him experience the floating, drifting sensation of the lights. Each evening he went out to stare at them. In March 1919, he purchased a biplane that had been used in the war, many of which had become available at cheap prices because the military no longer needed them.

A week after he took possession of the plane, he took off at dusk from the now overgrown airstrip where he'd trained pilots three years earlier. As the darkness thickened, he flew toward the lights. The sound of his engine receded into the gloom.

Neither he nor the plane was ever seen again.

56

In the dank complex beneath the abandoned airbase, Col. Warren Raleigh remembered seeing photographs of a dashing young man in a uniform, a strong-looking woman next to him, a biplane in the background. He remembered hearing about the Rostov lights and his great-grandfather's mysterious disappearance.

Raleigh's great-grandmother had raised her son alone, demonstrating the strength that had drawn her husband to her. Her only show of emotion came each night. While her parents took care of the baby, she went out to the area where her husband had disappeared. She watched the lights, waiting for him to return.

Night after night, winter and spring, she stared at them.

Inexplicably, her face became red and swollen. Blisters developed. One night, when strands of her hair began to fall out, she finally did something she would never have imagined doing—she took her son, moved from the once reassuring area where she'd grown up, and rented an apartment in noisy, disturbing El Paso. There she learned to be a seamstress, sewing at home while looking after her son.

El Paso led to Denver, Chicago, and finally Boston as she tried to get farther and farther from the lights. Despite the passage of years, she never remarried.

She died from skin cancer.

A voice interrupted Raleigh's thoughts.

"Sir, Fort . . . is . . . call . . . you."

He peered up from his desk. His earplugs muffled sounds. "Say again, Lieutenant?"

"Fort Meade wants you on the phone. Scrambler code 2."

As Raleigh reached for the phone on his desk, the lieutenant continued, "And even though it isn't night yet, we're getting extremely powerful readings."

Raleigh nodded. This time he didn't take the risk of removing an earplug as he pressed a button on his phone and engaged the scrambler.

"Colonel Raleigh here."

"This is Borden," a woman's voice said faintly. She was the director of the weapons research team at Raleigh's headquarters near the fortress-like National Security Agency in Maryland. "We're receiving unusually strong readings from the observatory."

"Yes, one of my people here just told me *we're* getting strong readings, also."

Borden's voice continued, "I reviewed the data parameters for previous versions of this study. As we know, the pattern's cyclical. Sometimes the signals are almost impossible to detect. Other times they're pronounced. But until now, the highs and lows have been in the same range. These are the highest readings we've ever seen— and that includes what happened where *you* are, back in 1945. The reason I contacted you isn't just to make a report. I'm asking you to reconsider your strategy." She paused. "Colonel, are you certain you want to stay at your location?"

Raleigh found the question touching. One of his many

secrets was that he and Borden met each month at a Baltimore hotel room, where they allowed themselves to pretend they had emotions unrelated to their careers. Her question wasn't merely about protecting the program. It suggested that she was actually concerned about his safety.

"Colonel, can you hear me?" Borden's voice asked.

"Yes," he finally said, "I hear you. Thank you for your input, but I'll be staying. All these years, this is where the program has been headed. Without a team on-site, we'll never know the truth. I can't leave."

This wasn't just where the program had been headed, though. It was where his *life* had been headed since he'd first heard about the lights when he was a boy.

FOUR

TRANSFIGURATION

57

Twenty seconds after the explosions, Page's cell phone rang. He and Tori were staring toward the sky in the direction from which the shock waves had come. He pulled the phone from his belt and pressed the answer button.

"Did you hear them?" Medrano's voice asked urgently.

"A small one, a big one, then another small one," Page replied. "From the northwest. The only thing over there is the observatory."

"That's what I'm thinking, too. Where *are* you?"

"The airport."

"Big surprise. I finally figured you were planning to use your plane tonight. A private plane can go just about anywhere, right?"

"Just about."

"The nearest Highway Patrol chopper is ninety minutes away. I can't wait that long. I want you to fly toward those explosions and find out what the hell happened."

"The problem is," Page said, "one of the places a private plane *can't* go is prohibited airspace."

"You're telling me the observatory's off-limits?"

"Usually a prohibited area has something to do with national security. I have no idea what that observatory has to do with any of that, but at the very least, I could lose my pilot's license if I fly in there."

"I can't go in there, either," Medrano said. "That's federal property. I don't have the jurisdiction to send in cruisers. Listen, I'll try to get permission from the FBI. While I'm waiting, can you at least fly along the boundary of that area—maybe get high enough to try to see what happened?"

"That I can do. I have a police radio in my plane. What's your frequency?"

Page wrote down the number, pressed the disconnect button, and returned his phone to his belt.

He looked at Tori. "This could be dangerous. You might want to think about not going up with me."

"Could you use an extra set of eyes?"

"Always."

"Then you've got company."

58

A bullet tore up dirt near Brent's left cheek. He flinched and ducked his head lower.

Where he lay was a sandy trough that might have been a dry creek bed. The parched land had absorbed the water from yesterday's storm except that there seemed to be a puddle under him, soaking him. Then he realized that what he felt was the wet crotch of his pants where his bladder had let go.

The only thing that kept him from panicking was the television camera. *I'm not going to lose this chance.* He angled it up toward the black smoke that billowed from the downed helicopter. Then he pivoted to the right and aimed the camera toward the smoking ruin of the news van.

Now comes the hard part—staying alive to show this to somebody, he thought.

Anita was sprawled between him and the burning van. Her head lolled, and she looked weaker.

He squirmed toward her, stopping when he was halfway there. The guard at the observatory had a large area to scan with his rifle. From this new position, Brent hoped to be able to ease the camera over the edge of the trough and record what the gunman was up to.

Need to do something. *I'm not just going to lie here.*

He took a deep breath, braced his trembling muscles, and cautiously showed himself. Through the camera's viewfinder, he saw the guard turning in his direction and raising the rifle. Brent managed to get down just before three bullets blasted dirt above him.

"Wouldn't pay attention to the sign!" the guard yelled from beyond the fences.

Brent had lost his handheld microphone. Now he relied solely on the shotgun mike attached to the top of the camera, although he had little hope that it would register the guard's voice from so far away.

"Had to come barging in!" the guard continued. "All I wanted was to listen to the music!"

Music? Brent thought.

"I *told* you to get out of here!" the guard shouted. "But you had to keep pushing! You had to keep me from the music!"

What in God's name is he talking about? Brent wondered.

"Trespassers will be prosecuted! That's what the sign says!"

More bullets sprayed dirt above Brent's head.

"And as soon as I get these gates open, I'll prosecute you to hell!"

Brent crawled toward Anita, whose dark skin should never have looked so pale. He untucked the pen that bound the tourniquet and loosened the cloth, grimacing at the sight of the blood that flowed from her left arm.

"Need to free the circulation from time to time. Otherwise you might get gangrene."

"Too much information," she said weakly.

"Sorry."

"Cold." Anita turned her head to the side and made vomiting noises, but nothing came from her stomach. "Heart's racing. Think I'm in shock."

Brent retightened the tourniquet. He strained to push a large rock toward her, propping her sneakers on it. "This is supposed to help."

"Where'd you learn all this?"

"I did a story about an emergency first-aid team."

"And now you're an expert? Lord, I wish I hadn't asked. The camera." Breathing rapidly, Anita noticed that Brent had set it down so that it pointed toward them. The red light was on. "You're recording us?"

"Don't you want to be a star?"

For a moment, Brent thought he heard an approaching engine. His pulse raced with the hope that the police had heard the explosions and were coming. But at once the faint drone stopped, and he feared he'd imagined it.

He picked up the camera and hoped that the smoke and flames would shield him as he hurried to the front of the burning van. Staying back from the heat, he aimed the camera along the side and focused on the guard, who stood before the inside gate. He seemed to be studying it.

He's not sure if the fence still has any juice to it, Brent realized. *When the helicopter crashed onto the fence, did it cut off the electricity, or will he get fried if he touches the gate?*

The guard evidently decided not to take the chance. He swung toward the shed, ran past the truck piled with corpses, and vanished through the doorway.

"Anita!" Brent rushed over to her. "He went inside! I think he's shutting off the electricity to the fence. If I'm right, he'll soon come for us. Hurry! We need to move!"

She licked her dry lips and nodded. "Help me up."

After he lifted her, she hooked her unwounded right arm around his neck. He linked his left arm around her waist. Holding the camera with his right hand, he helped her waver along the dirt road.

59

The elevation of Rostov's airport was five thousand feet. Page climbed three thousand five hundred feet higher than that and headed west along the county road that, according to his aerial map, formed one boundary of the observatory's prohibited airspace. That altitude provided a good perspective on the flat, sparse grassland off to the right.

Tori adjusted the microphone on her headset.

"Two columns of smoke." She pointed.

Even at a distance, the white observatory dishes were obvious, including the one that was tilted sideways and aimed toward the southeast. One section of smoke was on the left side of the dishes, very close to them. The other was in front of the dishes, rising from a dirt lane that led from the observatory to the county road.

The dark smoke reminded Page uncomfortably of the gasoline tanker he'd seen explode in Santa Fe, just four days earlier.

As he guided the Cessna along the boundary road, he and Tori came parallel to the fires on their right, gaining a closer view. She removed binoculars from Page's flight bag and peered through them, adjusting their focus.

"Wreckage near the dishes." She sounded more troubled. "Rotor blades. Looks like a helicopter crashed." She aimed the binoculars toward the lane. "The other fire's coming from a vehicle. A van. It's got a dish on it. Looks like a television news van."

Page activated the police radio.

"Cessna Four Three Alpha calling Captain Medrano."

Immediately Medrano's voice crackled through Page's headset. "Go ahead."

"We're seeing what appears to be a downed helicopter

next to the observatory. It and a television news van are on fire."

"*What?*"

"It isn't clear what happened. I told you prohibited flight areas usually involve national security. Do you suppose there's some kind of special government project there? The kind terrorists would want to attack?"

"The FBI must be worried about the same thing," Medrano's voice said starkly. "They gave you permission to take a closer look. They also gave me permission to send police cars in there."

"Understood. I have clearance to enter."

He banked to the right toward the columns of smoke. Through the canopy, the white dishes got bigger.

Tori kept staring through the binoculars.

"Do you see any survivors?" Page asked.

"No. Wait. Yes. But not at the helicopter. At the van. I see two people stumbling along the road. They're heading in our direction. A man and a woman. It looks like the woman's hurt."

As Page flew closer, they came into his line of sight. Struggling along the dirt lane, the man held the woman up with his left arm. He was carrying something in his lowered right hand.

"Is that a television camera?" Tori asked in amazement. "My God, that's the TV reporter who's been looking for us."

The woman's knees bent. She slumped, dragging the man down with her, both of them toppling to the ground.

Tori adjusted the binoculars. "The woman's covered with blood."

Medrano's voice blurted through Page's headset.

"The FBI has rescinded your clearance! Turn around! Get out of there!"

Page frowned at Tori. "What's going on?"

He was about to press the police radio's transmit button, but Medrano kept talking.

"You must be right—this has something to do with national security! And somebody with influence must be involved! A special team is being sent in!"

Page kept flying toward the observatory.

"Do you copy?" Medrano's voice demanded. "Your clearance to enter the prohibited airspace is no longer valid! Turn around!"

"The police radio's been acting up lately," Page told Tori. "All I hear is static."

"Yeah, I don't hear him, either."

Page gestured toward the man and woman who'd toppled onto the lane. The woman was sprawled on her back while the man knelt beside her, doing something to her left arm.

"How long do you think it'll take for that special team to get organized?" Page wondered. "The nearest place they can come from is El Paso. Maybe farther away than that. My guess is it'll take at least two hours for help to arrive. That woman might be dead by then."

"*Do you understand?*" Medrano's voice was loud enough to be distorted. "You do *not* have clearance to enter that airspace!"

Page shut off the radio. "It keeps overheating, too."

Beyond the burning van, he saw that three high fences encircled the observatory dishes. An open-backed truck was parked near a shed-like building.

The dishes loomed. At a thousand feet, Page flew over them, made a turn, and headed back toward the man and woman sprawled on the lane.

As the plane went over the observatory, Tori peered straight down.

"That truck near the small building," she said.

"What about it?"

"I think I saw . . ." She stopped suddenly.

"Your voice sounds strange. What's wrong?"

"Corpses in the back."

"Corpses?"

"A *bunch* of them," Tori said.

Page immediately banked to the left. He flew in a circle and returned over the dishes, heading toward the truck. This time he positioned the plane so he could look down from his side.

In the back of the truck, bodies were dumped on top of one another, legs and arms splayed in every direction, so that he couldn't count them. Some wore tan uniforms, others white lab coats.

"Jesus," he said.

As he neared the couple on the lane again, the man looked up in desperation, but what Page concentrated on was the lane itself. Made of dirt, it appeared to be flat, but that didn't mean there weren't rocks or potholes that could blow a tire or snap off wheels, causing the plane to flip.

"Tori, is your seat belt tight?"

"Is there any other way for a seat belt to be?"

He pulled back on the throttle, causing the plane to lose altitude. At the same time he eased back on the yoke, tilting the nose slightly upward, reducing speed. To reduce speed further, he lowered the maximum flaps.

The plane sank toward the ground. At sixty knots, Page leveled the aircraft above the lane and felt it settle.

In most landings, he protected the nose wheel by touching down on the two main wheels first. For this kind of landing, however, the objective was to stop in the shortest distance possible, which meant there wasn't time for the front wheel to settle gently onto the lane. Instead Page landed on all three wheels. The moment he felt the jolt, he pressed his feet on the brake pedals and pulled back on the yoke. He came to a stop a mere two hundred feet from where he'd touched down.

In a rush, he shut off the aircraft's engine, vaguely aware of the clinking sound of seat belts as he and Tori unbuckled them. He opened the door, jumped to the ground, grabbed a first-aid kit from under the back seat, and ran toward the couple on the lane.

Tori was next to him, matching his urgent pace.

They reached the man and woman, and yes, the man was the television reporter, looking more haggard than ever, his ear bloody, his suit and blond hair caked with dirt. But Page didn't have time for any more details as he crouched next to the woman and tried not to think about the quantity of blood that soaked her clothes.

"Keep your head down!" the reporter urged.

"What happened to her?"

"She was shot! Keep your head down!"

"Shot?" Page unzipped the first-aid kit.

"The guard might be back by now." Ashen, the reporter looked over his shoulder toward the observatory.

"A *guard* shot her?" Tori asked in confusion.

Page studied the necktie that served as a tourniquet.

"Did *you* do this?" he asked the reporter.

"It was all I could think of."

"You probably saved her life."

Page stared at the huge, ugly exit wound. He thought he saw bone. No time to clean it.

"Tori, open these packets."

While she did, he pulled a small roll of duct tape from the kit.

"I'm sorry I don't have anything for the pain," he told the woman.

She didn't reply. Her eyes were half open.

Tori handed him the open packets. He squeezed antiseptic cream into the wound and covered it with a wad of blood-absorbent material.

"Scissors," he said, fumbling through the kit. "Need scissors."

"Use this knife." The reporter pulled one from his pants: a black folding knife with a thumb button on the side of the blade. "It's hers."

Page sliced off a section of duct tape. He wrapped it around the woman's arm, then cut off another section of tape and applied it, too.

"I'll cut while you wrap," Tori said, taking the knife and the tape.

As he applied more tape, creating a pressure bandage,

a red light caught his attention. It was on the television camera, which the reporter angled in his direction, evidently recording the scene.

Page couldn't allow himself to be distracted. He finished the pressure bandage and undid the tourniquet, waiting to see if blood would flow past the tape.

Dirt suddenly pelted him, accompanied by a distant *crack*ing sound.

"What the . . ."

More dirt struck his face. Amid further distant *crack*ing sounds, he saw puffs of dust rising from the road.

"Somebody's shooting at us."

"Oh, shit, the guard got the gates open. He's coming," the reporter moaned.

"Why is he shooting at us?" Tori asked. "Why are there corpses in that truck?"

Page stared past the burning van toward the huge dishes. The gates to all three fences were now open. A man stood outside the third gate and aimed a rifle, which bucked from the recoil.

Dirt exploded on the lane. The *crack* from the shot echoed.

"We're just out of range," Page said.

The man stepped forward and fired again. After a moment, a bullet tore up dirt a little closer.

"We need to reach the Cessna!" Page said. "Hurry! Before he gets closer!"

He put his arms around the injured woman's legs and shoulders, lifting her. The smell of her blood was strong as he charged along the lane. Even though she was thin, she felt heavy, her hips sinking, her feet and arms flopping.

The reporter ran ahead of him, carrying the television camera.

Tori reached the Cessna's passenger door and yanked it open, tilting the seat forward. Page stooped beneath the high wing and eased the wounded woman into the back seat.

"Get in there!" he told the reporter. "Buckle her seat belt! Buckle your own!"

As he hurried around the back of the plane, he heard Tori helping the reporter climb inside. A frantic glance down the lane showed him that the guard was running in their direction.

The guard stopped and fired. Dirt flew near the Cessna's tail.

Somewhere in that dirt, a bullet's ricocheting, Page thought.

He drew his pistol and aimed extremely high. If he fired straight ahead, his bullets would drop to the ground before they had a chance to come anywhere close to the distant target. By aiming high, however, he gave the bullets an arc that increased their range. Much of their force would be lost when they landed, but Page hoped they would strike near enough to the gunman to make him pause.

In rapid order, Page pulled the trigger six times. Six clouds of dust burst from the lane in front of the gunman, making him stumble back. Immediately Page ran along the left side of the plane and yanked open the door, scrambling inside.

Tori was in the passenger seat, fastening her belt.

Page jabbed the master switch, turned the ignition key, and worked the throttle. Abruptly the propeller spun, roaring. When he released the brakes, he felt the Cessna bump along the dirt lane. The two additional passengers added weight, reducing the engine's power.

Come on! Page thought. *Move!*

Feeling the Cessna bump faster along the lane, Page imagined the guard racing to get within range. He braced himself for bullets that would tear through the rear windscreen and slam into his back—or that would damage the rear wings and make it impossible for him to get the Cessna into the air.

"The plane's blowing dust!" the reporter shouted from the back. "I can't see the guard!"

Which means the guard can't see the plane, Page thought. *But that won't stop him from shooting toward us.*

Their speed reached fifty-five knots. Page pulled back the yoke and felt the aircraft leave the ground. He stayed low, wanting to gain more speed before he went higher. Right now distance was the key, not height. When he thought he'd gone a sufficient distance, he eased farther back on the yoke and pointed the plane's nose toward the horizon.

He was abruptly aware that his shirt was soaked with sweat.

"Tori, take the controls."

He put on his headset. It muffled the engine's roar as he activated the radio system.

"Taking back the controls," he said.

He couldn't contact Medrano on the police radio. After all, his excuse for entering the prohibited airspace was that the police radio had failed. Instead he used the plane's standard radio. Although Rostov's airport didn't have a control tower, he hoped someone in the office would hear him.

"Rostov traffic. Cessna Four Three Alpha has an injured passenger. A gunshot victim. We need an ambulance at the airport. My ETA is five minutes. Rostov."

"I hear you, Four Three Alpha," a voice said through Page's headset. It belonged to the man in the frayed coveralls who'd given Page his rental-car papers. "I'll get that ambulance."

Page tilted his head toward the reporter in back. "How *is* she?"

"Unconscious. But it looks like the duct tape sealed the wound."

To Page's right, the stock pens outside Rostov came into view, as did the courthouse on the main street. People and vehicles seemed everywhere, exploring the town before night settled and they went to the viewing area.

He descended toward the airport northeast of town, but not before he took a hard look at the collapsed, rusted hangars and the cracked, overgrown airstrip on the abandoned military airbase in the opposite direction. There wasn't any sign of the vehicles he'd seen on the base the evening before. Beyond the ruin of the airbase, he frowned toward the boulders that looked like giant cinders strewn in a chaotic semicircle, all that remained of the volcanic rim that had spewed them to the surface eons earlier.

60

Lockhart lay on the ground and spoke into the radio.

"The plane's taking off. There's a lot of dust, but I can see that the guard's still running and firing."

"Shoot the son of a bitch," Raleigh's voice ordered.

"I'm not within accurate range, sir."

"Get closer."

"Yes, sir." He scanned the sky. "It looks like the plane escaped."

"By tomorrow there'll be no way to contain this. If I hadn't put a quarantine on that place, there'd be police cars all over there by now. I don't want anybody guessing what that facility really does. After you take care of the guard, destroy all the equipment in the observatory. Make it look as if he did it."

"Yes, sir."

Remaining low, Lockhart watched the guard continue firing toward the departing airplane—he kept squeezing the trigger even after he ran out of ammunition. As the lowering sun made the dust look scarlet, the guard glared toward the sky, then turned and took long, angry strides back toward the first of the three fences.

Lockhart was to the guard's right, just behind him and about two hundred yards away. Bullets from an M4 could travel that far, but Lockhart couldn't depend on where they would hit. To stop the guard, rather than merely startle him, he needed to get closer.

Satisfied that he wasn't in the guard's line of vision,

he stood, tucked the radio into the duffel bag that hung from his shoulder, picked up his M4, and broke into a run. As the man passed the burning van and got closer to the observatory, Lockhart increased his pace, the duffel bag bumping against his side. His thick-soled shoes crunched on the pebbly soil, but the breeze was blowing in his direction, so the slight sound wouldn't carry.

He couldn't allow the man to reach the door to the shed. He strained his legs to their full length. Charging across the scrub grass, he ignored the sweat that dripped from his face.

The guard reached the first gate.

Lockhart raced nearer.

The guard reached the second gate.

Lockhart had seen the difficulty that the guard had experienced when trying to shoot through the three fences. Continuing to rush forward, he simultaneously veered toward the lane.

Need to shoot through the open gates, he thought.

A hundred yards.

Abruptly the guard stopped walking toward the tiny building.

Does he hear me? Lockhart worried.

The guard turned, but instead of looking in Lockhart's direction, he came back and reached for the first open gate. As he started to close it, he froze at the sight of Lockhart racing toward the lane.

Lockhart stopped, raised the M4, fought to control his breathing, and leveled the rifle's sights on the target. His exertion made his arms unsteady. Years of combat training enabled him to brace his muscles and keep the barrel from wavering.

The guard raised his weapon and tried to shoot first, but nothing happened—he'd used all his ammunition when he'd fired at the airplane. He turned and ran toward the middle gate.

Lockhart pulled the trigger. The selector switch on his rifle was set to deliver bursts of three shots. The first group missed. He took a deep breath, held it, and fired again.

The guard lurched but kept running. He passed through the second gate and headed toward the final one, each frenzied step taking him farther away, making him a more difficult target.

Lockhart fired another burst, and again the guard seemed to lurch. But he made it past the open-backed truck, disappearing into the darkness beyond the shed's open door.

Cursing, Lockhart fired into the void of the door. His ammunition ran out, so he ejected the empty magazine, pulled a fresh one from his duffel bag, slammed it home, freed the bolt, and fired yet again through the open door.

Then he realized how out in the open he was and what an excellent target he made now that the guard had been given the opportunity to reload. He darted to the left of the lane, stopping where the three lines of fences provided some cover, and dropped to the ground, making himself a smaller target.

Unfortunately, while the fences gave him some protection, potentially deflecting bullets, they also protected the guard.

Lockhart studied the open door.

I hit him twice. I'm almost positive. He's probably bleeding to death in there.

The void taunted him.

Sure. It's just a matter of time. I'll wait for a while and let him bleed out. After that, there'll be no problem getting inside.

Right. No problem.

Abruptly the door was slammed shut.

In the weakening light, Lockhart stared at it. Cautiously he stood, walked to the lane, and went through the three open gates. He looked for blood on the lane but didn't see any.

I didn't hit him after all. He just stumbled.

Aiming his weapon, he approached the closed door. It was solid metal. Yesterday, when he'd arrived with Colonel Raleigh and the team, he'd noticed how thick it was. He had no doubt that it locked automatically, just as he had no doubt that similar thick metal lined the entire concrete structure. The pad next to the door would require a specific sequence to unlock it, and it wouldn't matter if the colonel knew the numbers that had been used yesterday—the guard would almost certainly have changed that sequence by now.

Even if I had grenades, I wouldn't be able to get through that door, Lockhart thought.

He studied the ground again but didn't see any blood.

He walked to the open-backed truck and smelled the corpses before he saw them.

To vent his frustration, he shot the security camera above the door and a security camera on one of the fence poles. There were plenty of others to destroy, and he did so, one after the other. Now the guard wouldn't be able to see what he was doing, but the destruction didn't really accomplish anything because Lockhart had no way of getting inside.

The colonel isn't going to be happy.

Lockhart waited several seconds before making himself reach for the two-way radio in the duffel bag.

61

Page landed as softly as he could, keeping the nose wheel off the ground as long as possible so the injured woman wouldn't feel a jolt. He taxied from the runway toward the airport's adobe office, where the man in frayed coveralls stood waiting.

After shutting off the engine, Page quickly got out, tilted the seat forward, and eased the woman from the back seat. She remained unconscious.

The man in the coveralls rushed to help.

"The ambulance is on the way," he said as they set her gently on the pavement, using the Cessna's shadow to keep her out of the sun.

Page heard the wail of approaching sirens.

"The Highway Patrol's on its way, too," the man said.

Page didn't look forward to *that* conversation.

Tori and the reporter joined them.

Tinted by the red light of the sunset, the reporter faced him.

"I didn't get a chance to introduce myself." He had the television camera on his shoulder, and it took some effort for him to hold it with his left arm while he extended his right hand. The sleeve of his suit coat was torn. "Brent Loft."

"I know who you are," Page said.

Loft missed his tone, evidently pleased that Page recognized him. "And I certainly know who *you* are."

"Excuse me?" Page asked.

"You have red hair," Loft said, turning to Tori. "You're the couple I've been looking for—Daniel and Victoria Page, from Santa Fe. I've done my homework. You stopped the shootings on Thursday night."

"Is that camera still on?" Page asked.

"It's worthless if it isn't."

Page had been through so much that his emotions nearly overwhelmed him. His need to shield Tori almost made him yank the camera from Loft's hands and hurl it onto the concrete.

The approaching sirens helped him keep control.

He took a deep breath.

"Can't this wait? It's not something we want to talk about right now. We saved your life. With luck, we got your friend back here in time. Isn't that worth something? Give us a break."

Loft glanced in the direction of his unconscious companion and nodded. As he turned back to Tori, the sirens wailed closer.

"I have only one question."

"You expect me to believe that?"

"Really. Just one question."

"What is it?" Tori demanded. "I'm tired of hiding from you. Let's get this over with."

"I can understand how your husband was able to do what he did. He's a professional, trained to take charge in emergencies. But you're a real estate agent. In your place, most people would have panicked. Somehow *you* found the strength to pick up a pistol and stop the gunman. Your courage was remarkable. How on earth were you able to do that?"

"There wasn't a choice," Tori answered. "He was trying to kill my husband." She looked directly at Page, then back to the reporter. "How could I not have tried to protect my husband?"

"So you're saying it was love that gave you courage?" Loft asked.

"Yes." Tori looked again at Page. "Love gave me courage."

Loft lowered the camera and studied each of them. "Thank you for saving Anita and me."

The sirens became terribly loud. An ambulance sped into view and skidded to a stop next to the airport's office, followed closely by a Highway Patrol car. Attendants jumped from the ambulance, hurrying to unfold the wheels of a gurney. One carried an emergency kit as they rushed toward the woman lying on the pavement.

Medrano got out of the patrol car, put on his Stetson, straightened to his full height, and took powerful strides toward Page.

His voice was strong. "I told you not to fly into that area."

"That's news to me," Page said. Next to him, the ambulance attendants put an oxygen mask over the woman's face and attached an IV line. "You said the government gave me clearance to ignore the restriction."

"And then they revoked it. I warned you to get out of there."

"If you told us to leave, we didn't hear it," Tori said. "The police radio stopped working."

Loft stepped forward, balancing the television camera on his shoulder, focusing it on Medrano.

"Captain, I'm Brent Loft from First-on-the-Scene News in El Paso. This couple did an amazing thing. At great risk to their lives, they landed their aircraft on hazardous terrain at the observatory so they could stop a guard from killing us. In fact, as you can see, he'd already shot my partner. They loaded us on their plane and took off. The entire time, I was afraid the maniac would fire another grenade at us."

Medrano was taken by surprise. "Grenade?"

"He'd already used one to shoot down a helicopter. Then he fired one at our van."

"Why was he firing grenades?"

"I have no idea, any more than I know why he piled all those corpses onto the back of a truck."

"Corpses . . . in a *truck*?"

"A lot of them. Enough to fill it. He kept babbling about wanting to listen to music." Loft continued aiming the camera. "Something bad is going on over there, Captain. You need to get your men to that observatory before God knows what else happens."

Medrano opened his mouth to say something, then decided against it. He hurried to his cruiser, where he reached for the microphone on his police radio and spoke urgently into it.

Loft lowered the camera and aimed it toward the ambulance attendants as they lifted the woman onto the gurney.

"How's she doing?" Page asked.

"Lost plenty of blood," an attendant answered.

"She'd have lost more if it weren't for the guy with the camera."

"I'll use that quote when I edit this," Loft said.

He stepped quickly over to the ambulance and began talking to the attendants at the open doors. He used his free hand to gesture persuasively. The next thing, he climbed into the back.

Page shook his head. "I hate to say this, but I think we're going to be seeing a lot more of him on television."

Siren blaring, the ambulance rushed away.

The man in the frayed coveralls came over to them. "I'll help you push your plane to a tie-down spot."

"Actually, we're going up again," Page told him.

The man frowned toward the dimming sky. "Never liked flying at night."

"We still have something to settle. Am I right, Tori? Or maybe you don't feel the need any longer."

"More than ever," Tori said. "Let's finish this."

62

The hum had become so intense that it felt like a drill boring into Halloway's skull.

Soon, he thought. *Soon I won't hear it any longer. Soon the only thing I'll hear will be the music.*

But despite his determination, he needed all of his willpower not to be distracted while he finished rigging the booby trap. The design—learned in Iraq—consisted of two trip wires. The first was stretched across the upper part of the stairs. If an assault team somehow managed to force the door open up there, they'd respond to their training and check for traps. After they spotted the wire and the grenades it was attached to, they'd disengage it, then proceed down the stairs. The second wire—in shadows, stretched across a lower part of the stairs—was the killer.

As he worked, the hum made Halloway's hands want to shake, but he refused to let that happen. Grinding his teeth, he tied the wire to a cluster of concealed grenades. Satisfied that the work had been done correctly, he carefully descended the remainder of the stairs.

At the bottom, he increased speed along the hallway and entered the surveillance room, where he saw that even more screens had gone blank. One of the few that was working showed the man who'd shot at him as he raised his M4 and fired.

Another screen went dead.

Well, that's okay, Halloway thought. *I wasn't going to be watching the monitors anyhow.*

He picked up his reloaded M4 and went down the hallway to the door marked DATA ANALYSIS. Inside, he'd already placed five other M4s on a table, along with numerous hundred-round magazines and a small stack of grenades. If an assault team tried to stop him from listening to the music, he planned to show them just how furious that would make him.

The room still smelled of death, mostly because of the dried blood that covered the floor. But Halloway didn't have time to clean it. Anyway, when the music started, the scent of cinnamon would replace the stench of the blood. Because he didn't know how to manipulate the electronic instruments, he'd kept all of them on, their panels glowing continuously.

The only switch he felt confident using was the one that activated either the speakers or the headphones, and the only knob he knew how to control was for the volume. While he'd prepared the booby trap, he'd kept the sound coming from the speakers. It had been loud enough that he could hear the static from a distance. More important, he'd been able to hear growing hints of music emerging from the static. Those half-heard alluring echoes were what had made him capable of working despite the agony of his headache.

Now the music was more than just hints and echoes. Strengthening, it drifted and floated. Halloway felt its eerie tones lifting him. The pain of the drill boring into his brain mercifully receded. The hum diminished, overcome by the sensual melody that again brought the taste of orange juice and vodka.

He closed his eyes. The woman he danced with whispered into each of his ears. Kissed them. Drew her tongue along them.

It left his ears wet. He put his hands to them and opened his eyes long enough to see what was on them.

Blood was dripping from his ears.

63

Raleigh finished yet another phone call in a successful effort to keep law enforcement away from the observatory. The voices in the urgent conversation had sounded distant because he couldn't take the risk of removing his earplugs now that it was almost dark outside and the static on the audio monitors was beginning to resolve itself into music.

The words "national security" were a powerful invocation. With the cooperation of the FBI, Raleigh had again stopped the Highway Patrol from entering the restricted area. He'd arranged for equipment to be delivered that would allow an assault team to break into the observatory. After they eliminated the guard and cleaned the facility so that outside agencies couldn't question its true purpose, Raleigh would make sure the bastard's autopsy revealed a high blood level of crack cocaine, explaining his psychotic behavior.

With one crisis dealt with, but anticipating more, he set down the phone, stepped from the command center, and surveyed the eight men poised in front of the numerous electronic consoles. Their faces reflecting the glow of instruments, they turned dials, refining and adjusting the incoming signals. In response to his orders, they'd turned off the audio capability of their monitors. Their earplugs were firmly in place.

Raleigh thought about his great-grandfather, who in 1919 had flown toward the lights and never been seen again. His great-grandmother had taken her two-year-old son and moved to Boston, but despite the distance that she'd put between herself and the lights, she hadn't been able to keep them out of her thoughts. Her memories of the lights and her husband became the bedtime stories she told her son, who grew up dreaming about them. When he was twenty and skin cancer finally killed his mother, he hitchhiked all the way to Texas. He needed to hitchhike because the Great Depression continued to ravage the nation. Using his legs and his thumb was the only way he could afford to make the trip.

His name was Edward. His mother's story about his father's disappearance had so obsessed him from when he was a child that he was drawn to Rostov the way religious people are drawn to holy places. It took him three months to get there. When he finally arrived, his belt was cinched so tightly that it barely kept his pants up. His shoes had holes in them. His shirt was tattered. His face was browned by the sun.

The dry-goods store that Edward's mother had told him about was still in business—although barely, judging from the meager samples in the front window. A bell rang when he opened the door. A tired-looking, gray-haired man and woman looked questioningly at him from behind a counter. Despite their age, he could see the resemblance immediately.

"I'm your grandson," he announced.

They gaped. Before they could ask any questions, he said the thing he had wanted to say all his life.

"Tell me where to go to see the lights."

They gaped even more.

Edward helped at the dry-goods store. He also found part-time jobs, painting barns and repairing wooden sidewalks in exchange for new shoes, clothes, and the extra food his grandmother needed to prepare. In Boston, meat had been a luxury, but not in cattle country. His grandmother's beef and potatoes helped him regain the weight he'd lost on his trek.

Every night Edward borrowed his grandfather's battered Chevrolet pickup truck and drove out to see the lights—or to try to see them, because they didn't appear.

"Are you sure they're real?" he asked his grandparents. "Have *you* ever seen them?"

"Yes," his grandmother said, and his grandfather nodded in agreement. "It's been a while since we tried, though."

"My mother swore she saw them a lot."

"At first she couldn't see them, either," his grandfather explained. "It took quite a while."

"My father believed in them enough to risk his life," Edward said, beginning to feel angry, as if something were being hidden from him. "So where are they? Why can't *I* see them?"

"Some people just can't," his grandmother said matter-of-factly.

"Why not?"

"No one knows."

That left him feeling more exasperated than ever.

On the days when he couldn't find work, he hiked through the area where the lights were said to appear. He stood where his father had built the airfield during World War I. Weeds and grass filled the unpaved runway, the length of which was just barely visible. The adobe buildings that had functioned as hangars were piles of dirt. He studied the distant rim of black boulders that looked like huge cinders—the aptly named Badlands.

He stared to the south toward Mexico.

"No one ever found the wreckage of an airplane?" he asked his grandparents.

"Some of his former students tried. They flew fifty miles—all the way to Mexico. A couple of them actually flew *into* Mexico. They went back and forth in what they called grids, but no one ever found your father or his plane."

"But nobody just *disappears*."

"The wings were covered with linen and hardened by shellac. If the plane crashed and burned, the debris could have been blown away by the wind."

"And his body?"

"Coyotes. God bless him, John's bones could have been carried off."

"I want to see the lights."

"Maybe you're trying too hard."

The next day, Edward dug postholes on a ranch until he earned enough to buy a bottle of whiskey—something that wasn't easy to locate because even though Prohibition had ended four years earlier, Rostov had voted to remain "dry."

At dark Edward drove out to the old airfield, sat on the ground, opened the bottle, and began sipping. Until then the only alcohol he'd ever sampled was beer, but the chance of obtaining beer in Rostov turned out to be even slimmer than that of finding whiskey. Besides, he wanted something strong.

It burned his throat. He felt its heat go all the way to his stomach. He gagged and almost threw it up.

At least it acted more quickly than beer would have. Because he wasn't used to it, he didn't need much before he felt off balance, as if something in his skull were tilting. Soon his tongue felt thick. His eyes became heavy. The moon and stars went out of focus.

"Come on!" Edward shouted. "Let me see you!" His words were slurred. "I'm not trying hard anymore! I'm relaxed! *More than* relaxed!" He laughed giddily and took another sip. "Hell, I'm drunk. . . .

"Drunk as a . . . skunk . . .

"Damned . . . stinkin' . . . drunk."

He closed his eyes. Fought to open them. Closed them again.

And passed out.

The night brought a cool breeze that wavered Edward's hair and caressed his cheeks. He dreamed of being on a boat, floating on a current. His mind drifted, rising and falling.

He woke to the glare of the rising sun. But when he managed to lift his heavy eyelids, he saw darkness off to his right. The stars and the moon were still there, but mostly he saw darkness.

On his right.

On his left, the rising sun persisted, and when Edward lifted his painful head from the dirt on which he lay, he saw that the sun was, in fact, a floating ball of light.

Groggy, he watched it divide, becoming red and yellow. The two orbs dissolved into four, adding blue and green. They split into eight, adding orange, purple, brown, and a blinding silver. Pulsing closer, they grew larger, their shimmer more intense.

There was something else, some kind of sound he couldn't identify, a hiss or hum or possibly distant music, as if from a radio station that had faded almost beyond hearing.

Even though his mother had said that the lights had frightened her the first time she'd seen them, Edward hadn't expected to have the same reaction. After all, the lights had caused his mother and father to fall in love. If it hadn't been for the lights, Edward would never have been born. His father had been so mesmerized by the lights that he'd done everything possible to try to find where they came from.

But as the colors of the lights increased before him, dispelling the darkness, what Edward felt wasn't the fear his mother had described. It was worse than that.

It was terror.

His mother had been a fervent churchgoer. Each Sunday, she'd made Edward go with her, always staying at the back, coming in late and leaving early so that people wouldn't see the lesions on her face.

He recalled very little of those Sunday mornings except his impatience to go and play—and a particular sermon that the minister had delivered. The subject was Christ's transfiguration, a word that Edward, then ten years old, hadn't understood but that he asked his mother to repeat several times afterward until he memorized it—because the sermon had made an unnerving impression on him.

In the gospels, the minister had said, Christ took three of the apostles to the top of a mountain, where he transformed himself into his true radiance. His clothes became as brilliant as the sun. The light was so blinding that the apostles fell to the ground, lowering their eyes in fear. When they finally looked up again, Christ had changed back to human form.

"Rise," he told them. "Don't be afraid. Don't tell others about this vision."

The minister had used this passage to explain how glorious heaven would be, how brilliant and spellbinding. But that hadn't made any sense to Edward. How could something be both glorious and terrifying at the same time? It seemed to him that heaven should make someone want to rush toward it rather than fall to the ground in fear.

That story about Christ's blinding light gave Edward nightmares—perhaps because it merged with his mother's story about the lights and his father's disappearance. In years to come, he would often think about it. After his mother died, he even spoke to the minister about it, although the minister didn't seem to get his point, which was that it might not be so easy to tell the difference between good and evil. If a vision of goodness made the apostles afraid, was it possible that a vision of evil would make them walk toward it? That would be logical because evil was tempting. But in a sane world, shouldn't evil be terrifying and goodness tempting? Why was everything reversed?

"That's God's way of testing us," the minister said.

"But why do we need to be tested?"

"Because our first parents were tested and failed. We are their fallen children. We need to prove that we won't repeat their sin."

"The choice ought to be clearer," Edward persisted. "The story only tells me that it's hard to know the difference. If Christ showed the apostles a vision of heaven, shouldn't it have been so wonderful that he'd have urged them to spread the word? Why did he tell them to keep it a secret?"

"That passage isn't clear."

"How's this for a theory, Reverend? What if heaven's so radiant that it's *terrifying*? Maybe people shouldn't know what it's really like until they finally get there and it's too late to back out."

"I'll pray for your soul."

Now the brilliance of the lights made Edward as frightened as the apostles had been at the sight of Christ's heavenly radiance. He told himself that his reaction was wrong, that he ought to be entranced by the shimmering beauty he was finally seeing.

I came all this way and tried so hard to see you.

You're glorious. I ought to feel awestruck.

Maybe his fear was a sign of how truly *good* the lights were, he thought. But then he was struck by something more than awe.

The lights changed. Clouds of the darkest thunderstorm suddenly churned within them. Lightning flashed at their core. As thunder punished his ears, he saw a figure amid the clouds, a young man in a uniform who looked like the photographs Edward had seen of his father. The man held out his hand, beckoning for Edward to step into the clouds and join him.

Edward screamed. Turning, he ran.

Without realizing it, he charged along the airstrip that his father had built and had flown from countless times, years ago. He stumbled, falling on stones, scraping his jaw. He scrambled to his feet and ran harder.

He heard a wail and realized that it was coming from him, that he couldn't stop screaming.

The next thing he knew, people were all around him, grabbing him, trying to calm him. He'd raced all the way back to town and had been so frenzied that he hadn't realized how far he'd gone. Standing in the middle of the main street, he was surrounded by townspeople, most of whom wore nightclothes and held lanterns or flashlights.

"Edward, what's the matter?" his grandfather asked in alarm. "What happened to you?"

"Clouds. Lightning," Edward blurted.

"What's he talking about?" someone asked. "Look at the stars. The sky's perfectly clear."

"Lights. Clouds in the lights."

"I smell whiskey."

"Thunder. Saw a man in the clouds."

"... reeks of it."

"My father."

"Look at the blood on his chin. He's so drunk he fell down."

"Edward, where'd yozu get the whiskey?" his grandfather demanded.

"Good's terrifying," Edward blurted. "So bright . . ."

"Too drunk to make sense."

"Where's my truck, Edward? Did you wreck my truck?" his grandfather asked sternly.

"Evil feels welcoming," Edward raved.

His grandfather shook him. "Answer me, Edward. Where's my truck?"

"Well, I've got better things to do than waste a good night's sleep on a drunk," someone said. "Come on, Sarah. Let's go back to bed."

"Saw my father," Edward persisted.

"*Damn it*, Edward, just be honest and tell me if you wrecked my truck."

The next morning, Edward walked to where he'd left the truck, near the old airstrip. For a long time, he stared toward the southern horizon. Had he been so drunk that he'd hallucinated?

No, he didn't believe that. He was convinced that the whiskey had long since worn off by the time he'd seen the lights.

I wasn't drunk when it happened. I know it! I know what I saw.

He started the truck, drove back to town, left it outside the dry-goods store, and hitchhiked two hundred miles to El Paso, where he joined the Army.

From that moment he had one ambition—to read the reports his father had written about the lights. Edward had no doubt that those reports would be hard to obtain, but he was certain of something else—that the son of a revered World War I ace would advance quickly in his military career.

He judged correctly. It turned out that many officers of importance had served with his father during the expedition into Mexico, and later in France and Germany. By 1942, after Pearl Harbor and America's entry into World War II, Edward had risen quickly to the rank of captain in Military Intelligence, a branch he'd pursued because it gave him the best chance of learning where his father's reports were located.

On a rainy October afternoon, after having searched in Washington, D.C., and at the Presidio in San Francisco, Edward uncovered hints that took him back to El Paso's Fort Bliss. From a disintegrating box in a musty Quonset hut filled with hundreds of similar long-forgotten boxes, he withdrew documents that his father had written twenty-four years earlier.

They were yellow with age. The words looked painfully typed. The ink on his father's signature had turned from blue to brown.

Edward read the reports, then read them again. And again. The text was revealing, especially the section in which his father maintained that the lights had somehow caused his student pilots to attack one another in night training. His father had become convinced that somehow the lights could be used as a weapon.

64

Anita had an IV line leading into her right arm. Prongs from an oxygen tube filled her nostrils. Behind her, a beeping monitor indicated her pulse, blood pressure, and heart rhythm.

"The doctor says you need surgery, but you're going to be okay," Brent told her, sitting next to her bed.

She managed to nod and raise her eyelids slightly, groggily attempting to see him. Her dark skin was only slightly less pale.

"The bullet broke your arm," Brent continued. "The doctor says that's why the pain feels so deep. The bone needs to be set."

Again Anita managed a slight nod.

"They're going to take you to the operating room now," Brent said. "When you wake up, I'll be here. That might not be the most thrilling promise. Maybe I'm the last person you want to see. All the same, like it or not, when you wake up, I'll be here."

Anita tried to raise her uninjured arm.

"Save your strength," Brent said.

She reached weakly for his hand.

Brent held it.

"You did damned good today," he told her. "You never stopped trying. You never gave up. I promise—you'll win an Emmy. You deserve it."

Her hand drooped. After easing it onto the bed, Brent heard footsteps behind him. Two nurses entered, ready to wheel her to the operating room.

He went out to the echoing corridor, where hospital visitors gave him troubled looks as they passed him. His torn coat sleeve flopped at his side. His hair was rumpled and dusty. Dirt and blood smeared his suit.

His producer waited for him. "You really want to go

on the air looking like that? You'll scare the hell out of some of your viewers."

"Good. Let them realize what it takes to get a story."

They walked quickly toward the elevator.

"Did you see the video I got on that camera?" Brent asked.

"Dynamite. We're editing it now."

"I'll do a commentary. We could use sections of it tonight, then run all the footage as a one-hour special." Brent pressed the elevator's down button. "The other stations won't come near us in the ratings."

"How are we going to connect the lights with what the guard did?"

"We don't need to. Run the stories back to back. Viewers will make the connection on their own. We won't be accused of misrepresenting. Get me to the viewing area. I have a feeling this story's about to become even more sensational."

"Sharon's anchoring the show at the moment," The producer braced himself as if he expected an outburst.

Brent nodded. "Why not? I've been hogging the camera. She deserves more airtime."

"That's a surprising answer, coming from you."

"One thing Anita made me realize is, sometimes two people can get a better story."

Brent looked down the hallway toward where Anita's gurney appeared, the nurses wheeling her from the room.

"Is she really going to be okay?" the producer asked.

"The bullet didn't just break her arm. It shattered bones," Brent told him. "The doctor warned me that he might not be able to save it."

65

In the gathering darkness, Page and Tori climbed into the Cessna. Behind them, the airport's office had a light over the door. Other lights gleamed through the windows. Page was careful not to look in that direction. Human eyes needed thirty minutes to adjust fully to the dark. Bright light could ruin night vision in an instant, with the result that another thirty minutes would be required.

The only color of light that didn't compromise night vision was red. As a consequence, the two flashlights Page kept in his flight bag came with a choice of lenses, clear or red. He switched to the latter and used a cord to hang the flashlight around his neck. Tori did the same.

In the dark, human eyes had difficulty seeing anything that was straight ahead. For that reason, Page focused on murky objects to the right and left, doing a slow scan to make sure it was safe to switch on the engine.

"Clear!" he shouted through his open window, warning anyone in the vicinity to stay away.

He turned the ignition key, and the engine roared to life. He used his left thumb to press the radio button on the Cessna's controls, speaking into his headset's microphone, addressing any active planes in the area.

"Rostov traffic, Cessna Four Three Alpha is taxiing to one five."

He tested the brakes, did another scan of the shadowy area around him, and guided the plane along the yellow taxiway line.

"Tori, the way you answered that reporter's question ..."

"I told you this afternoon. For the first time, I feel as if I understand you. Maybe I should have asked to go along with you in your police car so I could get an idea of what you go through each day. The terrible things people do to one another."

"I didn't talk about them because I didn't want you to feel what *I* do."

"Thank you for trying to shield me." She fell silent for a moment, then spoke again. "Whatever the cancer doctors say after my operation on Tuesday, whether my life is going to be short or long, I can't imagine not sharing it with you. And I don't want you to stop being a policeman. You're too good at it. Now quit talking and get this crate in the air."

Page taxied past the indistinct shapes of airplanes in the tie-down area and reached the entrance to the runway. The final checklist helped him to calm his emotions and concentrate on the task ahead.

He radioed his intentions, then increased speed along the runway. At fifty-five knots, he pulled back the yoke. The plane rose through the darkness.

Looking down, he noticed a steady stream of headlights moving toward the blocked-off observation area. The vehicles were parking along the road in a line much longer than the one the evening before. The viewing area had floodlights pointed toward the concrete barriers, presumably to emphasize that the place was off-limits. The lights from three helicopters showed where they hovered, keeping a safe distance from one another. Listening to their radio communications, Page learned that they were television news choppers.

"A wonderful clear sky," Tori said. "Look at the glow from the streets and houses in Rostov. And there—headlights from cars driving in from Mexico. I can actually count six pairs."

Page banked the Cessna in a slow, gentle circle, using the floodlights at the observation area as a reference.

"How high do you plan to go?" Tori asked.

"Enough to get above everything," he answered.

"Sounds like the way to run a life."

66

The concrete barriers were wide enough for Medrano to stand on. Raising his left hand to shield his eyes from the glaring floodlights, he watched in dismay as the crowd got larger.

"This area's closed!" he shouted through a bullhorn. "Turn around! Drive back to town!"

Amid the clamor of the crowd, someone yelled back at him, "This road's public property! My taxes paid for it! I've got a right to stay here as long as I want!"

"It isn't safe!" Medrano responded. "I'm telling you, go back to town!"

"You know where *you* can go?" somebody shouted. "To hell!"

People stretched to grip the top of the barriers and climb over.

"What is it you don't want us to see?" a woman demanded. "What are you hiding?"

"Turn off those damned floodlights!" a man complained. "They hurt my eyes!"

"Yeah, those aren't the kind of lights we came for!"

No sooner did police officers pull one group of people off the barricades than another group tried to climb them.

Three helicopters roared above the viewing area, keeping a distance from one another, aiming their landing lights and exterior television cameras toward the commotion.

I don't have anywhere near enough officers, Medrano thought, surveying the chaos.

Somebody yelled, "If you won't let us over those barricades, we'll go around them! My wife's got Alzheimer's! We're here for the miracle!"

Medrano watched helplessly as hundreds of people headed down the road and veered toward a field on the right. But some went in the opposite direction, toward the abandoned military airfield, and that was one place Medrano definitely couldn't let anyone go.

"Stop them from getting onto that airbase!" he shouted to his officers. "They'll blow themselves up!"

Jumping from the barricade, Medrano bent his knees as he landed on the road's gravel shoulder. Breathless, he straightened and ran toward the base. There, a man and a furiously barking German shepherd warned people not to climb the barbed-wire fence.

Suddenly the floodlights failed. People shouted in alarm. As darkness enveloped him, all Medrano saw were the residual images of the glaring lights imprinted on his eyes.

Somebody must have sabotaged the generator! he thought.

But it wasn't only the generator. Automobile engines and headlights suddenly failed. In place of the helicopters' hectic thumping, the only sound from the air was the whistle of slowing rotors.

Medrano flinched from the sound of a massive crash. It took him a stunned moment to realize that one of the helicopters had plummeted to the ground. The impact echoed from the field on the opposite side of the road, accompanied by a soaring fireball.

A second crash reverberated from the same direction. Medrano crouched sightlessly, worried about where the third crash would occur.

On the road. There wasn't one impact but several as the final helicopter dropped onto cars, crumpling and shredding metal as rotors tore into asphalt. An explosion knocked him backward.

67

Raleigh watched the chaos on the monitors. The night-vision capability of the outside cameras made the panicked crowd have a surreal greenish glow.

Did that cop really believe all he needed to do was put up concrete barriers and everyone would stay away?

Floodlights had gone dark. Cars and their headlights had become inoperative. Helicopters had fallen from the sky. Just one explanation could account for all that—a massive electromagnetic pulse, similar to one from a nuclear blast, had sent a power surge through all the electronic equipment in the viewing area, destroying it.

Exactly as predicted, Raleigh thought. He'd reinforced the outside cameras and the entire underground facility with multiple layers of electromagnetic shielding. The office behind him had three times the amount that the rest of the building had.

"Sir, the readings are becoming more intense," a member of his team said, watching a computer screen.

Despite his earplugs, Raleigh thought he felt a slight vibration. Or was he imagining it?

He glanced toward the shielded door to the command center.

"You're channeling the signal through the dish above us?" he asked.

"Yes, sir. The signal's being relayed to the observatory and then up to a satellite. The satellite is beaming the signal to the White Sands Missile Range. But I don't know if the circuits can handle this much power. We've never tested them at this level before."

68

July 23, 1942.

"Anybody here know what nuclear fission is?" the general in charge of the emergency intelligence meeting asked.

Like the other officers at the long metal table, Capt. Edward Raleigh did not.

"I'm not sure *I* do, either," the general admitted. "Apparently if you smash two sections of uranium together, and you do it with enough force, you can create a bomb with more power than anybody's ever imagined. Some scientists argue that the explosion could set off a chain reaction that would destroy the world, but most conclude that it could be controlled to the extent of vaporizing a city."

"General, with all due respect," a colonel asked, "you're serious about this?"

"Three years ago, Einstein wrote a letter to the president alerting him that tests had validated the theory. Apparently Einstein's contacts in the European scientific community warned him that the Germans were stockpiling uranium, and moving aggressively forward with nuclear-fission research. At that time, of course, we weren't in the war, but now we are, and the president's about to order a top-secret program to create a nuclear weapon as soon as possible.

"The scientist in charge will be Robert Oppenheimer. He was a Red sympathizer during the '30s, so the FBI's doing a thorough background check. Our job will be to maintain security at a place called Los Alamos in New Mexico. It's marked on the map behind me."

A major went to the map and indicated the exact spot. "Santa Fe and a few other towns are a half-day's drive away. Otherwise there's nothing but ranches in the area."

"Which we're confiscating," the general said. "Los Alamos is a boy's camp in the middle of nowhere. Oppenheimer went there when he was a kid. It's on top of a mesa, with one road up and one road down, easily contained. Oppenheimer's thinking about using that mesa as the principal site for designing the bomb. *We're* going to make sure nobody eavesdrops."

"Sir, there might be another out-of-the-way place that's equally suitable," Edward took the opportunity to say.

The general looked unhappy about being interrupted. "And where would that place be?" he asked impatiently.

"West Texas. Outside a town called Rostov. Nothing's there except millions of acres of ranchland. We built an airstrip there before we entered the last war. It was a good place to hide the pilots we were training so the Germans wouldn't suspect how actively we were preparing to help the Allies."

"Oppenheimer's got his mind set on Los Alamos."

"Rostov may offer another advantage," Edward pressed. "There might be fission already occurring there."

The general began to look interested. "Continue, Captain."

Edward focused his remarks so that they related exclusively to nuclear fission. He described his father's reports and concluded by saying, "There's no doubt the lights are powerful. Ultimately my mother died from the skin cancer they gave her. One theory is that they're caused by radioactive elements in the soil. If the rays can be channeled, and used as a weapon . . ."

The general held up a hand, cutting him off. "Put it in writing. I'll submit it to Oppenheimer."

"Yes, sir."

But Edward knew what happened to reports.

A week later, during the next meeting, the general announced that Los Alamos would be the primary site for designing the atomic bomb.

Edward contained his disappointment.

Then the general surprised him by adding, "The Germans are pursuing the development of a second major weapon."

The room became silent.

"It may be related to nuclear fission, or possibly it's based on a totally different principle. All we know is that since Germany invaded Norway in 1940, they've sent a disproportionate number of soldiers there—a half-million occupiers in a country of two million people. Many of those soldiers are in a position that strategically makes no sense—surrounding a small valley in the middle of Norway. The valley's called Hessdalen."

The general looked directly at Edward. "Reports indicate that those soldiers are providing security for scientists investigating strange lights that appear there."

"Lights, sir?" Edward tried not to show the emotion building inside him.

"With effects that apparently range from mass hallucination to religious rapture. Some people went blind from looking at them. Others became violent—even murderous. Still others developed cancerous lesions. There's no telling if any of it is real, but Germany's committed to exploring those lights as a possible weapon, and once they get interested in something, you know damned well we need to do the same. Even if the lights are bogus, all Hitler needs to do is start the rumor that he's figured out how to use them as a weapon and deploy it anywhere he wants. Sometimes psychological warfare can win more battles than tanks."

A colonel spoke up: "Sir, are these lights similar to the west Texas phenomena that Captain Raleigh was talking about?"

"That's the conclusion the president came to. If Hitler's using them as smoke and mirrors to distract us from his nuclear-fission program, we can do the same thing. Captain Raleigh, you're ordered to take an exploratory team to whatever this town is in west Texas."

"It's called Rostov, sir."

"To prove how apparently serious we are, two of Oppenheimer's researchers will accompany you. They'll send equipment from the University of Chicago. The Army Corps of Engineers—which is building the Los Alamos facility—will contribute a dozen men. There'll also be a rifle platoon to make a show of providing security. If it turns out there *is* something useful about these lights, so much the better, but I'm willing to bet that the main thing we'll accomplish is to drive Hitler crazy by making him think we're not only committed to this project but actually making progress. As a bonus, you'll act as a diversion from what's happening at Los Alamos."

Before the end of the month, Edward's team flew on a C-47 military transport plane to Fort Bliss, then drove ten trucks of men and equipment to Rostov. As soon as they reached the old airfield, they set up tents and unpacked electronic instruments, activating a generator to provide an independent source of power.

Oppenheimer's researchers scanned the ground with Geiger counters but couldn't find any trace of radioactivity.

"You'll need to scan a lot more ground than that." Edward pointed past the Badlands. "The lights come from way over there."

"I hope we made a big enough fuss about getting here," one of the researchers said. "German spies keep watch on Oppenheimer and anybody associated with him. Since we're here, word is bound to get back to Germany." The gangly, bespectacled man scanned the featureless horizon. The only things in sight were two jackrabbits and five scattered cows trying to eat the meager grass. "Hell, *nobody* would bother to come here if it wasn't desperately important."

The sunset was spectacular. As darkness thickened, the air cooled, making them cross their arms across their chests.

"So, where are the lights?" a soldier asked.

"They don't always come out. Give them time," Edward answered.

"Anybody got a smoke?"

An engineer went into the sizable main tent and leaned his watch toward one of the glowing instruments. "It's 9:20. This has been a long day. If something doesn't happen by 10 o'clock, I'm heading for my cot."

"You might need to give the lights more time than that," Edward said. "They don't exactly appear on a schedule."

"Well, wake me if you see Hitler's new secret weapon. Not that it'll be easy to sleep with that generator droning."

"And the static coming from that directional radio," a researcher said. "Doesn't matter what frequency I use. That's all I receive."

"No, there's something in the background. But I can barely hear it."

Somebody chuckled. "Probably a Mexican radio station playing mariachi music."

"Look, what's that over there?"

"A shooting star. Wow. Haven't seen one since I was a kid. I've been living in the city for so long, I almost forgot what they look like."

"There's another one."

"No, that one's not a shooting star. It's too low on the horizon, and it's lasting too long."

"A bunch of them. They look like skyrockets. I bet we're seeing fireworks from across the border. Does anybody know if it's a Mexican holiday?"

"Hey, whoever's in that tent, stop turning up the volume on that radio. The static's hurting my ears."

"Nobody's in the tent," one of the researchers said. "The static's getting louder on its own."

"And the fireworks are getting brighter," a soldier said. "Look at all those colors. They remind me of the Northern Lights. I saw them once when I was a kid and my dad took me camping on Lake Michigan."

"But these are to the south. And they're awfully low on the horizon," an engineer reminded him. He turned and stared toward the tent. "Are you sure nobody's screwing with that radio? Now the static's louder than the generator."

Abruptly the static ended.

So did the shooting stars or the skyrockets or the Northern Lights—or whatever they were. The horizon turned completely dark.

So did the glowing instruments in the tent. The generator stopped droning.

"What the hell happened to everything?"

"Gentlemen," Edward said, "welcome to the lights."

69

Page frowned when something changed on the ground behind the Cessna. The glow of the spotlights abruptly went out.

Tori noticed it, also. "Something happened behind us."

He banked the aircraft to the left and returned in the direction from which they'd come. But the landscape no longer appeared the same. "Where's the observation area? I don't see the floodlights."

"Not only that," Tori said, "I don't see any headlights. There was a whole line of traffic a couple of minutes ago. Now the road's invisible. And the helicopters—I don't see *their* lights anymore, either."

"Their radio transmissions have stopped," Page told her, puzzled.

Below them, a fireball suddenly illuminated the darkness. Two other explosions followed. Startled, Page saw the twisting impact of a helicopter crashing onto vehicles at the side of the road, its distant rumble reaching him. Huge chunks of metal flipped along the ground. The spreading flames revealed specks of people racing away in panic.

"God help them," Tori murmured.

Shock waves bumped the plane.

"Maybe we should head back," Page managed to say.

"No, it can't be a coincidence. Somehow what's happening down there has to be connected to the lights. We came up here to do something—if we don't finish this now, I don't think I'll ever have the strength to try it again." Tori paused. "I want to find the truth."

"Whatever you want," Page assured her. "We're in this together."

"Yes." Tori savored the word. "Together."

Avoiding the updraft of the flames and debris, Page flew south toward the murky horizon.

"What are those dark lumps ahead?" Tori asked.

"The Badlands."

Tori pointed. "Something's beyond them."

"I don't see anything."

"Faint red lights. Three of them."

Page concentrated. "I still don't see them."

"They're getting brighter."

"Where are they coming from? Give me a heading."

Tori looked at the indicator. "One hundred and forty degrees."

"All I see is blackness."

"They're dividing. They're even brighter now. They're changing from red to blue and green and yellow. How can you possibly not see them?"

"Maybe if I went lower."

"They're dividing again."

Page eased back on the throttle. The aircraft gradually descended, the sinking, floating sensation reminding him of what he felt when he saw the lights.

Except that *this* time, he didn't see them.

"So many now. They're like a rainbow rippling across the ground," Tori said, her voice strange. "They're moving toward the observation area."

"I'm as open as I can possibly be. Why can't I see them?"

As Page descended farther toward the darkness, all at once he *did* see the lights. It was as if a veil had dissolved, but the colors weren't rippling the way Tori had described.

They writhed in anger.

"Something's wrong." Page shoved in the throttle and raised the nose.

A yellow filament shot up, like a flare from a solar storm. It lengthened until it snapped free, condensing into a twisting mass that sped higher.

Climbing, Page banked to the right.

The light kept coming.

He banked to the left.

The light did the same.

Transparent, iridescent, pulsing, it suddenly filled the cockpit. Page could no longer hear the plane's engine. Instead he heard a rushing wind. Shades of yellow swirled around him. Images flickered.

He saw an aquarium filled with wavering plants and a model of a shipwreck, but the plants were actually cuttlefish, their tentacles resembling ferns, and parts of the shipwreck were more cuttlefish that had cleverly camouflaged themselves to match their surroundings.

And now his father was pointing toward more and more cuttlefish, and his mother, who would die from breast cancer within the year, was smiling because her husband and son were getting along for a change.

And Page heard a voice within the rushing air. It was his father.

"Sometimes we need to learn to see in a new way."

The engine stopped.

The yellow vanished.

Without warning, Page found himself in darkness, his night vision blunted by the residual image of the light. He strained his eyes, desperate to see out through the canopy. With relief, he found that the difference between the glow of the stars and moon above him and the darkness below him was enough for him at least to identify the horizon.

The ground straight ahead seemed darker than the areas around it. Lumpy.

Page frantically realized that, trying to escape the pursuing light, he'd become disoriented and turned the aircraft toward the Badlands. The silence was dismaying. Normally his headphones muffled the sound of the engine, reducing it to a drone. But now he heard nothing.

The instrument panel was dark. The radio was dead.

His father had told him repeatedly what to do in case of an engine failure. The first thing was to put the aircraft into a glide. At a speed of sixty-five knots, the Cessna would lose a thousand feet for every nine thousand feet that it glided. In theory, this provided enough time to choose a location for an emergency touchdown—ideally a field, or even a road. During the day, the options would be visible, but in the dark, it wasn't possible to know if a stretch of blackness was grass or rocks or a chasm.

At least the moon and the stars made the dark lumps of the Badlands look different from the flatness around them. Page kept the Cessna gliding at what he could only estimate was sixty-five knots. With the airspeed indicator not visible, he needed to rely on the feel of the aircraft, on thousands of hours of judging how it handled at various speeds.

They continued to drop.

"Tori, make sure your seat belt's tight! Just before we touch down, open your door! The impact of landing might twist the fuselage and wedge the door shut!"

He decided not to add, *And trap you inside.*

To minimize the possibility of a fire, Page twisted the fuel selector dial to the off position, sealing the fuel lines. The closer they got to the ground, the more his eyes worked sufficiently for him to distinguish the lumps of the Badlands.

Tori saw them, too.

"Will we clear them?" she shouted.

"That's the plan."

"A damned good one."

The Cessna glided lower. Time stretched. A minute felt like forever.

"My skin feels burned," Tori said.

Page frowned, touching his cheek. "So does mine."

"I saw my father," she said.

"What?"

"When the light swirled around us, I saw my father. I was a little girl. He was dragging me to the car. I hit him, trying to get away so I could look at the lights."

"I saw *my* father, too."

The dark ground sped closer.

"I love you," Tori said.

"I love *you*."

The boulders loomed.

"Brace yourself."

Skimming over the Badlands, Page thought he felt a wheel strike something. At once the uneven darkness was gone, replaced by what seemed to be grassland. But anything could be under the Cessna—rocks that would snap the wheels and flip the aircraft, or a fence that could do the same thing.

They were over the old military airbase, Page realized. Floating, he tried to hold off landing as long as possible, not only because that made for a theoretically softer impact but because as long as they were still in the air, they remained alive.

He couldn't help thinking about the unexploded bombs below him.

70

Blood dripped from Halloway's nostrils. He stopped dancing long enough to wipe the back of his right hand across his mouth. Seeing the red liquid on his knuckles, he felt troubled, but only for a moment. *That* blood didn't matter any more than the blood trickling from his ears did.

The woman in his arms mattered.

The glass of vodka and orange juice, always full—that mattered.

Most of all, the music mattered. Halloway remembered his youthful dreams of becoming a rock star, of having the world at his feet, of being able to give orders and do anything he wanted. He'd practiced with his guitar until his fingers had calluses. He'd written song after song. He'd followed rock bands from city to city, doing his best to be indispensable, buying drugs for them, getting girls for them, trying to persuade them to listen to his songs and maybe record them and maybe even let him sing in the background because good buddy Earl deserved repayment for all the favors he'd done.

Pretty soon, *he'd* be the guy people followed and got girls and drugs for.

But one city became another and another, just as one band became another and another, and one day Halloway realized that nobody was ever going to record his songs, just as they damned sure weren't going to let him sing. What was he, some kind of moron, that he didn't grasp that they were laughing at him and using him?

He went back to Providence, worked as a busboy in a restaurant, got his girlfriend pregnant, and joined the Army. The next thing he knew, he was killing people instead of singing to them.

The sadness of his life spilled over him as he danced to the heartbreaking music. His eyes blurred with tears. When he used his right hand to wipe them, he managed to see that there was a lot more blood on his knuckles than there'd been a minute ago. Frowning, he used his *left* hand to wipe his eyes. Seeing red liquid on those knuckles, he realized that blood was streaming from his tear ducts as well as his ears and his nose, but that didn't matter, either—because then it occurred to him that his eyes were blurred for another reason.

He smelled something other than the cinnamon hair of the woman. Coughing, he looked toward the hallway beyond the open door, but he couldn't actually see the hallway.

A haze filled it.

71

Lockhart piled more dead grass and tumbleweeds on the fire he'd built over the air-circulation pipes. The area around him blazed from spotlights that had been activated at sunset, casting a grotesque glare over the huge dishes. The lights were so powerful that he felt their heat.

Or maybe it was the heat from the fire, which rose about five feet into the air now. After shooting every surveillance camera Lockhart could find, he'd searched the area for another way to get into the complex.

Damn it, the place is airtight, he'd thought.

Immediately he'd realized that of course the facility couldn't *possibly* be airtight. There had to be pipes to pump the air in and out. Otherwise people inside would suffocate.

In the end, Lockhart discovered three sets of them, hidden among the dishes.

He didn't have matches. Muzzle flashes from his M4 had done just fine, however. First he'd piled dead grass and tumbleweeds over the pipes. Then, shooting into them, he'd had no trouble starting fires.

The trick was to keep hurrying from one fire to another, constantly adding more brush. It quickly became obvious which pipes were which. Smoke was sucked into one and blown upward from another. Even though the night air was pleasantly cool, the effort soaked his shirt with sweat, but he'd never felt more satisfied by exertion.

Thinking of the corpses in the truck and the threat the bastard inside was to the mission, he inwardly chanted, *Come on, baby, burn.*

He imagined the crazy prick trying to breathe through a wet towel while he coughed his guts out. Sooner or later, the outside door would open. Lockhart had a distant view of it as he rushed from fire to fire, focusing exclusively on the intake vents, throwing on more dead brush. Lumber left over from a construction project made the flames dance higher. He kept looking at the door. The moment Halloway showed himself, Lockhart would teach him why it was a bad idea to ruin things for the colonel.

The fires roared. But Lockhart now heard a louder sound. Staring toward the west, he saw the lights of a swiftly approaching Black Hawk helicopter. *Finally*, he thought. *The colonel said the equipment would arrive that would get me through that door.*

He grabbed his M4 and ran. The landing pad had been destroyed by the wreckage of the exploding chopper. He stood under a floodlight and waved both arms to get the pilot's attention, then motioned toward the area just beyond the open gates. Soon the Black Hawk settled onto the lane, its nose pointed through the gates toward the steel door of the concrete-block shed.

"What took that chopper down?" the pilot shouted as the Black Hawk's rotors whistled to a stop.

His face tightened as Lockhart explained.

A special-ops team leaped from the side hatch, assault rifles in hand.

"You're telling me that truck has corpses piled in the back?" the pilot demanded. Seeing three coyotes leap from the truck, things dangling from their mouths, he shook his head in disgust.

"The colonel said you'd bring equipment we could use to get through that door," Lockhart said. "What have you got? Claymores? Detonator cord?"

"For this guy, I've got something better."

A minute later, the chopper lifted off, hovered a hundred feet above the lane, and fired a rocket.

From a safe distance, Lockhart watched with joy. He'd wanted something to get him through the door. But this was so much better. With a satisfying roar, the rocket blew the whole damned concrete shed into pieces.

72

Brent stood on the motor home, describing the chaos of the crowd below him. Mindful of what had happened the night before, he'd almost decided to do his commentary from the ground or from something modestly higher.

But how the hell would that look? I'm supposed to be the toughest reporter in the business, and I do my spot on a picnic table?

Even so, every time the crowd jostled the motor home and forced him to correct his balance, he remembered what it had felt like to plummet to the ground. No camera operator had enough of Anita's determination to be willing to get on the roof with him. The producer had finally put a remote camera up there. It and the handheld cameras among the crowd, as well as the nose camera on the chopper, would provide ample coverage. But there wasn't any question where the viewers' attention would be—with the guy risking his life on the motor home's roof while all the other television reporters looked like wimps, doing their spots from the ground.

When the floodlights went out, Brent made a dramatic moment of it.

"Did somebody sabotage the lights?" he asked before realizing that his own lights had gone out, also—not to mention the lights on the cameras, the cars, and the choppers.

Jesus, don't tell me I'm off the air.

Blinded by the sudden darkness, he groped toward the ladder at the side of the motor home. People banged against the vehicle, shouting in panic. He wavered, reached the ladder, started down, and froze as helicopters plummeted to the ground, bursting into flames.

Shrapnel flying past him, Brent hugged the ladder and waited for the shock waves to subside. His eyes were level with the motor home's roof. He looked directly over the concrete barrier toward the field beyond the viewing area.

A glow approached.

At first Brent thought it was the residual image that the broadcast lights had imprinted on his eyes. But then he realized that what he saw stretched a hundred yards from right to left. The glow got bigger and closer, so strong that it dispelled the darkness, a tidal wave of colors rushing angrily across the grassland toward him.

Maybe the microphone is still working!

He spoke frantically into it. "Tonight this reporter is seeing the most powerful manifestation yet of the Rostov lights, stretching across my field of vision and approaching the crowd that has gathered here."

The glow became harsh.

"Lightning appears to be flashing inside it! The effect on the spectators is tremendous."

People in the crowd wept, wailed, and prayed. But the sounds they made weren't loud enough to shut out the growing hum of the lights speeding toward them.

"The air's getting hotter!" Brent shouted. "Grass is catching fire! Wait a minute, something's racing from the lights! The microphone's almost too hot to hold! My face is . . ."

He screamed.

73

When the Black Hawk blew the concrete shed apart, Lockhart and the assault team whistled in approval. A hole gaped, pointing the way downward.

"Now let's toast the son of a bitch!" Lockhart said.

Without warning, all the floodlights went off, plunging the area into darkness. Tensing, he told himself it was only because of the damage the explosion had inflicted. But before the chopper could land, its lights went off, also.

So did its engine.

Abruptly losing altitude, it walloped fifty feet onto the ground, rotors whistling, skids snapping. The only illumination was from the fires.

No, I'm wrong, Lockhart thought. To the southeast, where the abandoned military base was located, a glow attracted his attention. Even with his eyes straining to adjust to the darkness, it was impossible to ignore.

"What the hell is that?" a member of the special-ops team shouted.

"I don't know, but it's getting brighter! And it's coming this way!"

"Hit the ground!"

For an instant, Lockhart thought it was a missile streaking toward them, but as he landed on his chest, he realized it was a beam of light. The light was composed of spinning colors—red, green, yellow, blue. It shot from the horizon, hissed across the ground, and radiated heat as it passed over him. He smelled smoke from his hair and swatted out embers.

Throwing sparks, the light struck a satellite dish that was tilted sideways in the direction of the airbase. At once the light was redirected so that it rocketed upward from a dish pointed toward the sky. It reminded Lockhart of

World War II movies in which powerful spotlights searched the sky for enemy bombers making a night raid.

Though it was only one beam of light, the multicolored radiance hurt his eyes. It soared higher, stretching toward heaven until it reached something up there and threw off sparks before it suddenly blazed on a downward angle, streaking toward something on the ground far away to the northwest. It left a tube of pulsing light that continued to crackle over the ground and pointed upward from the dishes.

"I'm on fire!" somebody yelled. His teammates hurried to swat at the man's flaming clothes.

Lockhart held his hands over his ears. The beam of light hissed and crackled, but there was another sound—static that might have been a hum that might have been high-pitched music, threatening to split his eardrums.

74

July 16, 1945.

Just before dawn, the first atomic bomb was detonated outside Alamogordo in remote southern New Mexico. As the blinding, mushroom-shaped fireball rose thirty-eight thousand feet into the air and burned ten thousand times more fiercely than the exterior of the sun, the project's director, Robert Oppenheimer, recited a passage from the *Bhagavad Gita* in which God reveals his true, awesome, terrifying form to a disciple.

"'If the radiance of a thousand suns were to burst at once into the sky, that would be like the splendor of the mighty one,'" Oppenheimer quoted. "'Now I am become Death, destroyer of worlds.'"

At the same time, all telephone and radio messages ceased to be acknowledged by or sent from the military airbase outside Rostov, Texas, two hundred and fifty miles southeast of Alamogordo. Of particular concern was the status of the facility *beneath* the airbase, where research on an alternative weapon of mass destruction had been in progress since 1943.

After six hours of attempts to reestablish communication, the Army sent a P-40 Warhawk fighter plane on a reconnaissance mission from Fort Bliss. It arrived at 2 in the afternoon. Flying over the airfield, the pilot reported no activity whatsoever.

"I see open hangars. Trucks and aircraft at the side of the runway. A B-24's at the end of the runway, looking as if it's about to take off, but the propellers aren't moving. In fact, *nothing's* moving. I don't see any people."

Ordered to land and investigate, the pilot banked into a final approach. At two hundred feet, he finally did see something moving—a man in uniform staggering down the runway's centerline. The pilot performed an emergency go-around and watched the man in uniform continue staggering until he collapsed at the end of the runway.

After landing, the pilot did a quick scan of the area but still didn't see any people among the motionless trucks and aircraft. He rushed to the man he'd seen collapse. The man was semiconscious, moaning. His uniform had a colonel's insignia and was covered with blood. His face was burned. Identification in a pocket revealed that his name was Edward Raleigh.

The pilot ran to a truck, hoping to use it to drive Colonel Raleigh out of the sun, but the truck refused to start. Every other vehicle also refused to start. The best he could do was give the colonel elementary first aid and struggle to carry him into a hangar. There the pilot found the corpses of numerous military personnel, all of whom were covered with blood from their ears, noses, tear ducts, mouths, and other orifices. Some faces had hemorrhaged so badly that their skin had disintegrated.

The corpses were in positions that suggested a desperate effort to take cover, huddling against walls or aircraft or equipment. At least twelve soldiers seemed to have shot one another. Moans led the pilot to a few survivors, all of whom were bleeding, semiconscious, and delirious.

When the pilot radioed his report, he was told to stand by. Ten minutes later, an authoritative voice told him, "Stay where you are. Try to help Colonel Raleigh. Do not go anywhere else on the base. Two C-45s are being dispatched with a medical team. After they arrive, return to Fort Bliss and report immediately for debriefing. With that exception, do not discuss what you've seen with anyone. I repeat—do not go *anywhere* else on the base."

While the first C-45 did in fact carry medical personnel, the second brought a security team whose purpose was to investigate the integrity of the underground facility. A similar scene of devastation awaited them: most of the men dead from burns and hemorrhages, a few survivors moaning in pain. Again some victims seemed to have shot one another. Blood covered the walls.

Within three days, the airbase was shut down. The official explanation for the deaths was that a massive fuel leak had caused a devastating fire. The planes and other equipment were removed to various other bases. The entrance to the underground facility was sealed. Signs warned trespassers about unexploded bombs.

75

Lockhart and the special-ops team hurried away from the beam of light. Clutching their M4s, they reached the hole the rocket had made when it blasted the concrete shed. Stairs led downward, where a glow revealed smoke.

"We came with tear-gas capability," the special-ops leader told him.

They pulled gas masks from their equipment backpacks. Motioning for him to stay back, they hurried down the stairs.

Lockhart crouched to protect himself from the heat that the beam of light gave off.

"I see a trip wire!" a voice yelled.

"Step over it! Stupid bastard should have hidden it better!"

Lockhart heard boots clattering farther down the metal stairs. Without warning, he was thrown back by the force of an explosion below. *Another trip wire!* he realized. Landing hard on rubble, he groaned from the pain. Screams at the bottom of the stairs dwindled until the only sound was the hiss-crackle-hum from the beam of light.

And the unearthly music, which now had an eerie, throbbing quality. He had believed that it came from the beam of light, but now, as he squirmed shakily to his feet, it was obvious that the music echoed from the bottom of the stairs.

He picked up his M4, moved to the gaping hole, and looked cautiously down. The glow beyond the smoke showed him that the stairs were now a tangle of twisted metal and bodies.

Outraged, Lockhart slung his assault carbine over his shoulder. The right banister dangled from where its metal was anchored in concrete. It wobbled when he put his weight on it. Holding his breath, sweating, he climbed down the railing, hand over hand.

At the bottom, he tried not to cough from the bitter smoke. After surveying the mangled bodies, he had no doubt that there was nothing he could do to help.

He took a gas mask from a dead man and put it on. It made him feel smothered, but at least it stifled his need to cough. The smoke drifted past its lenses.

The music continued pulsing.

Some of the corpses had grenades. Lockhart took a few, then unslung his M4 and inched forward, ready to shoot at any movement.

The glow from the walls intensified. He inched along a hallway, reached an open door on the right, and threw a grenade into it, quickly ducking back. Amid the glare of the explosion, he heard glass and metal blowing apart.

He continued through the swirling smoke and reached

an open door on the left—the source of the music. Pulling a pin from another grenade, he was about to free the arming lever when a weak voice came from inside.

"Don't. I'm sick. All I want to do is listen to the music. Let me die listening to the music."

"You're Halloway?" he replied without moving into the doorway.

"Used to be."

"Used to be? That doesn't make sense."

"Do you like vodka and orange juice?"

"You're still not making sense."

"You don't taste vodka and orange juice?"

"All I taste is smoke."

"The first time I got drunk, it was on vodka and orange juice," the weak voice said, its owner having trouble breathing.

"Well, this'll be your last," Lockhart replied angrily.

"Please . . . just let me listen to the music a little longer. It's all I have." The voice sucked air. "I can't even dance any longer."

"I don't know what the hell you're talking about, but I guarantee your dancing days are over." Lockhart continued to hold the grenade, his fingers over the arming lever. "You shouldn't have messed with the colonel's project."

"The colonel's a prick."

Lockhart hesitated. "You're right about that."

He was suddenly aware that the floor felt unsteady.

"Did you ever want to be a rock star?" Halloway managed to ask.

Lockhart had once heard a man breathing through a

hole in his throat. That same liquid wheezing sound was what he now heard.

"Rock star? Wasn't high on my list."

"What did you want to be?"

"Never thought about it." Unbidden, Lockhart remembered the Harley-Davidson he'd left a couple of miles away.

As he prepared to throw the grenade, he frowned, feeling the walls tremble.

"I didn't know it was possible to bleed from so many places at once," Halloway murmured, his voice sounding more gurgly. "I'm pretty much dead already. Just let me go listening to the music."

Amid the smoke, the roof vibrated, a chunk of concrete dropping from it. Lockhart had the sense that everything was somehow connected to the music.

He imagined riding the Harley.

The floor shifted enough that he had trouble keeping his balance.

"Yeah," Lockhart said, "Colonel Raleigh's a prick. What you did, was it worth it?"

"Hell, yes." Halloway coughed up something thick.

"Hell's where you're going. I doubt there's music, though."

Lockhart threw the grenade into the room and stepped back, putting his hands over his ears. The blast shook him. He heard flying debris clatter from the room. What he didn't hear any longer was the music.

The corridor kept trembling. As more chunks fell from the walls and the ceiling, he turned and hurried as quickly as he could through the smoke. Hand over hand, he climbed the wobbling metal banister, fearful that it would snap.

At the top, he heard the crackle-hiss-hum of the beam of light and emerged into its hovering glare. When he threw away the gas mask, he noticed that the air had the odor of an electrical fire.

The earth vibrated.

He ran through the three open gates, charging along the lane. All he could think of was the motorcycle and how he'd love to ride it forever.

He stretched his legs farther, racing faster.

When he was about a mile from the observatory, he felt the heat of an explosion behind him. The shock wave made him stagger. He looked over his shoulder and saw the observatory erupting. The dishes blew apart. The most dramatic detonation took place in the sky, like the hugest skyrocket he'd ever seen. But it seemed much farther away than a simple rocket could go.

The only explanation he could think of was that a satellite was exploding.

76

Raleigh felt a vibration.

"Does the floor seem unsteady?" he asked the men in front of the electronic instruments. The earplugs made his voice sound distant.

"Everything's starting to tremble," a man acknowledged. "I'm hearing some kind of hum."

"Push your earplugs in deeper."

"They're in as far as they'll go."

"Then use the noise-reducing headphones."

Raleigh and the rest of the team put them on.

"I still hear a hum," the man said faintly.

On a video monitor, Raleigh saw the flames from the crashed helicopters. Otherwise the area was dark, people reacting in panicked confusion, the green of the night-vision camera making them look grotesque. Another monitor revealed how out of control the German shepherd had become. Jaws snapping, it lunged at its trainer.

Shoot it, Raleigh urged.

The trainer did in fact reach for a pistol under his shirt, but the dog's snapping jaws made him lurch back and fall. The trainer fired once into the air as the animal leaped over him, yanked the leash free, and rushed into the night.

"The hum's getting worse," someone said, his voice thickly muffled.

"The table's rattling."

"Jesus, my nose is bleeding."

The signal's too strong! The shields aren't working! Raleigh thought in alarm.

On a different screen, a tidal wave of light streaked across the rangeland, igniting the grass beneath it. A beam shot from it, rocketing toward the old airbase. It reached the hidden dish and sped through it in the direction of the observatory.

Abruptly all the monitors went dark, the shields on the cameras failing.

A man's eyes dripped blood.

Raleigh backed away.

"Turn off the equipment!" somebody yelled.

"No!" Raleigh shouted, continuing to step back. "Keep everything on as long as possible!"

"My ears!"

Someone vomited blood.

Raleigh reached the entrance to the office, stepped inside, closed the steel door, and locked it. The room had three times the electromagnetic shielding that the rest of the facility had. He hurried to the monitors on his desk and watched the men outside.

Some realized what Raleigh had done and rushed to the door, pounding on it. The frantic movement of their lips showed Raleigh that they begged to be let in. A man picked up an M4 that had a grenade launcher attached to it and pushed the others away.

He fired at the door.

Raleigh felt the concussion. On the monitors, he saw the smoke from the explosion and the damage the shrapnel had done to some of the team. But the door was intact. Screaming silently, the man fired another grenade, again with no effect on the door. But the pain that the explosion and the shrapnel inflicted on the rest of the team made someone pick up his carbine and shoot the man who held the grenade launcher.

The man with the carbine then shot three other members of the team, proving that the force associated with the lights did indeed provoke irrational violence. Testing that theory was why Raleigh had made firearms easily available to them. A moment later, the man dropped the carbine and pressed his hands over his skull, his face contorting in agony.

The monitors on Raleigh's desk went dark, the shields on the cameras failing.

Raleigh sank to the chair behind his desk. Stunned, he tried to tell himself that he'd truly never believed he would actually need to take refuge here. The shielding on the rest of the facility was so massive that he'd been confident it would hold. But there'd been only one way to test its limits.

He looked at his watch. It was 9:47. *A long time until sunrise. But hey, no big deal. I've got food and water to get through the night. It shouldn't be a problem to wait until after dawn before I leave.*

The overhead light dimmed, the generator failing.

Stay calm. If the generator fails, that's no big deal, either. I'll just put my head on the desk and do what's normal at night: sleep. The time'll speed by.

Those poor bastards out there . . .

The lights went out. Raleigh found himself immersed in the deepest darkness he'd ever experienced.

I'm safe. That's what matters. In the morning, I'll have all the light I want.

Sleep.

When Raleigh put his head on the desk and closed his eyes, he saw imaginary speckles that seemed to be on the backs of his eyelids—a trick of the brain. He opened his eyelids, and the darkness seemed thicker.

A slight ringing in his ears made him uneasy until he

decided that the ringing was normal when ambient sound was blocked.

It's there all the time. Normally other sounds mask it.

Even so . . .

Could I be hearing the lights?

No, he couldn't allow himself to panic.

Think of something else.

Like what?

But the answer came automatically.

My grandfather.

77

Edward Raleigh never recovered from whatever had happened to him at the Rostov airbase on July 16, 1945. The officers who wrote the Army intelligence reports felt relieved. A man in a state of permanent catatonia wasn't likely to tell anyone about a weapon of mass destruction that might be more powerful than the atomic bomb.

With the awesome success of Oppenheimer's project, the president and the military decided there wasn't any point in trying to develop a backup, especially when its elements were so little understood and so destructively unpredictable.

And unreliable. The lights didn't reappear for two months, and then only dimly.

Japan's unconditional surrender reinforced the decision. One superweapon was sufficient to control the world's destiny. But then the Soviets developed their own atomic bomb, and as the nuclear race intensified, the research done at Rostov was so well buried that it was forgotten.

Edward Raleigh spent the next twenty-five years in an Army mental hospital, visited every day by his wife, whom he'd married while he was stationed at the Presidio in San Francisco in 1939. Their son was named Robert. A devout Roman Catholic, Edward's wife refused to re-marry. To do that, she would need to divorce her husband, and she believed that a divorce would damn her soul.

In 1970, the mounting expenses of the Vietnam War forced the U.S. military to cut back on full-time medical care for personnel whose treatment went as far back as the two World Wars. Edward's wife moved him from the hospital to her apartment, where her life gained greater purpose as she devoted herself to taking care of him.

By then her son was twenty-nine and himself a father with a son named Warren. Growing up, Warren visited his grandfather and was by turns horrified and fascinated by the bearded old man who sat unmoving in a rocking chair in the living room, always wearing pajamas and a housecoat, always watching television—although if his grandfather was aware of anything he watched, no one could tell.

Warren was thirteen when a stroke killed his grand-mother. At the funeral, everyone said she had been a saint. He never forgot how intensely his parents talked about what to do with the "old man," as they called him.

"We don't have room," his mother insisted, while his father, a warrant officer in the Army, argued that they didn't have the money to put the old man in a facility.

In the end, Grandfather came to live in their small

unit at Fort Bragg, and Warren was given the responsibility of taking care of him after school while his mother went to her part-time job at the base's PX. Warren didn't mind. His friends were allowed to come over, and they weren't *too* grossed out by the wrinkled, shrunken, white-haired, white-bearded old man. He just sat there, watching whatever television programs they decided to watch.

He never moved on his own, but he could be made to walk if he was prompted, and he could be made to chew if food were put into his mouth. Also, he was pretty good about going to the toilet. All Warren needed to do was lead him into the bathroom every two hours, pull down his pajama bottoms, sit him down, and come back five minutes later. If the old man needed his rear end cleaned, Warren used a wet brush. Disgusting, sure, but Warren discovered that he could get used to a lot of things in exchange for the new video game his father let him buy every week.

One day after school, Warren was alone—which was what it felt like whenever he was in the living room with his grandfather—playing a video game that had a lot of floating, drifting balls of light. His grandfather shocked the hell out of him by speaking.

"The lights."

Warren dropped the video game control, turned toward his grandfather, and gaped.

"I saw them," the old man said.

"You can talk?" Warren asked in astonishment.

His grandfather didn't seem to hear him. Instead the old man just kept talking, his voice hoarse. A lot of it

Warren didn't understand— stuff about Texas, an airbase, lights, and an underground research station.

"Rostov." Whatever *that* meant.

"Ears bleed. Nose. Tear ducts. Burns. Time sped up. God help me. Alice." That was the name of Warren's grandmother. His grandfather began to weep.

Warren ran to get a Kleenex and wiped his grandfather's bearded face.

"It's all right, Grandpa. I'll help you. What are you trying to say?"

Warren's grandfather stopped talking then. It was days before Warren realized that when he'd wiped his grandfather's tears, he had stood between his grandfather and the balls of light in the video game.

His parents thought he was lying.

"No, he talked for five minutes," Warren insisted.

"What about?"

Warren told them.

"Lights," his father said. "My mother talked about the research he'd been doing down in Texas, something about lights."

"Texas?"

"Outside a nothing town called Rostov. *His* father had something to do with lights, too. Way back in the First World War. I never figured it out."

"Aren't there some letters?" Warren's mother asked.

"Letters?"

"Between his father and mother. I remember Alice showed them to us. According to her, Edward treasured anything to do with his father because he was just a toddler when his father disappeared," she said. "Some of the letters came from France during the First World War. They mentioned something about lights."

"Yes, I remember now. Where did we put Dad's stuff?"

After a twenty-minute search, they found the letters in the bottom of a box in a closet. They took them into the living room and clustered around the white-bearded figure in his rocking chair.

"Yep, look at this," Warren's father said. "'I dream about the lights. I can't wait to come back and find them.' January twentieth, 1918. Wow. Dad, what do you know about this?"

But Warren's grandfather was again catatonic.

The next afternoon, as Warren played the video game, his grandfather pointed toward the floating, drifting lights and began to tell a story that he'd kept locked within him since 1945—about a secret facility under a remote airbase in Texas and a weapon of unknown power.

Spellbound, Warren felt as if electricity straightened the hairs on his arms. From then on, he told his friends that his father had chores for him to do after school. He hurried home and put on the video game. As the floating, drifting balls of light appeared, his grandfather talked increasingly about the lights.

But one day, when Warren rushed home, his mother met him outside and told him to be quiet because his grandfather was asleep in the bedroom. This disappointed Warren because he wanted to hear more about the lights and what had happened that terrible morning in 1945.

He played a video game, got bored, and decided to see if his grandfather was awake. Opening the door, he found that the bed was empty. A window was open.

He called his mother, who hurried home. Although the two of them drove along every street on Fort Bragg, they couldn't find him. Military policemen widened the search. The police outside the base widened the search even farther.

Hospitals, shelters, churches, parks. Warren's grandfather wasn't at any of them.

"How the hell can an old man disappear?" Warren's father demanded.

"I think I know where he went," Warren said.

"Maybe he figured out where Alice is buried and decided to visit her," Warren's mother suggested.

"No. He went to Rostov," Warren said.

"Rostov? Texas?"

"The airfield where he got hurt. He's always talking about it. I think that's where he went."

"How could an old man get to Texas?"

"I'm not saying he got there. I'm just saying I bet that's where he went."

The police sent a missing-person bulletin to Georgia, Alabama, Mississippi, and Louisiana, all the states between North Carolina, where Fort Bragg was located, and west Texas.

Three days later, the Rostov police chief phoned. Yes, Warren's grandfather had managed to get there. He'd been found at the old airfield.

He was dead.

78

Raleigh felt the table beneath his head begin to vibrate. In the darkness, he straightened. The room seemed warmer, enough to make him sweat.

Of course it's warmer, he thought. *The generator failed. The air conditioner isn't working.*

But if that's the case, then the air-circulation pump isn't working, either, he realized. *The only oxygen I can get is in this room.*

The darkness made him imagine that the room was smaller than it was.

Relax. Take slow, calm breaths. There's plenty of air.

The ringing in Raleigh's ears persisted, aggravated by the earplugs. The noise-reducing headphones pinched the sides of his head. Sweat trickled from under them. He wiped the sweat away with his hands.

Thirst made him wish that he'd thought to put bottles of water on the table while the light was dimming. When he came to his feet, the darkness intensified the scrape of the chair. He turned to the left, extended his arms, and shuffled across the floor, pawing the empty space. Sooner than he expected, his fingers touched the smooth metal of the filing cabinet.

No problem.

The bottles of water were in the top drawer. He groped inside and tucked three of the bottles under his left arm. He gripped two energy bars with his right hand and shuffled back toward the desk.

He bumped a sharp corner. Cursing, he quickly set down what he carried and rubbed his throbbing hip.

The accumulating humidity made his nostrils moist. After wiping them with a handkerchief, he felt his way around the table to where his chair again made a screeching sound. He took three long swallows from a bottle of water, wiped moisture from his lips, tore open the wrapping on an energy bar, and suddenly felt queasy.

The water he'd swallowed had an aftertaste, as if there were metal in it. Was it starting to turn bad?

Will it make me throw up?

The metallic taste became stronger.

Sweat trickled down his face. As the table continued vibrating, the darkness seemed less absolute, perhaps because his eyes were adjusting. He could almost see the water bottles.

Of course. I've always had great eyesight.

The blackness developed shades of gray. He definitely saw the outline of the bottles. That was the good news. The bad news was that the ringing in his ears was sharper, and the metallic taste almost made him gag.

The bottles were coming into view, but a haze surrounded them.

Damned sweat's getting in my eyes. He wiped them with the back of a hand, but the bottles remained blurred, even though the gray of the room was now so pale that he could see a hint of the table.

And the energy bars.

And his hands.

The effect was similar to the way night fades just before

dawn. Through blurred vision, Raleigh was able to distinguish the filing cabinet. He saw walls and the metal door across from him, everything still hazy.

Again he rubbed his eyes to clear them of sweat. The room was now light enough that he could see colors, the orange wrappers on the energy bars, the blue labels on the water bottles, the red on his hands.

Red?

Drops of blood covered the table. His shirt was blotched with it. In dismay, he realized that the metallic taste hadn't come from the water and the moisture on his face hadn't been sweat. It was blood running from his tear ducts and his nose.

He screamed.

The illumination came from the floor, the walls, and the ceiling.

Raleigh lunged toward the door, unlocked it, and yanked it open. A glare made him shield his eyes.

The team lay before him. Covered with blood, those who were still alive groaned. One man had the strength to aim his M4 at him.

Raleigh stooped to grab the carbine with the grenade launcher but didn't need to use it—the man with the M4 passed out, his gun clattering to the concrete floor.

Raleigh charged over the bodies, yanked open another door, and raced into the chamber where the now useless Suburbans were parked. The glare was even brighter as he hurried toward the stairwell that led to the surface.

If I run fast enough, maybe I can go far enough.

I wasn't exposed as long as the rest of the team. Maybe I won't bleed out.

Chest heaving, he pounded up the stairs. He reached the door to the outside, turned the knob, rammed his shoulder against it, but couldn't make it budge. He jabbed numbers on a pad next to the door, entering the unlock sequence, but the door still wouldn't budge.

Of course! Raleigh thought. *Without electricity, the code pad can't work!*

Wailing uncontrollably, he hurried down the steps, raised the carbine, and fired a grenade at the door. The explosion threw him off balance. When the smoke cleared, he saw that the door hung askew. A glare showed beyond it.

As blood dripped from his face, he rushed up the stairs, entered the ruins of the hangar, and sprinted outside. Behind him, a massive light intensified, but straight ahead lay the darkness of the road.

Keep running!

He managed only three long, frenzied strides before something bounded from the darkness and struck his chest, knocking him onto his back. Jaws snapped at his neck. The German shepherd. Its face was bloody. In a frenzy, the dog drove its teeth toward Raleigh's neck. He grabbed its throat, trying to push it away. It clawed and writhed. He couldn't keep hold of its blood-slicked fur.

About to tear into his throat, it suddenly stopped and stared beyond his face. The blood on its muzzle reflected churning lights. With a yelp, it spun and raced into the darkness.

Raleigh struggled to his feet and staggered forward. The impact of falling had knocked his headphones off. The flow of blood had loosened his earplugs. Without their protection, he heard a hiss-crackle-hum behind him.

And something else.

The motor of an airplane.

Of all the stories his grandfather had told him, the one that haunted him the most was about how Raleigh's great-grandfather had flown a World War I biplane toward the dark horizon in an effort to learn the origin of the lights. As a boy, Raleigh had imagined that biplane going farther and farther away, getting smaller, receding into the distance, becoming only a speck.

Vanishing.

My great-grandfather.

Turning, he was nearly blinded by a wave of lights speeding toward him. In the distance, grassland was ablaze, the flames adding to the glare, the smoke reflecting it. He gaped toward the twisting colors, the dominant hue of which was orange and reminded him of the sun.

Something moved inside them.

A biplane swooped into view, its orange at first indistinguishable from that of the flares around it. The biplane had two seats, one behind the other. In the rear seat, a young man worked the controls. He wore a uniform and goggles. Even at a distance, it was obvious that he was handsome.

He had a mustache. The tail of a scarf floated behind him.

Before Raleigh understood what he was doing, he started along the old airstrip. He knew he ought to run toward the road, but ever since the age of thirteen, all of his thoughts had been about the lights and their secrets.

When he was eighteen, he'd come to this airbase and searched it, finding a way into the underground facility. Like his grandfather, he'd joined the Army with the purpose of rising through military intelligence. At last he'd gained the authority he needed to track down his great-grandfather's reports about the lights, to follow clues that led him to his *grandfather's* reports about the lights.

The biplane swooped nearer.

Without warning, the engine stopped.

The biplane disappeared. It was instantly replaced by a small, single-wing aircraft, a Cessna, the engine of which was silent, its propeller fluttering uselessly. Raleigh saw a man and a woman through the canopy. Their faces were twisted with fear.

The plane was about to crash.

79

One moment, Page was trying to guide the Cessna over the Badlands and onto the murky grass. The next, swirling colors enveloped the plane. If time had seemed prolonged during the gliding descent, it became even more so now.

The Cessna appeared not to be moving.

A beam of light shot from the colors that pulsed on the right side of the aircraft. It produced so much illumination that he could see the collapsed hangars of the old airfield. The beam of light streaked into one of them and angled toward the northwest in the direction of the observatory.

In the distance, the beam surged into the sky, deflected off something—a satellite, Page guessed—and rocketed toward the ground even farther northwest.

"I hear an engine!" Tori shouted.

"It isn't ours!"

A shadow passed through the colors on his left.

"Another plane!" Page yelled.

Not just another plane. A biplane of a type that dated back to World War I. A young man with a mustache and goggles was behind the controls in the rear seat, the tail of a scarf fluttering behind him.

Other images swirled within the colors: a man herding cattle, a woman on horseback riding along a dark road . . .

A handsome young man—James Deacon—leaning against a fence, staring toward darkness.

A teenager on a motorcycle racing across a murky field.

Soldiers holding their heads as if they feared their skulls would explode.

Edward Mullen shooting toward the lights, then firing into a crowd.

Tori sitting on a bench at the viewing area, gazing spellbound toward the shadowy distance.

At once all the images vanished, including the biplane. Its engine could no longer be heard.

The Cessna resumed its glide. The lights, which were now behind it, provided enough illumination for Page to see the weeds and dirt on the old runway.

"We're coming in short!"

The ground rose swiftly.

"Someone's ahead of us!" Tori yelled.

"What?"

"There's a man staggering along the runway!"

Page saw him then. Wavering, a man gaped at the Cessna, his head and clothes soaked with what had to be blood.

"Tori, get your door open!" Page yanked up the lever on his own door and pushed. He saw rocks among the weeds before the runway.

The Cessna couldn't stay in the air any longer. He pulled the controls back, raising the nose, hoping to keep the front wheel above the rocks. The left wheel struck and collapsed. He felt the plane drop on that side. The left wing dragged along the ground, then buckled. Snagging, it caused the fuselage to twist to the left.

The propeller struck earth, a blade breaking off and flipping away, the torque yanking the engine out of its housing. Dust billowed over the canopy. As the fuselage kept tilting violently to the left, Page found that he was lying on his side. The snapping and grinding of metal was matched by the crunch of the plane skidding over dirt. The shock of stopping would have slammed Page's chest against the controls if his seat belt and shoulder harness hadn't been tight, but even so, the snap of his chest against the harness made him feel as if he'd been punched.

He had trouble breathing.

"Tori," he managed to say, "are you all right?"

She didn't answer.

"Tori?"

"I think I'm okay."

Thank God, Page thought. "We need to get out in case there's a fire."

His door was wedged against the ground. In pain, he managed to free his seat belt and harness.

"Climb through your door!"

With the fuselage on its side, Page was able to half stand and help Tori unbuckle her harness. He pushed at her hips, helping her get through the door on the right. Wincing, he pulled himself up, squirmed through the open door, crawled over the side, and dropped to the ground.

His chest ached, but the pain hardly mattered when he smelled aviation fuel.

"Run!" he shouted. But Tori didn't need encouragement. She charged forward onto the old runway. Flanking her, Page ran as hard as he could.

Ahead, the man they'd seen on the runway had collapsed. Without hesitation they knelt beside him, turning him onto his back. Even with all the blood, Page knew he'd seen this man before. On the previous night, he and Tori had driven past the abandoned airbase. A man in his forties, bald and sinewy, with rigid shoulders and an air of authority—he'd been unlocking the gate.

"Can you stand? Page asked. "We need to get you out of here."

The man mumbled something that sounded like "great-grandfather."

Page and Tori lifted him to his feet, guiding him along the old runway. The beam of light continued radiating through one of the hangars, streaking toward the northwest, soaring into the sky, then angling down toward something on the far horizon. The air was filled with a hiss-crackle-hum that smelled like an electrical fire. Page felt his hair standing up.

Struggling to get the man to the road, Page looked over his shoulder, and was stunned by how much brighter the lights were. Explosions tore up ground in the distance: bombs from long ago. The grass fire spread toward the runway. When the flames reached the Cessna, the fuel tanks erupted, sending a fireball into the sky.

The hiss-crackle-hum became unbearable. As heat from the beam of light threatened to set Page's clothes on fire, the sky was abruptly filled with what seemed a gigantic skyrocket, higher and farther away than any fireworks could reach. It sent huge trails of sparks flying in every direction.

"What the hell is *that*?" Tori asked in amazement.

The sparks radiated high and low, far and wide across the heavens. Blazing tendrils showed every color imaginable, so massive a display that Page was stopped in his tracks, awestruck.

The sky seemed on fire.

At once the ray of light ceased.

It vanished at the same time as a blast lit the horizon, off in the direction of the observatory. The colors drooped in the sky. The sparks fell, their luster fading. As the hiss-crackle-hum went silent, the only illumination came from the grass fires.

Coughing from smoke that drifted over him, Page found that he was able to move again. He and Tori urged the man through the darkness. They reached a fence, lifted the man over it, passed between parked cars, and sank onto the road.

A new sound filled the night. The sound of hundreds of people crying.

"Great-grandfather," the man said.

People stumbled past them. Some got into cars, but the vehicles wouldn't start. Others called the names of loved ones. Pleas for help from God or somebody, *anybody*, blended with moans. A crowd gathered on the road, plodding along it, people looking like refugees from a war zone as they made their way toward Rostov. Sirens wailed from the direction of the town.

The fires showed Medrano climbing onto a pickup truck.

"Everybody stay calm!" he yelled. "We'll take care of you! Help's on the way!"

Page looked at the stranger they'd set on the road. His face was dark with blood.

"Hear those sirens? Just hang on, and you'll be okay," Page tried to assure him.

The man didn't respond. At first Page worried that he had died, but then he saw that the man's eyes were open, unblinking, staring at something that might have been far away, or else locked in his mind.

Page reached over and gripped Tori's hand. "You're sure you're okay?"

"We're alive," she answered. "Can't get much better than that."

The siren blared closer, red and blue lights flashing in the dark.

80

Anita woke periodically in the night, gradually recovering from the effects of the anesthetic. This time, when she opened her eyes, sunlight drifted between slats in blinds, revealing the hospital bed she lay on. Her left arm was in a cast, the weight of which added to the deep pain in her arm.

"The bullet did a lot of damage to the bones in your arm," a voice next to her said with effort, "but they were able to save it."

Anita looked to her left and found someone in the room's other bed. She recognized the voice—it was Brent's—but she couldn't see his face, which was covered with bandages.

"I told you I'd be here when you woke up," he said, his voice muffled. "I'm a man of my word."

Anita frowned. "What happened to you?"

"I chased that story until it caught me."

Still groggy from the drugs she'd been given, Anita said, "I don't understand."

"I got too close to it." Brent's voice dropped. "I got burned by it."

"Burned?"

"I don't think I'll be going to Atlanta. In fact, I don't think I'll be coanchoring with Sharon anymore, either. But given what the story cost us, I can guarantee that you and I will get that Emmy."

Anita tried to sit up. She was desperate to make sense out of what he was saying.

"You were burned?"

"The doctors aren't sure how bad the scars will be. They talked about skin grafts and specialists. If I'm lucky, I might be able to do some investigative reporting as long as my face is in shadows when I'm on camera."

Anita couldn't speak for a moment.

"*Lo siento.*"

"Since I'm probably going to be in El Paso for quite a while, I guess I'd better start learning Spanish. What did you just tell me?"

"I'm truly sorry."

"Thank you. We made a good team."

"We're *still* a good team," Anita said.

"All the same, I think you'd better start looking for another partner."

"Do you like Mexican food?"

"I don't know what that's got to do with anything, but the truth is, I tried the stuff once and hated it."

"That's because you didn't eat in the right place. You haven't tasted anything till you dig into my mother's chicken enchiladas."

81

"A massive electrical storm?" Costigan leaned back behind his desk. Although he wore his uniform and gunbelt, he still had the bandage around his head. It made him look vulnerable.

"A huge cell of dry lightning. That's what the feds say happened," Medrano told him. "All kinds of government types got involved, particularly the FBI and the National Science Foundation. The NSF runs the observatory. Or used to. The facility blew up last night."

"From dry lightning." Costigan looked confused. "Is that even possible? Could something like that disable the power systems in a couple of hundred vehicles? Not to mention several helicopters and a Cessna?"

"Whether or not it's possible isn't the point. That's the official explanation for what happened, and with all the television cameras disabled last night, we don't have pictures to prove otherwise."

"What about the satellite that exploded? Half the southern United States saw it."

"Space debris blew it apart. What looked like sparks was the wreckage burning as it entered the atmosphere. The fact that it happened at the same time as the dry lightning is entirely coincidental. There's no way the government'll admit that it was experimenting with a weapon that uses electromagnetic energy."

Church bells rang across the street, announcing the start of the Sunday service.

"A weapon?" Costigan frowned. "You think that's what was going on?"

"I was there, and I promise you that what I saw wasn't dry lightning. I can think of only one thing that stops engines and generators and everything else that depends on electricity or magnets. You know anything about astronomy?"

"Enough to tell the difference between it and astrology."

"Ever since I was a kid and saw my first comet, I've had a telescope," Medrano said. "I subscribed to *Astronomy* magazine for as long as I can remember. Black holes, supernovas, spiral nebulae. They're all pretty sexy. But solar storms are my personal favorite. I don't dare look at the sun through a telescope, of course. I need to rely on films taken by special cameras in observatories. Solar storms give off flares that look like the flicking end of a giant whip. They can get as hot as a hundred million degrees. They radiate the electromagnetic energy of ten million atomic bombs."

Costigan listened intently.

"They tend to run in eleven-year cycles," Medrano continued. "From almost no activity to spectacular eruptions. At their peak, the electromagnetic waves have so much strength that when they reach Earth they can knock satellites out of orbit, shut down power plants, and turn television broadcasts into static. The Northern Lights are caused by them. What I saw last night looked like a combination of the two: Northern Lights and solar flares."

"Solar flares. An awful long way from the sun."

"I'm not saying they *were* solar flares. I'm just saying that's what they looked like. An electromagnetic burst from somewhere on the ground would explain a lot of what happened last night."

"But what caused it?"

"That's another way of asking what the lights are. Here's a theory. The Earth's core is hotter than the surface of the sun." Medrano shrugged. "Maybe there are fault lines around here that allow electromagnetic waves to find their way to the surface."

Costigan thought about it. "As good an explanation as swamp gas, quartz crystals, radioactive gas, and temperature inversions, I suppose."

"Well, whatever's going on, I won't let this get any worse," Medrano said. "Most visitors have had enough and are going home on their own. But just to make sure, as of tonight we're blocking the road. Anybody who wants to drive in that direction will need to take a long detour. The viewing area, the portable toilets, the roadside plaque, the concrete barriers, the parking lot—everything's being removed. That place will look like just another section of a field by the time we're finished. Meanwhile, the feds are cleaning up the mess at the observatory and the airbase. We'll probably never know what went on there. They won't let us in. And we'll never officially know what happened at White Sands last night, either."

"White Sands?" Costigan asked. "The missile range?"

"Yeah, it's all over the news, and the conspiracy theorists are having a field day. Some kind of ray hit a target at White Sands—a mockup of a town. I think we can guess where the ray came from. Apparently it destroyed the mockup town, blew apart the monitoring station, and obliterated a half-dozen other buildings five miles away, not to mention taking out the electricity for the entire base, including the batteries in their vehicles. The ray was too visible for them to deny it happened. Reports are that twenty military technicians were killed. Civilians watching the night sky from Alamogordo claim they saw a blinding light. The Army attributes all this to a massive explosion at a munitions depot. The explosion was caused by dry lightning, they said."

"That dry lightning sure gets around." Costigan's features were suddenly creased with exhaustion.

"Are you okay?" Medrano asked.

Across the street, the church bells kept ringing.

"Maybe I'll stroll over there later," Costigan said. "It's been a while."

The police dispatcher knocked on the open door. "Mr. and Mrs. Page are here to see you."

"Show them in."

When Page and Tori stepped into the doorway, Costigan smiled. "It's good to see you, even if you do look a little sunburned."

"So does Captain Medrano," Tori said.

"Seems we're in the land of the midnight sun," Medrano replied. "We discussed your phone call. You're right that we're going to need you here to fill in some of the gaps. But at the moment we have plenty of other details to take care of. So if you can get back here in ten days, that'll be fine. Mrs. Page, you mentioned that you're going to have surgery Tuesday morning in San Antonio. Will ten days give you enough time to feel strong enough to travel?"

"We'll see," Tori said.

"We can always set up a video conference call, if necessary. I hope it isn't anything serious."

Page and Tori didn't reply.

82

The Falcon 2000 jet took off from the airbase at Fort Bliss and started its four-hour flight toward Glen Burnie Airport near Fort Meade, Maryland. It was piloted by Army Intelligence personnel, who were also affiliated with the NSA. Its passengers were a medical team and Colonel Raleigh.

The colonel stared straight ahead, his eyes blinking occasionally, but otherwise making no movement.

"How long has he been like this?" someone asked.

Because Raleigh was catatonic and couldn't turn his head, he wasn't able to identify the speaker.

"Apparently since twenty-two hundred hours last night," someone replied. That man, too, was out of Raleigh's line of sight.

"What's wrong with him?"

"The best I can say right now is trauma-induced paralysis. I don't know if it has a physical cause, a psychological one, or both. He'll need to be tested."

"Considering the mess we found in that underground facility, I'm not surprised he freaked out."

"Not a very scientific term, but yeah, basically that's what happened. He freaked out."

"Do you think he can hear us?"

"I have no idea. His ears were bleeding. There might have been permanent hearing loss. Or else the shock of what happened might have put him in a state of psychological disassociation."

"Yeah, but the thing is, what *did* happen? The cameras down there stopped working. The digital recordings were all wiped. All we've got are the bodies. Except for the men who were shot, those other poor bastards bled to death before we got to them."

"Unless the colonel starts communicating, we might never know."

Incapable of movement, Raleigh kept staring straight ahead.

The hiss of the jet engines gradually changed to the drone of a propeller and a piston-driven motor. The interior of the Falcon dissolved, giving him a back-seat view of a biplane skimming above a dark field while stars glistened.

He wore goggles and a scarf, one end of which fluttered behind him. He worked the controls and drifted toward the horizon.

Ahead, colors shimmered, beckoning.

83

The waiting room had plastic chairs linked together. A television was bolted to an upper corner of the room, tuned to the *Home and Garden* channel. At the entrance, a hospital volunteer sat at a desk and wrote down the names of people who came in, letting them know that coffee, tea, and water were available on the table behind her.

Page sat next to Tori's mother. After a while, their tension kept them from making small talk. Page flipped through a two-month-old issue of *Time*, then looked at the television, where a woman wearing gloves and holding a trowel gave viewers a tour of her flower garden.

"How long do you suppose it'll take?" Margaret asked, looking pale.

"I guess it depends on what they find and how much needs to be removed."

"My poor baby," Tori's mother said.

A woman wearing a surgical gown and bonnet walked into the waiting room. She scanned it, saw the two of them, and came over. Her expression was difficult to read.

It's far too soon, Page thought. *Something's gone wrong.*

The woman sat next to them. "There's been a mistake."

"Oh, dear God," Margaret said.

"Maybe Tori's films and records got confused with someone else's," the surgeon continued. "Or maybe there was something wrong with the equipment when the tests were given."

Page sat forward. "I don't understand. What are you saying?"

"Your wife doesn't have cancer."

"What?"

"There's no trace of it."

Page felt off balance.

"A mistake?"

"That's the only way I can explain it. Her mammogram and CAT scan both show a sizable mass that might have spread to the chest wall."

Tori never told me it was that serious, Page thought.

"But that mass definitely isn't there now," the surgeon

said. "On occasion, tumors go into remission, but they don't just vanish in a week. Somehow the equipment must have malfunctioned, or your wife was given someone else's results. We're working to find out what happened."

"My wife's going to be all right?" Page managed to ask.

"She should be fine, and I can tell you for certain that she doesn't have breast cancer."

Tori's mother wept.

84

Page had his own theory.

Equipment hadn't malfunctioned. Records hadn't been mislabeled. Test results hadn't been misrouted.

Back in Rostov, while he'd been buying a fresh shirt and jeans in a clothing store, he'd heard a customer ask a clerk about the lights.

"My wife has diabetes," the customer had said. "We heard this place makes miracles happen, like at Lourdes. If she sees the lights, she'll be cured."

At the time, Page had thought, *Cured? Wouldn't that be nice?*

And now it had happened.

Tori had been cured.

→→ ←←

They returned to Rostov for the further questioning and to sign their statements. By then Costigan no longer had the bandage around his skull, and his short gray hair revealed a scar along the side of his head.

"Haven't seen any sign of the lights since everything happened," Costigan told them. "Captain Medrano and I drove Harriett Ward out there. If anybody can be depended upon to see the lights, it's her. She says they're gone. What's the phrase she used? 'In remission.'"

"Yes," Tori said. "In remission."

Page took her home to Santa Fe—but it didn't seem like home any longer. She said she kept thinking of Rostov, dreaming about the lights, and Page was dreaming about them now, too.

The insurance payment for the crashed Cessna helped him buy a thirty-year-old replacement. A year later, Page and Tori flew back to Rostov. They rented a car and drove to Costigan's office, where the police chief was coughing from what he said was a bad summer cold, although Page had a strong idea about the true source of this ex-smoker's cough.

"We're thinking about moving here," Page said. "Any chance you have a job open?"

"A deputy's pay isn't much."

"But the cost of living here isn't much, either, and I can earn some extra cash as a mechanic at the airport."

Costigan cleared his throat. "Truth is, there might be an opening for *my* job."

"I'm sorry to hear it," Tori said, looking closely at him.

"Don't be," he said with a smile. "I learned a long

time ago, nothing lasts forever. But I'm not ready to go yet, so for the time being, the deputy's job is yours if you want it."

"I do," Page said.

"And we've got so many artists moving here from Austin, Santa Fe, and Sedona, the real estate market's picking up," Costigan told Tori. "I don't suppose it'll surprise you that there's something about the colors here that attracts them. I think you could earn a living."

"I'd like to try," she responded. "One thing I know— we won't be lonely here. We made some good friends."

"You did indeed."

→→ ←←

Six months later, Page became the police chief. After Costigan's funeral, he and Tori drove out to where they guessed the viewing area had been. Medrano had meant what he'd said—once everything was removed, the place looked like just another section of a field.

They arrived at sunset, got out of the car, and watched the horizon. As the darkness settled, they saw the headlights from cars approaching from Mexico. They saw a shooting star. They saw a hint of a shimmer beyond the Badlands.

"You think that's the start of the lights coming back?" Page asked.

"It might be," Tori answered. "Harriet says they have cycles, weak and strong. Maybe she's right. But I guess I really don't need to see them. Even back in town, I can *feel* them. That's enough."

"*More* than enough," Page agreed. "They match what people bring to them. If you need something to believe in, they'll inspire you, but if you built a wall around yourself, you won't be able to see them. If you're angry, they'll make you angrier. If you want to turn them into a weapon, they'll use that weapon against you and make you realize just how terrifying a weapon can be."

"Plus, if you hope hard enough for a miracle," Tori said, "they can make one happen."

The headlights of a car approached. It pulled up next to their car, and a man rolled down a window.

"Hey, isn't this where those weird lights used to show up?"

"Lights? Don't know anything about them," Page said. "We're just admiring the stars."

"Probably a lot of bunk anyhow."

"So we hear," Tori said.

The car drove on, its taillights fading into the darkness.

"Want to head back?" Page asked.

"I'm ready. If that shimmer out there is in fact the lights, we've probably seen enough."

In the car, Page hesitated before turning the ignition key.

"What's wrong?" Tori asked.

"Just remembering what this place used to look like, what I felt when I saw you on the bench, staring toward the horizon. I almost lost you. But because of the lights, that didn't happen. What *they* are to you, that's what you are to me. I love you." Page made a point of saying that every day.

Emotion filled him. "Did you ever read the plaque that was at the side of the road?"

"No. I figured it would be touristy, like it was written by somebody in the Chamber of Commerce."

"Not quite," Page told her. "As near as I can recall, it said, 'Welcome to the Rostov lights. Many people have claimed to see them, but no one has ever been able to explain them. If you're lucky enough to experience them, decide for yourself what they are.' Well, I know what they are to me."

Page kissed her.

AFTERWORD:
SPECTERS IN THE DARK

On November 7, 2004, I paged through the Sunday edition of my local newspaper, the *Santa Fe New Mexican*. Although I don't normally read the travel section, the headline for one of its articles caught my attention.

LIGHT UP YOUR LIFE
TINY MARFA, TEXAS, BOASTS WEIRD
NATURAL PHENOMENA

The caption for a ghostly photograph referred to "mystery lights."

I couldn't resist.

Reprinted from the *Washington Post*, the article described how its author, Zofia Smardz, had taken her family to Marfa, a small town in west Texas, searching for strange lights that are visible there on many nights throughout the year. It's difficult to tell how far away the lights are. Magical, they bob and weave, float and waver, blink and glow, appear and vanish.

As the article pointed out, no one can say for sure what causes them. Perhaps quartz crystals absorb the heat of the day and give off static electricity when the rocks cool at night. Perhaps the lights are formed by radioactive gases. Or perhaps temperature inversions in the atmosphere refract lights from faraway vehicles. Whatever the explanation, the lights have been in west Texas for quite a while. As far back as the 1880s, a rancher noticed them and assumed they came from Indian campfires, except that when he searched in the morning, he didn't find evidence of any campfires.

The article's author described her visit to the area's viewing station. Along with her husband and two boys, she stood at the side of a country road and stared toward the dark horizon, pointing excitedly when the lights made their dramatic appearance. On occasion, however, she saw the lights when her family didn't, or else her family saw the lights when she saw nothing. A similar contrast happened when other tourists joined them. Some people were transported by the lights, while others couldn't see what all the fuss was about.

I finished my coffee, tore out the page, and went to my office, where I put the article among others on a shelf of research materials. I've been doing this for decades, stacking items that intrigue me, waiting to discover which of them calls to my subconscious.

It didn't take long for the Marfa lights to do exactly that. During many nights in the final months of 2004, just before I went to sleep, a persistent image kept appearing in my imagination. A woman stood at a viewing platform at the side of a road, staring spellbound toward alluring lights on a dark horizon. Unlike the author of the Marfa-lights article, this woman was not accompanied by her husband and children. Although married, she was alone. Having stopped while driving to visit her mother, she was so obsessed by the lights that nothing else mattered to her, including the husband who came looking for her.

That was all I had, and as 2005 began, I didn't even have that—the image stopped appearing in my imagination. I'm used to ideas not being ready to reveal themselves completely, so I worked on other projects: *Creepers*, *Scavenger*, and *The Spy Who Came for Christmas*. Periodically, though, I removed the article from the stack on my office shelf. Rereading it, I felt compelled to do increasing research until I had a thick binder crammed with notes.

I learned that Marfa isn't the only place where the lights appear. Three other locations—the Hessdalen valley in Norway, a remote part of the Mekong River in Thailand, and a rugged area in northeastern Australia—have similar phenomena. In Australia, they're called the Min Min lights, and when an Australian fan got in touch with me through my website, I asked if he knew anything about the lights.

It turned out that the fan, a police officer named Daniel Browning, had actually experienced the lights.

My dad, Robert, and I were out near a town called Muttaburra in central Queensland, doing some kangaroo shooting about 30 years ago. Muttaburra was a tiny little town (10 houses). Dad was a professional "roo" shooter. We were doing some shooting at night by spotlight. We were out in the middle of nowhere—no houses or roads anywhere nearby.

We saw a light. It was just suddenly there. We didn't see it coming at all. It just appeared and shadowed us. It did not seem to get closer or move away. It just stayed the same distance from us, moving with us. The thing wasn't on the ground or high in the air. It just sort of hovered. It lasted about 10 minutes, and what makes it vivid in my memory is that it shook my old man up. He knew we weren't remotely anywhere near homes or vehicles. This thing really had him worried, and then it was gone.

With that image drifting through my mind, I came across the DVD version of one of my favorite movies, *Giant* (1956). Directed by George Stevens, it stars James Dean, Elizabeth Taylor, and Rock Hudson in an epic about a Texas oilman's multidecade feud with a prominent cattle family. To my amazement, a documentary informed me that a lot of the film had been photographed in Marfa, the same town where the lights appear. Moreover, a subsequent Internet search revealed that James Dean had been fascinated by the lights. He'd dragged his costars and his director to the viewing area, but he turned out to be the only one who could see them.

These elements worked on my imagination until, almost three years after that November morning when I'd come across the newspaper article, I was again visited by the image of the solitary woman who stood in the darkness at the side of a road, staring at the mysterious lights. But now I had another image: a man flying a single-engine airplane (I had recently started private-pilot lessons). To this I added the giant dishes of a radio observatory (there is in fact an observatory near Marfa) and the ruins of a military airbase from World War II (an abandoned airbase does exist outside Marfa, near where the lights appear).

I wasn't sure how all these items could be connected. Even so, I suddenly couldn't wait to begin. I made a list of all the elements I wanted to include, creating my own versions of people who in actuality had seen the lights: the rancher in the 1880s, the schoolteacher in the 1910s, James Dean in the 1950s, and the crowd involved with the ghost-light hunt in the 1970s. Yes, there really was a ghost-light hunt. A surprising amount of "reality" is in *The Shimmer*.

Of course, it's an alternate reality in the same way that Marfa and Rostov are alternate versions of a town in west Texas. Marfa is supposedly named after a character in Dostoyevsky's *Crime and Punishment*, whereas I named Rostov after a character in Tolstoy's *War and Peace*. Despite the parallels, no one in *The Shimmer* is meant to be identified with anybody in Marfa, although I hope that this novel makes you want to visit Marfa, which has come a long way since its cattle-town days and is now a picturesque artists' community similar to Sedona, Arizona, and Santa Fe.

In one respect, however, reality needed improving. Outside Marfa, the famous ranch-house set for *Giant*, which I call *Birthright*, was indeed only a facade. Although it appeared to be an entire, grand building, if you walked behind it, you found only open grassland. Over the years, that fake front disintegrated until only its support beams remain, and they won't stay upright much longer. Because of my fondness for *Giant*, in *The Shimmer* I allowed the movie set to endure.

For more information about this novel's background, search the Internet for "Marfa lights." You'll find over half a million sites. The more you learn, the more you'll understand what I meant earlier when I wrote that a surprising amount of "reality" is in this book.

ACKNOWLEDGMENTS

Many thanks to Hank Phillippi Ryan, an investigative television reporter for Boston's NBC affiliate. A multiple Emmy winner, Hank is also the author of a thriller series that features a female investigative reporter much like herself. *Air Time, Prime Time*, and *Face Time* are some of her titles. Hank made room in her busy schedule to teach me about technical details of television reporting.

Thanks also to Larry Haight and Paul Dwyer of Sierra Aviation in Santa Fe, New Mexico. Their patience and professionalism in teaching me to fly a Cessna 172 are much appreciated. Experienced pilots will recognize that, for reasons of drama, I simplified some elements of flying.

In addition, I'm indebted to the following people:

Roger Cooper, Peter Costanzo, Georgina Levitt, Amanda Ferber, and the wonderfully supportive group at Vanguard Press/Perseus Books;

my editor, Steve Saffel;

my publicist, Sarie Morrell, and my Internet guide, Nanci Kalanta;

my agents, Jane Dystel, Miriam Goderich, and the rest of the good folks at Dystel/Goderich Literary Management.

They light my way.

—*David Morrell*

ABOUT THE AUTHOR

David Morrell is the award-winning author of *First Blood*, the novel in which the character of Rambo was created. He was born in 1943 in Kitchener, Ontario, Canada. In 1960, at the age of seventeen, he became a fan of the classic television series *Route 66*, about two young men in a Corvette convertible traveling the United States in search of America and themselves. The scripts by Stirling Silliphant so impressed Morrell that he decided to become a writer.

In 1966, the work of another writer (Hemingway scholar Philip Young) prompted Morrell to move to the United States, where he studied with Young at the Pennsylvania State University and received his MA and PhD in American literature. There he also met the Golden Age science fiction writer William Tenn (real name Philip Klass), who taught Morrell the basics of fiction writing. The result was *First Blood*, a novel about a returned Vietnam veteran suffering from post-traumatic stress disorder who comes into conflict with a small-town police chief and fights his own version of the Vietnam War.

That "father" of modern action novels was published in 1972 while Morrell was a professor in the English department at the University of Iowa. He taught there from 1970 to 1986, simultaneously writing other novels, many of them *New York Times* best sellers, including the classic spy trilogy *The Brotherhood of the Rose* (the basis for a top-rated NBC miniseries broadcast after the Super Bowl), *The Fraternity of the Stone*, and *The League of Night and Fog*.

Eventually wearying of two professions, Morrell gave up his tenure in order to write full time. Shortly afterward, his fifteen-year-old son Matthew was diagnosed with a rare form of bone cancer and died in 1987, a loss that haunts not only Morrell's life but his work, particularly his memoir about Matthew, *Fireflies*, and his novel *Desperate Measures*, whose main character has lost a son.

"The mild-mannered professor with the bloody-minded visions," as one reviewer called him, Morrell is the author of more than thirty books, including such high-action thrillers as *The Fifth Profession*, *Assumed Identity*, and *Extreme Denial* (set in Santa Fe, New Mexico, where he lives with his wife, Donna). His *The Successful Novelist: A Lifetime of Lessons About Writing and Publishing* analyzes what he has learned during his almost four decades as an author.

Morrell is the cofounder of the International Thriller Writers organization. Noted for his research, he is a graduate of the National Outdoor Leadership School for wilderness survival as well as the G. Gordon Liddy Academy of Corporate Security. In addition, he is an honorary lifetime member of the Special Operations Association and the Association for Intelligence Officers. He has been trained in firearms, hostage negotiation, assuming identities, executive protection, and offensive/defensive driving, among numerous other action skills that he describes in his novels. With eighteen million copies in print, his work has been translated into twenty-six languages.

Morrell is a three-time recipient of the distinguished Bram Stoker Award, the latest for his novel *Creepers*. Comic-Con International honored him with its prestigious Inkpot Award for his lifetime contributions to popular culture. International Thriller Writers gave him its career achievement Thriller Master award. You can visit him at www.davidmorrell.net.